S0-AHT-437

S I M O N & S C H U S T E R

NEW YORK LONDON TORONTO SYDNEY TOKYO SINGAPORE

DAYS OF DRUMS

A NOVEL

PHILIP SHELBY

S I M O N & S C H U S T E R
Rockefeller Center
1230 Avenue of the Americas
New York, NY 10020

This book is a work of fiction. Names, characters,
places, and incidents either are products of the
author's imagination or are used fictitiously. Any
resemblance to actual events or locales or persons,
living or dead, is entirely coincidental.

Copyright © 1996 by Philip Shelby
All rights reserved,
including the right of reproduction
in whole or in part in any form.

S I M O N & S C H U S T E R and colophon are registered trademarks
of Simon & Schuster Inc.

Designed by Karolina Harris

Manufactured in the United States of America

2   3   4   5   6   7   8   9   10

Library of Congress Cataloging-in-Publication Data
Shelby, Philip.
Days of drums: a novel/Philip Shelby.
p.   cm.
I. Title.
PR9199.3.S5117D39   1996
813'.54—dc20   95-31045
CIP
ISBN 0-684-80177-9

What I heard that day were not muffled cries of grief nor solemn words

but the drums. Those were days of drums.

—A British journalist's observation

on the funeral of John F. Kennedy

March 30–April 1

LAMONT Fleming, agent in charge of the Secret Service detail, liked what he saw. For the past hour he had watched the dog teams work their way in from the perimeter of the Westbourne estate, named Oak Farms. It was almost April, and the foliage across the hundred acres of prime Virginia hunt country was still bare. On the ground, the brush was light, affording little or no camouflage. Underneath a thick carpet of last fall's rotting leaves, the earth was soft. Depending on a man's weight, footprints would sink deep and stay around for a long time.

Besides the dogs, there would be a helicopter on patrol, equipped with infrared and heat-seeking scopes; a mandatory chase car; along with a little surprise in the form of a small but powerful generator tucked away behind one of the gate's stone pillars. As soon as Senator Charles Westbourne, the senior senator from New Hampshire, and his guests, also members of the Senate and known collectively as the Cardinals, passed through, the gate would be charged with twenty thousand volts of electricity. On the practice range, the effect on a remote-controlled attacking vehicle had been devastating.

Fleming pulled up the collar of his nylon windbreaker against the raw wind, heavy with the scent of thawing decay. He was a short, bandy-legged man with a muscular torso and thick forearms. A twenty-year hitch with the Marines was etched on his perpetually tanned face. His eyes never stopped moving, like those of a great horned owl.

For five of his six years with the Secret Service, Fleming had been posted abroad, specializing in embassy security. Back stateside, he could take one look at a building and tell whether it was safe—or could ever be made safe. His expertise was gold to the Service.

Fleming had no problem with the main house, a three-story red-brick Federal with a dark-green slate roof and black shutters. Its construction was solid, and it had been meticulously combed. The staff had been given the night off. A caterer used frequently by the Service had provided finger food, to which the Cardinals could help themselves.

The meeting would take place in a room at the back of the house, an elegantly appointed, masculine library with French windows and doors that opened onto a stone terrace. All that glass had bothered Fleming, so he'd had the octagonal conference table moved next to a solid wall. To take out one target would require leveling the entire room with a rocket launcher.

Prior to leaving for Oak Farms, Fleming had sifted through the last six months' worth of threats by letter and phone. Westbourne's enemies were a disparate bunch: zealous antiabortionists who stalked doctors, radical environmentalists, the white supremacists who didn't much care for the senator's position on gun control. The most recent threats had been checked out by Service field offices: Those individuals considered physically dangerous were under continuous surveillance. All were accounted for at this hour.

Fleming's gaze drifted across the pond to the guest cottage. A simple chalet A-frame, it stood on a low knoll commanding a view across a stream-fed pond to the main house. Up until a few hours ago, it was to have been vacant. Then Fleming had been informed that the cottage *would* be occupied. A female acquaintance of the senator's would be arriving late that afternoon.

She was to be checked through and escorted to the cottage—which by that point would have been searched and sealed—and left there alone. The surveillance teams that would have used the cottage were to take up positions outside. The director told Fleming to requisition another vehicle to keep his men out of the cold.

Fleming was moving across the terrace, closer to the pond, trying to decide whether one more four-by-four would be enough, when his cell phone went off.

The monitor at the Command and Control Center in Washington was on the line with an answer to Fleming's earlier call. The agent Fleming had asked about, who was supposed to have reported by now, was unavailable. According to the monitor's records, the agent had been assigned elsewhere, but his name had never been struck from the Oak Farms active-duty roster. Nor had a replacement been scheduled.

Fleming cursed softly and requested the monitor to send a warm body chop-chop. He would not go into this night with anything less than a full team. The senior people in the Service constantly monitored the fortunes of the country's top political figures. Like the director, Fleming was privy to the rumor that Westbourne was considered a leading contender for his party's presidential nomination. But a shadow had crept over the seemingly illustrious senator from New Hampshire. How dark or potentially scandalous, Fleming couldn't say. Still, maybe that was why the President himself had expressed a personal interest in the security of Oak Farms.

From his nest in the partially submerged duck blind, the killer had been watching Fleming. The agent had focused in the right direction but on the wrong object. The cottage was not the immediate danger area. Right now Fleming could tear it apart board by board and it wouldn't matter.

Nor was the killer concerned that Fleming might pay particular attention to the duck blind. There were three of them around the pond. None had survived the winter intact, and all were half buried in the muck of the reeds. Which was why Fleming's detail hadn't bothered with them.

The one the killer was using was farthest from the main house and in the worst shape. Two days earlier, well before the Secret Service advance teams had arrived, he had drained it as best he could and set a waterproof tarpaulin across a plywood base supported by two-by-fours. He had scattered clumps of decaying leaves and reeds on the cover, then had returned at dawn today, before the on-duty Service teams were in place. The hollow was just large enough for him to stretch out in, and he knew the isometric exercises that would prevent his muscles from cramping. He was dressed in army-surplus foul-weather gear—a nylon jumpsuit stuffed with down, the kind used in maneuvers in the Alaskan tundra. He'd brought water and chocolate and a half pint of brandy. He paid no attention to the things that crawled and skittered across his face in the darkness. There was nothing poisonous in or around the pond, nothing like he'd had to endure in other ambush sites.

The killer removed the stick he had used to raise one of the boards of the blind, allowing him a head-on view of the manor. The image of Fleming on the telephone was eclipsed by familiar darkness. The killer could not know the details of the call, but he was unconcerned. He had been in the blind for almost ten hours. Soon the afternoon would disappear and he would sleep, dreaming of other places, where he had rested in the boughs of trees or lain covered to his eyelids in river mud. Then it would be ten o'clock, and he would rise. He had already made certain adjustments to the lock on the back door of the cottage. He knew exactly how close the roving patrol would be. By then the agents would be cold and tired. Their watch would be almost over, their attention focused on the light and warmth of the big house. They were such little details, human details, insignificant except for the fact that on each of them whole lives would turn and be extinguished.

Such thoughts sent a frisson of pleasure through the killer. The acts he would perform on the senator, while the victim was still alive, freed his soul from his frozen grave, sent it soaring across a universe whose stars were as sharp and white as splinters of bone. There was no beat left in that heart that once might have cared, no memory of pity or compassion in a mind that had long ago turned on itself.

ONE

1

WYATT Smith, the director of the Secret Service, was a man out of a sepia photograph. Whip thin, with a handlebar mustache, he had the hard eyes of a riverboat gambler. He favored dove-gray suits, the coat cut a fraction longer than fashion dictated, the usual buttons replaced with ones inlaid with mother-of-pearl. At his throat was a bolo tie.

Smith was in his office, behind a desk that had once served as a Sante Fe mission refectory table. On the speakerphone, the Command and Control monitor was still trying to explain the roster snafu that had left Oak Farms short one agent.

Smith could have told him the truth but instead continued to listen, his eyes lightly closed. Blood pounded at his temples, driving shards of pain into his skull. He forced himself to breathe deeply, slowly. In the course of his career he had twice taken bullets meant for his charges. The fragments of one shell were still lodged between the sixth and seventh vertebrae of his spine, too close to the spinal cord to be surgically removed. Wyatt Smith was never without pain; on the bad days, his back felt as though it were on fire. Smith's fingernails were clipped to the quick so that he could not tear at his flesh in his sleep.

The monitor had exhausted his possibilities, and in the split-second silence Smith heard a roar, like thunder over the horizon.

"I'll look after it."

Smith's South Texas drawl imparted confidence, underlined it with authority. The monitor didn't ask why the director wanted to go hands-on in this situation. He was glad to be rid of the responsibility.

Five minutes passed, and Smith had no idea where they'd gone. During his last physical he had lied to the Service doctors, brushing off their queries as to whether he was suffering from blackouts. He sat up in his chair, back straight, shoulders back. His mind was clear, like the sky after a deluge. He knew he sounded perfectly normal when he buzzed his secretary.

"Kathy, get hold of Frank Suress. Tell him to pick up Tylo."

Holland Tylo hadn't expected to be met when she stepped out of the jetway at Washington's National Airport. She was as much relieved as surprised. The lawyer sitting next to her on the Atlanta–D.C flight had still been dogging her as they deplaned. Holland heard a sharp intake of breath—a squeak, really—as the lawyer almost collided with a tall, impeccably dressed man with a bemused smile on his lips.

"Hello, Holland. Friend of yours?"

The lawyer backed around Holland, muttered something she couldn't catch, and dashed into the crowded concourse.

"I guess not," said Holland, looking over Frank Suress's shoulder.

She badly wanted to throw her arms around him but wasn't sure if he was alone.

Suress took her elbow and steered her behind the ticket counter at the gate. Holland felt his black eyes caress her—gypsy eyes, she called them, because of the way they shone when they were making love. The cologne he was wearing—her birthday gift to him—rushed through her senses as he kissed her.

"Only three days, and you missed me that much," Holland murmured into the side of his neck, lips nibbling on the strawberry birthmark. She wouldn't let him go when he broke the embrace. "I want to go home—now!"

Suress craned back his head, his breath whistling over her hair. "I wish we could. Smith wants to see you."

The flush of anticipation building inside Holland cooled.

"A glitch in Atlanta?" she asked quickly.

"Atlanta's fine. You brought it all home. Smith sent me by to save time." Suress glanced at her carry-on. "That all you have?"

Holland nodded, and Suress effortlessly hefted the garment bag on his shoulder.

"What's going on, Frank? Is it Razorback?"

Razorback was the Service code name for the President, who was a fan of an Arkansas football team of the same name.

"No. But near enough. The director will fill you in. If I decide you're up to it."

Suress didn't say more until they were through the concourse and moving toward the blue generic sedan parked in the shrine of the white no-loading zone. Holland didn't take his last words personally. Standing Service orders declared that, like pilots, agents coming off one post were never immediately assigned to another unless there were special considerations. Holland thought about that as Suress dropped her garment bag into the trunk. She was also curious as to why Suress had been sent to make the evaluation. He was in charge of Service details that were assigned to the capital's top-ranking diplomats and visiting dignitaries. This was donkey work for him.

As Suress got behind the wheel and turned to Holland, he saw her wary expression. He slid close to her.

"Don't read anything into my being here. Smith picked me out of a hat, is all." He cupped her cheek. "And I wasn't about to say no."

Suress negotiated his way out of the airport and onto 395 to the Beltway.

"Tell me about Atlanta," he suggested.

Frank Suress spent less than three minutes in the director's office at Service headquarters, located in a nondescript office tower on 1800 G Street N.W. When he came out he gave Holland, seated in the waiting area, a discreet thumbs-up. Passing her by, he mouthed the words *I'll call you.*

Holland was still smiling when she discovered that Suress had been blocking her view of the door to Smith's office. And there was Smith, with his inscrutable expression and eyes like wet river stones.

"Come on in, Tylo."

Smith had his back to her, but he was following her movements in the reflection of the tall windows that fronted G Street.

Tylo was eight months out of the Academy, older than most rookies, twenty-eight. Her law degree from Georgetown accounted for that. Smith remembered her from the Service graduation ceremonies. She was taller than most women, a five-ten frame carrying the supple body of an athlete. She'd had her ash-blond hair cut in a soft wedge, which suited her oval face with its slightly pronounced cheekbones. The overall effect would have stayed simply at beautiful, were it not for the eyes. Green, shot through with gold flecks, they were her first line of defense against the world, discouraging intimacy, always watchful, very careful. Smith had known others with eyes like that, people who had been carelessly cuffed by life, had pulled themselves back up, hurting but tougher, more cautious when the healing was done.

Tylo was one of these, a loner who, Smith reckoned, might never be able to shake the chill from her bones because of what had been done to her. For her, the Service was not a vocation. It was sanctuary.

Smith wondered just how much Frank Suress really understood about this woman who shared her bed with him. He suspected it wasn't as much as Suress thought.

Holland followed Smith in, her eyes taking in the warm, comfortable room littered with Western memorabilia: bronze originals by Remington, Navajo and Yaqui pottery and wall hangings. Smith turned away from the window and indicated a horsehair-stuffed chair.

"Atlanta tells me you pulled their fat out of the fire."

"The cover stood up, sir. It was really very good. The rest worked itself out."

Holland wasn't one to preen. She knew what she'd accomplished. The Atlanta bureau chief had promised a commendation letter for her file. Holland had thanked him but doubted it would come close to her own glow of satisfaction.

Tylo's modesty was in keeping with the picture Smith had framed of her from the files. The operation down in Atlanta had been a counterfeiting sting, and it had started to unravel when the female agent playing the role of the buyer was made by one of the bankers involved. They'd gotten the banker out of the way but couldn't risk using the agent any further. Atlanta put out a distress call for someone who'd been born and raised on the West Coast and could slide into the established cover. The Service had fewer than one hundred ninety women in Field Operations to choose from. It had taken the computer no time at all to spit out Tylo's name.

Smith had personally taken control of the project, watching as Tylo was primed and primped and sent in. He had spent two sleepless nights monitoring her progress, keeping reinforcements close by, gnawing on the cold knowledge that they could never react quite quickly enough if it started to go bad.

Yes, the cover had been good, but Tylo had made it better, slipped it on like a second skin. She was still wearing her props —navy designer skirt and jacket, double-breasted with chunky gold buttons, rich red-and-blue silk scarf, and butter-soft shoes— all of it bought on Service funds. She breathed power and radiated a hard-edged confidence.

Smith wondered if Tylo had rummaged through her personality to find something real, a peg on which she could hang this persona. It was all the protection she would have had, because the script had called for her going in unarmed.

Just like this one . . .

"We have a situation with Senator Westbourne," Smith said.

The mention of the name caused Holland to catch her breath. During his twenty years in the Senate, Charles Westbourne had chaired every important committee, served as counsel to three

Presidents, made history by helping push through bills of every stripe, from welfare reform to gun control. He was also that rare creature in politics—a plain-speaking man who eschewed dema-goguery, who remained untainted by scandal, and who had a se-cret way about him that made people trust him. He reminded Holland of another man she'd respected and admired, a man she still loved fiercely even though he'd been dead for fifteen years.

"Have there been threats against the senator?" Holland asked. She was surprised at how dry her mouth had become.

"No. But we're watching the lunatic-fringe antiabortionists and supremacists. . . . You made quite an impression on the senator when you worked him in Boston," Smith continued. "He sent me a note about you."

Holland blinked, surprised that Westbourne had remembered her and flattered by the compliment. She knew that individuals who regularly received Service protection had their favorite agents, ones they felt comfortable with.

Did Westbourne actually ask for me?

Smith read her mind. "Yes, Tylo. I thought of you because your name came up."

Holland took a deep breath, tried not to appear too eager. "Are there any special circumstances I should be aware of?"

"Not really. The senator's holding a meeting tonight at his place in Virginia. Most of the Cardinals will be there."

Holland caught the reference. A Washington gadfly magazine had dubbed Westbourne and a handful of other senators the Cardinals, a sideswipe at their enormous power and influence. The media had picked up the sobriquet, and it had stuck.

"Someone on the assignment desk messed up," Smith contin-ued. "We're one short out there. The meeting will run seven o'clock to midnight, give or take. The Cardinals will be going back to the city afterward. Westbourne may or may not do the same. There's a guest staying on the estate, in the cottage. A young lady by the name of Charlotte Lane. She works in Westbourne's office. She's been cleared."

The woman's name didn't mean anything to Holland, but now she understood why Smith wanted her there. An incident might occur that she would be better able to handle than a male agent.

Smith had a reputation for covering even the smallest contingency.

"The post will be inside the house," said Smith. "Fleming will brief you when you get there. Suress tells me you're up for this. Are you, Tylo?"

"Yes, sir."

"Know your way up there?"

Holland nodded. Smith came around the desk and offered his hand. His skin felt like worn saddle leather.

"Good luck."

Holland was at the door when his voice drifted up behind her. She felt a ghost of a smile on the words.

"You make that outfit you're wearing look good. Keep it if you like."

Three hours later, Holland had fought her way through the traffic on 66 and was cruising along a two-lane Virginia blacktop that had had a hard winter. She had to watch out for the potholes created by the frost and the snowplows.

Back at her Georgetown town house, she'd taken a long, hot shower to get rid of the traveler's grime. Frank Suress had called while she'd been in the bathroom. The answering machine had picked up his congratulations, and Holland listened as she nibbled on tuna salad. She was still thinking of him, missing him, when she began to dress for work: dark-green wool turtleneck, black cotton-twill slacks, new Nike Air Maxes that made her feel she was floating. The fifteen-shot SIG-Sauer was tucked along her left rib cage, covered by a well-worn leather jacket the color of maple syrup.

Holland followed the blacktop to Miller's Pond, a tiny community that serviced the area's country manors. She slowed at the single intersection, with its flashing yellow light swaying in the wind, streaking the windows of the arts-and-crafts stores, the old-fashioned pharmacy, the general store. As she left the hamlet behind, the Honda's headlights caught the weathered gray of split-rail fences. A cold white moon rode high above the dead silence of the countryside.

Holland took the crest of the hill fast. She still had her foot on the pedal when she was rolling down the other side and a pair of high beams stabbed through the windshield. Holland pumped the brakes and pulled over to the shoulder, mindful of the steep ditch. She had both hands on top of the steering wheel, her identification in her fingers, when the agent, holding a submachine gun, tapped on the window.

"Tylo?"

His cheeks were red from the wind; his voice was hoarse from tobacco. Holland waited until he checked her ID and received confirmation from the house. As she steered the car through the gate and up the drive, she noticed the portable generator humming softly and the thick medusa wire snaking through and around the bottom of the wrought-iron filigree.

There were four Lincoln Town Cars in the motor court, flanked by a pair of chase cars. Off to the side was a GMAC Suburban, a stretch utility vehicle for medical evacuation. Holland nosed the Honda next to a garden still covered with burlap to protect the bulbs from frost.

"Glad you made it," Lamont Fleming said, coming down the wide steps from the house. His handshake was warm and firm as he introduced himself. "The ride out okay?"

"Fine, sir."

"Someone fill you in on what's going on?"

"The director mentioned you were caught short."

Fleming nodded. "I understand you worked Westbourne before."

Holland wasn't sure what or how much Fleming knew about Boston. She wanted to be careful here. Some of the women she'd talked to said Fleming was tough but fair; he was happily married, which made working with him a lot easier. It mattered to her that Fleming shouldn't think she'd batted her eyelashes at Westbourne.

Holland gave him the short version of the Boston assignment. Fleming listened carefully, then asked how cooperative Westbourne had been. Holland replied that the senator had had no problem with procedure.

Fleming nodded in the direction of the house. "Go get yourself a cup of coffee, then I'll give you the walkaround."

Holland knew something about houses like these. There, in the marbled foyer, beneath the chandelier, was the round ebony table with its vase of greenhouse-fresh tulips. Farther along were the dual serpentine staircases and a short corridor that would pass through the pantry on its way to the kitchen, all spices and wood smoke from its own hearth. On either side of the foyer were the principal rooms, their sliding doors closed.

There was a difference, though, because this house had never been touched by the warmth of children or family. Holland felt a museum chill clinging to the sculptured moldings.

She went to the kitchen and introduced herself to the team of three men sitting at the table in the breakfast nook. A coffeepot was going on the butcher block in front of the hearth. Automatic weapons were propped up against the chairs, and she heard the chirps from the multiband radios. One of the agents offered to show her around, but she told him Fleming was waiting. She felt their eyes follow her out.

Holland didn't think anything of it. She'd never worked with this team, and a parachute agent was always treated as a distant cousin.

"Everything okay?" Fleming asked, as Holland stepped outside, a coffee mug cradled in her hands.

"Fine."

"Your post is behind the front doors. They'll be locked and bolted for the duration. You'll have a team by the library doors, two upstairs, a sniper on the roof."

Holland recognized the arrangement as a Level Three coverage, tight but not "waterproof," as it would have been had the President been involved.

"Let's walk," Fleming suggested.

They turned onto the path that followed the pond. Holland tracked the wavering reflection of light to the cottage windows. Her vision was excellent, and even at thirty yards she had no trouble seeing a woman step out of her underwear, lean back, her breasts swaying, and shake her hair loose. The woman reached for something on the bed, a towel, and wrapped it turban style around her head.

She's going to take a bath. . . .

Holland slipped a sidelong glance at Fleming, who appeared to be watching the smoke chugging out of the cottage chimney. His studious pose told her he'd missed nothing at all.

It was only then that Holland became aware of just how alive the night was, not with country sounds but with everything men used and did when they were hunting. The helicopter was making a run along the ridge, its high-intensity beam spraying the tree line. In a little closer were the dogs and their handlers. Beyond the sound of her footfalls Holland heard the quiet chatter of portable radios, like gossiping cicadas.

Fleming stopped short, bent down, and came up holding a thin, smooth stone the size of a silver dollar.

"Nighttime in the country spook you, Tylo?"

"I haven't been out like this for a while. Not since the Academy."

"Spooks me."

Fleming drew his arm back, then whipped it forward. The stone caught the water and skimmed straight down the path illuminated by the moon. It skipped only four times before Fleming's radio began squawking. The patrol on the other side of the pond had heard something. Fleming told them it was okay and to stand down.

"There's a team near the cottage," he said to Holland, then looked up at the moon as if to check the time. "They're starting inside. We'd best be getting back."

Holland couldn't shake the feeling that Fleming hadn't told her everything. A tiny but significant piece was missing from the tableau before her.

"Why is this a Level Three cover?" she blurted.

Fleming didn't break his stride, nor did he look at her.

"You know who's in there tonight? Baldwin, Robertson, Croft, and Zentner."

Holland couldn't make the connections.

"What's the one committee three of them—excluding Croft— sit on?" Fleming asked softly.

Senate Ethics . . .

"They move in whenever someone is suspected of having his hand in the cookie jar." He paused. "And *we're* here because the President wants us to make sure these good folks go about their work with no one disturbing them."

2

THE killer had heard them, beginning with the scrape of shoe leather on the gravel-lined path. Then the voices came closer, and he differentiated between the man and the woman and even made out a few words.

After the silence, something hit the water. The killer recognized the slap of stone on the pond, followed by the faint crackle of radios on the other side. Whoever had thrown the stone had unwittingly done him a favor, giving away the position of the team that, until this point, had not strayed too far from the cottage. Now they were far enough.

The killer counted off thirty seconds, then gingerly raised the top of the blind. The man and the woman had reached the house and were going inside. So the conference was beginning, and that left him three and a half, possibly four hours. More than he needed had he had to work quickly; enough time to make things pleasant for himself when he got to the girl in the cottage.

In a smooth rolling motion, the killer was out of the blind, the hatch replaced. They would find this nest, of course, and there was nothing he could do about the tarpaulin. But the ground sheet was pimpled rubber, like coarse-grade sandpaper. It wouldn't yield fingerprints. The nylon suit was tough, and he would leave no fibers behind. As the blind settled back in the reeds, the brackish water would take care of any skin and hair oils. He was not worried about the dogs. Even if they were closer they could not pick up his scent this near the pond.

Wading in hip-deep water, the killer pushed through the reeds as gently as if he were searching for the baby Moses. At the bank, he got on all fours, distributing his weight to prevent his boots from causing a sucking sound in the mud, and crawled to within ninety feet of the guest cottage.

Now it was all open ground, except for a tall maple close to the cottage. He raised his head to the wind and caught voices on the other side of the pond. He ran hard, the weight of his soaked clothing making his thighs and calves burn. He barely stopped at the tree; the field was still clear, and seconds later he was around the back of the cottage, kneeling next to a wooden trash bin.

The back door was an arm's length away to his left, the brass knob all spit and polish beneath the overhead carriage lamp. No light showed in the kitchen, and from the front of the cottage, probably the master bedroom, came the gentle throb of music.

The lock was more for show than security, the kind the rich install because they've put their money and faith into more expensive and elaborate forms of protection. That he had gone to work on its innards before tonight made it easy. He was inside in less than eight seconds.

The zipper on his army gear was also nylon, and it scarcely made a sound as he pulled it down and stepped out of the suit, pushing it out of sight into the corner where the sink met the dishwasher. The floor was broad-plank pine, smelling of lemon and warm to his feet.

He stood in the darkness, careful that his shadow didn't fall across the flowery curtains in the windows. Warm air from the ceiling duct flowed across his naked body, and he inhaled deeply, as much to smell the girl as to heat his lungs. He raised his arms over his head to almost reach the duct. He did not want to touch her with cold hands.

Because she was so young, he had expected harsh rock music. Instead, there was a pleasant folk song on the disc player. He imagined notes drifting around her like falling leaves.

First a shadow, and all at once he saw her, stepping lightly across the hall into the living room. She wore a man's casual shirt and nothing else, revealing a buxom, well-fleshed body. She was probably no more than twenty-one, one of those wide-eyed Wisconsin milkmaids who came to Washington with stars in their eyes and ended up on a congressman's mattress. When she stood on her toes in front of the bookcase, the shirt rode up her buttocks and he could see tufts of pubic hair. A natural redhead.

The killer slowly let out breath through his mouth. He waited until the girl had taken down a book and, frowning at the jacket, began walking back to the bedroom. His head moved forward slightly, nostrils flaring, as though her perfume was drawing him forward. He took one step, then another, and on his way warmed the blade of the knife against his cheek, ever the complete and thoughtful lover.

Someone had brought a dining room chair, one with armrests, out into the foyer and set it beside the front doors, where Holland was to stand post. She accepted the gesture in the camaraderie in which it was offered and tucked her purse under the chair. Standing post was not meant to be taken literally unless it was done in a public place. The agents by the closed library doors were also seated, one of them leafing through a car magazine, the other on alert. They would rotate every hour.

Holland hadn't brought any reading material. She was blessed with extraordinary patience, could tune in a part of her mind to her surroundings and let it shuffle along the baseboards and into corners like a bloodhound, searching for the tiny sounds that were out of place. The other part rested. It was the same capacity the best soldiers had, those who could sleep on command or walk thirty miles in a blizzard.

Holland knew a few tricks to keep her muscles from cramping. Twice an hour she went through those exercises, careful never to get into a position where she couldn't reach instantly for her weapon. Through the night she replayed the Atlanta operation, sifting for what she could keep and use from the experience.

At ten-thirty, Fleming made his walkaround. He spoke quietly to one of the agents by the library doors. The man rose, shrugged on his parka, and disappeared into the kitchen. Now Fleming was in front of her.

"Time to get some fresh air, stretch your legs."

"I'm all right," Holland told him.

"Sure you are. But humor me."

If she hadn't seen the other agent leave, Holland would have argued. Now she knew Fleming was only being considerate. Also, he didn't want agents on the inside perimeter to lose their edge, too easy to do if the surroundings were warm and comfortable.

"Five minutes, Tylo. I'll let 'em know you're coming."

The cold air felt good on her face. Holland waited at the top of the steps until she heard the patrols acknowledge Fleming's call that she was outside. She set out on the circular drive, debated taking the path beside the pond, then walked around the house instead.

This path was narrower and brightly lit by overhead floodlights. Holland picked up her pace, passed the side of the house, and headed for the gazebo at the edge of the back lawn. The boards crackled when she stepped up on the platform, followed by a low growl, panting. Holland stood very still until a voice called out softly, "You're clear."

It was enough adventure for one night. Holland retraced her steps to the back of the house, then swung around the side that faced the pond. The fieldstone terrace, empty except for two marble benches, was on her left, running at chest level. The lights from the library sparkled off the sheen of frost. The voices, when she heard them, seemed to float on lamplight.

"You can't do that, Charles. It's monstrous!"

Holland stopped short. It was a woman's voice, high pitched and ugly with anger. She knew the voice . . . it belonged to Senator Barbara Zentner of California.

"It doesn't have to be like this," Zentner carried on. "There's always a way to work things out. But you can't expect us to roll over—"

"You're still missing the point, Barbara. You have no choice *but* to go along. Now, that can be as hard or as easy as you choose to make it, but understand one thing: You want to talk ethics? I've already shown you where *that'll* take you."

Westbourne's voice had a smooth, patient tenor to it. *A prof trying to bring along a slow learner.* It faded beyond Holland's earshot, and she thought Westbourne must have been on his feet, pacing.

It was a basic lesson the Service drilled into you from day one: Whatever you hear on post, if it doesn't relate to the safety of your charge, you never heard it.

Holland resumed walking, forcing the words out of her mind, concentrating on what was important. The library's French doors were open, only a crack, but even that was too much. It was a security breach, and Fleming had to know.

"Who the hell are you?"

Holland was at the end of the terrace, radio in her hand, when the voice snared her. She turned as Barbara Zentner stepped through the French doors and peered into the darkness.

"Agent Tylo. Senator, those doors should be locked—"

"You make a habit of eavesdropping, Agent Tylo?"

Zentner was a short, thin woman in her early fifties, whose glaring characteristic was a head of frizzy orange-blond hair. She took two steps forward, enough for the floodlights to bathe one side of her heavily painted face.

Holland felt herself about to retreat, then planted her legs solidly.

"Please go back inside, Senator," she said firmly.

Zentner speared her with a venomous glare. A reference flashed through Holland's mind, how the media had dubbed Zentner the Hatchet because of the way she treated everyone, from reporters to witnesses before her committee hearings.

There were other voices now, asking questions. Holland watched Zentner hesitate, trying to decide which way to go. Then she backed away, never taking her eyes off Holland, slammed shut the doors, and yanked the drapes closed.

Holland didn't realize she'd been holding her breath until it all came out of her in one billowing cloud. She turned and continued back to the house. There was nothing she could do about the cold that had rattled up and down her spine.

．　．　．

A few minutes before midnight, word that the meeting was over was transmitted to all sixteen agents simultaneously. The helicopter pulled away from the perimeter and set up post nine hundred feet above the driveway, halfway between the main house and the gate. The dog teams began to return to their trucks, while drivers fired up the limousines and chase cars. The radio chatter was brisk.

"Four are headed back to the city," Fleming announced when he entered the foyer. "Westbourne's staying over."

The quality of his voice made Holland think he was none too happy about this last development but that it had not come as a complete surprise.

"Tylo, you stay with Westbourne when he comes out," Fleming said.

Holland shouldered her handbag and moved into an alcove beneath the staircase. Here she could watch without necessarily being seen. She had no wish to step into Barbara Zentner's gunsights again.

The senators filed out in silence, coats on, no smiles, congratulations, or last-minute pats on the back. There was an air of matters unresolved, a bitterness to their set, angry expressions. Beneath it all Holland thought she detected fear, even defeat. Her thoughts drifted back to the snatches of conversation she'd overheard.

Why would the Ethics Committee be hounding Westbourne?

Holland ventured back into the empty foyer. Outside, she heard car doors slam and the crunch of tires on crushed stone. Voices grew faint, then disappeared. The library doors remained closed when Fleming came back inside, rubbing his hands.

"Don't tell me. He's still in there?"

Holland nodded. "Not a peep."

"Go talk to him," Fleming said brusquely, moving down the hall toward the kitchen. "I need to know where he intends to spend the night—if I should pull back the team at the guesthouse or leave it there."

Holland walked to the library doors and knocked twice. She was appreciating how fine the cherrywood smelled, when she thought she heard a voice. She turned one of the handles. Charles

Westbourne was seated behind a desk at the end of the room, facing the doors. The library was well lit, and Holland had no difficulty making out the smaller objects in front of him: an antique inkwell, a colored glass paperweight in the shape of a seahorse, a sterling-silver letter opener, and, side by side on the oxblood leather blotter, two magnetic diskettes. On the left corner of the desk was a state-of-the-art computer.

In that split second, Holland realized Westbourne *hadn't* called her to come in. His head was bowed, fingers touching the diskettes, when he suddenly sat up, glaring.

"Senator, I'm sorry. I knocked . . . I thought I heard you say come in."

Westbourne's anger melted away, his face once again the one seen on hundreds of television interviews and magazine covers. He was a handsome man, achingly photogenic, very fit, with soft gray eyes, the mouth now slightly upturned in that famous grin. His detractors admitted he could charm the pitchfork from the devil, something even a Kennedy had never been credited with.

Westbourne sat back and ran a large, fine-boned hand through thick silver hair that tumbled onto the collar of his country shirt and cashmere cardigan.

"Agent Tylo," he said, turning up the smile just a notch. "Boston. Three, three and a half months ago?"

"I'm flattered you remember, Senator."

Holland felt herself gravitate toward him. It was a rare and powerful gift for a politician, to make a stranger feel included, cared about.

"What can I do for you?" asked Westbourne.

"We need to know if you'll be spending the night here or at the guesthouse, Senator."

The reply was tender but underlined with eagerness. "The guesthouse, Agent Tylo."

"Fine. I'll pass that along."

"Stay a moment, would you?"

Westbourne lifted an envelope from the stationery holder. For a second he seemed to hesitate, then he scooped up the diskette on the left and dropped it into the envelope. He sealed it, then put the second diskette into the breast pocket of his shirt, and stood.

"Are you going back to the city tonight—well, this morning, given the hour?"

"Yes, Senator."

"Would you do me a small favor?" He held up the envelope. "One of my secretaries is waiting to transcribe this. Has to do with a bill that's coming up on the floor this afternoon. Could you drop it off on your way? As long as it's no imposition."

"None at all, sir."

Holland accepted the envelope, made sure the magnetic diskette, two and three-quarter inches in diameter, was resting at one end, then folded the container. She unzipped her handbag, found the almost invisible "mad money" pocket sewn into the lining, and slipped in the envelope.

"You have good taste," Westbourne commented, watching her.

"Thank you."

Holland didn't think it necessary to tell him that this particular handbag, an original Hermès, had been bought as part of her camouflage for the Atlanta operation. Holland, who was hard on shoes and purses, ordinarily shopped for this kind of quality only during rock-bottom sales.

"Do you need a few more minutes, Senator?"

"No. I'm done here."

Westbourne plucked a sheepskin bomber jacket off an old-fashioned wooden coatrack and followed her out. Fleming was waiting in the foyer.

"The senator will be staying at the guesthouse," Holland told him.

Fleming nodded. "You know the way."

"Is it really necessary for Ms. Tylo to come with me?"

Holland and Fleming turned around and saw that Westbourne hadn't moved, his hands stuffed into the pockets of his jacket, one eyebrow raised to add emphasis to his question.

"It's protocol, Senator," Fleming replied. "Nothing more."

Westbourne seemed to weigh Fleming's words. Then he shrugged and went to the door, graciously holding it open for Holland.

. . .

She had to walk fast to get on Westbourne's flank. Her jacket was open, flapping lightly against her gun, and she brushed it back. Her eyes were roving, searching the shadows thrown up by the trees and shrubbery. She saw two figures on the path where it reached the cottage and dismissed them.

"Curious about this?"

Holland hadn't thought that he'd notice her staring at him in the dark. Out of the corner of her eye she'd seen him take his hands from his pockets, bring out something hard and shiny that he turned over in his fingers, like worry beads.

"It's a shell of some kind," she said.

"A cowrie shell. My wife found it on a dive in Fiji."

Holland sometimes read about the second Mrs. Westbourne in the society column of the paper. The senator had been a widower for sixteen years before remarrying. Then Cynthia Palmer had come along, and millions of women's hearts were broken. Many thought it was a natural match, the man who one day might be President and the socialite heiress to a candy fortune, who could finance his campaign. The fifteen-year difference in age between them added a certain cachet.

But recently Cynthia Palmer had stopped appearing at Westbourne's side. Washington gossips whispered it wasn't all hearts and flowers anymore. Holland remembered the girl in the cottage and that the lawmakers who had been here tonight sat in judgment over the conduct of their own. She had never heard one malign word about Westbourne and wanted to continue to believe in him. Holland came from people who put great stock in decency.

"Is there something you want to ask me, Agent Tylo?"

He was quick and caught her again. Holland thought back to the grim expressions of the other senators, asked herself what it was Westbourne could be hiding behind his easy smile.

"No, sir."

The two agents who had been standing post at the foot of the walk stepped apart to let them by. Holland was surprised that Westbourne headed for the back door. Then she saw the silhouette in the bedroom window, a reclining figure with one arm stretched out as though beckoning.

"Thank you for taking that material for me, Ms. Tylo," Westbourne said. "I hope we'll see each other again when the occasion warrants."

He was reaching for the doorknob when Holland touched his shoulder.

"I'm sorry, Senator. I have to walk through it first."

"And why is that? Wait. Don't tell me. Procedure."

Holland smiled lightly. "Afraid so."

She thought that would be the end of it, until he said in a formal tone, "Agent Tylo, my friend has been in there since five o'clock this afternoon. Your people saw her in and have been posted close by since that time. Do you honestly believe that she—or I— are in any danger?"

"Senator, I really have to do this. Please . . ." Holland brushed by him and stepped into the kitchen. Music played softly, and she recognized the folk song. The air was quite still, tinged with a lover's expensive fragrance, shot through with the scent of burning oak. The door closed, and she felt Westbourne standing behind her.

"My friend is young and somewhat uninhibited, Agent Tylo. I have no wish to embarrass her or myself."

The last words, *or you,* were left unspoken. There was no apology, no shame or regret. Westbourne came around and faced her calmly, a man very clear in his conscience.

When she thought about it later, Holland pinpointed that as the moment she capitulated. If it hadn't been for the silhouette, or the music and the crackling fire . . . If Westbourne had gotten angry instead of maintaining his dignity . . . If just the slightest thing had been out of place to give her the excuse she looked for . . .

Later on, too, Holland would curse herself for wasting time and precious concentration on this personal baggage. She should have been asking why, after a couple of minutes had passed, the young woman hadn't put on a robe and come out to them, or at least called to her man. . . .

.   .   .

He was listening to Westbourne and the woman argue in the kitchen. He recognized her voice from the time she and the other agent had walked by the pond. She was young, not only by her tone but in what she was saying. He was thinking that if she grew up very quickly, it might save her life.

The cottage bedroom was large, about the size of a hotel suite. Besides the king-size bed, night tables, and a dresser, there was enough room for a love seat, an ottoman, and a coffee table in front of the fire. He had arranged the girl on the love seat, and the configuration of the room required that Westbourne and the Secret Service woman would have to come all the way in before they saw her. The gun he had was fitted with a silencer. He could shoot both Westbourne and the woman before either screamed. But then he'd have little time to go to work on Westbourne, because soon the woman would be missed.

Now the woman was in the living room, her rubber-soled shoes squeaking on the pine floorboards. Westbourne had stopped talking. He was probably standing watching her, arms crossed over his chest. The killer wondered if Westbourne would later remember how this woman might have saved his life if it hadn't been for his impatience and his stiff dick.

He heard shower curtain rings in the second bathroom being pulled back, a low chuckle from Westbourne, a closet door opening and closing. She was through the second bedroom now. The killer crouched by the dresser, his arms extending slowly, the gun rising smoothly. After he'd finished with Westbourne's mistress, he had carefully washed and dried his hands. Other parts of him were still painted and wet.

He heard Westbourne say, "Satisfied, Agent Tylo?" Then hesitation on her part. He imagined her expression, pensive, her thoughts torn between duty and discretion. By now she might be wondering why the girl hadn't come out, or why it was so quiet. He saw the first shadow fall across the cream-white carpet and raised the gun barrel one more inch. Then Westbourne trampled on the silence.

"I think it's time for us to say good night."

His tone held just the right mix of condescension and weariness, that of a man who had been catering to a subordinate and now was tired of it. But this Agent Tylo did not give up so easily. The killer had counted to 1,005 before he heard retreating footsteps.

The door lock slid back home, then Westbourne laughed softly as he came back to the bedroom. His cardigan was already off, fingers working the buttons of his country shirt. His mouth went slack when he saw the girl on the love seat, then his legs were kicked out from under him and he fell down hard. The killer had the handcuffs on him as quickly as a bass strikes a lure. A piece of silver duct tape went across the mouth, another around the ankles. Westbourne's rolling, wild eyes reminded the killer of a steer locked in the slaughter pen.

The killer was breathing evenly in spite of the exertion. He propped up Westbourne against the base of the love seat and stretched his legs out. In front of the fireplace was a screen of tempered glass with an etched art deco design. The senator couldn't help but look at it, and when he did he saw the girl's reflection, what was left of her chest and face. The killer thought this might serve to encourage Westbourne.

The knife was out again, very close to Westbourne's eyes.

"Now, my dear Cardinal, tell me all about the sins you wish to absolve yourself of."

Holland found Lamont Fleming alone in the kitchen over a mug of coffee and a bagel. He gestured to her to sit.

"Everyone bundled up for the night?"

Holland nodded. All the way back from the cottage, she had been thinking she should turn around and finish the walk-through. Then she remembered how silly she'd felt opening closet doors and pulling back the shower curtain, Westbourne's amused silence a brand on the back of her neck. She should have ignored it, finished her job, not surrendered to his mocking presence. Holland was glad Fleming hadn't asked for details.

"The relief team is running late. It'll be another half hour before they get here."

Fleming looked at her, saw something in her face, and silently rose to get her a coffee. Holland thanked him and spooned in sugar for the energy.

"Who'll be staying on, sir?"

Fleming sat again and leaned back, the chair riding on its hind legs. "The patrol at the gate, the two in here. The team covering the cottage, in the four-by-four, is done."

Fleming paused. "If you don't feel like driving back, there's plenty of room here."

"Thanks. But I'd rather wake up in my own bed."

"Amen to that."

Fleming asked her about Atlanta, and they both laughed when Holland described the expression on the banker's face when the bust came down. Fleming told her a couple of anecdotes from his days in Germany with the Marines. The conversation served as a current that slowly but steadily drew Holland away from the cottage, settled her, focused her on the thought of home. When the relief team came in, stomping their feet in the foyer, she wanted to thank Fleming for having taken the time with her. He must have known what was coming, because he stuck out his hand a little too quickly and, with a firm handshake, said it had been good to work with her. She could tell he was embarrassed but also meant what he said.

The Honda was an icebox, but Holland didn't give the engine more than a minute to warm up. She thought she could deal with the cold for a couple of miles before the heater kicked in. Releasing the handbrake, she coasted down the driveway, into the darkness.

Holland shifted into second to slow at the gate, already open. The headlights caught the medusa wires, and she was thinking how ugly they looked, when the radio went off.

There was no screaming or shouting, just an insistent voice over the crackle.

"Redrun One, Redrun One, Redrun One."

Holland slammed the stick shift into reverse, gravel flying from underneath the rear tires. She spun the Honda around, the left fender catching something soft—a hedge, maybe. Her right foot slipped off the brake and slammed onto the accelerator.

Redrun One . . . Holland had heard it only in training. It meant a full-blown emergency, that security had been breached and the individual under protection was down. As she headed the car back up the drive, she remembered veteran agents boasting that they'd spent entire careers without hearing that squawk.

Holland didn't stop when she got to the house but twisted the Honda onto the path that led to the cottage. Twice the tires caught on the soft earth near the bank of the pond.

She jolted past Fleming, his legs pumping, and kept her eyes on the cottage, searching for a fast-moving shadow.

There haven't been any explosions, no gunfire. . . .

Holland skidded to a stop in front of the replacement team's Jeep Cherokee. The doors were open, and as she streaked by she saw that the shotgun and submachine gun mounts were empty. Her weapon in hand, she slipped into the cottage and began calling out, identifying herself.

Inside, the lights were blazing but it was very quiet. Holland was in the living room, moving with her back pressed against the wall, still talking. She heard a murmur, from the bedroom. As she moved in she could make out the word, only one, repeated over and over again like a litany:

"Jesus, Jesus, Jesus . . ."

One agent was on his knees, leaning over a larger copper tub meant to hold firewood. The other stood facing the French doors, his back to the room, one arm pressed hard against his nose. His breathing was noisy as he drew air in through the nylon fabric of his jacket.

Holland finally registered the stench, hanging in the air warmed by the fireplace. She threw back her head and sucked in a deep breath through her mouth. As long as she could hold it she could look.

Westbourne was on the carpet, his back against the love seat, hands manacled. His face was a bloody mask, the skin peeled back down the cheeks. The right socket was a hollow black cavity; the left eye stared directly ahead, its lid sliced away. Below the breastbone was a neat inverted Y incision that released the viscera. They had slithered out with the blood and lay in a heap in Westbourne's lap. If Westbourne had still been alive when this had been done to him, he would have died very slowly, in great pain.

The sight of the girl made Holland gag. But she clawed through her revulsion and terror, looking for what seemed out of place. The girl had been placed on the bed, facedown, with blood-drenched pillows stuffed underneath her torso. One arm had been arranged to trail onto the night table, and a hand now rested on what Holland first mistook for a small alarm clock. It was the alarm panel, with two buttons, one depressed and partially covered by the girl's hand.

Fleming was in the room now, pulling the sick agent to his feet and shoving him into the hall. He grabbed the other man by the elbow, kicked open the French doors, and pushed him outside. Holland didn't realize how hot she was until she felt the clean night air on her cheek. She moved to the source and stopped a few feet from the agent who was telling Fleming what he and his partner had found after they'd heard the alarm go off.

Then Fleming was on the cell phone to the Marine station at Quantico, ordering in the Rapid Reaction Force that trained there. His second call woke up the director. After that he realized Holland was in the room.

"This place was supposed to be secure!" he whispered hoarsely. "What the hell happened?"

3

IT was going on four o'clock in the morning, that time when body and soul are most vulnerable. Death had already come and gone, but in the big house Holland felt surrounded by it, a dense fog that kept pressing in on her.

The helicopters were gone too, but their clatter still throbbed behind her temples. They had swept the perimeter, using infrared and heat-seeking scanners, and come up empty. It was the dog crews that uncovered the blind, but there was no material from which to take a scent. Forensics continued to pore over the rubber tarpaulin. As agents drifted in and out of the house, Holland picked up snippets of conversation. The crime scene in the cottage hadn't yielded anything useful, not even an unaccounted-for fingerprint. Not that it seemed to matter. Everyone was fixed on how the killer had gotten in, gotten past the safety net. Then out again. Questions that were now Deputy Director Arliss Johnson's purview.

Johnson showed up with two teams, one of which immediately replaced Fleming and his crew. The other went to work with the FBI Rapid Reaction Force that had choppered in from Quantico. Holland thought the second team was more for show, to keep the Service from being bullied off the investigation.

Johnson's role was to question all security personnel assigned to Oak Farms. Holland remembered the procedure from her training. Johnson would start with those who had primary responsibility for the charge. That meant her, because she had escorted Westbourne into the guesthouse, and the two agents who had been stationed outside.

Johnson appeared fresh and alert when he stepped into the formal dining room where Fleming had sent Holland to write her after-action report. He wore a navy blazer several style seasons old, gray trousers, and a fresh white shirt. Droplets of water glistened in his hair, the residue of a hasty shower.

Johnson was standing in the shadow of middle age, tall and trim, with a swimmer's ropy muscles and the sun-seared face of a Louisiana shrimper, all planes and angles. His eyes reminded Holland of Confederate soldiers in photographs, the way their gaze seemed to follow you out of the picture. Johnson needed eyes like that. He was the head of the Service's Inspection Division, the sentinel who watched the watchers.

Holland felt a bitter shame when she saw Johnson's concern for her. He had been one of her instructors at the Academy, but there had been history between them long before then. Johnson had been close to her on that bloody day in Paris when her world had exploded. He had become her safe harbor, helped her heal and, later, coaxed forth what it was that would make her life whole again. It was Johnson who had shown her the sanctuary of the Service, had administered the oath she had now broken. At this moment Holland was startled to learn what was, really, an ancient truth: that one way or another we almost invariably betray those we hold closest to us.

"Take a pew, Holland."

Johnson sat himself down at the center of the dining table, which could easily accommodate twelve. He arranged his paperwork neatly in front of him and intertwined his long, thick fingers. His eyes continued to play lightly over her face, and Holland thought that was because six months had passed since they'd seen each other. She sensed Johnson wanting to reach out to her, and having to hold himself back.

"No," he said, knowing what her first question would be.

"There's no line on the killer. No name, no face. Given the time frame, we think he's within a hundred-mile radius."

Johnson's expression softened. "I'm sorry about what's happened to you, Holland." She knew the stats: only three percent of Service people ever lost a charge in the course of their careers. Most of the rest didn't even come close. "But believe me, you *will* get through this."

He paused. "Have you talked to anyone else?"

Holland shook her head.

What Johnson meant was had she spoken with either Hotchkiss or Siciliano, the agents stationed outside the guesthouse. Fleming had made sure to keep the three of them apart. It was standard practice, so that personnel couldn't cover for one another.

"Okay," said Johnson. "Give me a minute with this."

He picked up Holland's report and began reading. Holland looked away. Her heart was like a tiny captive animal battering against its cage.

"You're saying that you walked Westbourne back to the cottage," Johnson murmured. "He was anxious to get to his lady friend, didn't want you to go inside, but you did."

"Right."

"You entered through the kitchen door." He looked down at the report. "Okay. First you checked the living room, then the guest bedroom and bathroom, the hall closets. Now you're on your way to the master suite. You step inside, see the fire, the furniture in front, a small corner of the bed. You hear music but not the girl."

"Yes."

Johnson leaned forward. "What's missing?"

"I didn't go all the way into the bedroom." Holland thought her voice sounded like it belonged to someone else. "I didn't secure it. There had to be an en-suite bathroom, closets, maybe even an alcove or something. I never saw any of them."

Johnson pushed himself forward in his chair, poised like a high-platform diver, then slumped back. "Why?"

"Westbourne was on me about how embarrassing the scene in the bedroom could be. He said that after the girl had arrived, no one had gone in or come out of the cottage. I thought about that. The cottage would have been searched before the girl was allowed through. Westbourne told me about the post outside—"

"None of those things matter," Johnson interrupted, his voice painfully soft. Gone was the concern for a rookie who'd walked into a situation that got blood up to her knees; it was replaced by realization that the rookie had messed up big-time.

"Even if the cottage had been searched hourly, you were supposed to do it again before you left Westbourne in there alone."

"I know that," Holland said clearly.

In spite of her humiliation, she refused to bow under his gaze.

Johnson did a drum roll with the eraser tip of a pencil. When he had the pencil between his fingers again, without warning it snapped in two.

"Let's see if we can get a sequence," he said, oblivious to what he'd just done. "Pick it up from the time Lane gets here."

Holland took a deep breath, steadied herself. "The girl arrives at half past five. Before then the cottage has been searched and deemed secure. The post is inside or around it between the time of the search and her arrival. They vet her and let her in without going through it again.

"The girl stays inside, and there's no mention she ever went out. The post doesn't report any intrusion; ditto for the helicopter sweeps and dog crews. The conference begins here in the house, and everything is still deemed secure. After the meeting I escort Westbourne to the cottage. I go through everything except the master bedroom."

"Go on, play it out," Johnson urged her.

She took a deep breath. "It's dark by six or six-fifteen. The killer is already in the blind—who knows how he got there or how long he's been waiting? Westbourne and I are at the cottage at seventeen minutes past midnight. I leave ten or twelve minutes later. That's at least a six-hour window. The autopsy will tell us when the girl died, but that may not count for much."

"Why?"

"Because we don't know whether the killer hung on to her before he murdered her. He may have done it right away or else waited awhile."

"Why would he wait?"

"I don't know."

"I think that's the way it stacks up," Johnson said. "I also know that there were times when the post wasn't in the immediate vicinity of the cottage. You should have known that too."

Holland thought hard but couldn't make the connection.

"Just before the meeting started, you and Fleming were walking back from the cottage . . . ," Johnson prompted her.

"He skipped a stone across the pond. There were voices on the other side."

Johnson nodded. "They weren't *that* far away, but our boy could have made his move then. The kitchen door lock had been tampered with, not so that you'd spot it, but enough to save him five, ten seconds getting in."

Holland felt shaken. She replayed sliding in the key, turning the knob. Had anything felt loose in her hand? Had there been a rattle?

"The lock's not important," Johnson was saying. "The killer's already inside."

"So am I," Holland said softly. "Westbourne is dogging me, but I still check the rooms. When I get to the bedroom, everything seems normal. The music is playing. There's perfume in the air. I don't smell blood, so he couldn't have cut her up yet, at least not badly. Another couple of steps and I'd see him—"

"And he'd see you and you'd be dead," Johnson finished. "Along with Westbourne. The killer would have a gun with a silencer. He wouldn't risk hand-to-hand combat. He'd take you first, before you could reach your weapon, then go after Westbourne. Killing you would mean he'd have a lot less than the forty-three minutes to do his work. Fleming would have expected you back in the house in ten, fifteen minutes at the outside."

"The alarm," Holland said slowly. "When I found Lane, her fingers were on the button." She looked up at Johnson. "Lane *couldn't* have been alive. Not the way she looked."

Johnson grimaced. "He's very clever, this boy, in a twisted way. Remember the pillows underneath Lane?"

Holland nodded.

"We're thinking he put them there on purpose, lifting her and placing her hand on the alarm. Then he finished cutting her. As the blood seeped into the pillows they sank, bringing Lane down too. Eventually there was enough pressure on her hand to push down the alarm button." He paused. "That was his wake-up call for us."

Holland forced herself to take a deep breath. What Johnson had described was inhuman.

"How could he know how quickly the pillows would sink?"

"You've got to believe this wasn't the first time he's used this method. Anyway, a couple minutes either way wouldn't matter to him."

Johnson paused.

"The President is getting Smith's preliminary report with his morning coffee. This is bad, Holland. And what comes now doesn't get any better." He paused. "Now go home, get some rest, and report to Smith's office at four o'clock."

His expression, when he spoke, resembled something like regret.

The state police had pushed back the media caravans that choked the road in front of the gates. Holland slowed to let a trooper move the sawhorse, then darted onto the road, the Honda squealing past charging reporters with their minicams and blinding lights. She reached the interstate in time to catch the morning rush hour.

Her Georgetown town house had once been as elegant as its neighbors. Now the brick facade could have used sandblasting and the shutters and trim a new coat of black enamel. It was Holland's only legacy of home and family, a final refuge.

Inside, the chilly air raised gooseflesh. Holland didn't bother turning up the heat, even as she let her clothes fall behind her on the way to the bathroom. She cranked the shower to full force and closed her eyes as the hot water sluiced over her. For a few precious moments she lost herself to the steam and sweet-smelling soap. Then, as she was reaching for a towel, an image stabbed her.

Holland shivered violently through her tears, her fingers clawing at the faucets, the water drumming on her sobs. In her mind's eye she saw a perfect spring day in Paris. She was thirteen years old, her first time abroad, stepping out of a car in front of the cathedral of Notre Dame. The man in front of her took a few steps, then turned back, smiling and holding out his hand to her. That was when the first bullet had struck him. The second one caught him as he was pitching over, sending a spray of blood across Holland and the new dress he'd bought for her. . . .

That man had been Holland's father, Senator Robert Beaumont.

Holland crouched in the corner of the shower stall, the water beating on her bowed head. The semblance of peace she'd won hard over the years had been a precious, fragile treasure, tucked way in the tough shell of understanding that on that day in Paris there wasn't anything she could have done. Now, in the blink of an eye, she was back on that cold and stony road strewn with pain and doubt and second guesses. Holland wondered where she could possibly find the strength to walk it again.

4

IT was not yet 7:00 A.M., and Wyatt Smith had been in his office for six hours. Six hours earlier, he'd roused the President's chief of staff to tell him about Oak Farms. The chief of staff, nicknamed the Gatekeeper because he was so fiercely protective of his boss, had decided not to wake the President. He told Smith he would be at the White House in ninety minutes and expected to have as detailed a report as possible waiting on his desk. He would check the President's schedule and shoehorn Smith into a meeting as soon as possible.

At three o'clock this morning, Smith received the initial forensic report from Quantico. A half-dozen fingerprints had been found in the cottage. Most belonged to Westbourne, Charlotte Lane, Holland Tylo, Lamont Fleming, and the two agents who had searched the cottage, then had stood post outside. But one palm print remained unaccounted for.

Smith put that report aside.

At four forty-five, the photo fax peeled out the first close-up shots of the bodies and the wounds. The Johns Hopkins pathologist included a note on the nature of the cuts: They were uniformly jagged, indicating a distinctive nick or abrasion on the blade of the knife that had been used.

Smith had been waiting for that as well.

Smith told his secretary to hold all calls for five minutes. He took the Quantico and Johns Hopkins reports over to a bare worktable, set them down side by side, and reread both. Standing motionless, he gazed down at the words until he could leech nothing more from them.

It was eleven-thirty in the morning London time when Smith's call went through. He heard Dicky Venables' broadly accented greeting and thought the ruddy-faced Yorkshireman who headed up Scotland Yard's antiterrorist branch had been perched by the phone all along.

"Sorry for your troubles, Wyatt," said Venables. "It's all over the telly here."

"That's always the way it is with bad news. Listen, Dicky. I need, a favor, fast. I have a print, pictures of the wounds. Can you run them through your files?"

"Something in our bailiwick, you think?" Venables asked carefully.

"A detail I remembered from our conference in November. I'm reacting, but . . ."

"Send them along."

Smith was already pecking on the computer. Four hundred miles over Newfoundland, a Hughes Spectra satellite picked up the signal and flashed it into the Cheltenham station, which then relayed it to London.

"We should do very nicely with the print," Venables was saying. "The wounds are interesting."

"How long for a possible match?"

"Fifteen to twenty minutes for the print. The wounds will take a little longer."

"I'll be waiting."

There were enough calls to keep Smith busy, but he held one line clear for Venables. He was talking to the chief of staff when his secretary buzzed.

"That was quick, Dicky."

"Sorry to have to be the one to break this to you, Wyatt. Your hunch was better than you thought."

Then Venables went ahead and told Smith exactly what he'd expected to hear.

"We managed an ident on the blade too. It ties in perfectly with the print. Wyatt, are you there?"

"Yes, Dicky. Sorry. Can you give me background?"

Venables was way ahead of him. "The latest stuff is on the wire to you." His voice dropped a decibel. "This is all very fresh, Wyatt. I haven't shared it with the smart set at the Hoover bunker or Langley. We've been sifting through it ourselves, trying to make sense of it."

"I won't use you as a whipping boy, Dicky. Let me know if you come up with anything."

The Yorkshireman's laugh sounded tinny.

"We can't expect everyone to have your manners, now can we? Mind that you watch your back, Wyatt. Ta."

Two hours before Smith's appointment with the President, the secretary ushered Johnson into the director's office.

When Smith offered coffee, Johnson noted how deliberate the director's movements were. Smith swung his entire arm, shifted his body weight on the balls of his feet as he turned, to avoid twisting the spine. On the bad days, Johnson imagined, Smith could actually feel the grinding of steel against cartilage.

There had been a time when the two men had almost reached the cusp of friendship. They had been partners together out of the Academy and cut their teeth in the Counterfeiting Division. Both had applied for and been accepted into Executive Protection, and that was where Smith had outshone everyone. No one could better read a potential assassin's methodology, or lay down the protection blanket more effectively as a result. What the public knew about Smith's having taken two bullets was only the glitter. How Smith had identified and quietly intercepted almost thirty other potential killers in the course of his career was the stuff of awe and legend.

Their career paths within the Service diverged at that point, but Johnson never begrudged his former partner his stellar rise. Nor did he ever think—as others did, and whispered as much— that Smith was always prone to take one too many chances with his body, all but invited a bullet to find him eventually. Johnson had investigated both shootings that had taken Smith down. He knew the bullets would have come no matter who was covering that day, and concluded that if anyone other than Smith had been involved, the bullets might have gotten through.

But Johnson, then only a yearling at Internal Security, had been ordered to draft a second report, this one on Smith's fitness to remain in the field. Johnson's superiors had thought nothing of the assignment, coming on the heels of the surgeon's report. Johnson had spelled out the obvious, that Smith's wounds and his attendant condition would make him ineligible to continue in Executive Protection. To this day he remembered Smith's cold, expressionless gaze as, after the hearing concluded, he was awarded his commendation. Smith did not say a word to him throughout the presentation, and later, when Johnson tried to approach him, gave him his back.

The moment reminded Johnson of a fat greasy candle collapsing into its own pool of wax, taking with it the last of a cold, flickering light. Now he wondered whether Smith would seize upon the memory when the time came for Johnson to tell him about Holland. He wondered what it was he might chance to see in those eyes.

"You know what day it is today?" Smith asked.

"April first."

"The media are saying the excitable boy did his work on April Fool's. Just to rub our noses in it."

Johnson nodded. The sick little joke had been started by a hillbilly disk jockey out of West Virginia, and the tabloids had pounced on it.

"What's the situation out there?" asked Smith.

"Everyone's done and gone. Both houses are sealed. The state troopers are standing post to keep away the ghouls. Quantico is sifting through the physical evidence, such as it is. Johns Hopkins is doing the autopsies."

The director raised his eyebrows.

"We managed to reach Westbourne's wife in London," Johnson explained. "She was at Heathrow, waiting on the Concorde.

She told us to do whatever was necessary." Johnson paused. "I know—usually the family's skittish about cutting up the body. She didn't think twice."

"What about the Lane woman?"

"Next of kin was a sister back in Wisconsin. She was pretty far gone when I talked to her. The tabloid sleazos were already camped on her doorstep. I walked her through all the options— twice. She told me to go ahead and do what I thought was right."

Smith nodded. Johnson had that gift of getting people not only to do his bidding but to feel good about it. He was especially effective on the telephone, where one only heard a soft, soothing voice.

"The McNulty twins," said Smith.

For an instant Johnson registered only the non sequitur, not its meaning.

"Tommy and Sean?"

"Tommy. He belongs to the palm print. It's tempting to think Sean was with him, since they always work together."

Johnson heaved himself out of the chair and went to the window, where he pressed his burning cheek against the cold glass.

"You want to tell me about it?"

Smith did, beginning with the photos of the wounds and how they had triggered a detail he'd come across during a law enforcement conference in London. He talked about Venables and showed Johnson the reams of paper that had been faxed in from Scotland Yard.

"Who else knows about this?" asked Johnson.

"Marshall at the FBI, Peterson at State, Reynolds at CIA."

"Where's the hunt now?"

"As of an hour ago, state trooper barracks east of the Mississippi were turning out. Customs and Immigration are staking out ports from Galveston to Maine, the FBI's handling the airports. Airlines, Amtrak, and Greyhound have been wired photos. Their security people'll make sure employees coming off and going on shifts get a good look at them. Detective squads in New York, Boston, and Philadelphia specializing in ethnic neighborhoods are filtering through the Irish communities."

"We never got any advance warning," Johnson said suddenly. "How the hell can that be?"

Smith filled him in on what he'd gotten from Venables. For almost half of their tender twenty-four years, the McNulty twins had been among the best killers the IRA ever produced. They were so good and had lasted that long because they developed a genuine taste for their work. British paratroopers had been after their hides for years, because the twins especially liked to prey on patrolling soldiers. It was understood that when caught they were not to be afforded the luxury of due process of law.

But recently the leadership of the IRA had become sick of and, Smith reckoned, more than a little afraid of its own monsters. Three months ago, Venables had learned from an informer that the twins had been banished. But not defanged. They had offered their services to an extremist offshoot, the Brotherhood, and been accepted.

"Venables' best information had the twins lying low," Smith continued. "The Brotherhood hadn't made a move in months. The general thinking was they were short on guns and money."

"But not knives," Johnson said.

"That's Tommy's trademark. He always liked to work in close, and he's used that knife on British soldiers. That's how Venables ID'd it so fast."

"But why Westbourne?"

"I'm thinking the Brotherhood wanted to shit in the IRA's nest. Kill an American, someone like Westbourne, and contributions to the Cause will go south. Maybe it's the Brotherhood's first play to supplant the old-line IRA."

Smith paused. "We'll know more soon. Venables is beating the bushes hard."

"The Agency didn't have a line on this?"

"That the McNultys had switched? Maybe. That they were coming after Westbourne? I don't even want to think that."

"How much does the President know?"

"The Gatekeeper has everything we do."

"That means it's all over the Hill by now," said Johnson. The chief of staff had a bad habit of feeding tidbits to favored senators.

Smith let a beat of silence go by.

"Razorback'll be wanting to know if one or both of the twins made it onto the property *before* we swept it."

Johnson had been anticipating this. Now Smith had put the presidential imprimatur on it, and there was nowhere for Johnson to segue.

"We can't know for sure. Only Tommy or Sean'll be able to tell us that. The duck blinds are big enough to hold one man. The other two weren't used. We should figure only one McNulty in close. If the other was around, he was with the getaway vehicle.

"Forensics thinks he spent a lot of time in the blind. The earth was flattened, lots of compressed leaves and reeds. But then they say that could have been done if he'd stayed there four hours or forty."

Johnson paused. "Do we think the twins—or one of them—are still in the country?"

"It's been sixteen hours. Langley's been working with its friends in low places, covering Heathrow, Gatwick, and Dublin, Charles de Gaulle in Paris; Madrid, Frankfurt, and Rome. Not a peep. I'm inclined to think they haven't made it out."

Smith perched on the corner of his desk, one foot swinging lightly.

"Whatever you have for me, it can't be all good, right?"

Johnson took a deep breath, suddenly very annoyed that Smith could read him so easily. "There was a hole in the coverage. A pinprick, but—"

"Hotchkiss and Siciliano?"

"They're clean. Fleming's logs show they checked out the cottage before Lane got there, took her in, and kept their perimeter."

"They never saw or heard anything?"

"I sat across the table from them. They weren't lying or covering. They played it by the Book," Johnson said, referring to the Service's Standard Rules of Procedures and Practice.

Smith looked away. "But not Tylo."

"Not all the way."

Silently Smith held out his hand for the report, flipped it open at the dog-eared page.

"Says here Westbourne was on her case about her going into the cottage before him."

"I believe her," said Johnson. "She stated it as a fact, not something she was hiding behind."

"Just as well she came clean. No one on the Hill is going to want to hear how Westbourne may have contributed to his own death."

Smith slipped off the desk, thrust his hands deep in his pockets. "That's all of it?"

Johnson nodded and moved fast to cover what territory he could. He didn't care how it sounded. "Wyatt, I don't want her hung out to dry. Not if we're sure the McNultys were involved."

Smith fixed his gaze on him. "The calls have already started coming in from the Hill. People want to know what happened. More than that, they *don't* want to believe someone was actually good enough to get past us without a mistake having been made. You've been around that block, Arliss. They're looking for a guilty body, preferably a warm one."

Like the one I've just handed you.

Yet Johnson detected no malice in Smith's tone. The director's pain and flash of anger at being told an agent had let down the side sounded genuine. Johnson recalled that after Smith had been removed from field duty, he had remained unerringly polite and businesslike whenever he had to deal with Johnson. Smith could sit on his true feelings better than anyone Johnson knew.

"You have Tylo coming in later today?" Smith was asking.

"At four."

"Make it an hour earlier. I'll want to talk to her." Smith cut off Johnson's question with a warning glance.

"I have to tell the President about Tylo. You know I don't have any choice in that, Arliss. He'll want to know what I intend to do about her. . . ."

Johnson let the silence hang.

"I'll do what I can to make sure people understand the circumstances she was working under," Smith picked up. "It may count for something. I don't know." Another pause. "The hounds are baying, Arliss, and right now Tylo's the only bone I have."

5

HOLLAND managed a few hours of rest, waking up at one in the afternoon after a tossing, nightmare-ridden sleep. She rose and padded back into the shower. Only when she stepped out of the bedroom suite did she smell the aroma of fresh coffee.

She found Suress in the living room, a pot of coffee resting on a ceramic plate set on a low glass-top table. He came to his feet and wordlessly put his arms around her, his fingers combing through her damp hair.

"A little tough," he murmured, lips brushing her forehead.

"Big-time tough."

When Holland drew back, the top of his shirt was spotted wet.

"I'm so sorry," Suress whispered. "More than I can say. I should never have green-lighted you for the assignment, not right after Atlanta. . . ."

Holland drew back. "Atlanta has nothing to do with this. I was fine. Don't tear yourself up searching for excuses for me. You won't find any."

She nodded toward the coffee. "It smells too good to waste. Pour me some."

She settled in beside him on the couch and let him serve. The television was on, the sound mute.

"What's on the tube?"

Suress brought up the audio. "Something you need to see."

The feed was coming live out of CNN's Washington bureau. The reporter had rounded up a talking-head expert, a sad-faced young man from the Brookings Institute who had plenty to say. Holland started when the picture of the McNultys flashed on the screen.

Tommy and Sean, all of twenty-four years old, smiling for the cameras like it was some backyard party. Identical curly hair, worn long to the collar, the same needlelike nose and thin lips that seemed to curl over their teeth. Tommy was the one who practiced dental hygiene.

But it was their eyes that chilled Holland. Open wide, they stared out in a manic glee born not of courage but of idiocy. Those eyes could have stared down the devil.

"It was *them?*" she whispered. "No mistake?"

Suress shook his head. "We found Tommy's palm print."

The talking head was rambling on about classic sociopathic symptoms and manifestations, and that's when Holland's rage shut out his voice. There was nothing to explain here. She'd read enough about the McNultys' bloody exploits. They were Death's henchmen, killing for pleasure while spouting ideology and pocketing profit.

Which one of you was there? How close did I come to you?

Holland fiercely rubbed her forearm to get rid of the crawling gooseflesh.

"A palm print," she murmured.

"They got careless, we got lucky."

Holland looked up at him. "How much can you share?"

Suress told her how Smith had made the connection and about the evidence the British had provided that ultimately had linked the McNultys to the massacre. About the manhunt, he said more than Arliss Johnson had authorized, because the rules didn't apply to Holland anymore . . . even if she didn't know that yet.

Holland listened intently, filing away every scrap of information. Deep inside her rose a wisp of hope. Somehow she had to convince the director to let her in on the hunt. If she was given a chance . . .

Out of the corner of her eye she noticed Suress reach for the remote control.

"No, Frank. Leave it on."

"Believe me, you don't want to see this."

She snatched the remote from his hand and increased the volume. The coverage broke away to a news conference at the Senate media room. A gaggle of congressmen with the bright angry eyes of crows were clustered behind one of their own, a thin woman with pinched features and too much makeup. Senator Barbara Zentner's reedy voice spat the words out at the press corps.

"I have it on the best authority," the California Republican, chairman of the powerful Finance Committee, was saying, "that there was a breakdown in the Secret Service protection for Senator Westbourne. My sources indicate that the junior agent—a trainee, really—who was assigned to the senator did not strictly adhere to Service protocols. . . ."

A shudder worked itself through Holland.

"Where did she get *that?*"

Suress grabbed the remote and killed the power. Holland had jumped to her feet and was stalking up and down the room.

"How could Zentner know, Frank?" she repeated. "There was my report and Johnson's. Both went to the director. You don't think—"

Suress made a move to rise, but Holland shied away.

"Don't even think like that," Suress warned her. "Smith is a stand-up guy. There are lots of ways Zentner could have ID'd you."

"Name one!"

Suress bit his lip. Holland had no idea how swiftly the Service rumor mill worked. When someone under protection is taken down, the entire organism quivers from the shock. Details travel faster than gossip on a small-town party line. Suress himself had heard about the tragedy less than a half hour after it had occurred. And he'd been in bed, asleep.

"However it happened—and I tell you, it *wasn't* Smith's doing —the word is out," Suress said carefully. "There's nothing you can do about it—"

"Smith wants me in his office at three o'clock," Holland said suddenly. "He's going to pull the plug, isn't he?"

Suress had to look away. Holland's sudden realization, the terrible truth of what she had yet to face, wrenched his heart.

"Isn't he?"

"He's going to put you on administrative leave, pending a formal hearing."

Holland felt a hot flush creep up her neck.

"Section Fourteen, paragraph three-C of the Book" she whispered. "They're going to go through the motions, but in the end they'll throw me out."

"You don't know *what* the hearing will produce," Suress told her. "The McNultys' involvement puts a whole new spin on things."

Holland reached across and drew her fingernails over the back of his hand.

"Does it, Frank? Is that what you *really* believe?"

Holland stood firm in the face of Suress's protests when she asked him to leave. She needed to be alone, to compose herself for her meeting with Smith, concentrate on that and at the same time deal with the surges of panic and hopelessness.

Holland replayed each minute she'd spent in the guesthouse, and each time, she crashed against the same stumbling block: by not making sure that the bedroom was secure, she had been derelict in her duty. Any explanation, excuse, or possible reprieve died there.

But that didn't mean she couldn't help in the hunt for the McNultys. Right now Smith would need every warm body he could get his hands on. All she wanted was a chance—to try, to do *something*. When it came to the McNultys, Holland believed she was owed that much.

Holland went into the bedroom and dressed in the first clothes she plucked out of the closet. She forced herself not to leave the house until thirty minutes to her meeting, but traffic turned out to be light and she ended up having to wait in Smith's reception area. The secretary's brief glance and few words betrayed her pity.

"You may go in now."

Smith wasn't behind his desk, as Holland had expected him to be. He was seated on an old-fashioned nail-studded couch of green leather, his glasses dangling from his fingers. Holland was dismayed at how exhausted he appeared, like a patient whose medical treatment was slowly killing him.

"Are you okay—under the circumstances?" asked Smith, indicating a chair covered in pinto horsehair.

"Under the circumstances."

"Have you had a chance to follow developments?"

"Only what I saw on CNN."

"Good enough. They're in their vigil mode. Did you catch Zentner's piece?"

"Yes. 'Inadequate and inexperienced protection.' I was waiting for my name to come up."

"It has." Smith didn't elaborate. "So you know about the McNultys, then. There's not much more. The unidentified palm print in the guesthouse rang cherries. That and a peculiar nick in the blade of the weapon."

He was moving too fast, obviously wanting to get this interview over with, but Holland wasn't buying into that.

"Sir, how did Senator Zentner get her information?"

Smith pinched the bridge of his nose, then set his glasses back on. "Someone's been talking out of school, Tylo. The FBI's been huddling over at the Hoover Building all day long. I'm thinking that Zentner nagged them about you."

"There's something I need to know," Holland said slowly. "Was it my mistake? Am I the only one responsible?"

"You made the mistake of not going by the Book. That's what you're responsible for. No one can change that. Maybe things will look different when we catch up with the McNultys."

The words were tinged with regret, as though Smith hadn't really wanted to say them. Holland thought he was the kind of man who'd never been much good at raising false hope. Still, he had offered her something, and she was grateful for that.

"What is going to happen now?

She read his apology even before he spoke.

"There'll be an internal hearing about ten days from now. Bill Clements, the assistant secretary of the Treasury who looks after the Service, will chair. I'll be there, along with Arliss Johnson. We'll have gone through all the after-action reports to exactly determine your role. You'll be given a chance to say your piece, then we'll vote on whether or not to ask for your resignation."

"The outcome of that vote isn't really in doubt, is it?" Holland asked softly.

Smith did not retreat from her gaze. "No, it isn't. I'm sorry."

"What happens in the meantime?"

"As of right now you're on administrative leave. You can keep your badge for identification purposes, but there's no need to come into the office."

She knew he wasn't finished, but she had nothing to lose, except this last chance.

"I know you're hunting the McNultys. Everybody wants a piece of them, but we have to get to them first. You need every agent you have. I can help, if you'll let me."

For an instant Holland thought he might turn on her. Instead, all she saw on his face was the terrible weight of the burden she'd created for him.

"I might want to do that, Tylo," Smith said softly. "I might even think it's the right thing to do. But I can't let you in on this."

Smith rose, stuffing his hands deep into his pants pockets.

"It'll be the hardest thing to do right now, but I want you to think ahead. You're talented and capable. You're young. Don't let one mistake cripple you." He paused. "Later, when you've decided which way to go, if there's anything I can help you with . . ."

Holland felt an eerie calm about her. Now she knew exactly what she faced. She'd be able to deal with it. Somehow. Eventually.

The interview was over, and she sensed Smith was groping for a graceful way to see her out. Holland picked up her purse.

"Can I ask you a question?"

"Sure."

"I haven't read the classified stuff on the McNultys, but there's never been any mention in the media about their torturing their targets. Kneecapping, yes. But nothing like what was done to the senator or Charlotte Lane. It's the sort of thing that would be hard to ignore."

"I'm sure you're right, Tylo," Smith said, already moving to the door. "I'll have someone pick it apart, okay?"

For the first time since she'd been in Smith's presence, Holland was surprised. His rebuff bordered on rudeness, something Holland would have thought him incapable of.

TWO agents from the Internal Security Division flanked Smith as he stepped into the elevator. Halfway down to the garage, a microphone warbled softly. One of the agents pressed a finger against his earpiece, listened, then leaned toward Smith and whispered the message. Smith, who had been expecting the contact, was surprised it was so blatant.

"Tell them it's okay."

The Secret Service garage was a large, well-lit, spotless area that could have passed for a luxury-car dealership. Under fluorescent lights gleamed five identical copies of the presidential limousine, armor-plated and bulletproof. Against one wall was a brace of Service chase cars, fueled and tuned to perfection. Other vehicles, including Jeep Cherokee medical units, were on hoists, being attended to by mechanics. There were no pinups, cheesy calendars, or blaring radios, only soothing concert music drifting out from concealed speakers.

Smith's boot heels clattered down the metal catwalk. At the bottom, a few feet away from the director's Lincoln Town Car, stood a figure in an elegantly cut cashmere overcoat, a silk scarf, and calfskin gloves. He was in his early forties, and his features had a lumpy, unfinished quality that could have been mistaken for the aftereffects of recent plastic surgery. The waxed-out blue eyes rested under eyebrows that were almost white, the same color as the thin, expensively coiffed hair. The skin had a pink sheen to it, reflecting a recent sunburn or perhaps a drinking problem. Smith knew it was neither. James Croft, the senior senator from Illinois, head of the Senate Intelligence Committee, was a borderline albino.

"Good afternoon, Director. Although I guess it's not really that, is it?"

"I've had better," Smith replied coolly.

An agent held open the back door, and both men got in. The soundproof partition, darkened so that the driver couldn't read lips, was already up. Smith pressed the intercom button, and the sedan was rolling.

"Couldn't this have waited?" Smith demanded.

Croft chuckled softly. "I had to see you before you met with the President. Your secretary cut me off twice. If I didn't know better, I'd think you were trying to avoid me."

"There's nothing to tell," Smith said. "You already know what happened."

"But not *how*. That's what we're concerned with. We need to know what kind of fallout to expect."

Smith braced himself as the sedan turned sharply onto Constitution Avenue.

"There won't be any fallout," he replied, looking out the one-way glass at pedestrians who stared at the car.

"Suppose you give me the particulars and let me be the judge of that."

"Tylo has already admitted, in writing, that she failed to check the bedroom in the guesthouse. That's enough to hang her right there."

"So the internal investigation will begin and end with her," Croft murmured.

"*Any* investigation will do that," Smith snapped. "You won't even have to bother steering it."

Croft's brittle laughter mocked Smith. "Don't tell me you're having a crisis of conscience, Wyatt."

They were at the White House gates, and the driver had his

window rolled down, displaying identification. Smith waited until they were moving again.

"It's safe now," he said. "Do you understand that? No one has to worry anymore."

Croft debated if this was the time and place to rock Smith's fragile world with the revelation that there was in fact *a lot* still to worry about. He decided no. He'd give the director a chance to steady himself and get through this meeting with the President. Later, if Smith was needed again, Croft was sure he could count on his unstinting cooperation.

7

THE man entering the Four Seasons Hotel in Georgetown in the late afternoon attracted little attention from the staff. This was partly because of the cocktail hour rush and because the man was not a "face"—a political or entertainment celebrity. Nor was he one of the majors among the power brokers and lobbyists who huddle in the recesses of the hotel's mezzanine lounge. Floor security pegged him as a guest; the young female concierge thought him pleasant enough as she handed him a courier-delivered package the size of a paperback novel.

The computer had him listed as Mr. Alexander Bonatti, an executive with a San Francisco–based publishing house. The concierge, who was of Italian descent, thought his features were a little sharp, his skin hue a tad dark—almost Levantine. She put it down to his people having come from the Naples area, maybe even as far south as Sicily. What she really noticed about him were his hands, as he took the package. They were fine-boned, with long, smooth fingers, the nails carefully manicured and buffed. Here was a man who understood how important hands were to a woman, how she might want to be touched by such a fine, clean pair.

The man who was not Alexander Bonatti strolled through the

busy lobby to the elevators. He had a junior suite on the tenth floor overlooking the hotel gardens, and now he opened the French doors and stepped out on the tiny balcony. The pulse of the city throbbed pleasantly against his skin.

Among the fraternity that sought out his particular talents—some even said genius—he was called, simply, Preacher. The usual article was never used, and he did not correct those who addressed him by the single noun.

Preacher, born thirty-eight years ago in Pawtucket, Rhode Island, popped the staples of the package one by one. His dark features were a gift from his mother, a Spaniard from the Basque province. His taste for blood had been suckled at a different breast.

Preacher brought the contents of the package, a slender tome bound in fine calfskin, up to his nostrils and inhaled deeply. All the while, he continued to drink in the tempo of the city.

He had not been in this country for over ten years, made an exile who managed to spirit himself out just before that keenest of hounds had tracked him down. Ten years . . . So much had changed, yet equally much seemed painfully familiar. Preacher looked forward to exploring the dichotomy. The man who had come to him in Thailand had provided the very best papers. As an extra precaution, Preacher's real name and photo ID had been erased from the Watch List. The Immigration officer at LAX had welcomed Preacher home and actually made a casual salute. Preacher had been thrilled, even though he knew that the government flunky had mistaken the close-cropped, fit, casually dressed Preacher for an officer traveling in mufti.

Yes, it was so good to be back, to be doing what one did best—as that pompous ass Westbourne and his little buttercup had discovered. Preacher took great pride in his work, was intoxicated by it, especially when he could choose the method. Now that his principal task was half completed, he could turn his attention to how best to address the very personal matter he had waited ten years to deal with.

Preacher wondered idly if the object of his desire had any inkling Preacher was coming for him. *None at all.* But not because the man was stupid or careless. He simply could not countenance the possibility and at the moment was, Preacher surmised, quite wrapped up in other pursuits.

As Preacher looked over the city, he thought that today the self-confidence and bravado were down a decibel or two. At lunch, he had stopped off in an upscale sports bar. The television sets were going strong, and the crowd—young, moneyed, brash—was watching as eulogies poured forth from politicians of every rank and persuasion, from the President on down. Preacher didn't miss the anger in the clenched jaws and the fingers curled too tightly around cocktail glasses. It was harsh, unyielding, and demanding, the kind born of frustration in a people who wanted to lash out and punish. Preacher had witnessed the same emotion and reaction in New York after the World Trade Center bombing.

The phone chirped, and Preacher stepped inside, making sure to close the balcony doors behind him. He was expecting the call.

"Yes."

The voice on the other end of the line had been electronically altered, sounding as though the speaker were underwater.

"It did not go well."

"Westbourne preferred to suffer and die rather than give up the second diskette," Preacher replied. "There is nothing to be done when one faces a man like that. But you have the one diskette I took from him. Tell me where to look, and I will find the other."

"Unfortunately," the principal said harshly, "the diskette you retrieved was of absolutely no value to us. It contained office business, nothing more."

Even through the electronic distortion Preacher sensed the principal's rage. And something else . . . a veil of fear.

"Could the diskette still be in the house?" he asked.

"Doubtful, but we're looking. We believe that Westbourne may have given it to someone for safekeeping, to hold for him until the next day, when he could return it to wherever he was caching it."

Or else it was going to be delivered to him, Preacher thought. By someone who had no idea of what it was he or she was handling.

Preacher summoned up the images of the people he'd seen at

Oak Farms. The two agents around the house, the older man—
the one in charge. And the young woman . . . Westbourne had
called her Tylo.

"I need pictures and names." Preacher elaborated on what he
wanted.

"That'll be no problem," the principal said. "Do you really
think—"

"I don't know. *You* don't know. Maybe the diskette has already
been returned to its vault. Maybe Westbourne stashed it somewhere else. Send me what I asked for. Let me think about this."

"Very well. I'll get the material to you as soon as possible. I
trust you understand how anxious we are to put this matter to
rest."

"Yes. I believe I do."

Preacher hung up the phone, then took an imported beer out
of the minifridge. The cold pale lager felt good on the back of
his throat. He fished out a cigarette and evaluated his situation.
Preacher always made sure that his own flanks were covered first.

The most important thing was that the palm print had been
found and connected, along with the knife wounds, to the McNultys. Preacher considered that a tidy piece of work on his part.
Whatever are the twins thinking now? he wondered. He imagined
them stewing in some godforsaken rat's nest in Merseyside, trying
to figure out how to tell the world they were innocent. Going to
the local constabulary was certainly *not* an option. And if the
McNultys get hold of a sympathizer in the media, who would
believe them? No, on that count everything was fine.

As for the car he'd used to get to and from Oak Farms, that had
been abandoned in a Baltimore ghetto. By now it had surely been
stolen and was probably in a chop shop.

Preacher had taken a bus from Baltimore to Washington. He
had looked out the window during the entire ride, rediscovering
America. At the Washington depot, he had wandered into a
promising-looking alley and found a homeless person who could
make good use of the warm Arctic jumpsuit that had served him
so well in the duck blind.

The knife, with its distinctive notch on the blade, had gone into
the Dumpster behind the bus depot cafeteria.

The only thing Preacher found remarkable—and baffling—about events was Westbourne's unwillingness to talk. Preacher was something of an expert on pain. It held no terror for him. He never heard the cries of those he tortured and only dimly recalled the smell of their blood.

Preacher knew that Westbourne had suffered greatly under his ministrations. He had made it clear that the senator had only to tell him where to find the second diskette and the end would be swift. But Westbourne had not talked, not when Preacher made an example of the girl, not even when the flesh was being carved from Westbourne's own carcass.

Now Preacher understood why that had been so. Westbourne had been playing tricks, carrying a worthless diskette when he came into the guesthouse. Preacher could only imagine the measure of Westbourne's satisfaction when he realized that his torturer had accepted the diskette as valuable. It had been enough to sustain Westbourne through a terrible ordeal, and for that alone Preacher silently commended him. It wasn't often that the dead could spit at you from their graves.

But really, it was only a minor setback. Preacher poured out the last of his beer. The details he asked for would reach him in due course. Meantime there were other things to keep him busy. Preacher reached for the calfskin-bound volume he'd purchased at a smart bookshop and had delivered to the hotel. The gold letters on the spine read *Social Register.*

He found the entry he wanted, over half a page of small print. Preacher thought it made for fascinating reading.

Thirty minutes later, Preacher left the hotel and walked along M Street to Thirty-third Street in Georgetown. He crossed M Street, then took the steps that led down to the canal. At the water he turned left and weaved his way among the students and tourists who were taking advantage of the sun-dappled break in the foul weather. At the point where Georgetown Park met the canal, Preacher saw what, in another lifetime, had been an achingly familiar landmark.

The squat fieldstone building was all but invisible because of the tangle of vines across its face. Next to the polished black door was a plaque from the Historical Register, identifying the structure as a coach and ale house erected in 1779. Preacher pulled open the door and stepped into gloom smelling of sawdust, old timber, and bourbon.

At the Coach and Arms there was no patio with inviting tables and shady umbrellas to lure in the tourists. Locals who happened on the place quickly discovered that the decibel level of conversation dropped upon their entry. The bartender was amiable but hardly encouraging; the patrons kept to themselves. Few of the uninitiated stayed long enough to finish their drink. Later, they would wonder what was wrong with the place, and if they had asked the right person, they would learn that the Coach and Arms was, and had been for many years, the exclusive preserve of the Secret Service.

Whatever lunch crowd there might have been was gone. Only a few tables were still occupied, and the bar was empty. Preacher walked up, pushed aside twin stools, and ordered Barbière Haitian rum, double, straight up.

The bartender's eyes drifted over the tall, dark-complected man who kept his face toward the mullioned window. The bartender couldn't get a good look at it because of the light refracting off the thick glass. He was certain he hadn't seen the man before, but his physique and the way he carried himself, gliding, rather than walking, on the balls of his feet, gave him away. Not from the local post. Judging by the tan, transferred in from L.A. or even Honolulu.

Preacher curled his palm around the thick glass, warming the rum. He was not concerned about running into anyone who might recognize him. Even if he chanced to do so, his was quite a different face now from ten years ago.

But here all that had been lost could be remembered, turned over in one's fingers the way a man might examine an unexpectedly rediscovered treasure in a boyhood shoe box. For Preacher had once been a member of the fraternity that congregated here. The nicks and scratches on the weathered bar were like ancient scars on his own body. The low rumble of male conversation was as familiar as the surge of the sea through a shell. It was a life he had reveled in and that had been snatched away by one whose face floated in the pit that was Preacher's heart.

He lifted the glass and wet his lips with the rum. It was as warm as it needed to be. From his jacket pocket Preacher withdrew a pair of kitchen matches, the blue and red ends held tightly together. With his other hand he spilled the Barbière on the bar, at the same time flicking his thumb. White-hot phosphorus seared across his nail, but he waited another second for both matches to catch. He smiled dreamily into the golden pool of liquor, then put it to the flame.

Somewhere across a vast distance, Preacher heard the bartender shout. Chairs scraped across floorboards long ago stripped of their shellac. When suit jackets fell open, he could smell the oil from holstered guns.

Preacher had already turned, was walking out the door with the measured pace of a man who understands he will not be challenged. He had no doubt the patrons of the Coach and Arms would, after their shock, recognize his gesture. He wondered only how long it would take for the word to reach Arliss Johnson.

8

April 3

TWO days after the killings at Oak Farms, the flags in thousands of communities across the country flew at half mast. The governor of New Hampshire, the state Charles Westbourne had represented for twenty years, had declared it a day of mourning. Three hundred dignitaries, including the President, his cabinet and members of the business world, crowded into the chapel of Georgetown University for the funeral service.

Even under different circumstances Holland wouldn't have attended the ceremony. She watched CNN's live telecast while getting dressed. The subdued pomp and circumstance pricked the scar of old wounds. Holland switched off the set and left the house. For her, there was another way to try to make her peace with the man whose trust she'd betrayed.

Security in and around Georgetown was the tightest Holland had ever seen, with uniformed police on every corner. In the crowds it was easy to spot the deliberately anonymous men whose eyes never stopped moving.

As she made her way through the stop-and-go traffic, Holland imagined where Frank Suress might be at this moment. She pictured him in the chapel, moving deftly among ambassadors and consuls, eyes constantly roving, his hands never far from his weapon.

Holland felt a familiar knot forming in her stomach, being tightened by the fear she experienced every time Frank was in the field. They had talked about that, and now he felt the same way when she was standing post. The hint of danger added a certain urgency to their relationship, made them crave their love, devour it when they came together. Holland remembered Frank telling her that passion was what they had instead of worry. Each time they made love, they laughed at death. Afterward, when it was time to get back to the job, they were kind and considerate and tender with each other, always taking a few seconds for a last embrace. Just in case.

I should be out there with him. That's where I belong. That's the only place I really belong. . . .

Behind her a car horn blared. Holland spotted an opening in traffic and shot into it, only to come to a hard stop at the on-ramp to the Key Bridge. As she nursed the Honda along, she wiped her eyes with the back of her hand. When she looked up, she saw the driver on the right staring at her. He was nodding in sympathy, offering an encouraging smile. . . .

On the other side of the Potomac the wind freshened, gliding across the vast expanse of Arlington Cemetery. Holland arrived well ahead of the cortege, parked near the area dedicated to those who had fallen in Korea, and made her way up the gentle incline to an open space with stone benches arranged in a circle. This was one of the many "silent places" that dotted the cemetery, where the grieving could reflect and meditate.

The newspapers had written that at the family's request the graveside service would be limited to immediate kin. Only four limousines, surrounded by outriders and security, drew up behind the hearse. Holland watched as the mourners assembled and the coffin was carried to the bier. When all were gathered, the minister stepped forward and began to recite the Twenty-third Psalm.

Standing on the knoll, fifty-odd yards away, Holland bowed her head in prayer. Her lips moved silently, and from time to time she tasted the salt of those tears the wind hadn't been quick enough to dry.

Holland raised her head when the minister began his eulogy. For the first time, she took a good look at the mourners. Seated in front of the flower-decked coffin was Cynthia Palmer, all in black and veiled. She sat alone because the Westbournes had been childless. Holland found herself wondering if Palmer regretted that now.

Behind the widow, in a semicircle, were the family, three brothers and two sisters, whose faces Holland recognized from Westbourne's personnel file. They were all prominent in their fields, their names adorning the letterheads of prestigious law firms and giant corporations. There was a younger, bearded man among them, his collar turned up against the wind. He was standing off to the side behind the brothers, and Holland thought he must be someone's personal assistant, brought along to run interference.

And there was someone else—a woman in her late twenties or early thirties, her face thin and pinched. The wind had left red blotches on her cheeks, streaked by dried tears, and she was twisting a handkerchief in her fingers. Even from where Holland stood she could see the woman shivering. The black coat was strictly Kmart, with no lining, and the wind flapped it against her legs.

It took Holland a moment to place her: Boston, when Holland was working Westbourne. A woman who'd been in and out of Westbourne's suite. Mousy brown hair framing thin, homely features, a breathless air to her that had drawn Holland's attention. Judith Trask, Westbourne's principal researcher and speechwriter. Back then Holland had pegged her, not unkindly, as one of a recognized breed, the backroom drone who toils in obscurity, uncomplaining, feeding off that intangible sustenance of the powerful.

That Judith Trask was here made sense to Holland. But something wasn't quite right. At the core of the woman's grief Holland sensed nervousness. Something about those shifting feet, the way she kept looking around herself.

"Excuse me, ma'am. May I see some identification?"

Holland had been so intent on Judith Trask that she hadn't heard the man come up behind her. He was young, in his mid twenties, maybe, and light on his feet, like a quick shortstop. He wore jeans, a plaid jacket, and a cloth cap. The workman's costume would have worked, except for the gun butt peeking out from under the jacket, the tiny video camera hidden in his palm, and the FBI identification hanging from his neck, the letters in bold blue.

"Secret Service," Holland replied crisply. "The ID's in my purse."

His left hand had already drifted toward his gun, so Holland shrugged the purse off her shoulder, letting it fall open. In a smooth, unhurried motion she reached inside and plucked out the laminated card with her fingertips.

The FBI agent matched her features with the photo on the card and handed it back.

"Sorry about that, Agent Tylo," the agent said. He held out his hand. "Brad Norman, special agent, surveillance."

"I thought all the action was back in Georgetown," said Holland.

Norman grinned, making himself look sixteen. His drawl was pure Ozark.

"Yeah, well. Someone's got to do the scut work."

"They sent me out to see if anyone unexpected showed up," Holland improvised. "You know the faces down there?"

"Sure."

"What about the one with the beard?"

Norman lifted his head like a hunting dog, the tanned creases under his eyes making crow's-feet.

"Can't say he's familiar," he murmured. "I reckoned he was brought along at the last minute. You know, a spear carrier."

"Do you have him on tape?"

Norman tapped the camera. "Absolutely."

"Think you could send me a duplicate?"

"No problem. I can get you stills too, if you want."

Holland smiled. She wasn't interested in the bearded man; ask-

ing for the tape had just popped into her mind to make conversation. It was the image of Judith Trask that kept nagging her.

"If you like, I can bring it around later today," Norman was
saying, his tone hopeful.

That's when Holland remembered she didn't have a desk anymore.

"Better get it straight to my boss," she said, fishing out an auto-
body shop card. I'm up for rotation."

She scribbled Frank Suress's name and department on the
back. But Norman wasn't giving up that easily. He dug into his
pocket for his card and handed it over.

"Just in case you need anything done to the tape," he
said, offering her a toothy grin. "You know, enhancements,
whatever."

Holland thought he was sweet. She began to slip the card into
her handbag, her mind angling for some kind of graceful exit,
when suddenly she felt a sharp, slicing pain in her finger. Holland
jerked her hand back. Blood pooled on the tip of her right index
finger.

"Are you okay?" Norman asked, his concern verging on the
theatrical.

"Fine," Holland replied impatiently. "Must have been a pin—"

But it wasn't. Carefully, with her left hand, she fished down the
side of her purse, followed the zipper to the pocket sewn into the
lining, and found the sharp edge, damp with blood. Holland
tugged at it. An envelope?

*The envelope. The one Westbourne gave me, with the diskette
inside.*

Norman was standing over her, peering down like a curious
stork.

"Look, I've got to run." Holland stepped away. "You won't forget to send the tape, will you?"

"Count on it."

Holland waved over her shoulder without turning back. As she
walked quickly down the path, the fields of simple crosses a blur,
she silently chastised herself for her oversight. Only when she
reached the Honda did the obvious strike her: Westbourne had

said the diskette was Senate material, something about an up-
coming bill. Three days ago, that had undoubtedly been important. Now it was just one more minor piece of unfinished
business.

9

A small part of Preacher's attention was focused on the minister and his droning eulogy. Preacher had attended a fair number of funerals in his time and was familiar with this little speech. It was an accurate way to measure time without having to resort to the unseemly pulling back of one's cuff to sneak a peek at the watch.

Like Holland, Preacher had arrived at the cemetery ahead of the cortege, but he had used a different entrance. He thought it would have been more appropriate to pay his respects at the Georgetown chapel, but he wasn't prone to suicidal risks. This setting would do as well for what else he had in mind.

Preacher had spotted the undercover surveillance agent almost at once. He knew there would be a watcher and that he or she would have only rudimentary equipment, unlike the surveillance arsenal at the memorial service. So Preacher was not concerned if the camera caught a bearded younger-looking man. He had made only a few modest alterations to his appearance, but taken together they were extremely effective.

Nor was Preacher concerned if the family happened to ask who he was. Beneath his coat, clipped to the breast pocket of his suit jacket, was a laminated badge identical to the ones that had been issued to the FBI just this morning.

As the minister droned on about the righteous being made to

lie beside still waters, Preacher turned his attention to the woman the undercover agent had approached. She had her back to him but after a moment turned, her hand brushing away stray hairs from her cheek. Behind his sunglasses Preacher's eyes widened.

And what brings you here, young one?

Preacher was intrigued. The face of the woman standing on the knoll belonged to one of the photographs that had been delivered to his hotel room three hours earlier. Holland Tylo, twenty-eight, single, less than a year with the Secret Service and now disgraced, on the verge of being dismissed. What was she doing here?

Preacher chided himself. Her black outfit, where she was standing, gave it all away. Holland Tylo had not come here in any professional capacity. She was here to mourn. Or more accurately, that's what she *believed* she was doing. In fact, she was seeking scraps of forgiveness and redemption.

Preacher watched Tylo and the FBI agent talk. From Tylo's body language, it seemed the young photographer was making a clumsy pass at her. Preacher asked himself if this slip of a girl could really have some connection to the missing diskette. True, her record indicated that she was competent, exceptional in some areas. But her inexperience spoke volumes. Would Westbourne have even considered using someone like that to help him hide the diskette?

Preacher thought the possibility remote but did not dismiss it. After all, Westbourne had already proved himself a cunning bastard. It would be in keeping with his character to entrust the diskette to an unwitting guardian.

Unlike his principal, Preacher still believed that the senator had secreted the diskette somewhere at Oak Farms. But while that search continued, Preacher decided to review those who had come in contact with Westbourne that evening, the three veteran agents . . . and the rookie. If the diskette didn't turn up at Oak Farms, Preacher thought he might approach Holland Tylo first. She had, after all, been Westbourne's favorite. . . .

The minister's eulogy was losing steam. Preacher was now focused on Cynthia Palmer. She was starting to fidget. Now if she'd only turn around a little. Ah, lovely. . .

At a distance of a few yards, the veil didn't much matter.

Preacher appreciated the peaches-and-cream skin, the wide mouth, with lips whose full potential was subdued by flesh-colored lipstick. She wore her blond hair in a French braid, which he thought was fetching. Through black lace, her eyes appraised him unashamedly. When they grew wide, their blue more pronounced, he knew they liked what they saw.

Preacher smiled on one side of his mouth, offering what he thought was just the right amount of encouragement. His effort was rewarded as Cynthia Palmer shifted in her seat, affording him a perfect view of her long, taut calves.

Preacher waited until she had turned to the minister again before taking a few steps back. Only when she was out of his line of sight did he begin to walk diagonally toward his rental car, parked well away from the limousines.

Cynthia Palmer would be disappointed when she found him gone. She would be puzzled, more than a little intrigued. And very pleasantly surprised when he came calling on her at the Watergate apartment.

Preacher was very much looking forward to her company. He had many things to ask her, beginning with whether anyone had recently delivered to their apartment a small package for the senator. And if so, where that item might be found. It would all make for a stimulating interlude, for Preacher was sure Cynthia Palmer would prove quite the merry widow.

C H A P T E R

10

ARLISS Johnson had a two-bedroom suite on the top floor of the Windsor Arms. Located next to Georgetown University, it was the kind of hotel that the guidebooks described as "quaint" or "intimate." Johnson had been a tenant for twenty-two years and in the summer cultivated roses on his rooftop terrace.

It was three o'clock in the afternoon when Johnson slipped out of bed. He had been up all night, talking to people in different time zones and across the international date line. He'd had barely four hours' sleep. Johnson crossed the living room to the bathroom, showered and dressed quickly. A few minutes later, he was downstairs, walking through the lobby. The daytime concierge nodded and smiled but said nothing. At the hotel they knew who Johnson was and left him alone.

The air was scrubbed clean by the wind coming off the Potomac. Johnson turned off O Street and headed across the northwestern edge of the campus, in the direction of the university chapel with its tower clock. The paths he used ran through dense hedges and dark copses. Johnson had his face raised to the wind and his jacket was open, the SIG-Sauer riding along his ribs.

The area in front of the tower included a formal garden and fountains designed by Henry Moore. The gurgle of water from the fountains made it difficult to hear anyone approach. Not that it mattered. The man Johnson had come to meet was already there, smoking a pungent French cigarette.

"Hello, Robert."

The Irishman who stepped out of the shadows was a strapping man. Robert Cochran had once played for Ireland in the World Soccer Cup. The years had added layers of muscle to his torso, and nothing had ever been done about the mashed nose he'd gotten in a semifinal against Argentina.

"Top of the morning to you too, Arliss."

Because of the shattered cartilage, Cochran spoke with a nasal wheeze.

"Thank you for coming so quickly."

Cochran laughed. "Took the Concorde—that British piece of shit."

Robert Cochran had parlayed his sports fame into a thriving political career. A member of the Irish Parliament, he was a fire-brand loyalist who worked unceasingly for unification. Four years earlier, Cochran's teenage son had been picked up by British paratroops in Belfast as a suspected terrorist. A bomb had gone off in a pub frequented by soldiers, and the Brits were out for blood. Johnson had provided the British with evidence that cleared the boy and pointed at the real killers. Cochran never forgot that, even though his boy still walked with a limp, a me-mento of his four-day questioning at Castle Armagh.

"You said you want to know what our bad boys the McNultys are up to."

Johnson said nothing. In the past thirty hours he had pored over all the evidence Smith had accumulated on the Westbourne killing. It seemed watertight, especially with the British input.

But the motive nagged him. Johnson spent most of his time ferreting into the lives of Service agents who may have been se-duced by the easy money to be made from the counterfeiters they hunted. He understood a man's greed, the way a soul can erode when it brushes temptation one too many times. Motive was Johnson's beacon, and here he did not feel its light.

Westbourne was not a friend of the IRA, mainstream or provi-sional. He'd backed tougher laws to deal with the smuggling of weapons from the United States to Northern Ireland. But today

the laws remained as porous as ever, and money and guns continued to find their way across the Atlantic.

*So why kill him? Why run the risk of being identified—and the
fallout that would bring?*

Yet Smith was convinced, and he wasn't looking any further.

Cochran must have divined his thoughts.

"These are dark days for us, Arliss. Your people are calling us
savages, and all the Kennedys have red faces." He paused.
"You're worried about your little girl, aren't you?"

Johnson looked at Cochran. The Irishman's words had been
soft and sweet, because he knew that Johnson had been at Senator Beaumont's side when the bullet struck. Officially, the French
had been handling security. Johnson, who had been at the embassy at the time, had gone along because he and Robert Beaumont were old friends who'd first met as a pair of terrified
nineteen-year-olds in the killing fields of Qang Trei in Vietnam.
That morning in Paris, Johnson hadn't even been carrying his
weapon.

"What do you have for me, Bobby?"

The Irishman pulled an envelope from the folds of his overcoat.
He handed the pictures to Johnson one by one. Each showed both
McNultys looking suitably grim, staring at the camera, holding
an edition of the *International Herald Tribune.* The date on the
newspaper, March 30, was clearly visible. The background could
have belonged to any seaside resort along the Mediterranean.

"Friends of mine convinced the boys to cooperate," Cochran
was saying, "Not that they were too happy about that."

Behind the defiant expressions Johnson thought he detected
something else in the McNultys' eyes. Fear. To take on the British
was one thing; to stand accused of murdering an American senator went light-years beyond that. The McNultys knew they could
never run far enough or hard enough. It showed in their faces.

"The photos were taken with a special film so the time is
stamped on them," Cochran added. "Your people will tell you
there's been no tampering."

Johnson nodded. Cochran wouldn't take the chance of bringing
him phonies.

"The boys weren't in on this, Arliss. I'm not saying they have clean hands, but they didn't kill your man."

He turned away from the wind and lit another cigarette.

"Things are very hard for us, yes, they are. And they'll stay that way until you get the Brits to call off their dogs. Smith and Venables have been chattering away to each other like a pair of old dowagers—which surprises me, because Smith should know better."

"What do you mean, Bobby?" Johnson asked softly.

He felt as though the conversation had dropped to another level, like a tectonic shift deep inside the earth.

"I mean, Arliss, why is Smith plowing away at this thing? Why is he fixated on the McNultys?"

"Are you saying that he has other information?"

"He damn well should have by now!"

Cochran inhaled deeply, studied Johnson through the veil of smoke.

"Jesus, Arliss, you *don't* know, do you? You and I are mates, but I didn't have to beat my arse over here to hand you pictures. I came because I wanted you to tell me why the McNultys are still the prime targets, when your people already know they weren't anywhere near bloody Oak Farms."

"How can you assume we know *anything?*"

Cochran poked his finger toward Johnson. "And why are you thinking that *you're* the first boyo I've spoken to about this?"

The skin on Johnson's face grew hot.

"Who else have you told, Bobby?"

"James Bloody Croft is who. On my side of the pond I'm on the Parliamentary Security Committee. Same as he is over here."

It was going on five o'clock, and Johnson had planned to be back at the office by now. Instead, he was sitting on the brickwork that bordered the fountain, the collar of his jacket tucked against the back of his neck. The wind was holding, but the coffee Frank Suress had brought from the car helped. Johnson wouldn't have minded some brandy.

Johnson had thought twice about bringing Suress along as his long gun, to cover his back. Suress did not have much surveillance experience; on the other hand, the young agent was having a tough time with what was happening to Holland. Johnson knew about Suress's relationship with Holland, and that Suress had been making indiscreet comments about the way she was being treated. If those reached Smith, the director would tear Suress a new asshole. Johnson had to keep Suress close, protect him against misguided chivalrous instincts.

"James Croft?" Suress said into his plastic cup. "Cochran had already talked to him?"

Johnson had gone to the rendezvous miked. Every word he and Cochran exchanged had been overheard and taped by Suress.

"And the director never mentioned this?"

Johnson detected the anger behind his disbelief. Under other circumstances he would have warned Suress off, but he, too, had been wondering how much Smith knew and when the director had come to hear about it.

"Don't you find that strange?" Suress persisted.

"What I *don't* do is jump to conclusions," Johnson said, with an edge to his words.

Suress was silent for a moment. He was aware of Holland's and Johnson's shared history. He thought that by now Johnson, who was the lead investigator in this case, would have convinced Smith to at least keep Holland on active service pending an outcome. Now Suress thought he caught the sweet scent of total exoneration.

"Do you think the photos Cochran gave you are genuine?" he asked.

"Oh, yes. He wouldn't fool with that."

"That would mean someone set up the McNultys—and we bought the ruse."

And Wyatt made a mistake, Johnson thought. Could it have gone that way? Or had Croft, who knew about the evidence, not shared it?

Suress threw the dregs of his coffee across the grass.

"This changes everything, doesn't it? When the director hears about—"

"The director will hear about it when I decide." Johnson locked his gaze on the younger man. "And not before. Are we clear on this?"

The rebuke stung, but Suress let it go by.

"Yes, sir."

"I know your stake in this, Frank. But Holland has a lot more riding here than either of us does. Before I move, I have to be absolutely sure.

"I understand," Suress replied.

And he did, but he reckoned it wasn't in quite the same way as Johnson took it to mean.

11

ON her way home from Arlington, Holland stopped at Charles Westbourne's office in the Dirksen Building.

There was a funereal hush in the halls, even though they were crowded with aides, lobbyists, and the like. It was one of the few times Holland found the people here polite and civil. A young gofer pointed her in the right direction, and Holland drifted along in the stream until she spotted Westbourne's office.

Although the body had just been put in the ground, the senator's quarters had already been nearly stripped. Packing boxes were piled up head high. The furniture had been tagged and moved into the receptionist's area. Light-colored patches on the walls were hollow eyes where pictures had hung.

Holland twisted her way through the maze and poked her head into Westbourne's sanctum, its windows offering a panoramic view of the Capitol.

"Excuse me."

Holland thought the young Asian-American kneeling on the carpet over piles of office memoranda would have heard her coming. Instead, he started, whirling around and almost knocking off his wire-rim glasses in the process.

"What the hell do *you* want?" he demanded.

"I need to speak to the senator's secretary."

"Ah, jeez, I'm sorry. Didn't mean to snap at you. It's been that kind of a day."

He got to his feet, adjusted his spectacles, and held out his hand.

"Mike Woo, assistant to the senator—for all of three months."

Holland accepted his apology. "Holland Tylo. Secret Service. Do you have any idea where I can find the secretary? Or Judith Trask, the senator's assistant?"

"Actually there are—were—two secretaries," Woo told her. "Cathy, who's been here forever, is under sedation at Saint John's Medical Center. Bridget, who worked mainly nights, is halfway to California by now. She was scheduled to fly out right after the memorial service. As for Judy, I haven't a clue where she might be."

Holland bit her lip. "Damn."

"What's this all about?" Woo asked.

The words were on the tip of her tongue, but something made Holland hold back. While Woo had been talking, she'd noticed a couple of things that seemed odd. The carpet looked as if it had been peeled away from the floor, then hastily put back in place. The drawers to the senator's desk, the ones with locks, had what could have been minute splinters on them, as though someone had pried them open.

Where am I going with this? Holland scolded herself.

"Hello? Agent Tylo."

Holland shook her head. "Sorry."

"Don't mention it," Woo said. "I feel like a ghoul wading through this stuff. But I'm the only one left."

"What's going to happen to it?"

"Senate Records gets the paperwork and disks. General Services Administration handles the furniture. The personal stuff goes to the lawyers, who I guess will pass it on to the estate."

"What about the material the senator had been working on—new legislation, that sort of thing?"

Woo pushed his glasses up with one finger. "That probably falls into the laps of the cosponsors. Anything in particular you're looking for?"

Suddenly Holland wanted to be out of there. The room was too warm, the air oppressive. Everything around her reminded her of her failure. She could give Woo the diskette and be done with it.

But she didn't. She couldn't. Westbourne had made *her,* no one else, responsible. Holland felt she had this final obligation, and she would see it through.

"Thanks for helping me out," she said. "I'll call Cathy and see her when she's feeling better."

Woo shrugged. "Whatever."

Woo watched as Holland maneuvered her way through the front office. Only when he heard the door close did he move, flipping the bolt. He should have made sure it was locked. He'd been careless but lucky.

Woo turned back to the room. His eyes narrowed, and his cold, set expression banished the youthful innocence from his face. The room may have looked a mess, but in reality it reflected a careful grid search. Woo knelt, gripped the edge of the carpet, and pulled it back. He'd been instructed to look for a built-in safe or a hidden panel, a space that mightn't be any larger than a file card and only an inch or two deep. Woo had already searched the outer area and half of Westbourne's office. He was quick and meticulous and missed nothing, a reflection of his CIA training in black-bag jobs.

But even with that experience, Woo never considered that the object of his hunt had, for a fleeting moment, lain within a few feet of his grasp. The individual who was paying the former Agency employee to scour Westbourne's office for a diskette had never mentioned the name Holland Tylo.

Holland returned home and changed into jeans and an old cable-knit sweater. She made herself tea, then telephoned an old friend in New Mexico, who wasn't there to take the call. Holland ended up prowling the halls as her tea cooled, tapping the envelope against her thigh. She had never been good with things left unfinished.

She took her tea into the living room and called Saint John's Medical Center. The floor nurse informed her that Catherine McGraw was resting comfortably, following her collapse after hearing about Westbourne's murder. She was expected to stay in the hospital for at least a few more days.

Holland hung up, sipped her tea, and stared at the envelope. The only way to determine who should get the diskette now was to view it—in effect, to read Westbourne's confidential notes.

Uncomfortable with the idea, Holland rationalized that she need not watch the whole diskette. If Westbourne had been dictating, he'd mention a name right away; ditto if it was a memo. Then she could find out who was cosponsoring this bill and track him—or her—down.

Holland retreated into the den, switched on her computer, with its modem and speakers, and pulled up a chair. She tore open the envelope and loaded the diskette into her machine. If the information was stored verbally, she'd get it off the speaker. If Westbourne had written it down, it'd come on the screen.

It turned out to be both.

"Disk one. Journal entry one. September 27, 1984. Time, 5:15 A.M. The subject is Hubert Baldwin, senior senator from Tennessee, chairman of the Atomic Energy Oversight Committee. The matters concern Baldwin's agreements with the military to hide, falsify, and destroy certain documents pertaining to the testing of nuclear, chemical, and biological materials on unsuspecting military units as well as civilians from 1956 to the present."

The voice belonged to a younger Charles Westbourne, but it was unmistakably his. Holland also recognized Baldwin's name. Baldwin was a Cardinal. He'd been out at Oak Farms that night.

After a pause, a low, harsh chuckle. Then: "Baldwin should have gotten rid of this paperwork when he had the chance. Now he'll go looking for evidence he can't find. I wonder how long it'll take him to put two and two together and come knocking on my door."

The words as much as their pitiless tone chilled Holland. What in God's name was this? The computer screen flashed to life, as if in answer to her question.

The letters covered a twenty-year span, from the mid fifties to the mid seventies. Roughly half were from Senator Baldwin, some of them handwritten; the rest were from various officers in the Pentagon, ranking up to two-star generals.

The correspondence both shocked and revolted Holland. For two decades, Baldwin, who had been instrumental in expanding the Oak Ridge nuclear facility in his home state, had virtually turned it into a giant experimental lab for the military. The first tests had been a spin-off from the World War II atomic program. The facilities that should have been dismantled or at least scaled back—as the Pentagon had promised Congress—had instead been renovated and enlarged. Whole new medical wings had been built for soldiers who had been exposed to immense, even lethal, doses of radiation in the field. These human guinea pigs were then subjected to a variety of experimental treatments, almost all of them worthless, yet all causing excruciating pain and suffering.

At first the memoranda indicated that Baldwin was merely kowtowing to what the military had already begun. But then came letters and memos, written by Baldwin, badgering the military to expand the scope and number of its tests into other states. There were references to using some of the convict population, the lifers in Arizona's maximum-security state prisons, those beyond hope of parole or release. In Baldwin's opinion, these men could make one final and useful contribution to society by breaking rock in areas where nuclear testing had recently been conducted—to see how long they could last before succumbing to radiation poisoning.

Holland didn't think it could get any worse, until she reached the next part: how Baldwin intended to accommodate the military's desire to test chemical and bacteriological weapons.

The Korean War had demonstrated to the Pentagon how ineffectual bombs and bullets could be against a human tidal wave of invaders. A much more potent and paralyzing defense was needed.

Like Florida, Arizona had a large elderly population. But there was a crucial difference: Arizona was nowhere as densely populated as its sister state. Its towns were smaller, separated by miles of desert, well away from prying eyes. With Baldwin and then Senator Gaylord Robertson paving the way, the medical wing of the Pentagon began to infiltrate the state-run nursing homes and mental institutions. Patients who were feeble in mind or body or both found themselves on regimens of drugs whose existence had never been reported to the FDA. In carefully controlled experiments, unwitting subjects were injected with various strains of bacteria. Their reactions and resistance to them were carefully monitored, the results studied intently, adjustments made in the potency of the strains so that they would work much more quickly; in some cases, instantaneously.

By the time the testing had been scaled back and the programs dissolved, over fifteen thousand people had been victimized. From the charnel house records that swam before her eyes, Holland came to the sickening conclusion that none had survived more than a few months.

Senator Gaylord Robertson . . .

Holland craned back her head and closed her eyes lightly, visualizing a wizened figure who got around with the help of a wheelchair and a male nurse. He had a son, a cold, handsome man who had run for the Senate seat when Robertson died. Paul Robertson, another of the Cardinals . . .

Holland rose and discovered she was shaking. What was going on here? What was Westbourne doing with this evidence? Had he been planning to use it to expose Baldwin—or Robertson, if he had inherited his father's sins? Maybe both?

Snatches of an overheard conversation leaped into her mind:

"You can't do that, Charles. It's monstrous!"

"You have no choice but to go along . . . "

Holland worked furiously to put the words into context. *What* was monstrous? Had Westbourne revealed Baldwin's secret to the senators brought together at Oak Farms? Perhaps *he* had been the one threatening the Ethics Committee—not the other way around. And what was it *they* had to "go along" with?

Questions spun crazily through Holland's mind. She had stepped beyond the horror of the words she'd heard. The words were no longer disembodied, disinterested messengers. They were moving at her, crowding over her, working their way under her skin, making her an accomplice. They could now frighten, even terrorize her.

Abruptly Holland slammed the door of her consciousness on them. In their place a picture slowly came into focus. She was

back in Westbourne's office. He's behind his desk, looking startled, as if she's interrupted him at something. Two diskettes
are on the blotter in front of him. He reaches for the one on the
right—

*Then abruptly changes his mind! His fingers hesitate and pick
up the one on the left! He makes a mistake, ends up giving me the
wrong diskette!*

Holland slumped on the sofa, hugging her knees against her
chest. The contents of this diskette had nothing to do with any bill
or legislative business. *That* must have been on the diskette she'd
seen Westbourne slip into his pocket.

"He gave me the wrong damn diskette!" she said aloud in the
empty room.

When her voice curled off the walls and ceiling and back at
her, she heard herself almost laughing, the way people do when
they're about to spiral into hysteria.

Holland reached for the telephone, but the image of Westbourne's tortured body was quicker. A final question reared up:
Was this the kind of material that someone—an arcane department of the military, for example—would kill for in order to prevent it from ever coming to light?

In his office, Frank Suress stared balefully at the telephone, willing it to ring. He'd been waiting over an hour for the callback.
Too much time to think. Too many questions and issues to handle,
like trying to keep together a handful of oiled marbles.

Suress continued turning over the revelations Cochran had
brought with him. Maybe Arliss Johnson still had doubts, but as
far as Suress was concerned, the evidence Cochran had produced
was proof positive the McNultys hadn't murdered Westbourne.

*So who did? And if Croft knew about this evidence, why was
he sitting on it?*

Suress needed more information. To get it, he had stepped
beyond the pale. Johnson had specifically ordered him not to
discuss anything with Wyatt Smith. But he hadn't said, in so many
words, that Suress couldn't go elsewhere. Suress recognized frail,
dubious reasoning, but it was all he had to hold him to his course.

With Cochran's photographs and taped details in hand, Suress had expected Johnson to move quickly. Instead, nothing had happened. Holland remained in the wilderness, not only presumed guilty but already prejudged. If Suress could crack open the carapace circumstances had created around her, he could set her free. If he could make that happen, then nothing Johnson might say or do to him later on would matter.

Then the phone sounded and the caller Suress had been waiting for was speaking. Suress listened, thanked the man, and reached for his jacket. He had one hand on the doorknob when the phone warbled again.

"Frank. It's me."

"Holland. Listen, I'm just on my way out—"

"Has there been a break? Something to do with the McNultys?"

Suress hesitated. He badly wanted to give Holland a tiny bit of hope, but he couldn't say anything now. He chose his words carefully.

"Nothing new on the twins. I have something else I'm following up. Holland, I really have to get going."

"Frank, wait!"

Her voice was verging on panic, something Suress had never heard before.

"What's wrong, Holland?" he demanded sharply.

Her words, a stumbling rapid fire, left him in a daze. Westbourne had given her a diskette, and it contained files on Pentagon medical experiments on a civilian population?

"There's a lot more, Frank. Hours' worth of material. You've got to come over and see this for yourself. I—"

"Holland, slow down!"

There was a pause, then her voice, subdued now: "I'm sorry. But I need you to help me, Frank. This stuff scares me!"

"Have you spoken to anyone else?"

"No!"

"Okay. Sit tight. So far no one knows that Westbourne passed you the diskette. Let's keep it that way. What I have to do will take about an hour, ninety minutes tops. As soon as I'm done, I'll get over to your place."

The silence on the other end of the line told him his idea didn't sit well.

"Holland. An hour or two is *not* going to make a difference. What I need to do can't wait. I don't have a choice." Suress bit his lip, but the words got out anyway: "I might be onto something that can help you."

"Frank, tell me!"

"There's nothing to tell—yet. But the sooner I'm out of here, the sooner we can sit down with what you've found and figure out where to go next. I'll be there for you, Holland. I love you."

"Just hurry, Frank. Please," she whispered.

12

To the uninitiated the old Senate library was a rabbit warren of long, narrow corridors, sudden twists and turns that played havoc with one's sense of direction, and abrupt dead ends. As Secret Service liaison to the Senate Intelligence Committee, Frank Suress had become very familiar with its landscape.

At the end of a hall that seemed to run nowhere, Suress found a single door, painted over a hundred times and looking as if it opened onto a janitor's closet. Except that the door was reinforced with sheets of steel and had a state-of-the-art electronic lock. Suress swiped his coded card, pressed the correct numerical sequence, and was buzzed in.

A winding flight of stairs took him to a second level, where he stepped into a circular room, complete with dome ceiling, that could have doubled as an eccentric's library or a miniature observatory.

It was neither. Carved out from an architectural conceit and dubbed the Tower, it was the place where some of the most valued spies and defectors of the last fifty years had come to tell their tales to those elected representatives who worked in tandem with the country's intelligence services.

Suress looked around at the well-worn but comfortable sofas, the cigarette-scarred tables, and the single large desk, which had only a computer and a telephone bank on its surface. This place always unnerved him. No matter how thoroughly the air was re-circulated and scrubbed, he thought he could still smell the odor of treachery, suspicion, and fear.

"Good afternoon, Frank."

The speaker was James Croft, the ranking member of the Senate Intelligence Committee. Like Suress, he had the solid, compact build of a lightweight boxer. Suress thought that Croft must have had to become handy with his fists early on in life. His face was not pleasant to look at, and Suress couldn't help but wonder what cruelties Croft had endured growing up.

"Thanks for seeing me on such short notice, Senator," Suress said, shrugging off his coat.

Croft waved away the words with finely manicured fingers.

"How long have we been working together, Frank? Three years? More? I think we've made a good team."

Suress appreciated that. During his time on the committee, Croft had always treated Suress with friendly respect. He paid attention, asked good questions, went to bat for the Service when he was convinced it was the right—not the politically expedient—thing to do.

"So what's on your mind?" asked Croft, the sharp interest in his eyes belying his easy tone.

Suress took a deep breath. "Senator, are you familiar with an Irish national by the name of Cochran?"

"Robert Cochran? Sure. He's a thorn in the British side, but he and I get along."

Croft's misshapen mouth twisted into the only kind of smile he could offer. "Now you really have my attention, Frank."

Suress moved ahead. I understand that six days ago, Cochran spoke to you at length, from Ireland."

Croft's eyes narrowed. "You get very good information, Frank. Yes, as a matter of fact he did."

"Did Cochran, *at that time,* let you know that he believed two terrorists, the McNultys, constituted no threat to anyone in the United States, including Charles Westbourne?"

Croft leaned forward slightly. "We're beginning to tread in murky waters, Frank. Classified stuff. But I can tell you this: intelligence sources indicated to the committee that certain terrorist organizations were very interested in the current whereabouts and future travel plans of several high-level officials, including two senators."

"Was Westbourne one of those?"

"Yes. The reports we'd been getting indicated that certain factors of the IRA were not at all happy with Westbourne's attempt to modify our banking laws, which could choke American contributors to the cause. I was concerned enough to get hold of Cochran. He insisted that no threats of any kind were even being contemplated, much less on the drawing boards."

"Did you believe him?"

"I had no reason not to. Cochran knows better than to try to cross me."

"Do you *still* believe that, Senator, given that one of the McNultys' palm print was found at the murder scene?"

Croft fished out a package of cigarettes and offered one to Suress, who declined. Silent fans immediately drew the smoke into ceiling vents.

"Bottom line?" Croft said. "I can't believe Cochran would have lied to me or misled me. Still, I feel sick that maybe I was wrong in believing him—"

"No, you weren't, Senator."

Croft regarded him thoughtfully. "And why is that, Frank?"

"Because I've seen the evidence Cochran was probably referring to."

"The hell you say!" Croft whispered.

Suress knew that this was his last chance to salvage some of the trust Johnson had put in him. He could give Croft only the details that really counted—Cochran's photographs and some of the other particulars concerning the McNultys. But once he started, Suress couldn't stop himself. He needed Croft's help, and every detail was part of the currency with which he was willing to pay.

Croft listened without interruption. He had a second cigarette going by the time Suress was through.

"I can't believe it," he murmured. "Cochran coming up with photos, dates . . . You say Johnson believed him?"

"Cochran was very convincing, Senator."

Croft rose and paced the confines of the small chamber, his steps of equal length as though he was counting off the exact distance.

"You know what you're saying, Frank?" he said, his back to Suress.

Suress nodded, then looked up. "Yes, Senator. Someone had the balls—not to mention the time and resources—to *frame* two terrorists for Westbourne's murder. The real killers are still out there." He paused. "That's why I came to you, Senator. Cochran said you knew the McNultys weren't the threat. He redoubled his effort by providing us with the evidence. We've been hunting the wrong men, Senator."

"Who else knows about Cochran, Frank?"

"Only Arliss Johnson."

Croft spread his arms across the desk. "Okay. Let me try to get a handle—as discreetly as I can—on whoever's misleading us and why."

"Senator, I might be able to help you there."

"Put it on the table, Frank."

Suress hesitated. He'd been in such a rush when Holland called that he'd barely listened to what she'd told him, trying instead to calm her down and reassure her.

"The details are sketchy," Suress said, then described his brief conversation with Holland.

"Agent Tylo told me that the diskette contained records on medical experiments conducted by the Pentagon, along with references to Senator Baldwin," Suress concluded. "It sounded as if Westbourne had come across some massive cover-up and had evidence that could destroy a lot of careers and reputations."

Croft shook his head. "Do you realize how crazy that sounds?"

"Tylo isn't one to cry wolf, Senator," Suress replied firmly. "I have no reason to think she'd be making up any of it. If she says that's what's on the diskette, I believe her."

"Where are you going with this, Frank?"

"I'm saying that if the information on the diskette is as devastating as Tylo believes it to be, then maybe we have a *motive* for

Westbourne's murder. A motive might go a long way to pointing us toward the killers."

Croft thought about this. "Tylo has the diskette with her?"

"Yes. She's on administrative leave pending a hearing. Right now she's at home, waiting for me to get back to her."

Croft was silent for a moment.

"I want you to meet me at my office," he said finally. "Then we'll go for a little ride."

"Senator?"

"To see what your Agent Tylo has for us. Considering it seems to have put the fear of God into her, she deserves our attention, don't you think?"

Suress left the Tower. Croft waited a few moments, then quickly went into a room two doors down the corridor.

The three other Cardinals were present, seated around a horseshoe-shaped table set on a dais. Below were two desks and several chairs, arranged as in a courtroom. Behind them were three rows of benches. It was in this hearing room, over twenty years before, that the first high-echelon Watergate conspirators had tried to save their skins by offering testimony. Two of the Cardinals present had presided over those secret hearings.

Croft made sure the door was locked behind him. Judging by the set expressions, he concluded that the sensitive microphones hidden throughout the Tower had transmitted every word he and Suress had uttered. Good. That would save time.

"Seems like that Service pup has handed us a peck of trouble, Jimmy," said Hubert Baldwin, his Tennessee accent as thick as pine sap.

Baldwin was a Senate legend, a tall, heavy-set man whose craggy features could have been hewn from Mount Rushmore. He was seventy-two years old, got around with the help of a silver-tipped cane, loved his sour mash and cigars, and was working on his third wife, forty years his junior. Ruthless when it came to political infighting and seemingly indestructible, he had buried his share of political bodies and knew the locations of hundreds of others.

"It looks that way," Croft replied deferentially. He deliberately avoided any reference to the fact that Suress had mentioned Baldwin's name, and to the damning context.

"It would seem this whole thing is beginning to fray," Paul Robertson commented. "I wonder why *your* name was raised, Hubert. Would you care to enlighten us about these 'medical experiments'?"

He was the youngest of the three, in his late forties, handsome in the skin-deep way of a soap opera star. Robertson had inherited his Senate seat in Florida from his father. The power brokers finished Robertson's political education and set him up as a front man. No one was better at fund-raisers or getting out the retiree vote. But Robertson was more than just a pretty face. Those who crossed or angered him quickly discovered how unforgiving, even lethal, his mean streak could be.

"Ancient history!" Baldwin barked. "Buried and forgotten."

"Let's not get ahead of ourselves, Paul," Barbara Zentner suggested, stepping in when she saw Robertson's skeptical expression.

She was wearing a green silk suit that made her frizzy hair appear more orange than usual. Croft wondered how it was possible for someone to be so brilliant and at the same time so blatantly tacky. Yet Zentner was always being complimented on her appearance and taste in clothing. The senior senator from California, whose political cunning was given its respectful due, was not known to take kindly to constructive criticism.

"I agree that we're faced with something unexpected," she continued. "But it can be contained." She fixed her shiny predator's eyes on Croft. "Am I correct in assuming that, James?"

Croft was blessed with a quick, clear mind that functioned as well as any computer. Even as he'd listened to Suress he'd been weighing the variables, arranging and rearranging them, toting up the pros and cons of each possible action.

"Yes, you are, Barbara."

"Then please, share."

"From what Suress has told us, it's safe to assume that Westbourne himself inadvertently created this situation," Croft said.

"However, the important thing is that we now know exactly who has the diskette and where it can be found."

"*One* of the diskettes," Robertson cut in. "There's still another out there. And from what you told us, it's not to be found in Westbourne's office."

"True, and for the moment that will have to keep," Croft said patiently. "Our main concern is this Secret Service agent, Tylo."

"A rookie, no less," Baldwin rumbled.

"True. But that in itself will make getting the diskette much easier."

Baldwin's arthritic fingers kneaded the silver tip of his cane.

"Suress mentioned something about her being on administrative leave. Does that fit in?"

"Yes. And very nicely too. Here's a young woman who's just made a terrible mistake, one that cost the life of the man she was supposed to protect. She's devastated by the experience. Instead of standing by her, the Service has cut her loose. Her career is finished. With her record, she'd be lucky to get a job patrolling a mall.

"All this adds up to despair, hopelessness. It's a textbook springboard for suicide."

"What about family?" Robertson asked casually. "Someone who might actually care about what happens to her?"

"No one to speak of," Croft replied.

"Boyfriends?"

Croft smiled. "One of life's little ironies. She and Suress are an item."

He waited, wondering how long it would take them to make the connection and come to the subsequent realization.

"Suress has to go too," Zentner said at last. "Now that he knows something of what's on the diskette, he won't leave it alone —not with the girl involved."

"Suress isn't some rookie," Baldwin reminded them. "Whatever happens to him has to be foolproof. No comebacks."

"It's the same for both of them," Zentner said flatly. "As far as I'm concerned, they're joined at the hip."

Croft didn't get involved here. He'd already reached his conclusions.

"You have something in mind, don't you, Jimmy?" Baldwin said softly.

"I'd venture to say the same thing you have, Hubert."

Baldwin's rebuke carried the sting of the whip. "Don't get ahead of yourself, Jimmy. Not with me."

Croft reacted as though he'd been slapped. "Hubert, I only meant that our options are limited. And that we must act quickly."

Paul Robertson saw that Baldwin was spoiling for a fight. Too often lately, Baldwin was showing signs of his age, being moody, testy, stubborn. They didn't have time to stroke him right now.

"James is right, Hubert," Robertson said. He turned to Croft. "Go on."

"It appears that Tylo listened to only a fraction of the diskette. But that was hours ago. We have to assume that since then she's gone through it all. Since we don't know the contents or their chronology, we must also assume that besides Hubert, other names have been mentioned."

Croft let that sink in, pleased by the droop that had erased Baldwin's patrician smugness. Robertson and Zentner were no less worried but managed to disguise their fear. Croft realized this must be a new experience for all of them, to have someone holding the sword over their heads.

"Where's Suress right now?" asked Robertson.

"Waiting for me at my office," Croft replied. "I told him we'd go over to meet Tylo and see what she has. Before that happens I can contact—"

"We don't need the details right away," Robertson said smoothly.

He glanced at the others and got minute nods.

"We don't have to impress upon you how delicate the situation has become," Robertson continued. "And we have every confidence that you will render it harmless. To that end, just make sure your shooter doesn't fuck up."

Croft almost laughed at the crude attempt at bravado. Instead, he assumed a sober tone.

"You can count on that."

. . .

"I hate that little freak!"

Baldwin stared murderously at the door Croft had just passed through.

I'm sure the feeling is mutual, Robertson thought.

"He'll get the job done, Hubert," he said. "He *wants* to do it for us. That's all that should matter to you. To any of us."

"Without Croft we wouldn't have gotten in this far," Zentner added, then drove home her point: "And Westbourne would still be holding a gun to our heads with those White House ambitions he had."

She paused.

"Westbourne had us coming and going, Hubert. There was no way we could have gotten out from under his blackmail. But had we supported his nomination—as he needed us to—he would have later destroyed us politically."

Baldwin leaned forward and sent a wad of tobacco-colored phlegm smacking into the brass spittoon, a grudging admission that Zentner was right.

Over their long and illustrious careers, the Cardinals had profited handsomely—to the tune of millions of dollars—from their Senate seats. Westbourne had threatened their cozy arrangements with their leading supporters. His proposed tobacco taxes would have created havoc in Baldwin's home state and throughout the South. Zentner, along with California's economy, would have been further crippled by Westbourne's targeted military base closings. Robertson would have lost the linchpin of his support, Florida's powerful sugar producers, if Westbourne had abolished the quota on imports.

The Cardinals had acted on the most basic instinct: self-preservation. And the political gods had smiled upon them, sent them James Croft to be the instrument of their will. Baldwin knew he should not look at gift horses, yet neither could he contain his revulsion.

"I think Croft is getting too big for his britches," he whined stubbornly. "He's starting to think he's really one of us—"

"So let him have his illusions," Robertson said harshly. "What does it matter? You seem to forget, Hubert, that as long as Tylo and Suress are walking around, our collective balls are in Croft's hands. Until that changes, we treat him like an old pal."

Baldwin glared at the younger man. Barbara Zentner stepped between them. Baldwin was revolted by her red, pasty lips.

"Remember what you mentioned about no comebacks, Hubert?" she said, trying for a seductive tone and failing utterly. "Well, with Croft handling the details, none of what is about to happen can be traced back to us. Croft is our living, breathing guarantee of that. That's *all* he's worth to us."

13

FRANK Suress spent twenty minutes in Croft's reception area before the secretary told him to go in. The senator was behind his desk, telephone cradled against his shoulder.

"There's someone here I have to see," he said in a harried tone. "Let me put you on hold."

Without missing a beat, Croft looked up at Suress.

"This thing won't wait. I need another fifteen minutes at least. Why don't you go on ahead to Tylo's place, and I'll meet you there."

"Fine," Suress replied.

On his way to the Dirksen Building, Suress had stopped by his office and called Holland, quickly explaining that he wouldn't be coming alone. Her response sounded hollow and bleak, her relief strained. Suress was glad not to have to keep her waiting for Croft.

"Fifteen minutes," Croft promised, jabbing the blinking light on the telephone console.

Croft watched Suress leave and didn't speak until the door was closed.

"He's on his way," he said softly. "Take good care of him."

· · ·

In his suite at the Four Seasons, Preacher replaced the receiver in its cradle. He was dressed in tan wool slacks, chocolate-brown turtleneck, and hand-tooled Italian boots. A warm wool Burberry jacket lay beside him. He would blend in perfectly with his surroundings.

Preacher opened the Washington guidebook and carefully examined the warren of streets that crisscrossed Georgetown. Entry into the neighborhood was by one of two major arteries feeding in from the city center. Knowing where Suress would be leaving from, Preacher eliminated one point.

The fact that Georgetown streets were, for the most part, one way also helped. The number of approaches to Tylo's house was limited.

Downstairs, Preacher had the doorman flag him a cab. A few minutes later, he was cruising along M Street, through what used to be Georgetown's bohemian quarter after property values had driven out the espresso bars and counterculture paraphernalia boutiques. The street was now lined with upscale European-cuisine restaurants, trendy clothes outlets, and gourmet shops.

Preacher got out of the taxi in front of a sandblasted brick building that housed a northern Italian trattoria, and looked up and down the sidewalks. He was pleased. There were just enough people to create a cover, not so many as to get in his way. Traffic moved steadily, and there was a crosswalk at the end of the block that could prove useful. Preacher fell in step with the other pedestrians and made his way to the corner. He bought a warm chocolate-chip cookie from a vendor and waited.

Part of Suress's job was to know the shortest route between any two points in the city. Dent Place was the one he always used when going to Holland's house.

Something kept teasing Suress as he made his way along Thirty-third Street. It had started after he left Croft's office and stuck like a burr. No amount of coaxing seemed to bring it out, until Suress's peripheral vision began to track the street numbers ahead of him.

How can Croft get to Holland's when he never asked me for the address?

Suress had just begun punching numbers on the car phone when he heard a shout. There, at the crosswalk, stood a man wearing a wool sports jacket, motioning to him, holding up something that looked like a small wallet. Suress edged his car toward the curb. The man was twenty feet away, and what he was holding was identification. From this distance Suress could make out the bold blue letters: FBI.

Suress reacted exactly in keeping with his training. He had no reason not to trust the ID and, by extension, the individual who held it. His first thought was that the agent needed assistance. The man's expression was set, but the eyes darted up and down the sidewalk, searching for something, or someone.

Now Suress had his car at the curb, the door partially swung open. The agent was less than five feet away, still surveying the sidewalk traffic. Pedestrians walking by him gave a curious look and picked up their pace.

"What's going on?" asked Suress, halfway out of the car.

Preacher was turned partially away from him. Suress had both feet on the sidewalk. His right hand was moving to the inside of his jacket.

"Thank Christ I saw you," Preacher was saying. "There's a guy with a rifle—"

Preacher, never finishing the sentence, whirled around and faced him. The muffled pop was lost in the growl of traffic. The .22 bullet, expertly modified, penetrated Suress's abdomen, slicing through the liver and stomach and ratting off the left side of the rib cage, exactly as it had been intended to do.

Suress's hand never reached his gun. The pain he felt was like razor wire being dragged through his insides.

"Jeez, Frank. It's only four o'clock and you're already shitfaced. Come on, you can't drive like that."

Suress felt two powerful arms propping him up, then pushing him back into the car and across the bench seat. Preacher was beside him, behind the wheel, door closed. Beyond the windshield, Suress saw people passing by, completely unaware of what was going on.

With one hand on the wheel, Preacher steered the car back into traffic. He took the corner quickly, tossing Suress hard against the passenger door. Suress clawed through his pain, straining to reach the door handle.

"I'm sorry, Frank. But that just won't do."

Preacher kept his hand on the seat, the barrel of the gun slightly elevated, and fired again, catching Suress just under the shoulder. The scream in Suress's throat emerged as a gurgle. He felt very light and told himself he had to hold on to something, otherwise he'd float away. A lingering thought closed over him like a shroud.

How does he know my name?

Holland drew back the lace curtains on the tall, narrow windows that faced the front lawn. It had been almost forty minutes since Suress called, telling her that he would be bringing Croft along. No sign of them yet.

Frank's telling her that Croft was coming had taken Holland by surprise. Frank had added only that she mustn't worry. Croft was "intensely interested" in what was going on with her. Frank had dealt with Croft before. He could be trusted.

Holland barely had the chance to register this before Frank hung up. Later, when she thought about it, she remembered Croft as one of the men who had filed out of Westbourne's study that night at Oak Farms. Holland didn't know much about the man himself, except that he and his Illinois organization had been the decisive factor in the President's election victory. Croft was a heavy hitter. But Frank vouched for him, and Croft's name had never been mentioned in Westbourne's diary.

With the remote phone in her hand, Holland paced about the living room in front of the floor-to-ceiling bookcases. Her eye caught a volume of Greek tragedies, and the sudden irony pinched her. Thousands of years separated her from a time when the lives of mortals and gods were inextricably linked. But men had learned little in the interim, seemed doomed to repeat ancient mistakes. Holland felt as though she had committed a horrible mythic sin: She had acquired knowledge that she could neither deal with nor give back. She had been tempted by that most basic of instincts—curiosity—and succumbed to it.

It wasn't a stone tablet she'd read or a forbidden box she'd opened but a tiny diskette, whose secrets now infected her. Holland knew that the commentary she'd heard and the documents she'd seen were the truth, about Charles Westbourne, about some of the most powerful men and women in the nation. Driven by a desperate need to know, she had sat through the entire diskette. Now nothing could ever be the same again. Because its revelations terrified and angered her. Because she felt cheated and betrayed by those who had sworn to be guardians of the public trust.

But the terror did not stop there. As much as she'd already learned, there was still more knowledge out there for her. At the end of the diskette, Westbourne had said there was a second diary . . . somewhere.

And they'll come looking for the one I have, whoever they *are. . . .*

Holland understood now why Westbourne had had to die. But now she realized his enemies were legion. How would she recognize the one who already had blood on his hands?

Holland almost jumped as the phone in her hand rang.

"Agent Tylo? Senator Croft here."

"Senator. Is everything all right?" Holland asked nervously.

"Of course, Ms. Tylo. I'm just calling to say that Frank and I are running late."

Holland closed her eyes, trying to slow her pounding heart.

"Ms. Tylo? Hello?"

"Excuse me, Senator."

"I'm on the car phone. We'll be there in five minutes." Croft's words sounded strong and reassuring.

Static shot through the connection, and Holland lost him.

Okay. They're almost here. Just a few more minutes.

Preacher was two minutes from the town house when the car phone went off. He activated it, waited for Croft's voice, identified himself, and listened. The conversation lasted only a few seconds.

Preacher swung off into a side street and began circling the block. Holland was in position, but he didn't want to draw her guard by showing up too early.

Holland heard a crunch of tires as a car moved up her driveway. Through the window she caught a glimpse of blue.
Frank. Thank God.
Now someone was knocking.
The front door had a small stained-glass window, the design of a sunflower, cut into it. Beyond the yellow, brown, and black pieces all Holland could see was a blur. She flipped the dead bolt, then the lower lock, and had begun to open the door when it slammed into her, the heavy wood digging into the right side of her body, its edge cracking open the skin on her cheek and forehead. Holland felt as though someone had yanked her violently backward; she teetered as the pain shot through her, then felt her legs collapse under her.
Preacher was inside, his gun trained on Holland, who lay in a heap at his feet. He pressed the barrel to her temple and checked her pulse. Alive; semiconscious. He turned his head to take in the room. Nothing.
Preacher dropped to one knee, picked up Holland's limp hand, and pressed her fingers tightly around the butt and trigger of his gun. The latex gloves he wore would allow him to handle the weapon without disturbing her prints.
Next he grabbed Holland by the scruff of the neck and dragged her along the polished floorboards to the back of the house. Preacher peeked inside the den and smiled when he saw the diskette on the red rubber pad.

Frank Suress had no feeling below his waist, yet he could move his feet. His chest burned horribly, and he felt something warm and wet dribbling from the corner of his mouth. But his mind was perfectly clear. He remembered how his attacker had taken him down, how casually he had put the last bullet into him. He recognized that the house beyond the windshield was Holland's. And that the killer was no longer in the car.

A low moan, broken by a bubble of blood, spilled over Suress's lips as, slowly, he began to move.

"Look away from me."

Holland was sitting on the floor, her hands under her buttocks, her back against her desk. Her head throbbed, and she had to blink to make the dancing black spots go away. But she couldn't tear her gaze from the man standing a few feet away, one arm hanging straight down, the barrel of a gun pointed at her neck.

"Who are you?" she asked hoarsely.

"No one you need concern yourself about."

His voice was soft, almost seductive.

"What do you want?" Holland demanded, trying to put some steel into her words.

She reacted to her training, stopped thinking of where Frank and Croft were or what might have happened to them. Instead, she focused on the gun.

Preacher held up the diskette. "I have what I want." He slipped it into his pocket. "And I'm afraid there is no alternative for what I must do. You do not want to look at death, young one. Better to turn away, think of a lover or a beautiful memory. I promise you there will be no pain."

Holland almost responded to the hypnotic tone. Then she shook her head violently, and the pain snapped her back to reality.

"It doesn't have to be—" she began.

Preacher held a finger to his lips. He moved one step closer, the gun barrel coming up a fraction.

"All right. Fuck you!"

Holland hurled the epithet as though it were a solid object. Preacher recoiled, his body stiffening, and Holland made her move. Her feet struck out, catching him just above the ankles. Driven by her desperation, the force was enough to cause him to lose his balance on the polished hardwood.

Preacher roared as he went down, grabbing for Holland. Now

he had her by the ankle and was getting to his knees, the gun trained on the back of her neck.

The shot that boomed in the small room did not come from Preacher's .22 caliber. Holland stared up to see Frank Suress clutching the doorframe, his clothing soaked with blood, his Service automatic dangling from one hand. Holland gave one last kick, felt herself free, and scrambled toward him.

Preacher didn't bother to duck. The shot you heard was never the one that killed you, he knew. As he saw Suress trying to summon the strength to raise his hand, Preacher squeezed off two shots. A pair of red buttons appeared on the agent's forehead.

Preacher was on his feet. He heard the girl racing somewhere to the back of the house. The temptation to go after her, to punish her, was almost overwhelming. But he knew better.

Making sure he still had the diskette, Preacher cautiously retreated down the hall. He tossed the .22 on the couch and slipped out the front door. Preacher had already backed the car into the street when he heard the sirens.

Holland had pressed herself against the refrigerator, her weapon out, ready. She had heard the front door open and close, the car start up. Peering over the ledge of the kitchen window, she saw the killer behind the wheel. Holland raced for the door, flung it open, and crouched in a firing stance. Sixty feet away, the rear window exploded in a shower of glass, but the sedan kept going, fishtailing until it was out of sight.

Holland ran back inside and knelt beside Suress. She almost gagged when she saw the two bullet holes in his forehead, his eyes staring at her lifelessly. Her lips curled over her teeth, and she could do nothing but scream.

It was the sirens that cut through her agony. Holland stumbled to her feet and, still gripping her gun, teetered toward the open door. An unmarked sedan screeched to a stop in front of the house, followed by two more, seconds apart. Holland registered that the license plates belonged to the Service. She almost sobbed with relief when armed men piled out of the cars, their weapons trained on her.

"There she is! She's got a gun!"

The first two shots splintered the wood next to her face. Holland slammed the door shut and ran through the living room. Behind her, a fusillade sent breaking glass across the carpet.

"What are you doing?" Holland screamed. "Stop it!"

She raced through the kitchen, snatching her jacket and purse, fumbling with the lock on the back door. Somewhere behind her, the phone was ringing until the answering machine kicked in. Outside, the cold almost knocked the wind out of her. Holland staggered across the concrete patio. The voices were closer now, around the side of the house.

The gate lock was frozen with rust. Holland stepped back and shot it away. For a second there was silence, then gunfire erupted again, much closer this time. Holland took one last look back, then kicked open the gate. That it was still swinging, lopsided on its creaky hinges, was the only evidence that she'd ever been there.

TWO

14

THE cab was idling in front of the Hickory Dickory Dock, a bed-and-breakfast fashioned out of a renovated Victorian mansion that fronted the park on Volta Place.

Holland had been running hard, in the loping stride of a marathoner. Now she forced herself to scale back to a jog. A woman runner, head held high, eyes straight ahead, was a common sight in the neighborhood. But the sidewalks had become crowded with rush-hour pedestrians and she didn't want to draw attention to herself.

As she trotted in place at the corner, waiting for the light to change, her eyes fixed on the battered yellow Chevy cab across the street. The driver was a very tall black man, Nigerian or Senegalese, his skin gleaming like oiled walnut. He stood by the open trunk, bags neatly arranged on the sidewalk, waiting for the passenger to calculate his tip. On the steps of the bed-and-breakfast, a young woman in a flower-print spring dress shivered, glanced at her guidebook, then, dubiously, at her accommodations.

The light changed, and Holland moved fast to cut off a scholarly-looking man who'd been eyeing the cab. She swept around the front of the car and slipped into the backseat. The cab smelled of sweet nutmeg and an incense she couldn't identify.

"Off duty! Off duty!"

The driver, still outside, flapped his wrist at her, his other hand receiving the fare. Then Holland felt the car rock as the trunk lid slammed down. The driver slipped behind the wheel, making shooing gestures at her with his fingers.

"Woodley Park. You know where that is?"

"Off duty!"

Holland leaned forward and jammed a bill into his palm.

"Woodley Park."

The driver flinched at the sound of her voice. He looked at the fifty-dollar bill and, in a language Holland didn't understand, began conversing with the figurines and talismans glued to the dashboard.

She knew they would track down the driver eventually. They'd question him until he described the crazy woman who'd gotten into the cab in front of the Hickory Dickory Dock and told them where he'd dropped her off.

Who are *they*?

When she'd been running, Holland had used her ears, not her eyes, to determine how close the hunters might be. She was still listening, separating the various strains of traffic noise, fire engine claxons from the wails of an ambulance, probing for the distinctive sound of police sirens. Nothing yet. Every click of the cab's meter filtered another grain of relief into the hourglass of her hope.

Who *are* they?

The license tags on the cars that had drawn up in front of her house belonged to the Service. The men who had shot at her had to have been agents.

Could they have been responding to a distress call Frank had managed to send out? Had he somehow alerted headquarters that he was down and now his assailant was threatening another agent?

Holland shivered at the image of her cradling Suress in her arms, his eyes staring up at her, the two bullet wounds on his forehead looking like blood-crusted scabs. During her escape she'd been able to shut it away; now she could feel his soft hair on her fingers. . . .

"There she is! She's got a gun!"

The words the agents had shouted before opening fire jolted Holland. They were *not* there because Suress had put through a mayday, *not* because they knew she was in danger. They were not coming after a killer. They had been after her, *only* her . . .

Holland's knuckles were white where her fingers curled around the handgrip as the cab rocketed through a sharp curve on Rock Creek Drive. They were past Dumbarton Oaks, heading east, with Rock Creek Park ahead. Holland didn't bother scanning the traffic. If they knew she was in the cab, they'd converge on it, force it off the road.

My own people are after me. They want to kill me. . . .

Questions about how and why and *God, this really didn't happen to me, did it?* threatened what was left of her self-control.

You don't know enough yet. But soon, maybe.

Holland slammed the door on the whirlwind, coaxed up the image of the killer. He was what was important to remember, what she could use later.

Mid to late thirties. Slim but very strong, agate eyes against burnished skin, like a model ready for a photo shoot on a Caribbean yacht or backdropped by the white cliffs of the Aegean. A voice—American—that had almost made her savor death, belonging to a professional whose gun hand had been rock steady, who'd put two bullets into a man's forehead without taking deliberate aim. Very well trained, supremely confident.

But only in his abilities?

Something in his manner, and not just the absence of fear. The way he'd spoken, as if he had all the time in the world. That it was impossible for him to make a mistake and so she should look away from the gun, think of her lover or a beautiful memory . . . It was as though he had an aura around him, some magic that would always protect him, never allow anyone to stop him.

Protect him . . .

Who are you? Where did you come from? No, change direction. What I *know* is that you came for the diskette. You smiled at me, told me you had what you'd come for, then put the diskette in your pocket. *So you were there that night at Oak Farms. A few more steps, and I would have seen you . . . for that split second before you shot me.*

You murdered Westbourne. But you tortured him first. Why? It's the diskette again, isn't it? Westbourne didn't have it with him. No. That's not the sequence. He didn't have the *right* one, the one you wanted.

The one you were sent to get.

You knew all the security details, didn't you? That, and everything else you needed. Like the duck blind. It was cold and uncomfortable, but you didn't care. You were safe. Not even the dogs could find you there. And you knew there'd be dogs.

You jimmied the lock on the back door because that's how you had planned to go in. You heard Fleming skip the stone across the water, and the response from the field team. You knew then it was safe to make for the cottage.

And you knew Westbourne's mistress would be there. You had very special plans for her, made an example of her so Westbourne would give you what you wanted before you tore him apart like a doll. . . .

They were on Connecticut Avenue, almost at Woodley Road. The entrance to the zoo was across the street, on the right, but Holland wasn't looking at that.

"Stop here."

She had the door open even before the cab jolted to a stop, and ran across Connecticut on a yellow light. The afternoon was fading into ominous clouds, driven by a cold wind. Holland shouldered her way past the panhandlers and street people clustered near the grates in front of the metro station. The coins she was clutching for her fare felt hot in her palm. A last, terrible thought hounded her as she stepped through the gates and onto the escalator: *Who sent you to maim and kill? Who is your protection?*

Holland dashed for a departing train, wedging herself through the closing doors. It turned out to be the milk run that made a half-dozen stops before reaching the hub at Farragut North station.

For the first time since she'd fled her house, she felt safe. As long as she was in a crowd she was anonymous. They might have considered that she would run for the warrens of the metro, but getting hunters to blanket the stations this quickly, much less on individual trains, was virtually impossible.

At Farragut North, Holland melted into the pack heading for the southbound line. A moment later, she was safely in another car. The ride to Waterfront station lasted only fifteen minutes.

Walking swiftly and keeping her head down, Holland crossed Maine Street, heading for the park area that bordered the Washington Channel. On her left were the jetties of the Washington Boat Lines, from which the river cruises departed. In the distance were the lights of Fort Lesley McNair, and farther, those of Buzzard Point, where the FBI Hostage Rescue Teams were quartered.

Holland turned left and picked up her pace. The waterfront promenade was virtually deserted, and the wind bearing off the water knifed through her cotton jacket. She felt exposed and vulnerable. The cold was beginning to fuel her fear; fatigue was conjuring up suspicions that, she kept reassuring herself, were only illusions. She physically sensed the weakening of her grip on control.

The lights of the Francis Case Memorial Bridge rolled across the choppy waters. In the shadow of the bridge, Holland picked out the red, green, and blue pinpricks of light dancing in the darkness. She heard the clear peal of a ship's bell, the groan of timber and straining rope.

The Potomac Yacht Club had three hundred slips, occupied in roughly equal numbers by power yachts and sailboats. The club itself was a Palladian manor spread across a small knoll, backlit by gold floodlights. Holland caught the strains of an orchestra, snatches of women's throaty laughter. The mirage, with its promise of warmth and safety, was almost too tempting.

She skirted the great lawn and headed to the guardhouse, the only break in the wrought-iron fence that separated the property from the public promenade.

Holland knew the instant the guard heard her footsteps. She heard the whir of a mounted camera as it tracked her in the darkness. Holland turned her face to the water, hoping the camera would catch her only in profile, if at all. Out of the corner of her eye she saw the guard watching her. He wasn't the usual rent-a-cop; he belonged to the Capitol Hill Patrol, a special private force that watched over all the major nongovernmental buildings. She had been counting on that, on his making a reasonable assumption.

Holland already had the plastic card in her hand when she reached the gate. She swiped it through a slot in the lock and was rewarded with one green light. Holding her breath, she punched in five digits on the pad. To ensure security, the access codes were changed once a month. Holland couldn't remember when she'd received this particular number.

A second green light appeared, and the gate buzzed open. Holland stepped through, closed the gate, and kept walking. She glanced back once and saw the guard reaching for the volume control on his television. His computer would automatically log the time of entry and the visitor's name. But it wouldn't be her name. Holland was sure he was used to seeing young women arrive alone. A man might already be waiting, or else he would come later. As long as the woman had a card and the proper code, the whys and wherefores of the rendezvous were of no concern to security.

The slip numbers were illuminated by orange lamps, and Holland followed them to a forty-eight-foot, twin-mast Swan Nautor, hand built in Finland twelve years ago. She had been out on it during the summers, when the boat roamed the coastline from the Chesapeake up to Maine. Once, she'd helped crew it down to the Mexican Caribbean.

Holland stepped up onto the gunwale and jumped lightly into the stern. Crouching by the door behind the large chrome wheel, she slipped a key into the lock. Now she was inside the main cabin, switching on the generator, lights, and heat. Then she ducked into the master bedroom, kicked off her sneakers, and collapsed onto the bed.

She lay curled like a shrimp, exhausted but not daring to close her eyes. It wasn't the darkness she was afraid of but the images that lay beyond it. And then she saw the photograph on the night table bolted to the bed: she and Frank, all brown and bleached from the Mexican sun and sea, perched on the stern, arms around each other. Later, when the boat had returned to Washington, its owner had given Holland the access card and code. Holland and Frank, who had to maintain a certain discretion in their relationship, used it as their hideaway, far from the gossips and prying eyes. Nobody ever knew where they disappeared to on their days off; no one ever saw them together in public. *Swann's Way* had been their most precious secret.

Holland stared at the photograph until she remembered the last time she'd seen Frank, and then she couldn't look at it anymore. She could not mourn him now, for the barbed hooks of guilt she felt would paralyze her if she let them. Holland checked the time, then went into the head and scrubbed herself until the hot water ran out. In drawers beneath the bed she found underwear, jeans, and a sweater she'd left there.

Next she dragged the portable television out of its cabinet and plugged it in in time to see the opening credits of the six o'clock news. A pretty black woman launched into the lead story, about a gas explosion that had leveled a New Jersey apartment complex.

Croft's alive. . . .

Injury or death overtaking a U.S. senator would have preempted everything else. Holland had tried hard not to think of what might have happened to him, why he hadn't arrived at her house with Frank. But the questions persisted.

She reached back for that last telephone conversation. Croft saying he was in the car with Frank, five minutes from her house. Had Croft received some urgent summons that had caused him to get out of the car, just minutes before Frank was ambushed? It was the only reasonable explanation. He must have told Frank to go on ahead . . . never suspecting that the delay would save his own life.

Out there is a man who knows I exist. Croft agreed to come because Frank told him about the diskette. As much as he knew about it . . .

This fragile hope warmed Holland until the commercials were finished and the next story scrolled up on the screen. There was her town house, lit up like a stage set by police car high beams, purposeful-looking men in overcoats and trooper jackets trampling down the lawn. A breathless young woman clutching a microphone was going on about how a Secret Service agent had been killed in a counterfeiting raid gone bad. That was followed by a brief reference to a recent Service operation in Atlanta, hinting at a connection between the two, and the reporter switched tracks. Another agent, identified as Holland Tylo, was missing. No further details were available, so the reporter threw in a gratuitous remark about the possibility of Holland Tylo being an undercover agent who had been blown.

Holland couldn't believe what she was hearing. She switched to two other stations and found that both had identical spins on the story. As she skipped past a third, something caught her eye, and she backtracked. On WJLA she saw her house but from a different angle. The picture was jiggly, as if the cameraman was running. Then a close-up—Arliss Johnson, in profile, standing in front of her door, talking to a pair of D.C. patrolmen.

Holland didn't realize she was holding her breath until her chest began to ache. The snippet that included Johnson couldn't have lasted for more than a dozen seconds, but it seemed much longer. Terribly long.

How had Johnson gotten out there so fast? When an agent was brought down, it was the Service's Reaction Squad that hit the ground running. Not the Inspection Division.

Unless Inspection Division was already on the scene . . .

The thought dug into her brain like a fishhook. Holland could not believe that Frank, in his condition, would have tried to reach Division on the radio. With only seconds of life left, he would have hit the panic button to summon help.

Nor was the timing right. Counting back, Holland estimated how much time could have elapsed between the shooting and Johnson's arrival.

Not enough to put him on the scene so fast . . .

Which meant that the men who had shot at her were Inspection Division. However Frank's distress call had been handled, they had been the first to respond.

Holland struggled to free the hook. She knew she was in great pain, on the verge of trauma, and that she had to watch her thinking very closely. There were both real hobgoblins and tempting mirages in this landscape. She could not ignore logic and reason; she had to put a leash on her rampaging emotions.

Because none of this made any sense—especially where it concerned Arliss Johnson. Holland knew too many things about Johnson, the secret places where he dwelled. She kept telling herself that even if he had suspected the worst kind of scenario, he would never have dispatched anonymous enforcers to hunt her down.

But that's exactly what had happened. And who was standing in front of her door but Johnson? Holland wanted to believe that it was a terrible bureaucratic miscommunication. The shooters saw her and, under the circumstances of the call, overreacted.

Except that Arliss doesn't have men who make mistakes like that. Men who appear within minutes of the killer's arrival, seconds after he's fled. How convenient . . . They don't give chase. They try to finish what he began. . . .

Holland stared at the phone on its charging base next to the Loran and satellite navigation system. Service procedure dictated that she call in on the crash number, identify herself, report her condition and location, advise if assistance was necessary. That's what the Book said and what Johnson—who had drilled into her that procedure is what will, in the last resort, keep you alive—expected her to do. Somewhere beyond the brine and the rocking waters, in the siren-pierced night that lay over the city, Holland could feel him waiting, a phone warming in his hand.

"I can't do it, Arliss. I'm sorry," she whispered. "I can't let you find me."

Holland thought briefly about calling Senator Croft but decided against it. Croft would keep till tomorrow. Tonight, she needed someone who wouldn't ask questions, offer advice, or push her to act. Just someone who loved her, would reach out and embrace her.

Holland punched in a number in New Mexico. The woman who answered told her that Dr. Daniels was out of the clinic, expected back in four hours.

"Would you ask her to call *Swann's Way,* please."

"Swan's Way?"

"She'll understand," Holland said softly, then prudently broke the connection.

15

"I didn't want you to hear this through the mill," Wyatt Smith said.

He sat in his high-back chair, the ancient green leather shiny with wear and studded with brass upholstery nails that held it to the frame. Arliss Johnson caught the slight shifts as Smith arranged and rearranged his posture to try to ease the pain. Tonight, nothing was working. But Johnson said nothing. He valued silence, cultivated it, knowing that patience alone would coax forth its fruit.

"The late report came in," Smith continued "Tylo's fingerprints are all over the gun used to kill Suress. I talked to Powell at forensics. His people triple-checked."

"You're saying Tylo murdered him," Johnson said flatly.

"I'm telling you about the evidence. Have you heard from Tylo?" It was eight o'clock, three hours since the shooting.

"No."

"Any idea where she is?"

Johnson shook his head.

"You don't seem surprised about the lab's findings, Arliss."

"It's just one more piece that doesn't make any sense," Johnson replied. "Of course I'm surprised. I'm not going to tell Powell he's wrong. Given the circumstances, he wouldn't say word one unless he was a hundred percent sure. But you and I both know there are ways to put prints on a murder weapon."

"Is that what you think happened here? A third party involved?"

"I don't know what happened at Tylo's house. Yet."

Smith knew Johnson better than to press him. He'd return to that subject later.

"What about Suress?"

Johnson still couldn't quite believe that the man who'd covered him at his meeting with Cochran was dead. The blood, the body, the detritus, all were real. But it had happened so fast, wrenching Johnson from one image of Suress to another—a very able agent who was being torn apart by what was happening to his woman became a series of bumps beneath the paramedics' orange blanket.

"I've been going through Suress's file. There's nothing in it to indicate he might have been set up as a target."

"He worked diplomatic. Maybe he crossed one of our dusky-hued revolutionary brethren, unwittingly got involved in something they didn't want us to know about?"

Johnson let the director's racial slur pass. Smith had always had a strong dislike of Arabs. It had become more pronounced since the World Trade Center bombing.

"There's nothing in his 601 to indicate that," Johnson said. "We've been through his office and his home. Nothing. By midnight we'll have the contents of his lockbox at First Franklin, but don't expect much."

"It all comes down to Tylo again, doesn't it? I gather she and Suress were intimate. Maybe she's holding something for him. Or else he told her things."

Johnson didn't bother to ask how Smith knew about Holland and Suress's relationship. Smith had a point: maybe Holland did know "things."

"There's something else that doesn't make sense," Smith said.

As he turned to face Johnson, his bifocals caught light beams reflected off the illuminated building across the street.

"Why were your people shooting at her? How did that Reaction Squad get on the scene so fast? Witnesses hear a gunshot in

Tylo's house, and before the D.C. cops put in an appearance, your squad is there." Smith paused. "Arliss, did you suspect something was going to happen? Did you have her under surveillance?"

Johnson fished out a two-page report from his briefcase. He walked Smith through it as the director read.

"A call came in on the panic line at five-seventeen. We have the tape. The speaker is male, probably white; age is a problem, because he sounded like he was choking. We tried to match it with Suress's voiceprint, but there are too many anomalies. The voice could belong to anyone—except a female.

"The operator wasn't able to get an identifying unit number. All the caller said was that an agent was down and gave Tylo's address. There was static in the background, then he was back on: shots fired, woman involved. The whole exchange lasted less than six seconds.

"In a situation like that, standing orders dictate that the Reaction Squad move on the watch commander's authority. It did."

"And when it got there, there was Tylo at the front door, waving a gun," Smith said, flipping over the second page of the report. "Your people fired at her because they perceived her as a threat."

Smith got out of his chair and walked stiffly to the armoire that doubled as a liquor cabinet. He held up a bottle of single-malt Scotch; Johnson shook his head. Smith studied the bottle as though he were reading the label, then replaced it, unopened.

"Who do you think was on the panic line?"

"Had to be Suress. There was blood all over the inside of his car, including the radio mike."

"But we don't know the sequence," Smith snapped. "We don't know if Suress was shot inside the car first, then again when he stumbled into the house, or if it happened another way. We don't know why she turned the gun on him to begin with. Too damn much we don't know."

Smith returned to his chair.

"For the time being we're going to contain this thing."

"Contain it how?" Johnson objected. "The media're already all over it—"

"And for once that's working in our favor," Smith interrupted. "They were quick to link Tylo to Atlanta, so we'll keep playing that angle. It gives us an ironclad reason to shut out D.C. homicide and keep the investigation in-house."

"I don't think that's the right move, Wyatt."

"It's the only thing that might help keep Tylo alive long enough for you to find her. Because if I let this become a full-blown murder hunt, put it on the FBI, Virginia, and Maryland hot sheets, Tylo won't have a chance. Those boys would have to be told that Tylo might have killed a federal officer. What odds would you give her if she's spotted and tries to run?"

Smith moved his leg, and Johnson heard a click of a lamp switch. The light behind the desk dimmed.

"You're the best hope she has, Arliss. You're the one who knows her, knows how she thinks, how she might react. I just hope you didn't teach her all the tricks." Smith paused. "She's one of ours, Arliss. Please, find her."

The director was wrong on that point, about how well he knew Tylo. Johnson wasn't sure of that anymore but chose not to correct Smith.

As he passed through the deserted reception area, Johnson patted his jacket pocket, reassured when his fingers touched the microcassette he had lifted from Tylo's answering machine. The unit was one of the new ones, with two counters, one to indicate the last message received, a second to show the total number of messages, in case the listener wanted to scan.

The first counter had read zero, which would mean no recent incoming calls. That jibed with the fact that the tape had been rewound. But the second counter showed that there *had* been one message.

His footsteps crashing around him in the stairwell, Johnson pounded away at the questions: Who had listened to that single message—Holland, the killer, both? And would it have enough meaning for him, when he listened to it, so that he could reach into the night and bring her home?

CHAPTER

16

"I warned you about it, and you blew me off. Now your gun's gone and fucked up."

Senator Paul Robertson stretched his legs along the leather sofa in Croft's office. He wore a white poplin suit and fiddled with the brim of a planter's hat. Earlier, Robertson had glad-handed a retiree delegation—a "geezer gaggle." He always decked out in his plantation best for such occasions.

Croft poured another finger of excellent sour mash into Robertson's glass. His own drink remained untouched.

"The raid went off exactly as it should have," Croft said. "My man had his timing down. I've also been told that the cover story for the media will hold. As far as Inspection Division's concerned, Tylo's gone rogue. Their switchboard has a log of a call she made to Suress this afternoon; when he left for her place, he checked in with the dispatcher and gave her the address. Her link to him is solid.

"Best of all, no one saw a third man come or go. There's nothing surrounding the shooting that can be traced to my man."

Croft said "my man" as if he were talking about a valet.

"But the bottom line is, Tylo still has the diskette," Robertson said. "It wasn't found in her house."

Croft settled in a chair opposite the couch, leaning forward, elbows on knees.

"Listen, Paul. We're no further behind than when Suress went to her. Maybe even a little ahead. Tylo's alone now, running scared. It's only a matter of time before we draw a bead on her."

In a single fluid motion, Robertson sat up. "The others are none too happy about this, James: not knowing where that diskette is, what Tylo might do with it."

"Baldwin made that very clear."

"The old goat got to you, didn't he? Listen, Baldwin's rope is just about played out." Robertson's gaze became cold. "This is for your ears only, understood? It comes from a medical source who owes me. Baldwin doesn't have more than six, seven months left. Cancer. When's he's gone, there will be a lot of vacancies to fill. Bring Tylo home, and Barbara and I will make sure you have the pick of the crop."

Robertson rose, swirled the bourbon in his glass, and quickly drained it.

"The club door's open, James. All you need is the price of admission."

He smiled at Croft's intent concentration, saw the greed and dreams in the sheen of his eyes.

"I don't think Tylo can last more than forty-eight hours on her own," Croft said quietly.

"That's good. You stay in touch, hear?"

Croft was seeing Robertson to the door when the phone rang. It was the private line that bypassed his secretaries. Croft picked it up, listened, then said in a low, urgent voice, "Wait one minute, please. There's someone in the office. Let me get rid of him."

He gestured to Robertson to come back inside, pressing a finger to his lips. Then Croft said, "It's okay, Ms. Tylo. I'm alone now."

Robertson sank slowly into a chair, his eyes riveted on Croft.

"First of all, Ms. Tylo, are you all right? Are you hurt? No? That's a relief. I can't tell you how worried I was. . . . Yes, of course I heard what happened to Frank. I called you from the car, remember? Right after that my pager went off—something that couldn't wait. I had Frank drop me off at that coffeehouse near your place. . . . Yes, that's the one. I made my calls from there and then . . . Well, when I got to your place, it was all over."

Croft jammed a cigarette between his lips and lit it.

"What concerns me is *you*. Where are— Okay, I understand. Ask me whatever you want."

Croft listened, then said, "Frank told me you had information related to Charles Westbourne's murder. He said it was explosive —hard to believe, really, but he had no doubt it was genuine. And I had no reason to question his judgment. You want to tell me a little about that? No?

"Listen, Ms. Tylo. I don't know what really happened at your home. But Frank's dead, and you're obviously a fugitive. I'm willing to help you any way I can, but you have to give me something to work with. . . . No, I haven't spoken with Director Smith. Give me a reason and I will. . . .

"Let me ask you this: Can you stay where you are at least until tomorrow? Okay. . . . Believe me, I understand you're frightened. Like I said, I want to help you, but you have to let me. . . . No, listen to me. I'm *not* going to tell anyone you contacted me. As long as you feel safe, stay where you are. Get as much rest as you can. Tomorrow morning, call me, say, eight o'clock. Then you can tell me where you are, and I'll personally pick you up—alone.

"At the moment that's all I *can* do, Ms. Tylo. Believe me, whatever protection you need, you'll get. Not Service personnel, either. The FBI. And I'll be there with you every step of the way. . . .

"Okay. No, wait. Take down my home number, in case you need it tonight." Croft carefully recited the number. "Listen, Ms. Tylo—it's Holland, isn't it? Holland, just get through tonight. Tomorrow, all this will be over, I promise. . . . Yes, you too. Good night."

Croft sank back in his chair. His cigarette had fallen out of the ashtray, leaving a burn mark on the leather blotter. Croft dropped the charred filter into the wastebasket.

"Glad you were around to hear that."

"She didn't tell you where she is," Robertson said harshly. "You should have pushed her—"

"And lost her for sure." Croft shook his head. "Tylo's finding out she's not as tough as she thinks. She survived, and because of what happened, she doesn't want to trust anyone. *Except she has to.* That's the only reason she called. She's alone and frightened and reaching out. Had I tried to get more out of her, she would have shut me out completely."

Croft smiled. "She'll call tomorrow, Paul. She'll think it through but not for very long. The idea of safety, of having a U.S. senator in her corner—it doesn't get any better. In the end, she'll tell me where to find her."

"You didn't ask about the diskette."

"Didn't have to. She's smart enough to understand that that's the only thing she has to trade. Who better to share it with than the one person who can really use it to help her?"

Robertson thought about this. "It sounds good," he said at last.

"Dooesn't it, though?" Croft murmured. "The hare calling the hound for help."

After Robertson left, Croft threw away his untouched bourbon and eased the cork from a bottle of fine old Bordeaux. Allowing the wine to breathe, he wondered whether he should have told Robertson about Michael Woo. He decided no. Beneath his slick facade, Robertson was a grim, humorless Neanderthal, upon whom subtlety and irony were lost. Croft, on the other hand, savored just how close he'd come to Westbourne's secret, how it had unexpectedly popped up to within his grasp and how he had just failed to reach it. Not telling Michael Woo about Tylo had been a mistake—Croft erring on the side of caution. When Woo had reported the encounter, Croft blamed only himself. But maybe the fact that Tylo had survived her chance encounter with the man had been all to the good. If Woo had taken her then, Suress would still be around to ask questions.

Croft tilted the bottle and carefully poured a glass. The soft light from the desk lamp coaxed forth the wine's blood-ruby hue. Croft took a sip, savored, and smiled approvingly.

Oenophilia was only one of Croft's private and expensive pursuits. Like most of the others, it was paid for by the lobbyists and favor seekers. Unlike cash, material things left no trail; they were consumed and the vessels discarded. Including the women.

Croft knew this game and played it well. But he never flaunted his trophies, as some of his brethren did. He took his pleasures in private, working them as carefully as a potter does his wheel, so that afterward he was left with a sweet, burnished memory. And if others thought him stiff or overprincipled, Croft didn't care. He had long ago accepted the fact that in this life he would never be loved by a beautiful woman or be accepted by those whose measuring stick was pedigree and chiseled good looks.

Croft's constant companion was a hard truth—that the ugly and the deformed garner only pity and, in the political world, contempt. He had learned this during his party's last presidential nomination.

Months before the convention, Croft had been brought into the center of power, given equal voice with men who were already slated for cabinet positions. Intense whispered discussions about the choice of a running mate swirled like prairie dust devils in the humid Texas night. Croft had been questioned closely. Although he gave no sign, he was aware that the FBI was conducting a full-field background check on him. Whenever Croft looked at the candidate, he felt his own heartbeat. That's how close he believed himself to be to the man whose charisma and honeyed promises had bought Croft's support.

The Illinois delegation would put the candidate over the top; Croft had had no doubt of that. As far as he was concerned, the announcement that he would be the vice-presidential choice was a mere formality.

Then, the day before the decision was to be made, the candidate cut Croft off at his knees.

Croft had entered the candidate's suite unannounced and overheard a conversation between the candidate and his horse-faced wife.

"Brad, tell me you're not the teeniest bit serious about taking Croft on the ticket. I mean, really, the man is unbearable!"

"Not much to look at, is he?"

"And so slimy. Christ, my skin crawls whenever I have to shake hands with him. Plus, he's such a brown-noser!"

"He did deliver Illinois."

"You would have won them over without him."

"Maybe. But you're right about Croft. On television he comes across like the Elephant Man. Poor dumb shit. At least he has his Senate seat. . . ."

"Throw him some bones when you get into office, darling. But let's not take that kind of baggage with us, hmm?"

The baggage was abandoned at the station. The next morning the candidate had called Croft in for breakfast and given him the song and dance about how tough his decision had been, how sorry he was that Croft had lost out on the number two post.

Croft was very proud of the way he'd handled that, commiserating with the candidate's angst, assuring him he was prepared to serve him in any way possible. But throughout the convention and the victorious November campaign, Croft heard none of the thunder and ovation. The words he had stumbled across lay embedded in him like shards of glass. They pricked him now, reminding him of the lie behind Robertson's words. He stood no more chance of being included in the Cardinals' inner sanctum now than he had three months ago.

It had started then, at a pre-Christmas party, where he had been buttonholed by a drunk octogenarian senator who kept clutching Croft's lapel. Through the inebriated babble, something quite shocking had spilled out of the old man's phlegmy lips. Croft, who had mentioned he might be working with Westbourne, was told he should run like hell in the other direction. Westbourne was poison. He had unearthed terrible secrets about his colleagues and others in government as well as in private life. And he would not hesitate to use that information to corrupt and destroy.

"I know," the old senator had rasped, tapping his nose with his forefinger. "I've had to eat his shit for years."

Over the next few weeks, Croft dug into Westbourne's background. He traveled across the country to meet people who existed in quiet desperation, exiled from public life or shorn of their fortunes because they had not done Westbourne's bidding.

It was along this journey that Croft kept hearing about West-bourne's secret diaries, a trove of the sins and transgressions of his peers. A wisp of a plan had suggested itself to him; it took on substance when he was certain that among those who lived in Westbourne's shadow were the Cardinals.

Robertson, Baldwin, and Zentner had been cool to Croft when he first mentioned the diaries. The details he offered nudged them to admit that they had heard of them, but they discounted their importance. Croft said he was relieved. Obviously the Cardinals wouldn't be interested in his suggestion as to how the diaries might be obtained.

Zentner and the rest played into the gambit exactly as Croft had intended. They were not only interested but eager, as long as there was no possibility of exposure. So in somber, measured tones, Croft lied to them, mixing assurances with promises, and now he had his coconspirators, who were willing to trade Croft's delivery of the diaries for entry into their club.

Croft poured himself more wine and switched on his computer. The screen filled with photocopies of checks that Zentner had deposited in an offshore account four years earlier, when she'd been fighting for her political life against a surprisingly strong upstart opponent. Westbourne's voice drifted from the speaker, recounting how that money had mysteriously ended up in the opponent's private account on the eve of the election. The re-sulting scandal and the opponent's grisly suicide made a fascinat-ing narrative.

No wonder old Barb is salivating through her dentures, waiting for me to deliver.

Croft giggled at how easily Robertson had bought his lie. He and the rest of the gang did not deserve to be let in on this bit of fun: that the man Croft had sent to visit Westbourne—and later Suress and Tylo—had already delivered the first half of the West-bourne diaries.

In due course Preacher would find the second diskette. Of that Croft had no doubt. And of course Croft had no intention of shar-ing the contents of that, either. All he'd ever intended to do was to make Westbourne's weapon his own.

But now that weapon was much more potent than Croft had

dreamed possible. Because in addition to the oldies but goodies, Croft had come across another name, belonging to a disdainful, cruel man who had once dismissed Croft as a "poor dumb shit" and "the Elephant Man."

Croft sipped his wine and closed his eyes. Behind the thin, pink lids, which barely blocked the light, he imagined himself in the Oval Office. A computer was humming, and the diskette was spinning round and round, draining the lifeblood of the man who sat behind that very important desk, at the helm of the nation.

Two time zones to the west, in New Mexico, the sun began to drench the Sangre de Cristo Mountains in purple. Meg Daniels, an epidemiologist and senior researcher with the National Institutes of Health, braked the Land-Rover in front of the clinic on the outskirts of Santa Fe. She hauled out her field gear and toted it inside. The air conditioning in the reception area raised goose bumps on her skin.

"You look like something the cat dragged in."

Benjamin Zuckerman, who oversaw the clinic on behalf of the University of New Mexico, clucked his disapproval. From the beginning, Meg had pegged him as an anal retentive, and Zuckerman hadn't disappointed her. He was all forms and paperwork, and actually paled at the sight of blood. Whenever Zuckerman was looking for her, she told him she was in the pathology lab, a place Zuckerman studiously avoided.

"You're a swell guy, Benny," Meg said as she trooped by. "Here's the field report. We're still nowhere."

"Tell that to Washington. They're screaming for your D-47."

The D-47 was a weekly résumé she was supposed to file with the NIH. She was about a month behind. But there was nothing new to send in. The Indians kept going to sleep one night, waking up the next morning retching and feverish. Three had died; a dozen others were critical. The rest of the sixty-three victims were barely holding their own. Daniels, who'd been tracking the mysterious outbreak, hadn't been able to come up with any answers except one: It sure as hell wasn't because of a tardy D-47.

"I'm going to run some toxicology screens, Benny. We can talk there."

"Can't. Gotta run."

Meg kept walking, one arm held high, waving.

Meg pigeonholed the clinic as a kind of Frank Lloyd Wright meets adobe concept, crammed with medical miracle toys and the amenities of a fine resort. It was one of the few worthwhile pork barrel projects she had been assigned to. She entered her office, tiptoed around the paperwork strewn on the cool Mexican-tile floor, and dropped her clothes as she headed for the adjacent bathroom. It took her a good twenty minutes to scrub off the desert sand and grime.

Braless under a cotton T-shirt, Meg tugged on a pair of cut-off jeans, pleased about the five pounds she'd lost. Another ten had to go. She ran a brush through her short red hair, worked mois-turizer into her face, then padded barefoot to the computer. The E-mail signal was blinking. Retrieving a Snapple from her cooler, she watched the screen intently.

Pruitt, her boss, from D.C., speculating that the virus that was decimating the Navajo might be airborne. Had Meg found any anomalies in the water samples? It might also be a good idea to check the lung tissue of deceased. She was way ahead of him. No mention of her overdue D-47. Good for Pruitt.

Harry Riggs from UCLA Medical Center. The lung tissue she had FedExed hadn't revealed anything unusual on the first batch of tests, but he'd keep digging. Would she like to have dinner with him next week, seeing as his wife would be out of town? *I think not.*

From Andreas Neumann's secretary at Johns Hopkins, the sug-gestion that Meg check a 1992 outbreak of the so-called sleeping sickness among the Melati Indians in Peru. There, the clue lay in the annual spring arrival of field mice. Were the Navajo experi-encing any kind of rodent infestation?

Meg groaned. She'd missed the possible Melati connection. Leave it to Neumann, her seventy-six-year-old mentor, to re-member.

She was rummaging through her mental closet for what she'd read about the Peruvian outbreak, when the fourth and last message flashed on the screen. From the clinic operator: *Call Swann's Way.* In parentheses: *Caller said you would understand.*

She did.

Holland hadn't expected to reach James Croft on the first try, and she was glad she had succeeded. His tone had been comforting, concerned but not panicky, up to the minute on everything that had happened. Behind the strong voice, Holland had sensed someone reaching out for her, and now she wondered why she'd cut him off when he asked where she was, if she wanted to come in tonight.

She called up his image, Croft sitting behind a curved bench, one of eight senators at some committee meeting. Interservice Communications. Arliss had brought Holland along so she could get a taste of what it was like to grub for budget money on Capitol Hill. When she saw Croft for the first time, she was repelled by his lumpy, shiny face, and instantly ashamed, especially since he'd turned out to be a Service ally.

Holland slipped into the galley and heated up a can of soup. She wasn't hungry but knew that she had to eat. As she stirred the soup, she thought about letting Croft bring her in. Croft had the juice to help her, to protect her if necessary. Most important, he had Frank's testimony with which to weigh the truth of what she would tell him.

Her only reservation, which nagged at her, was that, bottom line, she didn't know anything about the man. His persona, yes. But not the man. Holland had thought she knew Charles Westbourne, that the man she had read about and the one she'd protected were one and the same. Westbourne's diaries had changed all that. Croft hadn't been mentioned on the diskette. There was no reason to think he was in any way connected to—

The phone warbled.

"Hello, old chum."

The connection was scratchy, the voice unmistakable. "Meg!"

Old chum . . . A Britishism Meg had affected during their senior year together in La Jolla. Meg, two years older and stocky then, digging for the ball during a lacrosse match, fending off the hoots

from the high school boys with her quick, clever tongue, crying
about their cruelty when no one except Holland was around. In
college she had bloomed, and some of those same boys had come
calling. But by then it was too late, for Meg had already set sail
into the world.

"Hear you got yourself in trouble, girl. You didn't get hurt at
Westbourne's, did you?"

"No."

"I called you earlier, left a message. . . ."

*When I heard Frank's car come up the driveway . . . I was going
to the front door, and the phone was ringing.*

Holland felt weak with relief. "It's good to hear your voice,
Meg," she said softly.

"So you're okay."

"Kind of."

"What the hell does that mean? Is Frank there with you?"

She doesn't know.

"Meg, I want you to listen to me."

Holland told her everything, beginning with the moment she'd
discovered that she was still carrying Westbourne's diskette. The
only part she omitted was the contents of the diskette. There was
no reason to tell Meg any of that. When Holland was finished,
there was silence on the line.

"Hey!"

"I'm here."

Holland could almost see Meg chewing on a cuticle, a childhood
habit she'd never been able to break, not even when she'd
painted her nails with pepper sauce.

"I'm sorry, Holland. Jesus God, you don't know how sorry I am,
for Frank, and you. . . . How could those assholes have shot at
you?"

"I don't know. Big-time crazy. Maybe I'll know by tomorrow."

"I don't like that part, either, you cozying up with this Croft
guy."

"He's a U.S. senator—"

"So was Westbourne."

"He can help, Meg."

"Maybe. But you haven't thought this through. What's your

alternative? And don't tell me you don't have one, because you've never done anything without leaving yourself an option."

Holland hesitated. "I was thinking of staying put for a day or two."

"Better."

"I don't have any money. I can't get to a bank. By now my credit cards are flagged."

"That we can take care of."

"I'm thinking that the guy who murdered Frank also did West-bourne," Holland said softly.

"Why?"

"He was so cold, Meg. The complete professional. Not a care in the world, because he'd planned every detail." She paused. "Two men killed by skilled assassins within days of each other. What are the chances of that happening?"

"The same as me winning the lottery. Holland, I don't want you to move until I get there."

"Meg—"

"Don't even start. Delta has a red-eye from Albuquerque to Atlanta. From there, I can be in D.C. by eight o'clock, nine at the latest. I'll stop at the bank on my way out to you, and we're done."

"I don't want you involved in this," Holland said, but the idea that her best friend would soon be with her was warm and comforting.

"What are you going to tell Zuckerman?"

"That I need to get into some NIH records. Not a fib, really. Neumann sent me something I can follow up on in Washington."

"How bad is it there?"

"People are still dying, old chum, and I can't figure out why."

"I know," Holland said sadly. "Listen. There are some things you have to watch out for."

At eleven o'clock, Croft paced his condo overlooking the Woodley Park Zoo. The view of the backlit spires of the National Cathedral failed to stir him tonight. He'd been waiting too long for the call.

"Preacher here."

Croft set aside his irritation. "We've tracked down a possible contact for Tylo. Her best friend is Meg Daniels, a doctor, working in Santa Fe on that Indian epidemic. A sharp lady—works for the NIH."

"Why did you say 'best friend'?"

"On the Service application, Tylo listed her as the one to notify in case of emergency. She's also the sole beneficiary on the life insurance."

"Have you talked to her?"

"Tried to. No one at the clinic out there knows where she went after she came in from the field. She's not answering at home, either."

"She's on her way here," said Preacher. "Check the airlines; the charters too. She's playing cavalry."

"It won't matter," Croft said. "She'll never make it in in time."

There was silence for a moment, then Preacher said, "You have something else."

Croft took his time, savored the moment.

"You're going to like this. I got a printout of all contact numbers Suress filed in the last six months. Nothing unusual except one: a marine operator number. There's no record of Suress's ever having shepherded anyone on the water. He's afraid of it—even got himself off the Princess Di visit when she cruised the Potomac."

"So Suress and Tylo had some sort of coop?"

"I think they were very careful and discreet about their fucking," Croft said softly. "Think they did it where no one would ever consider looking. You might want to trace that number, let me know where it leads."

"Forecast calls for heavy rain," Preacher said. "Dangerous time to be on the water."

17

JUST before dawn on April 4, the demons stalking Holland's sleep retreated. She lay still, but the twisted, sweat-damp sheets marked her torturous night's journey.

She'd been running from a tall, dark-skinned stranger, whose voice coaxed the will from her soul and turned her blood to water. Suress was there too, staring sadly at her with a perplexed expression as his fingertips rubbed two red spots on his forehead.

The images were gone now, taking her fear with them, slowing her heartbeat. The gun still lay next to her stomach; like a mother enfolding her infant, Holland knew exactly where it was. She never rolled on top of it, and sometimes her hand strayed to brush the warm carbon-composite barrel.

In that primal part of the mind that did not rest, Holland knew that beyond the darkness, men were hunting her. Had she been gifted with a "shining," a second sight, perhaps she would have known that at this moment Preacher was locked away in a cramped switching room at Bell Atlantic's district substation. The laminated FBI ID Croft had provided dangled from the breast pocket of his camel-hair jacket. Hunched over a computer keyboard was the night supervisor, tracking down the marine number Preacher had given him. The printer spewed out a single line of laser print. Preacher tore it off and smiled when he saw *Swann's*

Way, followed by the registered owner's name and Coast Guard identification numbers. He was well read in early-twentieth-century French literature and wondered if the name was coincidence or the mark of a properly schooled young woman.

Arliss Johnson knew the time because the wind shifted, carrying the scent of dewy rosebushes into his study. The blooms hadn't opened yet. Neither had the thoughts he had pursued through the night.

Dressed in an old wool bathrobe with a tartan design, he sat at his desk. The slab of walnut was laden with thick files bound with rubber bands, old letters stacked in shoe boxes, and a teetering pile of photo albums. Some of the material had been in his closets, but most of it he'd retrieved from a Maryland self-storage warehouse at one o'clock that morning.

Letters, photos, case files—these were what Johnson had in lieu of a family. They talked to him like living, breathing people and, like people, were sometimes pointedly unhelpful, no matter how carefully he probed.

Johnson dimmed the light a fraction to compensate for the dawn and hit the Play button on the cassette recorder.

"Hi, it's me. Got your message. Give your old chum a call."

Who was the "old chum" on Holland's answering machine tape? The unfamiliar voice belonged to a woman, young, sounding strong but anxious, someone not quite sure of the circumstances.

There was static on the line, so Johnson was thinking long-distance.

"Old chum" was obviously a close friend. The sentences were clipped, almost shorthand. Someone Holland had called recently, was Johnson's guess. But not from her house phone. He'd already been through those records.

She called on the run. From somewhere she stopped to catch her breath. She didn't use her calling card, but it was long-distance; she might have gotten change. A 7-Eleven, something like that . . .

Johnson listened to the recording one more time. He thought

he had, at one time or another, been introduced to all of Holland's friends, the few she had.

Johnson cleared a space on the desk and hefted the last filing box he'd brought from storage. His delay in searching it was deliberate, and he still questioned the wisdom of going through it. The box was stuffed with pain. In it were all the official records from both the American and the French intelligence investigations into the assassination of Senator Beaumont. Holland's father. Most of these had never been revealed to the public, and now, as his fingertips marched over the dulled edges of the files, the questions that had haunted Johnson throughout these latter years stirred once more. He remembered how righteous his outrage had been, how his tears had burned for his old friend and the daughter he'd left behind. He saw, too, the wreckage of his promises to track the assassin and tear the truth from his throat. No assassin had ever been found.

Johnson had learned a terrible truth in the months after Beaumont's death. Those close to an assassin's victim learn to live by a different code. They may come to know things, or think they know them, but before they can speak, a figure steps from the shadows and counsels silence. After the indignation and anger, the victim's family and friends are so persuaded. No one understands their acquiescence, the polite, tight-lipped fashion in which questions are deflected or pointedly ignored. After a time, out of respect, the questions cease.

But the doubts linger, or so Johnson believed. For who had not asked himself why Jackie Kennedy never railed against or protested the investigations into the President's death? Why had she retreated so quietly into her hard, shiny shell?

Because she was a member of that most exclusive of clubs: the survivors who know some truth, maybe all of it, but who can never speak.

Johnson sifted through the files until he found the packet of photographs wedged within the manila. He pulled this out and slipped a penknife under the gummy seal.

The pictures tumbled out like butterfly wings. There were four of them—three of Johnson and Robert Beaumont in Rome, and a fourth, much more recent, that showed Holland and another girl, arms draped around each other, as they stood on the parapet of a centuries-old fort in the Caribbean. Johnson wished hard and turned over the photograph.

Me and Meg/St. Thomas, 9/30/94.

Johnson exhaled slowly. He had it then, Meg's surname. Holland had mentioned it when he'd asked her about that holiday.

Two minutes later, Johnson had his top field investigator, Tommy Bryant, awake and listening hard. After Bryant repeated back the orders, Johnson turned to his computer and set it loose among the files of the National Institutes of Health. Meg Daniels's 601 personnel sheet sprang up, and Johnson was punching in the number for the Santa Fe clinic. His heart dropped when a sleepy supervisor explained that Dr. Daniels had left Santa Fe earlier that night. No, the supervisor didn't have her destination.

Where did she go? To Holland.

The next time Johnson spoke to Bryant, the field investigator was in his car, en route to pick up two of the six members of the Inspection Division's Reaction Squad. Johnson told him to get his people to National. A package needed to be picked up. The details were coming.

The enclosed sunroom of Croft's condo was a state-of-the-art gym. He was into his thirty-seventh minute on the Stairmaster when the phone rang. He grabbed a towel off the wet bar as he answered.

"I've tracked her. She's on a boat in the Yacht Club marina."

Croft thought he detected a certain eagerness to Preacher's tone, such as might belong to a gourmand about to indulge.

"Can you see her?"

"When she comes out." Croft heard a breath. "That is, if you want her to come out."

Croft's elevated pulse was settling. His thoughts danced like motes in the halo of the sun.

"Let's wait for her to call me." When Preacher did not respond, he added, "If she leaves, follow her. I don't think she'll stray far. To get to a phone, is all. You'll hear from me as soon as she hangs up."

"Your call," Preacher said, and broke the connection.

The towel draped around his neck, Croft reached for the pitcher of iced orange juice. He knew that Preacher was annoyed at being restrained, but that couldn't be helped. It *was* tempting to take Tylo when she was exhausted, let him go to work on her, then slip her into the grave.

She'll call because she has no one else. And that will be soon enough to see things done.

Such thoughts pleasantly reinvigorated Croft as he headed back to his machines.

Johnson's man spotted Meg as soon as she emerged from the jetway at Delta's gate at National Airport. Even without the photo Johnson had had faxed over from the NIH she would have been hard to miss, the full-figure woman in suede boots and an expensive parka, Navajo jewelry on her wrists. Her styled red hair had a sheen to it, and Bryant caught a whiff of shampoo as she swept by him, saucy green eyes roving but not really searching for a particular face.

Bryant didn't think she would have checked through any luggage, and she didn't disappoint him. He had five agents out front: one in a shuttle bus in case the woman headed for a car rental depot, two behind the wheels of cabs, one as a dispatcher, one in a pursuit car. She obliged him by getting into a cab.

"Okay," Bryant murmured. "Where to, lady?"

Bryant got his answer from his radio, set on the same frequency as the one in the cab. He heard her calm, clear voice say, "The National Institutes of Health."

This took Bryant by surprise. Woman flies across the country all night at the drop of a hat and ends up going to the office?

One of Bryant's men came on the radio, expressing similar puzzlement.

"Maybe that's where Tylo's meeting her. Or else she's already there. We'll know soon enough," Bryant said. Because Daniels's office had been already bugged, her phone tapped.

But something else irritated Bryant, something he couldn't work out, like a sliver of popcorn caught between the teeth. As his driver pulled into traffic three cars behind the cab, Bryant replayed the images he'd caught of Meg Daniels.

She's very calm. Not like someone who's rushing back to help a friend. Shit! Does she even know what's really going on?

Bryant shoved the question aside. One way or another, the woman would lead him to Tylo. If Tylo hadn't been straight with her, made up some story to get Daniels out here but not one so bad as to make her panic, she'd learn differently real fast.

In the back of the cab, Meg was pretending to read an article in *The New England Journal of Medicine* that she'd started on the plane. Holland had warned her that she might be followed, and the thought of that angered her. She reminded herself that she had followed Holland's instructions to the letter and thought that so far everything seemed okay, except her blood pressure.

The headquarters of the National Institutes of Health, a rectangle built in the sixties, with windows like the archer slits in an ancient castle wall, is not a particularly large building, nor is its layout complicated. However, it does have its secrets.

Meg got out of the cab and fell into the stream of personnel funneling through the front doors. She held out her ID to security and squeezed into one of the elevators. Her office was on the fifth floor, one of twenty glass-enclosed cubicles covered by ugly venetian blinds. It was eight-thirty, so Meg wasn't surprised that no one was in yet. She looked around her office, found that nothing appeared to have been touched—some things not even by the cleaning staff—and went into her lines.

"Shit! Couldn't you guys have put on the coffee?"

Holland had told her that the office might be bugged and that Meg would have to buy herself time.

Now she was back in the hall, jogging to the stairs, her boot heels skidding as she took the corners. In the lobby, she threaded her way through the office workers lined up at the vendors' coffee-and-Danish carts, and headed to the back of the building. She was just in time to see a uniformed guard unlock the bottom bolts of the doors to the NIH branch of First Deposit National Bank.

Meg scribbled out a withdrawal slip and, smiling, presented it to a young woman behind two inches of Plexiglas.

"I'd like it in twenties and fifties," she said sweetly.

She figured that five thousand dollars would be enough to get Holland started.

"Talk to me, boys and girls. Where is she?"

The "shuttle bus driver" was in the lobby, working the elevator crowds. There were two banks of four cars, facing each other, not hard to scout.

Bryant strained to get all the words from the background din. "Not in the lobby. Hasn't come down."

"All right, Maryanne. You're it."

Maryanne Jenkins was on the fifth floor, in the section where Daniels worked. Only four or five people had arrived. There was a lot of glass, empty space, and silence. Maryanne, who had known Tylo at the Academy and had taken a visceral dislike to her, thought it wasn't looking good. Daniels's computer was still cloaked in its plastic dust cover. Worse, she couldn't smell any coffee going, and now, as she turned the corner, she found the snack alcove deserted, the twin glass pots perched on top of the urn, empty.

Maryanne took a deep breath and got her voice under control.

"She's gone. She might be in the ladies' room, but don't wait for me to find out. Seal off the exits. Now!"

Meg moved purposefully out of the bank and onto the sidewalk. The street entrance was on the opposite side of the building from the main doors. She was sure no one had followed her into the bank, and no one had come out with her. Now she heard the hiss of pneumatic brakes being released and raced for the bus that was about to pull away from the curb. The driver stopped abruptly and flipped open the doors, and Daniels jumped on board.

"Thanks!" she gasped, handing him a five-dollar bill.

The driver looked at her sourly. "You're welcome, I'm sure." And pointed to the exact-change sign.

Holland waited until the graveyard-shift guard left before she stepped off *Swann's Way*. She tested the silence, then the things that broke it—the lapping of water against the bulkhead, the creaking of rope, the sails flapping in the wind. These were reassuring; more so because they were not broken by man-made sounds.

Holland scanned the nearby piers. All were deserted.

Waving to the guard who'd just come on shift, she buzzed herself through the gate, stretching and yawning like any early riser who's reluctant to get started with his morning exercise. The wind was stronger than she'd thought and cold coming off the water. Overhead, gray clouds shifted restlessly.

The air echoed with the slap of rubber against asphalt. The waterfront was a popular spot for runners, and Holland was glad to see so many diehards out there; she wouldn't stand out. Running in place to warm up, she scanned the area and saw nothing inappropriate. The secret of *Swann's Way* was holding.

It was a half mile to the snack bar, and Holland picked up her pace. The SIG-Sauer, strapped to her side, made her work a little harder, but that was okay. Falling in behind a woman in pink sweats, who ran with weights in each hand, she kept a measured distance, using the woman as a screen. Head high, eyes focused ahead, Holland scrutinized the runners coming toward her. Her hearing was tuned to sounds behind her, in case someone began pounding too close.

Four hundred yards into the run, Holland felt her blood singing, and her confidence inched up a notch. She had survived the night. Her attacker hadn't tracked her down. Very soon, if luck held, she would have money and the luxury of choice it afforded. Holland knew she was well overdue in calling Croft back, as she'd promised, but she didn't want to speak to him again until she was sure it was the right thing to do. She needed time and the advice of her friend.

The wind changed direction, and Holland caught the cloying scent of cinnamon. The snack bar operator knew his clientele. As she closed to within fifteen yards, she saw the gleaming espresso machine and racks of organically correct muffins. Holland deserted the lady in pink and veered toward the concrete embankment, gradually slowing her pace, eyes scanning fast.

A half-dozen joggers, all in expensive, logo-emblazoned outfits, stood around the counter, shaking chocolate or cinnamon onto their foam-milk coffees. Holland studied their eyes, determined the location of their hands. She scrutinized their costumes. It was hard to tell from this distance whether they were concealing anything. Most were carrying a few extra pounds under their loose-fitting sweats.

Now a couple drifted over to a plastic table and chairs. Three more runners arrived, armpits and backs spotted with wet black patches. A balding lobbyist type wearing a beeper came out of the men's room, glanced around quickly, and decided it was okay to scratch his crotch.

She's late. Too late.

A trickle of adrenaline jolted Holland's system. Standing this close to the other runners, she was exposed and vulnerable. She cast a quick glance to her left, where masts rolled back and forth like bobbing toothpicks, and remembered how safe she'd felt on *Swann's Way.*

One turn around the snack bar, then head for home. And don't think! She could have flown into heavy weather, and traffic's always a bear at this hour—

Holland registered the hair first, that regal red helmet that had always made Meg stand out. She was walking quickly along the serpentine path that cut across the park. She appeared so calm, carrying a large brown shoulder bag that made her look like a grad student.

Holland watched her go to the espresso bar, order a coffee, and take it to the table farthest from the stand. No one else appeared on the path. There was no movement in the trees or shrubbery. The channel hummed with the usual morning barge traffic. The sky was empty, but she heard the faraway drone of descending aircraft.

The other joggers were moving along now, most of them slog-
ging up the incline and disappearing into the park. The proprietor
of the espresso bar looked up as Holland drifted in. She smiled at
him and shook her head, and he went back to counting his money.

"Thought I wasn't going to make it, didn't you?"

Meg was on her feet, giving Holland a hard hug, straightening
out to look at her and take stock, then hugging her again.

"I don't know," Holland said softly, slipping into a chair. "I
couldn't be sure if they'd had enough time to connect you to me."
She gripped her friend's hand tightly. "Thank you."

"First things first." Meg reached into her bag, then slid an envelope toward Holland, who immediately stuffed it into her pocket.
"Five thousand. There's more if you need it." She paused. "And
they made the connection, Holland. Whoever *they* are." She
checked to make sure no one was within earshot. "Nothing I can
put my finger on, you understand? I didn't see anyone follow me
in from the airport, but I could *feel* them, always out of sight but
there just the same. My office looked okay, but I can't say for sure
no one had pawed through my stuff. I did what you told me, got
to the bank and the hell away from there once I had the money.
On the way down, I was really looking. I don't think anyone
picked me up."

"They would have netted us by now," Holland agreed. "You did
good, old chum."

Meg drained her coffee. "Let's walk. You have a lot of explaining to do."

They stayed on the path closest to the park, conscious of the
wind, turning their heads and lowering their voices whenever it
changed. Holland talked almost nonstop, unaware of the fear and
grief that rode on her words.

Meg Daniels was very bright. She had a thousand questions
and knew that not one was really important at the moment. Her
curiosity, her need for detail and elucidation, would have to wait.

"You don't have to go to Croft right now," she said. *"Swann's
Way* is safe. If they haven't found you there by now . . ."

"I know. The downside is that Croft will think I'm jerking him
around. Frank gave him a lot of reasons to believe in me, but I
can screw that up real quick."

"What does Croft stand to gain by helping you?"

Holland had thought about this, thought she had the practical answer.

"I think he's a stand-up guy. Otherwise Frank wouldn't have confided in him. But he's also a politician. If he has me to corroborate what Frank told him, the hunt for the diskette is heating up. I'll bet Croft thinks this could be bigger than Watergate."

"With you as Croft's not-so-secret Deep Throat."

At her friend's skeptical look, Holland explained, "This is Washington, and that's the way it'll work. It doesn't reflect on Croft."

"Maybe. Maybe not. I'm not sold on this guy."

"What's my alternative? Sure, I can hide, but for how long? And I won't be any closer to finding out who killed Frank. I *need* to know that, Meg."

"No. What you want is to take him down yourself."

"That too."

They walked on in silence, then Meg said, "Maybe I can help—"

"You already have." Holland had been waiting for this. "Now I want you to walk away. Go back to Santa Fe. I have to know that you're safe."

Holland recognized the stubborn set to her old chum's chin. In the end, Meg would go because Holland had asked.

"You're staying with Croft," Meg said flatly.

"Yeah. I've been listening to myself talk. I know what I'm hearing."

"Then I'll hang around a few days to see where the dust settles. I have some work at the NIH that needs tending."

Meg saw Holland's alarm, knew that it was triggered by what had happened to Suress. "You won't hear a peep out of me," she promised. "But if you need me . . ."

"It'll be good to have you close." Holland did not need more assurance than her friend's word.

"So what now?"

"Now I go back and call Croft."

Meg fished out a quarter.

"Do me a favor. Use the pay phone over there."

Holland, who had been tracking the fading sounds of the jog-
gers, suddenly realized how hushed the waterfront had become.
   "What is it, Meg?"
   "Damned if I know. This place gives me the creeps. Call and
get him down here before I change my mind and haul you off to
Santa Fe."

18

"HOLLAND. I was beginning to worry. Are you all right?"

"I'm fine, Senator."

She did not elaborate. She was listening to the pitch of Croft's voice, trying to detect nervousness or anger. But he sounded calm and reasonable, and he did not ask why she was so late in calling him back.

"Have you thought about what we discussed?"

"Yes, sir. I think it would be a good idea for me to come in with you."

"I'm glad to hear that, Holland."

Now there was a catch to his voice. The hesitation was split-second, but Holland had picked up on it.

"What is it, Senator?"

"The gun used to kill Frank. It had your fingerprints all over it."

"What?"

"Some people are saying you did it, Holland. They're not interested in the whys and wherefores. They want to go public with this, post it on the regional police bulletins."

She was trying to keep the images of Frank out of her mind. She saw herself going to the door, peeking through the leaded glass, seeing nothing. Then the door was in her face and she was down. How long had she been out? A few seconds? A minute or more? Now she saw something else, the killer, a few feet away, holding the gun on her.

He's wearing latex gloves. He hadn't needed to do that because he hadn't had to touch anything smooth. Not even the doorbell. He could have used a knuckle to press that. *Why would he wear gloves? Unless he wanted to preserve something on the gun.*

"I can explain that, Senator."

"I certainly hope so. When I heard about it, I called Smith to double-check. I didn't give him anything, but he's suspicious. He thinks you and I have had contact. I can stall him only so long."

"I understand."

"So how shall we work this, Holland?"

"Do you know the Washington Boat Lines terminal?"

"Yes."

"It'll take me about an hour and a half to get there. There's an area where the tour buses pull up."

"I'll be there. Have you thought about security?"

"We won't need them. Please, come alone."

"All right. Ninety minutes, Holland, and it'll all be over."

She walked to the beach, where Meg was waiting.

"You don't look so good."

Holland quickly went over what Croft had told her. Meg paled when Holland told her about the prints. "I'm meeting Croft by the boat line docks," she finished.

Meg rose. "Fine. The walk will do me good."

"Please . . ."

Holland turned away so that she didn't have to look at the sheen in Meg's eyes.

"You have my number at the office?" Meg asked.

Holland nodded. "I'll call as soon as Croft brings me in."

They hugged, then Meg turned, boot heels clicking off the blacktop. She felt the back of her neck tingle and abruptly turned around, but all she saw was Holland walking in the opposite direction.

. . . .

"Okay. They've split up. The redhead is heading through the park. She's out of it."

Preacher was using high-power field glasses, Israeli military surplus, three hundred dollars a copy. His vantage point was a knoll close to the yacht club, affording a clear view of the landscape below.

"Follow her," Croft instructed. "I'll be along when she expects me."

Preacher jammed the cell phone back into his pocket and quickly dismantled the long-range parabolic microphone, which opened and closed like a miniature fan. The equipment was year-old Agency issue. It had picked up every word Tylo had spoken. The rookie was making it almost too easy.

Preacher was about to move off the knoll, when the hairs on the back of his neck prickled. The nondescript sedan easing to a stop at the club guardhouse might be nothing more than an unmarked patrol. Or it might be something else.

Preacher's eyes went stone cold when he saw Arliss Johnson get out of the car. He had his ID in his hand, and now the guard was stepping out.

Oh, my . . .

The last time Preacher had seen Johnson was ten years ago, in a sterile white room in the bowels of 1800 G Street. Johnson had had him then. The schoolteacher with whom Preacher had had a one-night stand had been found along the Maryland shore. Johnson said there was a witness, a university geek who'd spotted a man shoveling dirt on a mound. The geek waited until the man was gone, then went to satisfy his curiosity. He dug only a few inches before discovering the bloody hand with its broken fingernails. When the forensics people got there, they joked about the vomit on the shallow grave.

The geek, actually an ornithologist, was a trained observer. The composite drawing a police artist had helped him come up with was better than a fair likeness of Preacher. Johnson had kept pounding away at that. True, it had been twilight and the ornithologist had admitted that his field glasses were not capable of light enhancement. Still, he was sure that Preacher was the man who'd stood over that grave.

Johnson had hammered at Preacher for six hours, but Preacher simply went away on him. The rational, logical part of him thrust and parried with Johnson; in his mind, he was soaring on the wings of memory. He knew that Johnson had no idea that his interrogation only heightened the intense pleasure Preacher felt. That, and the fact that he knew Johnson could never pin the grisly murder on him.

A search of Preacher's apartment produced no links to either the victim or the crime site. In less than twelve hours, Preacher's lawyer announced that the ornithologist had been receiving extensive psychiatric counseling and was on a regimen of heavy antidepressants. Subsequent tests confirmed that the geek hadn't taken his pills that day, an oversight that could cause dizziness, blurred vision, even blackouts.

Further investigation had made Johnson's job even more difficult. Preacher, in his fourth year with the Service, had a sterling record in Executive Protection. Before that he'd done three years in the Army, Green Beret. But his record there was so thoroughly sanitized that not even Johnson's long reach could get to it. And no one knew about the rest, the bodies of women decomposing in rain forests, riverbeds, and the stinking garbage dumps of third-world cities. No one had ever suspected.

Except Johnson. Who had Preacher suspended from active duty. Who began reaching out to men Preacher had served with, commanders who had given him his marching orders. Johnson plagued Preacher until he couldn't stand it anymore. He knew, was exactly sure, what Johnson intended: to push him to the brink and over it, make him confess or force him to act.

They had taken Preacher's credentials and gun but not his passport. They didn't know about the safe-deposit box stuffed with cash or the other identification he'd squirreled away. They did not know, as they watched on that sunny May afternoon when Preacher boarded a flight to California, that he would never come back. His itinerary, which he made sure Johnson could access, read Palm Springs via L.A. It mentioned nothing about the 10:45 Thai International flight to Bangkok.

Preacher remembered that moment at LAX, looking out the windows at the 747 parked at the gate. He knew he had no choice.

Johnson was relentless, patient, methodical, utterly without mercy. One day, perhaps very soon, he would excavate the truth about Preacher's bloody secrets, and Preacher could not allow that. Exile was his only choice.

Now he watched Johnson go along the slip to *Swann's Way,* step onto the gunwale, and disappear inside. A few minutes later, he was out again, looking frustrated and angry.

"Not there, is she, sport?" Preacher murmured. "But you are. And I'll be coming for you, Arliss. Oh, yes . . ."

James Croft did not take kindly to being lied to. Holland had needed nowhere near the hour and a half she'd claimed in order to reach their rendezvous point.

Fifty minutes had elapsed since their conversation. Preacher had called in again, reporting that Tylo had reached her destination and was sniffing it out. The idea of Tylo, so trusting and unaware, alleviated some of Croft's anger. This was good, because for a few crucial minutes she would be staring into his face. There could be no untoward expression on it for her to react to.

Croft left his condo lobby and soon was fighting the heavy D.C. traffic. In keeping with his dressed-down image, he drove a comfortable but unostentatious Oldsmobile. Croft slipped a compact disc into the upgraded stereo system and let the strains of a Bach Brandenberg Concerto ease his tension. He hoped that he would have the chance to rebuke Tylo for her lie before Preacher fell upon her. It would please him enormously to do so.

Bryant was in the glue but didn't know how deep. The minute he was certain his people had lost the Daniels woman, he'd called Johnson. Now Johnson sat beside him in the car across from the main entrance of the NIH. He hadn't said one word about Bryant's verbal report. Instead, he'd ordered Maryanne Jenkins to fetch some things off his desk. After his spectacular failure, Bryant wasn't about to ask for details.

"We can put out an APB on her," Bryant said hesitantly, fidgeting behind the wheel.

He wanted to smoke, but it had started to drizzle and the windows were closed.

"She went into the bank," Johnson said. "You'd already lost her by then. She came out with five thousand to give to Holland."

Bryant just listened. Johnson had all the details. He was thinking out loud, working through to something.

"How much more help can she give? There's the boat, now the money. How close will Holland pull her in? Not very, I think."

Now Bryant understood the gamble Johnson was taking.

"Christ on a sidecar!"

Bryant grabbed the top of the steering wheel, ready to propel himself out of the car. Because there was Dr. Meg Daniels, getting out of a cab, walking casually into the building.

"Hold on."

Bryant's head snapped around. Johnson was staring at Daniels, his face as still as an Aztec mask.

"We have to wait for Maryanne," Johnson murmured. "She'll be along any minute now."

It was like old homecoming week for Meg. Colleagues she hadn't seen in months were coming by, intrigued by her sudden reappearance. Meg gave them the sleeping sickness story, put bells and whistles on it by referring to Neumann, and left them stroking their chins.

All the while the cell phone in her white lab coat weighed her down like an anchor. She kept telling herself it was too early for Holland to call, but that didn't help at all. Now Pruitt, her boss, was on the line, asking her to come down to his office.

Meg gathered up a couple of files for show and set off. Pruitt would expect her to be gung ho, on the verge of a breakthrough. Why else fly across the country in the middle of the night?

"Come on in, Meg."

Pruitt was in his early forties, a trim, dapper man with a sunbeam personality. Which was why she knew immediately that something was wrong.

Pruitt rose and took her hand in both of his.

"It's good to see you, Meg. I'm anxious to know what you've

found out. We'll talk when you have . . . when these other matters are squared away."

Pruitt hurried out before Meg could reply, leaving her staring at the back of a tall, rangy man standing by the windows.

"Hello, Meg." He turned around. "Remember me?"

She did, recalling Arliss Johnson from Holland's Service graduation ceremonies. And she was aware of the history between him and Holland.

"Sure," Meg said lightly. "The first time Holland introduced us, I wished you were twenty years younger."

Meg knew why he was here. How he had tracked her so quickly didn't matter. She had to get the upper hand now. Arliss Johnson was a slippery character who could charm his way into your pants in no time flat. She noticed how his fatigued smile belied the urgency in his eyes.

"You must have been reading my mind," Johnson said. "I was thinking the same thing."

He thrust his hands deep into his pockets. "I don't have time to dance around this, Meg. This is what I know: Holland called you, and you jumped on a midnight plane. You got here, went to the bank, then went to meet her. From there I draw a blank. I have a lot of questions but only one that really counts: Where can I find Holland, to help—"

"Why were your people—Holland's people—shooting at her?" she cut in.

Johnson nodded, as though she'd just confirmed a suspicion.

"She told you what happened at the house," Johnson said. "You know about Suress. But there's a side to the shooting she can't possibly know about."

Johnson walked her through everything: the call from the as yet unidentified source, the Service's reaction, the almost fatal, tragic result. Johnson neither embellished nor indulged in mea culpa. He thought Meg would smell bullshit a mile off. He hoped she was keen enough to recognize the truth, not skirt around it out of loyalty.

"That's all I have," Johnson said. "That's all I could tell Holland right now."

He paused. "Why does she need that money, Meg? She's not

going to run. She's too smart for that. Besides, five thousand isn't enough to take her very far."

Meg did not reply, but neither did she drop her gaze from his eyes.

"Holland's done nothing wrong," she said. "It's you who's pushed her into a corner. Give her some time to—"

"I know she needs time," Johnson interrupted softly. "She's out there alone, frightened. I'm asking myself why she didn't come in with you. You could have rounded up a battalion of legal eagles in no time flat. I would have been lucky to get in to see her. But that's not what you did. You went to her, gave her what she needed, and came back here. Why? Because she argued you might be in harm's way? Okay. But maybe something else too. Maybe she convinced you that she had a plan to get out of all this, something that, when she explained it, made all the sense in the world to you. That's it, isn't it? Otherwise you never would have left her alone, not with that stubborn Scots mentality of yours."

Johnson waited a beat. "I need to know where she is, Meg. I already checked the boat. Wherever she's gone—"

And then Johnson caught himself, because something so obvious slammed into his consciousness.

"Whoever she's going to meet, Meg, might not be one of the good guys."

Jesus, he's quick!

Johnson was making all the connections, barreling ahead because he knew he was right.

But there are things he isn't telling me. Things he doesn't know. Like Croft . . .

And she saw something else. For the first time, Johnson seemed to falter, as though he was unsure of himself.

He never considered that she'd go elsewhere, break the loop. Now she's outside, and he's lost.

Johnson was looking at her, and she realized he saw this new, hard knowledge she had about him.

"Is Holland afraid of me? She doesn't trust me to bring her in?"

"Can you blame her?" Meg countered. *"She* doesn't know why people were shooting at her." She paused. "How did you find *Swann's Way?"*

Johnson flipped open a file on the desk and pushed a picture toward her. In the file Meg saw pink and mauve envelopes with Holland's handwriting, addressed to Johnson.

She knew what he was doing—what she'd inadvertently let him do: dredge up the good history between him and Holland, remind her, with Holland's own script, that there were years of trust there.

Meg felt herself teetering. The idea of Holland going to Croft had never sat well with her. She looked up at Johnson, saw his quiet expectation.

Suddenly the door burst open. Johnson turned quickly, but Meg registered his flash of anger.

"What is it?" he snapped.

Bryant had done the halls like a broken-field runner. His face was flushed and he was breathing hard.

"You need to see this. Right now."

Johnson turned to Meg. "Give me a moment." Outside, he faced Bryant.

"What is it?"

"Yesterday a guy came into the Coach and Arms. This is what he did."

Bryant shoved the single-page report at Johnson and kept on talking.

"Bartender says he did his act and walked away real casually. Everyone in the place was watching with their mouths open."

Johnson's forehead wrinkled as he read about the spilled Barbière rum that was set on fire. It was a symbolic act, sometimes carried out by Secret Service agents to honor the memory of a fallen comrade.

"For Suress?" he asked.

"That's what I thought. But the bartender said there was something off about this guy. He gave the investigating team a composite. They got it about thirty minutes ago and hit the panic switch."

Bryant unfolded a twelve-by-sixteen piece of heavy-grade artist's paper, watching as Johnson's eyes widened and his body stiffened.

"The bartender's sure?"

"Positive. He was Service for twenty-two years. His eyesight's better than mine." Bryant paused. "Once the investigating team knew what they had, they pulled the file."

"Where is it?" Johnson demanded softly.

Bryant picked up the accordion file he'd placed on a soft fabric chair, one of three that lined the hall outside Pruitt's office. Johnson held it in both hands, like some kind of talisman.

"Preacher's back," Bryant said. "Those scattered reports out of Southeast Asia about his being dead—all crap."

Bryant knew how Johnson had hunted Preacher, how he wouldn't let go of him because he believed Preacher was, in the depths of his heart, a stone killer. Johnson never believed the third- and fourth-hand accounts about Preacher's demise in some jungle backwater. Johnson would never believe that unless he had Preacher's corpse at his feet.

"Preacher did Westbourne, didn't he?" Bryant was saying. "Someone brought him home—"

"We'll talk about that later," Johnson said sharply. "Get hold of Customs and Immigration at LAX, San Francisco, and Seattle. Send them the composite and tell them to review the videotapes. They won't have whatever name he's using on the Watch List, so tapes are our only bet. Red-flag the Canadians too. He may have come through Vancouver."

"What about here in the city?" asked Bryant.

"Preacher did Suress too," Johnson replied softly. "If Westbourne had been his only concern, that wouldn't have happened. He's here for something else . . . someone else."

Bryant bit his tongue before the name could get past his lips. "I'll be done here in a few minutes, one way or the other," Johnson said. "Be ready to move."

Johnson slipped the file under his arm and went back into the office. Meg saw that he was different now. She'd never thought that he could look frightening.

Johnson stacked the things on Pruitt's desk to clear some space. Then he opened the file and unfolded the composite.

"I don't have time to get you to sign security papers," he said flatly. "I'll take your word that what I show you will not go further —ever."

He raised his eyebrows in question.

"You have it," Meg told him.

But she didn't want to know what he was about to tell her. Not any of it. She felt as she had when as a child she tiptoed along the bottom of the pool until the water was up to her neck and she was gasping, not really trusting her ability to swim.

"His name is Preacher," Johnson said. "He worked for the Service until we found out he had certain predilections. . . ."

"Predilections?"

"He enjoyed killing and torturing, mostly women. He fled the country before I could stop him. Reports had him dead, but he's surfaced in D.C. The ID's positive. I'm certain he took down Westbourne and his girl. I think he murdered Suress too."

Johnson paused. "He was in the house with Holland. Somehow she managed to get away from him. That's why she was shooting, had the gun in her hand when the cavalry pulled up.

"Who's to say what went on inside, but I think Preacher's not quite done. Maybe Holland heard him say something, saw him do something. Whatever, he's after her."

Johnson balled his hands into fists and leaned toward Meg.

"I don't know who Holland's meeting, or where. But she can't know that Preacher's close by—"

"If he's close by," Meg cut in.

Johnson nodded. "Sure. *If.* So here's the situation. It's your call. Do *you* think it's worth the risk not to bring her out? Because I can't help her if I can't get to her."

Johnson rocked back on his heels, his eyes latched onto Meg.

Meg stared at the composite. The face was accented by Latin features, full lips, delicate cheekbones. The eyes, friendly and kind, could have belonged to any one of the hundreds of young priests on the Georgetown University campus. Preacher . . . the name was apt.

Her fingers strayed to the file. She could take the time to read it cover to cover, but what good would that do. For a moment she thought it seemed too convenient for Johnson to have it right now. Then she recalled the desperation of the agent who'd barged in. That had not been an act.

Holland's out there. It's your call. She's waiting.

19

THE day's first tour buses were pulling up to the orange-painted cinder-block depot. Next to it was a quaint Colonial-style cabin that housed a cafeteria, ticket booth, and souvenir stand. Holland saw that the Japanese and European tourists were dressed for the weather, wool turtlenecks beneath warm coats and scarves. Visitors from the American heartland, thinking Washington was the South and dreaming of cherry blossoms, huddled in their light windbreakers.

Holland slipped in among them. She felt better now, surrounded by anonymous bodies. The walk along the esplanade to the Washington Boat Lines terminal had seemed longer than it actually was. There was still time to scout Croft's arrival.

She followed the crowds inside, wedged herself between a Japanese foursome at the cafeteria line, and bought a hot chocolate, which she took to a table by the window. At the water's edge, she saw three double-decker ferries lined up like docile behemoths. Holland scanned the crews working the ropes and readying the ramp. She didn't startle when it dropped to the pier with a metallic crash.

When the bell sounded, Holland fell in with the parade, moving as far as the ticket taker's booth. Then she veered toward the depot as another bus arrived, and she searched the faces of those

who stepped off. She thought she'd be all right as long as the
buses kept coming.

Walking back toward the cafeteria, she noticed a van angling
into one of the bus spaces. Across its side was the logo *Mott's
Tours and Excursions.* The windows were blacked out. Because
almost all tour-operated vehicles had tinted glass, Holland didn't
pay it any attention. She did not see the door open and a man slip
out.

Preacher was wearing glasses with clear lenses, a Baltimore Ori-
oles baseball cap, and a scarred leather jacket strewn with ancient high school football patches. He looked like a math teacher
who coached Little League on the side somewhere in the Rust
Belt.

Preacher had arrived at the waterfront before Holland. He'd
made a quick sweep of the area, chatted with the dockworkers,
and blended in completely by the time he spotted her. Preacher
watched the girl maneuver and thought she was very good. He
could almost smell her urgent need to be free of this terror, and
he waited to see if she would falter or panic. So far she was doing
all the right things—using the tourists for cover, keeping her back
covered, scouting a location where she might watch unobserved
as Croft approached. Preacher smiled when she settled on her
vantage point. He would have chosen the same one.

He had already counted three opportunities to kill the girl. That
she had gotten the better of him at her town house still rankled.
But Croft had impressed upon him that she had to be dealt with
in a way that would raise no suspicion; her death must be compat-
ible with the circumstances she herself had helped to create. This,
Preacher knew, would require privacy and his undivided attention.

Impatient, he checked his watch. Croft would be here in a few
minutes. Tylo was in place. It was time. He was eager.

To the left of the third ferry was a brick shed with a galvanized
tin roof. It was surrounded by fifty gallon drums of marine oil and

lubricants. The blacktop beneath Holland's running shoes was slick, so she moved cautiously.

The shed was a perfect cover, affording an unobstructed view of the parking lot. Holland chided herself for not remembering to ask Croft what kind of car he'd be driving. But there were few private vehicles in the lot. He would be easy enough to spot.

Holland checked the time. Any minute now. She was intensely aware of everything around her—the low rumble of the departing ferry, the sweet, nauseating odor of diesel fuel, the clatter of the ramp as it was winched off the pier. Then the ferry horn startled her. She never heard the footsteps behind her, felt only a stinging sensation at the side of her neck.

Holland's first thought was that she'd been bitten by an insect. She turned and saw the shadow, then her hand was reaching for her gun. But her muscles refused to respond. She moved slowly, as though pushing her way through molasses. Holland watched helplessly as her arm fell to her side. She opened her mouth to scream but heard only a dry gurgle. Her knees began to shake.

Someone scooped her up from behind, propping her up. Holland felt hot breath on her cheek, but she couldn't turn to see her attacker.

"You can walk," he said. "You can't feel your legs, but you can walk. Now!"

Holland saw one foot go before the other but had no idea how it was happening. They were behind the shed now, Holland's toes catching on the concrete dividers, dragging along the asphalt. Again she tried to scream but could not.

Then they were in the parking lot, skirting around the back of the buses, heat still coming off the engines. Ahead, Holland saw the van with its smoked windows. The side door slid back, and she caught a glimpse of a strong hand, nothing else.

She was spun around and pushed so that she was sitting with her back to the van's interior. Then her legs were lifted up and over, rolling her helplessly onto the floor. For a split second Holland saw but did not feel the nubby carpet against her cheek. As the door was rolling to a close, Holland summoned the last of her will and clawed at it, just in time to see James Croft step out of a nearby car.

20

CROFT made sure that his scarf—silk paisley over guards-green cashmere—was snug around his throat before he buttoned his topcoat. He was susceptible to any kind of illness and was especially careful in the raw, unpredictable weather of early spring.

Strolling among the tourists, he ignored the foreigners, sifted through the day-trippers. Croft didn't waste time on the families but searched out the singles in the ticket line, then inside the cafeteria. He peeked into the gift shop, saw the walls strung with T-shirts, glass cabinets filled with tacky miniatures of the Washington Monument and other landmarks. He spent a few minutes pretending to read the ferry departure schedule while watching the door to the ladies' room.

Where is she?

Croft drifted outside as another tour bus pulled up. The diesel fumes made his eyes water. He watched the new arrivals; saw that Tylo was not among them. After they'd trooped by him, he made a slow circle from the cafeteria to the parking lot and over to the water's edge, then up to the lot. If she was watching, she couldn't help but spot him.

As he circled the area again, Croft began to feel the cold creeping into his feet. His face, its skin extremely sensitive, felt frostbitten. This time when he looked around, he searched for Preacher.

He's taken her. Something went wrong and he had to take her.

In measured strides, Croft returned to the parking lot. He had the car's heater going full blast before he headed to the rendez-vous point.

"Okay. He's not coming this way. He's in the car, engine is on. He's out of here."

Holland didn't recognize the voice. Her eyes closed in reflex when the interior light came on, brighter than it should have been. Someone was moving her, big hands around her shoulders, as gentle as they could be in the confined space. Holland kept her eyes closed. She wasn't going to let them see her fear.

"Open your eyes, Holland."

First she gasped as she recognized the voice, then she found herself blinking at Arliss Johnson. He was trying to smile, but it came out as a grimace.

"You . . ."

Her mouth formed more words, but her vocal cords refused to cooperate. Johnson slapped a blood pressure cuff on her arm, pumped it up, and watched the needle as he let the air out.

"You'll be fine." He tilted up her head and held a plastic glass with a straw to her lips. "It's only water with a little salt. Doesn't taste very good, but it'll help you along. Swirl it around; gargle if you can."

Holland took a sip and felt the salty sting. She moved the water around her gums and ended up swallowing most of it.

"It's a very mild version of synthetic curare," Johnson said. "It paralyzes the muscles but doesn't affect the neurological system. It'll wear off fast, like novocaine."

Johnson turned to Bryant. "Give Croft some distance, but don't lose him. I don't think he's quite done yet."

Holland checked her body, wiggling her toes, stretching her legs, clenching her fingers, working her jaw.

"Why did you do this?" she asked, her words slurred.

Johnson helped her sit up. The van was a full surveillance unit, with captain's chairs that could swivel and lock. Holland brushed away Johnson's hand and pulled herself into a leather seat.

Johnson squatted in front of her. His eyes reached out to her, asking for understanding. But there was something else there, a spark of rage.

He's onto something bad.

"You were running from *me*," Johnson said. "When I found you, I couldn't take the chance you'd fight me." He paused. "I'm sorry for the way it came down, Holland, but I couldn't let you walk to Croft."

Holland looked through the smoked window and saw trees and grassy areas. The van was moving smoothly, against the traffic of cars and tour buses headed for the wharf.

"Meg told you where to find me," she said. Now her voice sounded clear, strong, and she rolled her head, loosening tight muscles.

"She didn't betray you," Johnson replied. "I showed her things."

Holland heard papers rustling, turned, and saw the composite. The surge of adrenaline that hit her killed the remaining effects of the tranquilizer.

Johnson nodded. "Yeah, it's the guy who came after you at your house."

He placed a file folder on her lap and began speaking fast, about a former Service agent called Preacher who'd gone rogue, who'd thriven on violence, who preferred to practice on young women. A finely honed assassin, expert tracker, very confident, supremely capable.

Very confident . . .

The phrase reverberated in Holland's head, shaking loose old thoughts.

What is your magic? Who is your magic?

"It's not you," Holland murmured. "It was never you."

"What?"

Holland shook her head. "Nothing. Cobwebs. Where are we going?"

"Croft came in for the meeting. He waited, didn't spot you, and left—"

"He's pulling over," Bryant said from behind the wheel. "What's the call?"

"Scoot by him, make a U-turn, park so we're out of his line of sight but where we can still watch him."

They were on the two-lane blacktop that snaked through the park between the channel and Water Street. It was a shaded road, indented with parking spaces for cars and Winnebagos to nose into. In open areas of wet brown grass were picnic tables, large metal drums for trash, and brick fireboxes with rusted barbecue grills.

Holland watched Croft's sedan pull into the rest stop. The van drifted by, then she heard the click of blinkers as Bryant eased it onto the shoulder. Three cars went past. Suddenly the rear tires dug into the gravel, and Holland was pinned against her seat as the van turned. Bryant slowed and drifted onto the opposite shoulder; Holland heard branches scraping the roof.

Swiftly Bryant was out of the van. He threw open the back doors, pulled out a duffel bag, then slammed them shut. Over the traffic, Holland heard the ratcheting and felt the van tilt. Now there was a jack under the van, a signal to passing motorists—or anyone else who might see the van—indicating what the problem was: a driver with a flat but with the necessary equipment to fix it. No one would bother them.

"Croft's stopping for a picnic?" Johnson muttered. "I think not. What's wrong with what you see, Holland?"

She took the Rangemaster binoculars from him, heard the electronic whir of delicate machinery as the lenses refocused.

The picnic benches were deserted. There were no shadows other than the ones cast by the trees, no glints of light in the shrubbery. Croft was out of the car, walking around the picnic area, his steps jerky as though the cold had locked his knees. He batted his gloved hands, not bothering to conceal his anger.

Then another car pulled in, a beige rental that looked ready for recycling. *There's nothing wrong—*

"Except the beige car is backing in," Holland said aloud. "Its front is toward the road, the way someone would park who was thinking of leaving in a hurry."

"Yes. Now, who is it?"

Johnson tried to wait, but he couldn't help himself. "Come on, now. Get out of the car. The senator's a busy man. He doesn't have all day."

"Sir . . ."

Bryant, who had returned to the driver's seat, was turned around. Holland looked at him for the first time, at his red, fleshy face and pug nose, the hard, intelligent eyes. She could tell he was aching for Johnson to cut him loose.

"There's a Nightingale on standby at Andrews. We can have her here in twelve minutes. The Rapid Reaction Force at Buzzard Point can move—"

Johnson shushed him with a wave of his hand. Holland knew that the Nightingale was a helicopter with PAVE LOW capabilities, meaning that it could go anywhere, anytime. But unlike PAVE LOW, it was a two-seater, strictly reconnaissance and surveillance. Nightingale could come up behind you, drift down, and you wouldn't know it was there until it sat on your shoulder.

"Anyone else but Preacher, sure," Johnson said. "But he's up on the hardware. Right now, even though he has no cause, he's watching for it."

Holland didn't clue in until the door of the beige sedan swung fully open and the man in the composite stepped out. She heard Johnson breathe deeply, the air catching at the back of his throat. Up front, Bryant slipped an Uzi from the rack under the dash.

"He'll spot Nightingale," Johnson was saying, sounding as if he were talking to himself. "And then he'll know the rest isn't far behind. Nightingale can't trap him, can't stop him from taking out Croft or using him as hostage. That would be his first play, a United States senator as a shield. If he couldn't do that, he'd jump on the first family that came down the road. I don't think— No, Holland!"

Holland felt his hand clamp around her biceps. Her fingers had already reached the handle on the panel door, and in another second she would have been out.

"You're okay, right, Holland? Not thinking of doing anything silly?"

Johnson released his grip, and Holland sank back into the chair. She could not tear her eyes from the two men who were talking to each other, puffs of white air billowing between them.

"Give him to me!" Holland whispered.

But if she'd been asked which one, she couldn't have answered. The one called Preacher, who had spoken to her as softly as a lover, who had shot Frank in the car, then again when Frank had staggered into her house? Or Croft, whom she had believed in, trusted to the point where she had offered up her life to him.

Croft, whom Frank had confided in, who gave Frank up to his butcher, who was Preacher's magic . . .

She turned to Johnson, wild-eyed. He was already on the phone, talking in a low voice to the Command monitor at Buzzard Point. The Secret Service got a faster response than anyone else from the FBI's Rapid Reaction Force dispatcher. Armed men in hard-shell armor, their black suits heavy with stun and flash grenades, tear gas, and extra ammunition, were pounding into vans that had florists' and bakeries' logos stenciled on their sides. Johnson was describing the car and the driver, then relayed the only route Preacher could take out of the park to reach 395, the Southwest Freeway. If they could bottle Preacher up, there was a chance of taking him. Units from Johnson's Inspection Division were on the way. Now Johnson looked at Bryant, who was on the second line.

"The boys and girls are rolling," he said.

Johnson was back on his call. "This is a hard takedown. No warning. Shoot for the limbs. I need him alive if possible. I need to ask him about some things. . . .

"Holland, what's happening out there?"

"Croft's back in his car. Preacher's . . . he's gone back to his. He's heading out first."

Johnson tapped Bryant on the shoulder. Metal screeched, and the van dropped heavily as it slid off the jack. Bryant straightened out the wheels, stepped on the gas, and made a textbook evasive maneuver that sent the vehicle into a one-hundred-eighty-degree turn. Behind them, horns blared.

"Okay, now," Johnson said quietly. "We'll fall in behind Croft, pass him if we have an opening between him and Preacher, slip right behind him, then slow down, separate them."

Johnson turned to Holland. "How are the cobwebs?"

"I'm fine."

"No knee-knocking?"

She shook her head.

"Okay, then. We might get lucky."

"Croft—"

"Not important now, Holland. We *know* where to find him. This will be the FBI's play, understand? You've seen Preacher up close and personal, but I know him better than that. He won't give us more than one chance."

Holland swallowed hard, then slipped her gun from the holster, dropped the clip, checked it, and slapped it back in.

Johnson watched her hands on the gun, searched for a tremor that never came.

Preacher drove along Water Street at a steady forty miles per hour. Even so, Croft kept falling behind, like a knee-jerk tourist.

Croft had been livid that Tylo had stood him up. At the picnic area, he'd badgered Preacher about his surveillance, the way he'd let her slip out of sight at the ferry landing. Preacher had had to remind Croft of his instructions—that he wasn't to intercept the girl but was only to follow her to the meeting point. It was not a criticism Croft had taken lightly.

Nor could Croft understand why, at the last minute, Tylo had gotten cold feet. He'd suggested that something might have spooked her, hinting that maybe Preacher's watch had been a little too obvious.

Preacher hadn't bothered to reply to that. By the same token, he hadn't thought it necessary to inform Croft about Arliss Johnson's having been on *Swann's Way* and that, contrary to Croft's predictions, he didn't think Tylo would go back there.

Did Johnson get to her first?

Preacher wasn't sure. The last glimpse he'd had of Johnson, he was headed back to the city. No one had tailed Tylo to the landing. If Johnson had even a suspicion that she might be in the area, he would not have left.

That Preacher had lost Tylo at the wharves hadn't bothered him. He had shared Croft's confidence that she would let herself be taken. But when he learned that she hadn't shown, Preacher's antennae quivered. He had scouted every vehicle that passed the picnic area, and now on the road his eyes darted into the windshields of oncoming cars.

Preacher heard the car horn first, two abrupt blasts coming from a driver who'd lost his patience. In the side mirror he saw the van with *Mott's Tours and Excursions* painted above the grille pull out, draw abreast of Croft's car, then rock slightly as it shot into the space in front.

Preacher smiled. The way the van rode indicated that the driver had no load. He was on his way back to the city to retread the hotel circuit, pick up a fresh load of sightseers.

Or maybe not.

Preacher had the van driver in his rearview mirror. He wasn't wearing a baseball cap with the company logo. He had on a sports jacket and dress shirt instead of a sweatshirt and windbreaker. Sometimes his lips moved, as if he was talking to somebody in the back but didn't want to take his eyes off the road. He wasn't a tour van driver at all.

Preacher was coming up to a turn and headed right. He crossed Maine Avenue slowly, giving himself a chance to see Croft swing toward Seventh Street, which would take him to Independence Avenue. The van stayed behind him.

Now Preacher knew that Johnson had tagged him. Which meant that he had gotten the girl. Which meant that she would have described Preacher to him. Or else Johnson had gotten his burning message from the Coach and Arms and was carrying around a composite the bartender would have provided.

Preacher made a left, heading toward the promenade where Tenth Street dead-ended.

Johnson wasn't alone. He had the driver and the girl in the van. Preacher hadn't thought he'd bring troops along.

Johnson had tagged him—it had to have been at the picnic area —and he would have shaken loose the Rapid Reaction Force. So far Preacher hadn't spotted any of their telltale step vans, the kind used by UPS and other courier companies.

And he'd have primed his own people who were out searching for Tylo. But here Johnson was at a disadvantage. He hadn't expected to snare Tylo, so he'd left the troops behind. Now he was following along, hoping Preacher would give him time to get them in place.

Not likely.

In the center of the circle was one of Washington's most famous fountains. Preacher had developed a particular fondness for it and had gone here often, early in the morning before the crowds. Now there were at least fifty cars parked around the fountain, with the usual assembly of gawkers and photo buffs lining up their sullen, runny-nosed kids for pictures. Preacher didn't want them. He wanted a . . . Yes, that nice-looking young Japanese couple in new, matching red parkas, getting out of a rented Lincoln.

Preacher pulled in beside the Lincoln, always watching. The *Mott's Tours* van was hanging well back, searching for a space. Then the traffic behind it began pulling around, creeping ahead, closing in the van.

Preacher quickly took off his jacket and put on a gray parka and knitted cap. Out of the car, he aimed a friendly smile at the couple.

"Hello. It's very cold today," he said in Japanese.

The young man looked startled. The girl began to giggle. Then they approached, surprised and pleased to hear their native language spoken perfectly by this American.

Preacher kept his peripheral vision on the van, which was mired in traffic on the other side of the circle. He chattered away in Japanese, praising the quality of the young man's camera, offering to take the couple's picture.

The Japanese man handed Preacher the camera, explaining about the buttons and knobs. The instant the couple's backs were turned, Preacher set the camera down on the hood of the car. In his hand was a slim six-inch blade tempered from the same steel used to make samurai swords.

Preacher was thinking about this irony when he came up behind the young man as if to put his arm around his shoulder.

"I can't see him! Goddammit, *I can't see him!*"

Holland had her face almost against the glass, as though that would somehow make a difference. Through the inching cars and people who strolled by the van she caught glimpses of Preacher's car. But not of him. She had her fingers around the door handle when the first scream reached her, more a plaintive cry by the time she heard it.

"Holland!"

She was out of the van and running, Johnson's shouts chasing her. Zigzagging through the crowds, shoulders low to absorb the collisions with the tourists, stiff-arming those who didn't get out of her way fast enough.

Holland saw onlookers first, standing in a semicircle, then the blood that was seeping along the asphalt. The couple lay face-down. The young man's wound was at the base of the neck, a thick slash that had cut right to the bone at the brain stem. The woman was nothing like Holland had ever seen, even on the autopsy tables during training. Her hair was fanned across the back of her head, and the jacket had ridden up just enough to expose the mass of blood at her abdomen. The fabric of her sweater had been shorn away. Swimming in the cavity were two perfectly severed kidneys.

Holland didn't realize she was on her knees, surrounded by the crowd, until someone grabbed her by the shoulders and pulled.

"We have to go," Johnson was saying urgently.

Holland tore herself away from his grip, only to collide with Bryant, who had come up behind her.

"We have to help them!"

Johnson reached out again. This time his grip was like a steel trap, pulling her through the moans and sobbing, through the red haze of blood that dripped across her vision.

Bryant, beside her, was speaking softly, urgently, to the 911 operator on his cell phone. That done, he dialed again. Holland heard enough to realize what was happening.

"You're telling the FBI to stand down? What about Preacher?"

Johnson spun her around to face him, nodded in the direction of the parked cars.

"Preacher's car is still there. The space beside it is empty."

Holland glanced over, saw the vacant slot, a shattered camera on the blacktop, bits of glass or crystal winking back at her.

"He used them as decoys, came up behind them, did his work, and took their car before anyone spotted him."

All the while he talked, Johnson kept her moving. Holland heard sirens in the distance.

"D.C. cops," Johnson said. "They'll do what they can. No one will have seen anything. No one will give any kind of description —or if they do, there'll be a dozen variations."

"But *we* know!"

"And Preacher knows that."

Johnson had her back at the van now. Bryant was climbing behind the wheel, firing up the engine.

"Preacher's gone to ground. Believe me, he's good enough to evade anyone. And we can't put his face on the wire. If we tell them about Preacher, we have to give them everything. I'm not ready to warn off Croft. Are you?"

Holland craned her head back so the tears wouldn't seep out.

"Preacher will go to Croft, tell him he's been tagged."

"No, he won't," Johnson said softly. "Because what's happened here has nothing to do with Croft. This is personal. This is something Preacher came back to do for himself. Unfinished business, Holland—Preacher's message to me in case I missed the first one."

21

THE building was on the eastern fringe of George Washington University, kitty-corner from the Lisner Auditorium. It was ancient red brick, worn down to the hue of dried blood, with tall chimneys and turrets poking into the sky.

Holland thought it looked like a secretarial academy from the turn of the century. She wasn't far off. The plaque from the Historical Society informed her that it had been a finishing college for young gentlewomen. A more recent one read: *The Stewart Center—Women's Shelter and Counseling.*

A trim, pleasant woman in her early fifties answered the door, introducing herself as Claire Cranston. She wore a floral-pattern smock over an Ann Taylor suit, and there was no jewelry on her fingers or wrists. Holland, hanging back with Bryant, was surprised to see the woman and Johnson peck each other on the cheek.

Johnson looked back at Bryant, who must have caught the message and led Holland up the stairs and into the house. Holland figured he knew the place well, as he steered her precisely through the foyer and sitting room, down a long corridor to a country kitchen, then into a birdcage elevator. The aroma of cooking food—goulash or beef stew—shot a pang of hunger through Holland.

"What is this place, really?" asked Holland over the clatter of the elevator.

Bryant stared down at her, his expression as soft as that of the man in the moon.

"You know Johnson pretty well, don't you?"

"He and my father were best friends."

She saw that Bryant was about to respond to that but changed his mind.

"Did you know Johnson had a sister?"

Holland shook her head.

"She lived in Texas. Her husband was ex-CIA and Johnson didn't find out that he beat her until it was too late. After that, he began talking to women in the service—ours, FBI, the Agency. The amount of abuse made him sick, so he helped get this place started. Claire—the woman downstairs—runs it. It's all low key, but she makes sure women in government know about it. Johnson's very good with the stock market. He borrowed on his pension, set up a fund, and now the place doesn't want for anything. In return, he shows up every once in a while with someone he doesn't want found. Claire used to be with DEA. She knows how to handle that."

They stepped out of the elevator and proceeded down a narrow corridor, in a renovated attic. Holland imagined that at one time it had been a jumble of tiny rooms for the live-in help. Bryant had to stoop to avoid bumping his head on the beams.

The room was bright and much larger than she had expected, with tasteful floral wallpaper and a four-poster of soft maple. It had the charm of a country inn, right down to the ornamental water jug and washbowl. But the air was musty, and Holland thought it had been a while since anyone had been up there.

Arliss's secret nest, where he brings sparrows with broken wings . . .

"What's your name?" Holland asked.

Bryant shifted from one foot to the other, as if she'd asked him too personal a question. When he told her, she said, "Thank you for getting me out of there."

Bryant smiled and busied himself with the coffeemaker. The

way he moved told Holland that he lived alone—a bachelor's
quick, familiar way around the sink and the minifridge.

"How are you holding up?"

Holland hadn't heard Johnson step into the room. He closed
the door behind him and looked around, pursing his lips, nodding.

"You'll be all right here. Claire will get you clothes—tell her
your size and what you want.

"The place is pretty empty now, only four women. No one
comes up here. The elevator won't work without an access code.
Claire will give you that." He gestured toward the phone. "It
has a permanent tap on it, but I don't think you'll be calling
anyone."

"Meg," Holland said.

"Right. And tell her I'm not the Evil Empire, will you?"

Holland watched him as he settled into a comfortable stuffed
chair and stretched out his legs as though he were at the beach.
She felt the weight of events upon him, past ones and those yet to
come, the burden of knowing he could neither change nor outrun
them.

"He didn't have to do them both," Holland heard herself say.
"Preacher could have killed one. He wanted a diversion, right?
Something to stop us cold, give him time to slip away." She
paused. "He didn't have to do them both."

Johnson accepted a cup of coffee from Bryant and said, "Yes,
he did. You remember the fable about the frog and the scorpion?
The frog carries the scorpion on its back across a river after the
scorpion promises not to sting it. Halfway across, the scorpion
does just that. As they're drowning, the frog asks, Why? and the
scorpion replies, It's my nature.

"It's Preacher's nature. Nothing more complicated than that.
He wasn't made into what he is. He just *is*. That's why when we
find him, he goes down hard."

"You said Preacher was sending you a message, in case you
missed the first one."

So Johnson told her about the incident at the Coach and Arms
and his history with Preacher. He abbreviated some of the details
of Preacher's predilections, things that were of no consequence

at the moment, but he omitted nothing about the man, the things
Holland needed to know if she was to recognize him again.

"He won't look the same," Johnson explained. "He'll come at
you out of nowhere. You have to spot his movement first. . . . And
he's working with Croft." The last sentence came out like a hiss.

Holland saw that Johnson was working hard to hold himself
back. Croft was the visible one, instantly available to them. They
could take him right now, and the thought was sweet, like heroin.

"We can and we can't," Holland said.

Johnson looked up at her.

"Croft, I mean. He's there for us, but we can't touch him."

Johnson was pleased but didn't show it. Holland had been set
up, betrayed, by a man who'd promised her sanctuary. Adrenaline had been replaced by revenge, but she was working hard to
keep a handle on it.

"Croft brought Preacher into this," he said. "We take that as a
given, yes?"

"Yes."

"Why?"

"I don't know. Frank didn't know. He trusted Croft, but he
didn't tell me anything about him."

Johnson saw her eyes glaze over when she spoke Suress's
name. He had to get her off that.

"I need to know what happened at your house, every detail."

"It doesn't start there. It began with Westbourne."

Holland had reached the part about Westbourne giving her the
diskette to deliver to his secretary and how it had turned out to
be the wrong one.

"You didn't mention any of this when I debriefed you," Johnson
cut in.

"Sure I did," Holland protested. "I . . ."

Did I?

She cast her mind back to that time, tried to push away the
confusion and turmoil that had erupted after Westbourne was
found. She focused on the library where she and Johnson had
faced each other, brought back his quiet, concerned voice, his
questions, and the answers he'd coaxed from her.

No, I never mentioned it.

She looked at Johnson. "I don't know what to say. Either it slipped my mind or I blocked it out. There was no reason for either to have happened. I'm sorry."

"In retrospect, what does Westbourne's having the diskette on him that night mean to us?"

"The senators who were there, with the exception of Croft and Westbourne, are on the Senate Ethics Committee. I'm thinking this is the ploy Croft used: He got the Cardinals to dig up some Ethics beef against Westbourne, real or imagined. It would have to be something good, something Westbourne would feel threatened by. So he brought out the heavy artillery. He brought the diskette with him—hell, maybe he gave them a sample—ready to use it if they pushed him too hard. Croft was counting on exactly that. He knew if Westbourne was pressed hard enough, he'd bring the diskette."

"Yeah. I think that's how it happened." Johnson paused. "So it doesn't matter, your not remembering the incident. It wouldn't have meant anything to me then. There was no context."

Holland picked up where she'd left off and brought Johnson along to the point where Preacher was inside her town house.

"He was hunting for the diskette. That's all he was interested in. Croft set Frank up by telling him he'd come with him to my place. But he had no intention of doing that and at the last minute backed out. By this time Preacher knew Frank was on his way. He intercepted Frank, shot him, and drove up in his car. I recognized it, didn't think twice about who was in it. Then he was through the door."

Holland drew in a deep breath.

"All he wanted was the diskette, and I had it out, just waiting. He should have been faster, killed me then and there, but he was so confident. He wanted a minute or two to dangle death in front of my eyes.

"But he'd made a mistake. Frank wasn't dead. He staggered in and got off one shot before Preacher took him down. He had got to me when he came through the door. I know I was out. He had time to wrap my fingers around his gun. He was planning to make it look like I'd committed suicide. The prints stayed because he was wearing gloves."

Johnson understood that he had all of it now. The sequence was complete. But he needed the why.

"Tell me about the diskette."

Holland began with Westbourne's funeral, where she'd found the diskette in her purse. She told Johnson about going to Westbourne's office in the Dirksen Building, finding it stripped and packed, with a staffer and Westbourne's personal assistant sorting through what was left. Johnson's eyes narrowed when she said she took the diskette home; they began to burn when she admitted to listening to its contents, the kind of travesty and betrayal she found there.

"Those fools!" he whispered.

"That's not all," Holland added, then told him about the reference to another diskette, the second half of the diaries.

She saw by Johnson's expression that he understood it all now, waited for him to walk her through the rest, to cement past and present.

"So Preacher, thinking he already had one diskette, tortured Westbourne for the location of the second. Westbourne held out, and then Croft, to whom Preacher had given the diskette, discovered the mistake. He pounced on the opportunity to make good when Suress mentioned you had it. But you're still alive; you've become a second party after the information. Croft drew you in, hoping to get you close. Maybe you knew the location of the second diskette, maybe not. If so, it was bonus time. If not, you had to die anyway. The field would be clear for Preacher to continue the hunt."

"He's so sly, Croft is. . . ."

"How did Croft get hold of Preacher? What's the history there?"

"We don't know." Johnson looked at Bryant. "You'll check that. Tear Croft apart—overseas phone bills, travel, bank wire transfers. Preacher was in Thailand. There has to be a trail."

Johnson didn't speak for a long time. He knew enough about Washington politics to realize their vampiric quality. You never knew what could rise from the ashes.

Johnson thought he knew what to do: go to Wyatt Smith, bring him up to speed, drop the mess on his desk. As chief of the

Inspection Division, he now had all the pieces in place. His department had a peripheral interest in the case because of Preacher. But Preacher was a killer and a fugitive. Technically, he was the property of the FBI.

Johnson could help Holland too. With everything she'd contributed, he could bring her back into the fold.

"We hand what we have to the director," he said. "This thing has mushroomed—"

"I'll get it for you."

Johnson stared at her.

"I can get the second diskette. Croft doesn't have it yet. Preacher has a split agenda, and that works in our favor. He's not ahead of us on this thing." She paused. "Let me get this for you."

"Holland, even if you knew where it was, we don't have the time to set it up."

"*No one* has the time. Preacher can't hang around Washington for long. He was supposed to be in and out and gone. If you give this to the director, he'll need time to decide which way to go on this. And we'll lose Preacher. For sure."

Holland's tone softened. "Besides, it's personal now. You and Preacher. Me and Croft. You'll never snare Croft with an official investigation. He'll come right back in your face, demanding proof we don't have. He'll set up some slick maneuver, force us to fight *his* way. . . . They'll both get away, Arliss. You know it."

"What if you beat Preacher to the diskette?"

"Then we might have the evidence to bring Croft down too. Westbourne must have had dirt on him, so we'll link him to everything that began at Oak Farms."

Johnson wasn't thinking of his career or of his loyalty to Wyatt, how both could be poisoned if he made the wrong call here. It wasn't the fear he had of Preacher. He could look at that, admit to it. There was something Holland wasn't saying, that rested on her words like a cancer.

"You're making yourself the bait. You're going out into the field and draw out Preacher. . . . You want him to come to you. . . ."

"He's going to come whether I want him to or not." Holland looked into Johnson's eyes. A calm lightness overcame her. "I'm counting on you to be there when that happens."

THREE

22

THE call came through on the private line in Croft's condo.

"Yes?"

"You broke your word, Senator."

"Holland?"

"You had Johnson out at the wharves. I saw him."

Holland had rehearsed the text. Sounding bitter and angry was no problem at all. If Croft had been in the room with her, she'd have torn his eyes out.

"You don't need to take that tone with me, Holland. If Johnson was there, I had nothing to do with it. And more to the point," Croft added, *"I* was there, looking for you."

"So you were. But I wasn't going to let myself be taken!"

"No one wants to *take* you, Holland." Croft's voice was filled with weary patience. "You're the one who contacted me, yes? Everything was arranged according to your terms. I offered you protection, you declined. I respected your wish. I kept my end of the bargain." Now a pause. "I still think you should come in."

He's so good . . .

"I'll have to think about that." She wanted to sound vague, to make him think that now that she'd vented her anger she was still afraid, out there alone. Which way would Croft play it?

"I don't know what to say, Holland. You'll recall that your fingerprints were on the gun that killed Frank. The police won't let that go. They haven't gone public with that detail, but that doesn't mean they won't. You need to come in for your own safety."

Croft paused again, and Holland waited.

Here comes the pitch.

"I'm still willing to help you, if you let me. Do it now, today, and we can begin to unravel this mess."

Holland caught a different edge to Croft's tone.

He has a schedule, and he doesn't want to waste time on me. Come on, give me something more!

"Maybe it's not safe for me to be seen right now."

"It's as safe as it will ever be."

"You make it sound like you're in a rush. Are you, Senator? Has something else happened that you should tell me about?"

Bite, dammit! Get pissed off with me. Let something slip!

"Holland, I remain deeply concerned for your welfare. The choice is yours: Accept my help or do whatever you feel you must. Just be aware of one thing—if I do not see you or hear from you by the end of the day, I am obliged to report my contacts with you to the police. After that I can be of no assistance to you."

Strike three.

"I'll get back to you, Senator."

The receiver rattled in its cradle. Holland's heart was pounding. She felt polluted, as though Croft's words had eaten their way under her skin. She waited a moment before turning to Johnson.

"I can't tell if he suspects anything, but it doesn't matter. We've lost him."

"The bitch is lying."

Preacher said this without rancor, merely as a statement of fact.

He was standing by the floor-to-ceiling windows in Croft's den, paneled with dark walnut, then tacked up with mementos, most of them framed photos of himself and political pooh-bahs. Preacher thought it a telling indicator of the man's insecurity.

Croft remained at his desk, staring at the phone, chewing on his fleshy pink lips.

Preacher had said nothing about Johnson's spotting him or about the subsequent chase. He didn't think Croft would connect him to the random killing of the Japanese tourists. But it wouldn't matter. Preacher planned to be finished and out of the country within forty-eight hours.

"I think you're right," Croft said at last. "Somehow Johnson tracked her down and got to her. But why would she hide that?"

The question was an easy underhand lob, and Preacher hit it out of the park. He didn't want Croft worrying Johnson the way he would pick at a scab.

"Johnson has a lot of things to piece together. He has the girl; that's his starting point. He has to ferret out how much she knows, how her prints got on the gun, and who she's talked to or met with since the shooting. I wouldn't be surprised if she gave out your name right off and Johnson ate it up. A fugitive cozying up to a U.S. senator? Inquiring minds want to know."

Preacher was rolling right along now.

"Johnson had Tylo call and feed you the lines. You came back with the truth—exactly what you'd offer her, what's still on the table, what'll happen if she doesn't come in with you. Johnson was listening to everything—taping too. Since there's no way you and Tylo could be working this together, he knows that she's telling the truth, at least where you're concerned. This gives her credibility, leads Johnson to believe anything else she gives him."

"But why wouldn't Johnson have contacted me directly?" Croft asked. "Why use her like that?"

"Because he's a crafty bastard. He had to know—without *your* knowing—how deep you were in this. And you came out smelling like roses. If you hear from Johnson again, it'll be a summons to a hearing where they make Tylo walk the plank."

"She decided to put her faith in Johnson, leave me twisting?"

"I wouldn't take it personally," Preacher said. "Johnson got the drop on her, put her between a rock and a hard place. Believe me, she'd give up her firstborn to get out from under there."

Croft fiddled with a sterling-silver letter opener.

"I did want her, though. She could have given us something to work with. She'll tell Johnson about the diskette!"

"Which still won't make any difference," Preacher said. "She has no proof that it even existed."

"What if she has a hunch where to find the second one? If she persuades Johnson to follow up?"

Preacher thought he'd like that very much. "Then she—or Johnson—will come my way, which will prove extremely inconvenient for either or both."

CHAPTER

23

AFTER Johnson and Bryant had left, Holland tried to sleep. Fatigue had seeped right through to her marrow. A hot bath had dissolved the cold but failed to uncoil the tension in her muscles. And nothing worked on the thoughts that continued to spin and explode in her mind, like a fireworks display at a county fair.

Her eyes were open when Claire Cranston came in, so softly that Holland caught her perfume before she heard a footfall.

"Would you like something to help you relax?"

Holland sat up, stretching her arms to reach her bare toes. "No, thanks. It's getting on."

She noticed that Claire's iron-gray hair, trimmed in a simple, elegant wedge, was damp.

"Is it raining?"

Claire set two shopping bags beside the bed. "Just a light drizzle. The coat I got for you has a big collar. It'll help some."

Holland began going through the purchases—underwear, sweaters, jeans, and thin-wale cords. The trench coat Claire had bought was almost professional-quality camouflage, brown-gray, and down-filled.

Holland wondered why Claire hadn't included an umbrella, then she remembered that the woman had been with the DEA. Field agents always have to keep both hands free.

"There's no reason you'd know this, but I met your father several times," Claire said quietly. "Twice in Colombia, when I was in the field office down there. He was on a fact-finding mission for the Senate."

Holland was very still, looking at her.

"I wanted you to know that he made a tremendous impression on me—on all of us. He was one of the best people this country ever produced. I still think about his death—it's something I'll never understand."

Holland nodded. She didn't intend to speak, knew that Claire wasn't expecting a response, but the words crowded her mouth. They came up, with bile, every time someone mentioned Robert Beaumont, and Holland, like the good soldier, had always swallowed them back.

"I think about it too. And for the same reason. Because the triggerman was never caught. Because no one knows who hired him or why. Because the investigation committee was a joke. We think about it because of restless ghosts."

Holland felt Claire's touch on her shoulder.

"The truth is still with us. It's a curious human trait, to want to record and catalog actions, the heinous ones. Evil is opaque, and it fascinates us. If you believe that, then you must believe that the truth within the evil will also be found."

The phone on the nightstand chirped, startling Holland. It was Johnson, at the office and talking fast.

"The name Brad Norman at FBI ring a bell?"

Holland thought hard for a few seconds, then stepped back from Johnson and his abrupt tone. A face floated up, the boyish grin punctuated by an overbite, a bashful, collegiate air, a need to be helpful.

"He was at Westbourne's funeral, photographing it for the faces. It was a make-work detail."

"Yeah. Then, maybe. Not now. He sent a package to Suress."

"I asked him for a copy of his tapes. I didn't have a desk by then, so I gave him Frank's name."

"Okay. Here's what we have. Most of the video is standard stuff —the widow, the family. But then he zooms in on the guy in the background. First I thought I was seeing things, but the lab blew up the frames."

She heard Johnson draw a deep breath.

"Preacher was at the funeral, standing next to the family, ten paces from Cynthia Palmer."

Holland put her palm against the mouthpiece so that Johnson wouldn't catch her gasp.

"He was on your case that far back. In a couple of frames he's looking right at you and this Norman."

Holland stepped hard on Johnson's conclusion. She didn't want to accept it because it meant that Preacher was some kind of vampire, looming in her shadow. She couldn't let herself see him that way, omnipotent, unstoppable, having her at his whim.

"I need to see the video," Holland said in a low voice. "And the enhancements." She checked her watch. "Now."

"Where are you going with this?"

"Maybe it's nothing. I won't be sure until I see the material. Please, Arliss."

"Thirty minutes," Johnson said.

"One more thing. How long would it take to tool up an ID?"

"Price in Documents could have it in two hours."

"Then do it. Please."

Holland hung up the phone and stared at the new clothes. Their fresh-from-the-store odor bothered her.

"I'll need a few other things," she told Claire. "Special pieces."

The older woman looked at her with sad understanding. "Yes. I can see that."

Johnson had not wanted to go to his office. Chances were good he would run into Wyatt Smith. Smith would ask him about the search for Tylo, and Johnson would have to lie. Lies tended to metastasize.

Johnson knew that he shouldn't care about this. Years ago, when Johnson's fitness report had helped get Smith removed from field duty, the director had closed off his soul, sealed it with the putty of unerring courtesy and professionalism, leaving Johnson no chance to break through.

Smith wasn't in. His secretary, flying by Johnson in the hall, breathlessly informed him the director had been called to the Oval Office. It was no secret that Smith and the current President were very close. Razorback liked to have Smith brief him on security procedures over clam chowder, and Johnson knew the Chief Executive would be doing a swing through the West Coast next week.

But there was a message on Johnson's E-mail. Smith wanted an update on the Tylo matter and would be back late in the afternoon; he wanted to hear from Johnson.

Johnson sifted through a few notes and memos, fobbed them off on his secretary with one-word replies, then headed down two floors to Documents Section.

The prime directive of the Secret Service is to protect the integrity of U.S. banknotes, so it employs the world's leading experts in the fields of engraving, paper, and document manufacture— and forgery thereof. Eugenia Price, third runner-up for Miss America twenty years before, took the snapshot Johnson gave her and held it by the edges, between thumb and forefinger.

"We seem to be missing a few things, Arliss."

Eugenia's soft drawl was Deep South. Her caramel eyes, set against flawless mocha skin, searched shamelessly among the wilds of Johnson's intentions.

"There's no paperwork on this."

It was carved in stone that a request for a new ID was accompanied by a half-dozen forms. In Johnson's case the forms could be reduced to two, one signed by him, the other by the director. Eugenia had heard that years back, when the Iraqis had been tooling up for a shot on President Bush, Johnson had actually gotten an ID on his own authority. But that had been a flash situation, and Eugenia hadn't been chief of Documents then.

"It's a temporary ID," Johnson said, looking her in the eye. "You can set it up so that it turns to mush in forty-eight hours."

Certain precautions had been developed for temporary identification. The photo was chemically treated so that after a specified time the paper and the image would dissolve. This had become policy when people began to "forget" to turn in their ID's, squirreled them away as souvenirs.

Eugenia was studying the photo. "I know this girl. Haven't seen her face-to-face, but I know her."

Eugenia had a memory like a bear trap. It had been less than a year since Holland had been issued her official ID. If she needed to, Eugenia could always match the photo against the one in the master file.

"I'll sign off on it if you like," Johnson said. "Or else you have my word I'll bring it back to you personally as soon as we're done."

Eugenia considered. She'd be on the receiving end of an official reprimand if anyone found out she'd cut a document without the paperwork. But the only way anyone could know was if there *was* any paperwork.

She had the name now: Holland Tylo. Eight, nine months back, the young woman had come through, eager to take on the world. Eugenia had also heard the scuttlebutt on Tylo, which was pretty graphic—downright sexist when it came from some of the men. But here was Johnson risking his pension for the girl.

Eugenia would go with Johnson's call every time.

"What's the name you want on this thing?"

"Beaumont—her father's name. She uses Tylo for personal reasons."

Eugenia's eyes widened as she made the connections.

"Okay. Same first name?"

"Yeah."

"What about rank?"

"Make it Investigator."

Eugenia smiled wanly. "Investigator" could mean anything. Which meant that the little girl could be headed for a world of hurt.

Johnson returned to the Stewart Center at four o'clock. When he entered Holland's room he saw that a small television and VCR had been set up on the shellacked pine coffee table.

"Where's Claire?"

"She went out to get some things. Do you have the tape?"

Johnson handed her the package. He understood the symptoms. Holland had withdrawn, living in that space inside herself where hunters dwell when they think they've caught a whiff. Johnson had been to such places inside himself, so he knew better than to disturb her or confuse her with questions.

Holland slipped the tape into the VCR, then sat cross-legged on the hooked rug. The camera jiggled as it panned the funeral party. First were the close-ups of the family: the brothers and sisters, the widow, Cynthia Palmer, looking quite regal in black and pearls, the wind trying to get at her French braid.

And there was Preacher, a little pudgy in the cheeks from what Holland guessed were theatrical latex inserts, a neatly trimmed beard to disguise the jawline. Too bad about the sunglasses. Holland thought she would have learned something had she been able to see Preacher's eyes.

Holland watched the tape three times. Preacher was on it for six minutes—less than she'd expected.

Then she rewound and watched the part where Preacher stood behind Cynthia Palmer. After a half-dozen times she cut it down to sixteen seconds of tape. A few minutes went by before she reached for the blowups of the stills. She shuffled through them slowly, letting them fall to her right. Only one made it to the opposite side.

Holland stared at the still as she rewound the tape. She hit the slo-mo button and watched the images crawl by. The definition was hazy but good enough for her purposes.

Her eyes flickered from the still to the tape. She was sure it was there. The still couldn't stand alone. It was part of a sequence.

And there it was. Holland jammed her thumb on the freeze-frame button.

"Preacher wasn't interested in me back then," she told Johnson, her eyes still on the screen. "He may have seen me, been curious about me or Norman. Maybe he even made Norman as surveillance and got a laugh out of that. But his attention was here."

Holland tapped her fingernail on the television screen, drawing Johnson's attention. There was Cynthia Palmer, half turned to the left, her fine long legs perfectly exposed, the black skirt riding higher than it should have done. The very ends of her lips were curled in a coyly veiled smile of lust.

To the left, in an over-the-shoulder shot, stood Preacher, staring at her brazenly, coaxing her desire with a smile of his own.

"It's April fourth," Holland said. "Tonight's the annual Red Cross Ball. Westbourne was a regular. It's in his file. Never missed one. I don't think his widow is so broken up that she won't attend. It's at the Omni Shoreham Hotel."

Johnson was punching in the numbers when Claire came in. Draped over one arm was a stunning black evening dress; in her hands were the matching shoes and purse.

The head of security at the Omni, Barclay Halliday, told Johnson that, yes, the fund-raiser was on for tonight. He balked when Johnson asked about the guest list. Halliday wasn't about to give that information to a stranger over the telephone.

Johnson finessed the man to stay on hold while he called the commander of the precinct in the Omni's district. Having worked with Johnson before, the commander agreed to a conference call with Halliday.

Five minutes later, Claire returned with a fax of the guest list. Johnson, still on the line thanking Halliday, handed it to Holland.

"Palmer's name is on it," Holland said, motioning to Johnson. "Ask him if he knows anything about individual security arrangements."

Halliday did. The A-list people, which of course included Cynthia Palmer, had their own retinue. Her driver for the evening worked for Boulder Security Services.

Johnson knew them. The group was headed by a former FBI deputy chief. His strength ran to industrial espionage and surveillance, but he had a small roster of former law enforcement officers who handled personal protection. Boulder advertised exclusively by word of mouth. It didn't do rock stars, entertainment people, or foreign politicos on the lam.

Johnson assured Halliday that the Service had no reason to think there was any threat to anyone attending the benefit; he was calling only because the Service had an arm's-length interest in Cynthia Palmer, given that her husband's killer had not yet been apprehended. Johnson gave all this in a weary tone that Halliday would recognize: a man being pushed by his boss to do some baby-sitting.

Johnson quickly finished up by saying that he'd be sending over an agent, just for the sake of appearance. Her name was Beaumont. She would introduce herself to Halliday when she arrived. After that Halliday needn't give her a second thought.

"You think he bought that?" Holland asked when Johnson was off the phone.

He shrugged. "I boosted his ego. We'll get a little bonus in that he'll be more alert now, put some starch into his own people."

"But you don't think Preacher will show up?"

Johnson shook his head. "*If* you're right—if Preacher is interested in Palmer—it's because of what she might know. Or what he thinks she might know. She's no good to him dead."

He looked at her keenly. "Do you think she'll open up?"

"I've heard she's an ice queen. But I'll get further than a man."

"We'll be outside in the van."

"It might not end at the hotel. I may have to go home with her. It'll be her play."

Johnson shook his head. "Up to a point. The van will be there, and you go in miked. If I find it slipping away from us, I bring *both* of you in."

Johnson glanced at the dress, a simple little thing that probably cost a thousand dollars, accessories not included.

"Let's see how it fits."

24

CHESTER Rawlins had served twenty-one years with the Chicago police, ten of those on SWAT, his final two on the mayor's body-guard force. That last posting had gotten him easily into Boulder Security.

Rawlins had a custom-made wardrobe. He projected a cheerful, confident air that was reassuring to his clients. He could do this because of his imposing size. After years of being the first one through killers' doors, Rawlins thought that his usual assignments these days—watching over little brown men in fluttering robes—were easy duty. Then there were peachy assignments like this, from Boulder's roster of old-time clients.

Rawlins wheeled the limo into the motor court and braked fifteen feet in front of the car up ahead, which was off-loading. Rawlins never allowed himself to get boxed in. He had trained for three weeks at the race track the FBI leased from the Bondurant car racing people in Arizona. He could maneuver the two-and-a-half-ton Lincoln like a sports coupe.

After checking both side mirrors, his eyes settled on the rear-view. Having never squired Cynthia Palmer before, he pitied the poor bastards who drew her on a regular basis. She was a bitch on wheels.

Palmer had been late coming down from her penthouse condo.

He hadn't thought much of it until she'd brushed by him into the car and snapped, "Get your ass in gear!" Rawlins, a good Lutheran, had blinked.

On the way to the Omni, she carped nonstop. Rawlins was driving too slowly; he'd chosen the wrong route and now they were sitting in traffic; the heater wasn't working properly—it was like a sauna in the back.

Rawlins tried to tune her out, but the woman was relentless. Finally she got on the phone and started jabbering to someone named Betsy. Rawlins was delighted at the opportunity to raise the privacy divider.

No one had warned him about Palmer's brittle personality. The assignments director had said only that she was a long-standing client, and underlined that Westbourne's killing changed Palmer's status. The Secret Service and the FBI were both on record as saying that the hit had not been political. Personal payback had also been ruled out. But what *wasn't* said—was barely whispered, even—was that the murders could have been the work of a serial killer. The director had gotten secondhand accounts of the condition in which the corpses had been found.

"Whoever did Westbourne and his fluff favors the knife," he'd told Rawlins. "If it is a wacko, then it's highly unlikely he'll be coming back for her. Thrill killers don't stalk families; they do 'em in one shot.

"The feds don't think Palmer's in any danger. I have them cold on that. Nor did Palmer request Secret Service cover, as she could have. Guess you can't blame her.

"What I'm saying is, stay sharp and don't let anyone get too close unless you're sure she recognizes them. Hotel security's been beefed up, and D.C. police will be there, so once she's inside she'll be fine. In fact, she doesn't *want* cover inside."

That last comment hadn't sat well with Rawlins. Now he was glad to be off the hook. If he'd had to go in with Palmer, she would have made him fetch.

Rawlins tapped on the gas, and the limo rolled up to the Omni main entrance. He was out fast, watching as the doorman, dressed in a ridiculous Beefeater uniform, reached to open the back door. Cynthia Palmer swung her legs out—her best asset, Rawlins thought—gave everyone a two-second look, and stepped out.

"I'll be back here in two and one-half hours. And I'm *punctual.*" Her words were like a glancing blow.

Rawlins's reply was indecipherable. He got back into the Lincoln and eased into the VIP area, which was crowded with limos, the drivers in topcoats banding together for a smoke.

Rawlins was very fit for his age. He was proud that he could bench-press the same amount as he had in college. He did not enjoy sitting on his duff. Normally he would have taken a walk to burn time and calories. But not on this watch, when Palmer could change her mind and want to leave early.

Rawlins decided to check out the other drivers. They had begun introducing themselves, when, out of the corner of his eye, Rawlins spotted a man standing at the edge of the steps to the hotel lobby. He wore a navy-blue topcoat and a cap with a shiny visor. His hands were clasped in front of him as he stared off into space. Rawlins had seen that look many times at the Vietnam Memorial.

Although Preacher gave no sign, he knew Palmer's driver had made a connection, recognized him as a breed apart. Rawlins—Preacher knew his name—would make small talk with the other drivers first. When he tired of that, he would come Preacher's way, ask him what security outfit he was with, whom he was driving.

Preacher had a story ready for him. He was sure that Rawlins would enjoy it for as long as he was alive.

Holland entered the hotel through the underground entrance, Johnson's surveillance van with its smoked windows rolling down the incline, Bryant at the wheel, tires squealing on the polished concrete floor.

Johnson admired her dress, but it had its drawbacks. The microphone hadn't been the problem; it went underneath the bow on the right shoulder strap. But the dress was too skimpy to hide even the small, flat Beretta he'd had Holland try on. Johnson bridled at sending her in unarmed.

"Preacher's not going to be there," Holland reminded him now.

"This is an insiders' party. Invitations went out weeks ago. Besides, there's a receiving line. Marjorie Woolworth is handling it personally. These are three hundred of her closest friends."

She paused. "The staff areas and kitchens are covered, right?"

Johnson nodded. "Halliday laid on extra bodies to walk the service quarters."

"Then we're okay."

Holland thought her words sounded confident enough. She didn't want Johnson to glimpse behind them, where clusters of fear huddled, whispering to her.

Bryant had the door open, his hand out to help her. Holland was moved by the courtly gesture. Ahead of her was a steel-sheathed fire door with *Kitchens* stenciled in yellow. Her heels smacked off the concrete like rifle shots.

"You see anything that looks like him—even a hint—you call."

The concern in Bryant's eyes shot through her. She would have reached out and touched him had they been alone.

"I will."

He opened the steel door, and Holland stepped by him, into a short corridor.

"Don't worry about introducing yourself to Halliday," he said. "Johnson's handling him right now. He doesn't want Halliday crowding you."

Bryant went through the swinging kitchen doors fast, leading with his shoulders. At the same time, he scooped Holland around so that she was on his flank, protected by his body.

The kitchen staff had seen this kind of thing before. The babble disappeared, leaving only the sounds of cooking. Chefs and helpers backed up against fridges and hot tables, eyes following the woman in black, making sure they were nowhere near the big man who flew by them, one hand riding lightly on his holstered weapon.

They knew the Service hated kitchens. Too many sharp knives and cleavers, narrow confines that restricted movement, cubbyholes that could be used as ambush sites.

When Holland and Bryant reached the doors that opened onto the ballroom, she felt the eyes of the waiters on the back of her neck.

"You're up," Bryant said softly. "Okay?"
She nodded slightly. "Let's get this done."

Holland was alone on the floor, except for the waiters fussing with finishing touches on the sixty round supper tables. The action now was on the mezzanine level, where the strains of a jazz quintet drifted over small talk. A handsome banner, anchored by two trellises of red and white roses, proclaimed the Red Cross charity. As Holland moved up the carpeted staircase, she saw the banner billow lightly in drafts of warm air.

Holland had scanned the guest list in the van. Although Cynthia Palmer's name appeared by itself, she had expected the widow to be escorted, probably by an old family friend. Instead, she had arrived alone.

A signal that she was mourning and needed her privacy? Holland didn't think so.

She wished she had a better handle on Palmer. The background sheet Johnson had given her was stuff from the society and financial columns—polo ponies, and how well Chocolate Tarts, Grandfather Palmer's famous candy, was doing now that the Eastern European market was adding to the hundreds of millions already in the family coffers.

All Holland really knew about Palmer was what she'd gleaned from those few seconds of video: the woman's sly smile at Preacher, knowing what he was looking at and giving him a better view of it. Not a flattering portrayal of the grieving widow. Holland had heard news commentators describe Cynthia Palmer's "grace in the face of tragedy," elaborating on how she had "fought her grief with love she still carried, like a torch, for her husband."

But was love there? Had her love—if there was any left—forgiven him his infidelity? Could she forgive her husband for dying next to his mistress and so humiliating her?

Holland thought if she had just a few kernels of truth, she would know how to approach Cynthia Palmer. She would not get more than this one chance.

The mix was moneyed, older, those from the West Coast fashionably tanned, the Easterners pale. Holland coaxed up the right smile as she wended her way through black-tie and designer pandemonium. She found Palmer standing next to the railing, swathed in a Galanos original, studded with diamonds and emeralds, surrounded by courtiers and ladies-in-waiting—Marjorie Woolworth herself among them—tilting her head this way and that to catch what they said, then offering them her long, lovely throat as she laughed. No, there was no grief in those eyes that flitted from face to face like butterflies picking at pollen, no remorse or loss in the tiny intimate gestures that encouraged and applauded.

But there was trouble, in the form of Lawrence Ross, who was walking up to Palmer, the retinue parting obediently. The way Palmer was gazing at him, he was obviously the consort of the evening, whispering something in her ear that made her clap delightedly, then turning back to the other guests, making sure no one had missed the intimacy.

Holland knew Lawrence Ross by reputation. He came from old money and possessed one of the the keenest legal minds in the country. When Presidents—past or present—had conflict-of-interest matters or skeletons suddenly rattling in the closet, Ross was the man they called.

But it wasn't Ross's legal prowess that bothered Holland—it was his infuriating possessiveness. There was no way she would be able to get to Palmer, with the lawyer draped all over her.

Holland pictured Johnson and Bryant in the back of the van, the big reel-to-reel tape recorder on superslow. They were hearing everything she heard. She could find some privacy, talk to Johnson. Maybe he had a way to pry Palmer loose.

No, not Palmer. But he can do something else.

Holland stepped back and turned to face a marble column that soared from the ground floor to the gallery above her.

"Mike-mike."

The plastic receiver in her ear vibrated, indicating that transmission was good.

"Mike-mike," Johnson acknowledged.

"Lawrence Ross is her escort. I need you to get him away from her."

"Done. Mike-mike."

Johnson was quick. Holland had barely gotten herself back into the mix, when a hotel employee—one of the managers, judging by his suit—came up to Ross. Holland couldn't pick up what was being said. Ross was at first annoyed, then resigned. He whispered to Palmer, who patted him on the arm. Then he followed the manager down the stairs.

Okay, Margie. Do your thing.

Marjorie Woolworth, the hostess, now had Palmer all to herself, which Palmer clearly was not thrilled about. The matron steered her to one of the small salons that lined the mezzanine. This one had been hastily done up in Red Cross colors and had a beautiful Louis XIV writing desk as its centerpiece. Two women were working at an adjacent desk, opening envelopes from contributors. Holland thought the charity would do very well tonight.

Woolworth shooed the two other women out and closed the doors, giving Holland a pointed look. Holland thought Woolworth's maneuver was slick: Get the widow alone, give her a gander at the checks her friends had ponied up, and let conscience do the rest.

Holland was wondering how long it would be before Woolworth began the nudging, when the salon door flew open. Woolworth emerged, smiling like a sleepy alligator; when she saw Holland again, she quickly closed the door behind her and began stalking.

"Can I help you, please?"

Her tone indicated that she had no idea who Holland was but very much wanted to know. The mixture of Grès perfume and champagne breath was distinctly uncomplementary.

From an invisible slit in the side of her dress, Holland palmed the new ID Johnson had tooled up.

"United States Secret Service, Mrs. Woolworth. Can I see you over here for a moment? Thank you."

Holland mixed courtesy with firmness and kept one eye on the salon door.

Take your time, Cynthia, she prayed.

Holland was aware that people like Marjorie Woolworth, the old D.C. crowd, were not impressed by federal credentials. The circles in which they moved always had security on the periphery. Holland went with the soft pitch.

"There's nothing to be alarmed about, Mrs. Woolworth. I think you can appreciate that Mrs. Westbourne is receiving extra attention—"

"Of course I can. And if you people had done your jobs, maybe that wouldn't be necessary!"

Holland took the slight, tried to ignore its sting. "Mrs. Westbourne indicated to us that she had a second destination tonight. There's been a complication, and I need to talk with her. I would be very grateful if you could arrange for us to have a few minutes undisturbed. Mrs. Westbourne will probably want to use the phone."

Holland saw the older woman's hesitation. She had a plum contributor in there, but the business of the check was probably concluded. With Palmer otherwise engaged, Woolworth wouldn't have to waste time stroking her. She could be out scouting fresh quarry.

"I *suppose* that would be all right," Woolworth said. "You do understand I need that room . . ."

"As I'm sure Mrs. Westbourne does. And, Mrs. Woolworth? If you could refrain from mentioning this—"

"Oh, please! You people think we're all morons. I expect ten minutes will suffice."

With that, the formidable Marjorie Woolworth set sail for new plunder.

Holland moved fast to the door. She was inside, fingertips working the lock, as Cynthia Palmer looked up from lighting a cigarette.

"Hello. Margie send you?"

Her tone was bored, her attitude indifferent. In her hand she waved a blue check.

"All done."

Holland held out her identification, caught the slight wrinkle in Cynthia Palmer's brow.

"I know you, don't I?" Palmer said slowly, letting the check flutter to the carpet.

Holland did not drop her gaze. "I was the agent assigned to your husband the night he was murdered."

Sparks of recognition crackled in Palmer's eyes. For an instant Holland thought the woman would actually strike her. Instead, Palmer's fury turned to ash.

"Yes . . . I saw your picture on the television." Palmer studied her, a matron's critique of a runway model. "You've lost some weight."

"I suppose," Holland said carefully.

"What are you doing here? How did you get in?"

Holland took advantage of the opening. "Mrs. Woolworth told me where to find you. She was kind enough to give us some privacy."

"I'll bet that was because you didn't tell *her* who you were." Palmer stabbed out her cigarette, lit a second one. "So now you can tell me just what the hell is going on."

Holland had nothing but a watered-down version of the truth to go with, and she had to use it all in one shot. She hoped it would be enough.

"Our investigation shows that during his time in public office, your husband compiled detailed records—a political diary, you might call it. There were two parts to it. We have one. We need to find the second part."

Cynthia Palmer's cold expression held for an instant, then splintered, letting Holland see the anger and pain and surprise.

"A political diary? What the hell are you *really* talking about?"

Holland went in swinging.

"The entries in the first part of the diary are sensitive. We've determined that some of those mentioned might have used extreme measures to get that information away from your husband."

Palmer drew deeply on her cigarette, then threw her head back. A low sound, a moan or dry chuckle, rode up her throat with the smoke.

"Yes, the diaries . . . Say it like that, and they sound so—so innocent. I told the son of a bitch they were poison. I told him that!"

Okay. Be really careful here.

"We have names, Mrs. Westbourne. Lots of them. But there are references that carry onto the second diary, another diskette. Do you—"

"I *told* him that!" Palmer muttered, repeating herself. She seemed not to have heard anything Holland had said. "I told him that sooner or later he'd come up against someone who wouldn't put up with that shit, who'd knock his ass up between his shoulders. But Charlie always knew better."

Holland shifted gears on the fly.

"Your husband was a powerful man, Mrs. Westbourne. He didn't need this kind of information—"

"Dirt, you mean."

"He had his career," Holland continued, working like a blind person, fingertips tapping across Cynthia Palmer's raw psyche.

Palmer shook her head.

"You have his stuff and you still don't get it? Christ, it's right there in front of you!"

"Your husband had . . . higher political ambitions?"

"Very good, Ms. Beaumont. And those ambitions have very special, very *expensive* needs."

"Money?"

"Hard to believe, hmm?" Palmer jabbed her cigarette in the glass ashtray, sparks flying on veneer three centuries old. "You think, Here's this brutally handsome, pedigreed fucker who not only has his own money but a rich wife. A *very* rich wife. One who can help him outspend any opponent who comes down the pike.

"But Charlie didn't have nearly enough to buy into the White House. He *needed* my share. And he knew he'd never get it!"

Holland worked with Palmer's rage, kept stoking it.

"The diaries were to make up for what you wouldn't give him," she said quickly. "He was using blackmail instead of money."

"He loved the Oval Office more than anything. Sometimes I would look at him and he'd have that faraway expression and I could tell he was already there, behind that desk, giving commands on how to run the planet."

Sweet Jesus!

A thought seared through Holland's mind:

She hated him. She knew he'd been stepping out on her. She knew the girl would be there in the guesthouse and that he would go to her, would make sure they were alone. . . .

But she was terrified too. . . .

Holland stared into Cynthia Palmer's face, saw something there that she thought she recognized. Something that had meant so much to her and all the other women who'd attended that particular Service training session.

"You were frightened of him, weren't you?" Holland said softly. "He was a ladies' man, and you knew that. So you told him he wasn't going to get any of your money. That's how you were punishing him. . . ."

Holland paused. "And he didn't take kindly to that. The other women, the humiliation he forced on you, that wasn't the end of it. There was more. . . ."

Two fat tears rolled down Cynthia Palmer's sculpted cheeks as she turned around and opened the shoulder clasp of her evening gown, letting the right side fall away almost to the small of her back.

Three of the bruises were old. The fresh one, greenish yellow, was the size of an oyster. Two bones of the rib cage had telltale bumps. They had knitted as well as could be expected.

"Why?" Holland whispered.

Palmer shrugged her dress back on. "I knew he was a beater and a cheat when I married him," she said matter-of-factly. A rictus of a smile appeared on her lips. "So what does that say about me, hmm?"

Palmer hesitated.

"I also knew what he was doing to people. He'd gloated about it. Sat there in front of the fireplace swigging cognac, laughing about how he'd crucify old Bob or Harry if they didn't come across. He loved to say how for the first time in history the presidency wouldn't be bought. Not even contested. They'd *give* him the office, on a platter, and ask if there was anything more they could do. . . ."

Holland watched Palmer run her fingertips over her ribs.

"In the end, I let him infect me too. Because I saw that no one could stop him. Hell, I don't think anyone wanted to anymore. They'd lived with his threats for so long, they thought that with him finally in office the pressure would come off a bit, they could get their piece of the action."

"Why?" Holland asked again.

"Because I wanted it *too*," she whispered. "After everything he did, I still wanted to be Mrs. President. The First Lady . . . the First Victim. He made it so I *couldn't* give it up, not after every-thing—I fucking well *earned* that!"

Holland wanted to reach out to her, embrace her, let her cry out the poison. But she couldn't do that.

"Do you know where the second diskette is, Mrs. Westbourne? Is it in your home?"

And Cynthia Parker would have told her. Holland could see the words forming on the trembling lips, the need for the truth to be said at last, shining through the veil of a grief no one recognized. She would have had it all, but the doorknob was rattling, being worked by a heavy, angry hand. Knuckles rapped on the wood, then a profundo bass voice, more indignant than concerned:

"Cynthia, are you all right? It's Lawrence. Cynthia . . ."

"Mrs. Westbourne—"

Palmer's eyes snapped open so wide that Holland saw their whites. The bond that had been created between them cracked apart like an ice floe splitting in two.

"Get the hell out of here!"

Holland flipped the lock on the door, but her eyes never left Palmer.

"It's not over yet, Mrs. Westbourne."

"Don't call me that! Don't call me by his name!"

Her shrieking brought Lawrence Ross crashing into the room. He looked wildly from side to side, focused on Palmer leaning on the desk with one arm, half turned away. Holland caught all of his fury.

"Who the hell are you?"

"Secret Service." Ross snatched Holland's credentials from her fingers. "We need a few more minutes—"

"The hell you do! Have you been *interrogating* her?"

"Mike-mike! Get out of there, Holland. Now! Don't butt heads with him."

Holland pressed her finger to the earpiece. Ross kept his arm around Palmer's shoulders as he glowered at Holland. At the door stood Marjorie Woolworth, her mouth a perfectly round O. Holland heard concerned voices behind Woolworth.

"Get out, Holland!"

She ignored Johnson's voice. She didn't want him to fight her. He couldn't understand what he was asking of her.

But Ross is in the way, and now I've lost her. He'll gut me if I give him the chance.

Holland stepped up to Ross and yanked her ID from his fingers.

"I'm not through with you yet!" he roared, cheeks mottled with rage.

"You interfered with the duties of a federal officer, sir. I'll take up this issue with my supervisor."

That stopped Ross in his tracks, not because of the threat but because he was incredulous that anyone would speak to him like that.

Holland cast one last look back at Palmer.

"It's not over yet, ma'am. I'm very sorry."

Marjorie Woolworth stumbled out of the way as Holland exited the room. The crowd at the door, trying to get a better view, stepped on one another's toes.

Holland walked the gauntlet swiftly, her head bowed. She felt the lust of their curiosity, the stuff of scandal they feasted on, like a brand on the back of her neck.

25

''SHE was with me. Very close . . . Everything would have been all right if Ross hadn't barged in.''

Holland was seated on one of the swivel captain's chairs, in front of the motionless reel-to-reel tape recorder.

Johnson watched her carefully, wondering if she realized how she looked. Her right arm rested on her knee, her palm cupped, as if she were holding something in it. Maybe it was Cynthia Palmer.

Johnson had had time to replay the last few minutes of tape before Holland reached the van, breathless, eyes flashing. Her anger had a special quality to it. Johnson felt it shimmer off her, knew he had nothing to say that would help. Her anger swelled not only because she'd come so close to coaxing out Cynthia Palmer's secret but because of the dark truths she had discovered about Palmer. And Westbourne. More so about Westbourne, Johnson reckoned. Holland had given her loyalty to a man who had turned out to be a blackmailer and an abuser, tainted and unworthy. He thought Holland's mourning and guilt had been cauterized, like a white-hot iron pressed against an open vein, leaving her swollen with contempt.

"I can get her back," Holland said.

"Ross won't leave her now. I don't know what he has in mind, but he'll play the gallant, shield the overwrought widow."

"She came here alone, she'll go home alone," Holland said stonily.

"So?"

"I want to go to her, after we're certain she's home for the night."

Johnson shifted in his chair. The air in the van, even though it was double filtered, was shot through with the fumes of the hotel's underground garage. He tapped Bryant on the shoulder.

"Get us outside, where we can see the motor court."

Johnson wasn't giving any odds on Cynthia Palmer's being alone tonight. By moving the van, he was giving Holland a chance to see that for herself.

Johnson had what he thought was a bigger problem. Ross wouldn't let slide what had happened. If the confrontation had been private, maybe. But not when it had occurred in front of Marjorie Woolworth and her crowd, watching as a wisp of a girl cut him off at the knees.

Johnson would have to do some damage control. Ross was powerful enough to get Wyatt Smith on the phone without calling in a favor. He'd tell Smith about a young agent called Beaumont, and Smith would link the name to Holland. The director would immediately start scouring the field for Johnson.

Take care of it now. Go in somber and properly regretful. Take him aside and give him some song and dance about an overzealous recruit. Chirp apologies, ask for his confidence and cooperation. He can't resist a marker, and he'll snap at this one if you package it like it came out of Tiffany's.

Johnson made that decision as Bryant pulled the van into the far end of the motor court and slipped out from behind the wheel to deal with a car jockey who was strolling up, ready to evict them.

Is Holland right? Does Palmer know where the diskette is?

Johnson couldn't be sure. Palmer knew about the diaries. But she hadn't reacted positively to Holland's mention of a second diskette. The way Johnson interpreted her words, Palmer knew that the blackmail *existed,* but not necessarily in what form or quantity.

I have to send Holland back to her.

He shifted in his seat.

"I have to go inside and make things nice with Ross," he said. "If I don't, he'll be headhunting when he gets out of bed tomorrow. Maybe sooner."

"There was nothing I could do—" Holland said.

"I know. But there's something you *can* do now. Stay put until I get back and we can talk."

"What if Palmer leaves—"

"She won't. It's too early. You know the etiquette these things run on."

Johnson was out of the van. "Fifteen, twenty minutes tops. Ross isn't the hardass he likes to think he is."

Holland watched him walk away, wind snapping at his pants, shoulders angled to keep the draft off his neck. She slipped into the front seat, set her eyes on the entrance to the hotel, and replayed Cynthia Palmer's bleeding words.

Time was falling all around Preacher, like notes from a heroic symphony. The music only he could hear was reaching its crescendo. Chester Rawlins would soon hear it too, the thundering finale of timpani and crashing cymbals. It would be the last thing he heard.

And here was Rawlins, getting out of his car and plodding toward him, right on cue.

It had been easy to befriend him. Rawlins thought Preacher was a *buddy*. He'd been intrigued by Preacher's account of his time with the Green Berets but, as a fellow professional, had refrained from nosy questions. Now Preacher thought Rawlins was ready for a cup of coffee. There was an upscale deli just around the corner. You could get there even faster through the alley that ran alongside the hotel.

"So how about that coffee?" Preacher asked.

"Sounds good to me."

"Two minutes and we're right back here. Only warmer."

Rawlins laughed. He had very small teeth for such a big man. Preacher was thinking about that when Rawlins's beeper went off.

"Here. Use mine." Preacher offered him his cell phone. He was curious about the call.

Rawlins was first puzzled, then a little piqued. "Could have told me that sooner," he groused. "But good luck to whoever gets her."

"Gets who?" asked Preacher, taking back his phone.

"Palmer, that Rockefeller bitch. Something must be up. The Secret Service's taking over."

Preacher did his best to look impressed.

"Look, I'm not going home right away," Rawlins said. "You want to meet for a drink when you're done?"

"Can't," Preacher said. "My ride's got me booked until two. Between you and me, I think he's going to play hide the salami in the back with his date."

Rawlins laughed. "Amen to that."

Preacher pocketed the card Rawlins gave him, promised to call on his day off, and got rid of him. Rawlins was getting into his car when Preacher's phone rang.

"There's been a change of plans."

"I gathered that."

"You have the backup?"

Preacher glanced at the limo he'd rented. "Yes."

"There's a surveillance unit at the hotel, in the motor court. But right now they have other things on their mind."

Preacher immediately conjured up the image of Holland Tylo. He very much wanted to ask if she was close enough for him to introduce himself.

Instead, he said, "Soon they'll have plenty more to keep them occupied."

The twenty minutes Johnson said he would need had passed. Bryant offered Holland a refill from the coffee thermos, but she shook her head. She didn't want to take her eyes off people streaming underneath the marquee.

Private cars rolled up, mostly rentals driven by tired business-men, squashed road maps on the front seat. There were also taxis and occasional stretches. In the far corner of the motor court, the pride of limos that would ferry the charity ball crowd waited. Once in a while a driver would get in and fire up the engine to get the heater going.

And now one was moving out of the pack, swinging around the motor court, braking at the foot of the red-and-gold carpet. A Beefeater hurried forward, reaching for the rear door.

"There she is."

Holland opened the door of the van.

"Tylo! Don't!"

Bryant had both hands on the wheel, the fingers of one hand curled around his plastic coffee cup, squeezing it so that it was almost oval. Holland knew he wouldn't have a chance to stop her if she ran, and that he knew it too.

"You know where I'm going. Wait for me outside Palmer's place."

"We can't protect you out there!"

"Palmer's there alone. I know what to watch out for. She doesn't."

Bryant watched her trot toward an off-loading cab, one hand against her thigh to keep the wind from playing with her dress. The jacket she'd thrown over her shoulders, something Bryant had found in the back of the van, was incongruous with the evening wear, but it effectively hid the gun she'd strapped on.

It's Johnson's fault, Bryant thought. He should have known Tylo would bolt if Palmer came out. And Johnson had gone in without a mike, wearing only a beeper. It was the kind that vibrated, not squawked, but even so the interruption could come at a bad moment if Johnson was still dealing with Ross.

Bryant let out a soft expletive and punched in the beeper number. As soon as the call registered he was stabbing the buttons again, waiting for a woman to pick up.

Expecting to have to wait for her driver, Cynthia Palmer thought she could vent some of her fury on the lummox, but there was the car idling at the foot of the steps. Palmer gritted her teeth when the doorman clumsily tipped his hat and in the process grazed her cheek.

The privacy window was up, which was just as well. Palmer depressed the intercom button and said, "Take me home."

The jerk she anticipated never came. The car drew away as smoothly as a sailboat into the dawn. Palmer settled into the deep velour, stretching her legs, wiggling her toes in front of the warm air sighing through the floor vents.

That little Secret Service bitch—what was her name? Beaumont. All that talk about Charlie's diaries. Thank God Ross and that cow Marjorie hadn't heard *that!*

She fished out a cigarette and fired it up with her Cartier. Beaumont had caught her by surprise, when all those feelings she so carefully kept away from her world had been left unguarded. Tonight was supposed to have been fun. To gossip, spend a little money, test the social waters behind the condolences. Maybe even get laid. Certainly Ross had been plenty eager.

But Beaumont had hit her between the eyes with the diaries, telling her they were out, implying that they could be the motive behind Charlie's death. Not exactly the conclusion of a rocket scientist. From the moment she'd learned of Charlie's murder, while having breakfast at the Savoy in London, she knew the reason for the killing.

She was also aware that there were two parts to the blackmail material. One night when he'd had too much Armagnac, Charlie had bragged about how clever he was, not placing all his eggs in one basket. Charlie was hopelessly clichéd without a speechwriter.

During the short flight from London, throughout the kid-glove handling by the police and FBI and the hopelessly maudlin outpouring of concern from her friends, Palmer had held on to a single hard, shiny question: Had the diaries, all or part of them, been found and taken by the killer?

She'd measured every question directed at her with that stern scale and had come to the conclusion that no, the killer, or whoever sent him, had not come away with the prize.

She laughed shortly. Not only had she been wrong about all the clever, pathologically ruthless bastards who would have wanted the diaries, but it turned out that a greenhorn agent had somehow gotten her hands on one of them.

What do I know right this moment? What do I have to work with?

Beaumont obviously knew about the diaries—she dropped enough hints about the contents. Which meant that the Secret Service—Beaumont's superior or whoever—also knew.

Question: Had Beaumont or anyone else in the Service spilled the beans?

Not damn likely. Whoever had heard the tape, or whatever format Charlie had used, *knew* they were handling political plutonium.

And they were thinking that someone mentioned in the diaries could be the killer. Logical enough, but who cares?

Palmer had pruned away the thicket of the situation and now had the fine, hard trunk: Whatever the Secret Service had, however they had come across it, it was now, by virtue of Charlie's will, her personal property. . . .

The only nettle was this: Why had the Service sent along that Cinderella in her pret-a-porter when something like this should have been dealt with privately?

Unless whoever had sent the girl had thought that Palmer would be shocked enough, made distraught enough by the mention of the diaries, to blurt out where the second diskette might be.

I wish I knew. . . .

She had already emptied every lockbox she knew about, checked the penthouse condo thoroughly, gone to the Belmont Club and done her grieving widow act, which got her a private audience with Charlie's locker. That left only Oak Farms, and she was sure that unless Charlie had buried it on the property, it wasn't to be found up there. Now she thought she might have been too hasty; when the ground firmed up, she'd walk the woods to where Charlie had his private places—"secret places," he called them.

But first she had to get hold of Beaumont. She would demand that the girl bring her the diskette already in her possession. She was certain Beaumont would hedge, bump her up to her superior. But Palmer had long ago mastered the art of dealing with Washington underlings. Unless they were really persistent or stupid, there shouldn't be any need to involve Lawrence Ross.

And how delicious it'll be if Larry's name has been mentioned!

The lights of the condominium tower crawled across the tinted glass. Palmer didn't notice, until the car tilted forward, that it was on the ramp into the garage. She was reaching for the intercom when the lummox spoke.

"Just a security precaution, Mrs. Westbourne. Instructions from the office said we go in this way."

Who cares?

Palmer was thinking about the girl, Beaumont. What was it that had happened between them in that instant, to allow all of her defenses to crumble like a sand castle?

Palmer had never talked that way in front of anyone, certainly not Marjorie Woolworth or any of her clones. They could detect weakness or trouble better and faster than any man. Their power lay in hoarding little secrets until they became large and powerful enough to snare victims. Among one another they were like crocodiles in slumber that struck out viciously when the first drop of blood hit the water. Cannibals all, they created and re-created their pecking order on a mountain of bones.

Yet there she was, calling Charlie poison, admitting to so much on a tide of anger, revolt, and revulsion, displaying her scars.

Why?

Because pretty Beaumont doesn't have to live here. She's a clean, fresh girl, gloriously unmarked, though not without her own secrets.

Maybe I was once like her. Or maybe not and just think I was. If I had had some of her seed and refused to barter it away, I might have been okay.

She was still thinking about how she needed refuge from that cold, brittle planet where she dwelled, when the car eased to a stop.

The door opened, and when she was out, the driver had his back to her. She heard the snap of a lighter, smelled the tobacco. She reached into her purse and found the key card for the elevator. The building had top security, including elevators that went only to the floor indicated on the card's magnetic stripe.

The doors opened and Palmer stepped in, turning around to face front. There was the car, engine off and ticking as it cooled. Bluish smoke hung in the air, but she didn't see the driver . . .

Until he was in the elevator, and she realized he was a different man, with frenzied eyes but movements as smooth and graceful as a dancer's. Her neck felt as though it were being crushed in a vise. Light was fleeing from her eyes and her last thought was how powerful he was. Because with his other hand he plucked the key card and swiped it through the slot, and now the elevator doors were gliding closed.

26

BRYANT watched through the windshield as Johnson came out of the hotel, taking the steps two at a time. When his boss was closer, Bryant saw the furrows around his eyes and knew things hadn't gone well with Lawrence Ross. Now Johnson was looking directly at him, and at the empty passenger seat, and his eyes were dangerous.

"When did she bolt?" he asked, climbing into the van.

Bryant checked the digital display on the dash.

"Twelve minutes. I suppose I could have slapped handcuffs—"

"She went to Palmer's. Let's go."

"I got on the horn to Maryanne," Bryant said. "She got a new ride in the divorce settlement, one of those fancy Jeep Cherokees. She'll pick up David Cobb on the way. . . . Maryanne carries a shotgun, and Cobb never goes anywhere without his Uzi. They're probably reaching Palmer's condo right now. . . . The Jeep is a lot better than a surveillance car. It fits the neighborhood. I told them to look like a pair of cheating spouses."

Johnson grunted and braced himself as Bryant swung the van into traffic.

"How did it go with Ross?"

"He was a royal pain in the ass. I think he had intentions on the widow Westbourne."

"Is he going to make noise with the director?"

"He already tried. Smith wasn't around."

Johnson didn't elaborate. Only a half-dozen people besides the President were aware that Wyatt Smith was seeing a surgeon at Johns Hopkins once a week. He had reached a critical point with the bullet lodged in his spine. If left there, it would soon damage the spinal cord, and Smith would be paralyzed.

The only alternative was the knife. The bullet could come out, but afterward Smith would still run the risk of losing the use of his legs, be confined to a wheelchair for the rest of his life.

Johnson knew that Smith had to decide very soon, if he wanted to have a choice at all. He did not want Smith's time intruded upon by a pompous ass like Ross, so tonight he'd dined on crow, promising the attorney he personally would handle the issue of "Agent Beaumont" 's conduct.

Something continued to nag at Johnson. Ross's behavior had been true to form for a Beltway Brahmin, yet something had been missing.

Holland had volunteered a lot of information to Cynthia Palmer. Ross, the confidant, had used none of it in front of Johnson. And Johnson knew that Ross could have grilled him much harder if he'd had the right information to stoke the fires.

So Ross had consoled and comforted Palmer, stroked her with questions, and the widow had given him nothing. Why?

If Holland had hit pay dirt, made Palmer think about things she'd either dismissed or overlooked . . .

Johnson reached for the phone on the console and called the concierge of Palmer's condo complex. The man knew what was going on on his turf. Palmer's limousine had just pulled into the garage.

Johnson told him that Palmer was expected to go out again. A Secret Service detail would want to park downstairs as well. It would help if someone met the agents at the garage door. ETA was seven minutes.

Glancing at Johnson as he finished the call, Bryant shifted in his seat and put a little more muscle on the accelerator.

. . .

From the outside, the security at Riverview Towers looked good.

When Holland's cab drew up in the circular drive, a jacketed valet stepped forward. Behind the front doors, lined with slabs of bronze, was a second man, watching. At the lobby desk stood the concierge. They were big men, polite in the gruff, heavy way of ex-cops or of ballplayers who'd missed out on the easy life of endorsements.

Holland looked up at the twenty-four stories of granite, marble, and copper, the surrounding grounds protected by an ornate wrought-iron fence, black paint gleaming off the spikes. In corners of darkness she picked out the roving red eyes of security cameras, wondered if they were the kind with motion sensor capabilities.

A killer, even a thief, would have a tough time. But to someone like Preacher, the building would be nothing more than a stack of fancy, million-dollar chicken coops.

The doormen didn't recognize her as a resident, so she wasn't buzzed in until she offered up her ID. The lobby could have been a salon at the National Gallery, marble hung with tapestries, art, and unusual Han pieces in Plexiglas cases.

Holland noticed the concierge staring at the sports jacket slung over her shoulders.

"I have something for Ms. Westbourne."

Holland was startled by the concierge's response.

"Of course." With a flourish, he produced a key card. "You know it's Penthouse One. The elevator is an express. Please return the card when you're finished."

The concierge walked her to the bank of elevators.

"Has anyone called on Ms. Westbourne tonight?" Holland asked.

"No. She arrived twenty minutes ago. Her car is still downstairs. We're *very* careful about our residents' movements."

Holland ignored his smug tone.

The ride up made her think of the Service's training school in Beltsville, Maryland, where she'd practiced getting "hostages" out of a shaft. The Beltsville elevator had been an industrial cage, and it moved faster than this one.

Holland cleared her mind of everything: Bryant, Johnson, the uncomfortable shoulder holster against her side, how cold her toes were in the evening shoes. She called up the last words she'd spoken to Cynthia Palmer, the cadence and tone she'd used. She replayed everything Palmer had said to her and panned it for nuggets she could use. She didn't want to give Palmer a chance to think after she opened the door.

Holland imagined the big penthouse, Palmer sitting in the dark with the sprawl of city and river lights beyond the tall windows. Curled up in a favorite chair, the drink in her hand making her palm cold and wet, she was staring at a crackling fireplace or maybe a hearth, as cold and empty as her soul.

The elevator was slowing. The doors opened silently, and Holland stepped into a small, circular foyer with a rosewood table holding an exquisite floral arrangement. On the left was the fire escape door. Holland tested it and found it locked.

Directly in front of her were the double doors to the suite and, at waist level, a glowing button that was the bell.

Johnson spotted the Cherokee parked across the street from the condo tower, along a tree-lined street that fronted a small park.

The anticrime lights were good, and he easily made out the couple in the front seat. Johnson thought Cobb would be having the rougher time of the two. He was newly married, and Mary-anne was busy exploring her newfound conjugal freedoms. She was the one halfway turned toward Cobb, one arm draped across the back of his seat.

Bryant finished talking to the valet, who'd run up with the key for the garage doors.

"Has the other agent arrived?" Johnson asked, leaning across the console.

"Yes, sir. We let her go right on upstairs."

Johnson smiled tightly. He could have walked an elephant up there with dollied-up credentials and an attitude.

The garage was brightly lit and had recently been whitewashed.

There were fresh black lines for individual parking spaces and clean lettering for the owners' names. The limousine was parked lengthwise in front of the elevator doors, in a loading zone marked off in yellow.

Bryant hopped out and went up to the car. The front seats were empty. He rapped on the back window, thinking the driver was cooping.

Bryant opened the door and checked inside, then looked back at Johnson.

"Was she sloshed and needed help getting upstairs? Maybe he was carrying something for her."

"Go up to security," Johnson said tightly. "They have cameras in the elevators. Check the tapes."

Holland didn't have to use the illuminated button. The doors to Cynthia Palmer's suite were ajar.

Holland pushed one open, hearing the rustle of wood on carpet. She was in the foyer, standing under recessed lighting, on a small Chinese carpet that covered the pale-pink marble floor.

Holland slipped off her shoes, shrugged off the jacket, and swept the gun into her hand.

The wall on the right was dominated by a large abstract painting; on the left was the living room. Flame from the gas-fed fire lapped at the granite hearth and teased the edges of a Kirman rug. The only other light in the room came through the floor-to-ceiling windows that faced the city landmarks.

Palmer's perfume hung in the air. Holland stepped left, saw the dining room off to the right, a hall running in the opposite direction.

The hall was a gallery of Chagalls, the rampaging oils backlit by museum lights. On the right was a bedroom, a small Laura Ashley guest suite. Next to it was an office, with the silhouette of a delicate writing desk and a modern high-back chair on a cream carpet.

Holland froze and blinked. A shadow fell across the carpet, grotesque limbs that seemed to be reaching out for her. She took one more step, saw that it was a Giacometti sculpture.

Now she faced another set of doors, one of them open: the master suite. The lights were on. Off to the left, water ran into a basin. Vaguely human sounds came from the bedroom proper.

From the proportions of the apartment, Holland knew that the master suite would be enormous: at least one walk-in closet, a bathroom with a separate water closet and a large linen space, the bedroom itself, which could be L-shaped. So many places for Preacher to hide . . .

He'll come at you when you least expect it. You have to see him through the camouflage. . . .

The thing in the bedroom began keening, and the high pitch cut through Holland. She pretended it was something else, the wind whistling through the planks of a country cabin, and bolted through the door. She kicked closed the door to one of the walk-in closets and turned the button on the handle, locking it. With the gun trained to her left, she took three quick steps and bolted the entrance to the second closet.

In the bathroom, water was running into one of the two sinks set into a custom-appointed vanity. Holland flipped the faucet handles, and the keening grew louder. She threw open the doors to the water closet and the shower, then moved toward the bedroom.

In front of her was a horizon of city lights. A stronger light, in the alcove to her left, fell across a comforter that had been dragged off the bed. It was a four-poster, with gleaming brass pillars and orbs.

As she stepped forward on the plush carpet, reflections in the windows began to give up the secrets of the room. There, on one post, and now another, were cords, the thick nylon kind used by climbers. A pair of feet were stretched between the posts.

Holland realized she was breathing through her mouth. She did not want to take that last step, because the smell told her what she'd find. Suddenly she was catapulted back to the guesthouse at Oak Farms and its bedroom of dripping red walls and the stench of warm copper pennies.

Cynthia Palmer lay spread-eagled, her wrists bound the same way as her ankles. The bed was a California king, and Holland saw where the arms had been pulled out of their shoulder sockets so that Preacher could bind her to the posts.

Holland felt blood squish under her feet, through her nylons, run between her toes. She was polluting the crime scene but kept moving, kneeling by the bed, one arm held out straight, the barrel of the gun on the door.

This is when he'll come for me, out of the camouflage. . . .

Except the entry was the only way in. There were no closets in the bedroom; the dresser, love seat, and television were pushed up against the wall.

Cynthia Palmer's head rolled toward Holland, eyelids fluttering, mouth open. She was barely breathing, yet the keening continued, as though forced from the pit of her stomach by some obscene bellows. Holland looked at the sheet that covered Palmer up to the bottom of her breasts. It was sodden with blood, giving it the texture of wet cheesecloth. Holland didn't touch the sheet; she knew what she'd find underneath.

"Mike-mike! Mike-mike!"

Johnson and Bryant were here by now, Holland was sure of it. The microphone frequency was still good. Any second now she would hear Johnson whispering in her ear.

"Mike-mike!" she repeated.

Holland's gun hand wavered as despair stole her strength. *Where's Johnson?*

"Help me . . ."

Holland started when she heard the woman's groan, saw Palmer's eyes boring into hers. The face and neck had been left untouched, not a blemish or a drop of blood. Holland imagined Preacher sitting beside her, looking into her face, perhaps stroking her with one hand while the other guided his knife.

Palmer's eyes moved from side to side. "Help *you* . . ."

Slowly, without shifting her gaze from the bedroom entrance, Holland climbed onto the bed and gently brought her ear to Cynthia Palmer's lips.

A heartbeat later, she heard the muffled pop of a silenced pistol and the splintering of metal and wood.

.   .   .

In the garage, Johnson was slowly circling the limousine. Whatever the driver was doing was taking too long, and Bryant should have gotten back to him by now. He looked intently at the long black car as if trying to divine from it what was wrong, and so he did not remember that his microphone set was still on the van's center console, where he'd left it before going in to talk to Ross.

Johnson opened the driver's door and slipped across the leather seat. He remembered Bryant checking the car and again wondered what the hell he was doing. Impatient with himself, he jerked down the visor.

It was smooth velour, with no clips to hold the registration papers that were usually stashed there.

There was no center console, because that's where the driver's phone had been installed.

There was no registration card tucked in the visor above the passenger seat. No Boulder Security cards, stationery, gas or toll receipts in the glove box . . .

But tucked underneath the passenger seat, almost out of sight, was a small, flat object. Its blinking light drew Johnson's eye.

He eased back, dropping to his knees so that he was almost eye level with the object. It looked like a portable CD player, five inches square, with a smooth matte-black finish. Its light continued to pulse.

Johnson heard no telltale ticking. There were no wires connected to the box. It appeared not to be fixed to the floor but to have been placed there almost casually, the way any driver would stash it away from thieves.

Johnson brushed his fingertips across his lips, blowing warm air on them. Slowly, he reached forward and touched the sides of the box. There could be a spring he wasn't able to see, or a pressure trigger that would detonate the bomb in his face. Johnson lifted the box a half inch and started to bring it out. He had it halfway out from under the seat when he saw the counter. A digital readout was flipping back red numerals. It was down to twenty-six seconds.

Johnson felt for a clasp or slide, some way to open the counter. Instead, he found dry, hard ridges of epoxy where the housing had been sealed.

Twenty-three seconds.

Johnson set the device on the carpeted mat, then ran to the van, wrenched open the door, and snatched the microphone.

"Mike-mike! Mike-mike! Holland, get out of there, now! *Now!* Preacher's been up there. He's wired the place!"

His desperation caromed off the concrete, spinning into oblivion. Johnson had taken two steps toward the stairwell when a rumble made him look up. He thought of the time he'd been out in Los Angeles, sitting at a bar, when a 5.2 aftershock hit. It was as though a giant palm had smacked into the building, sending a shudder through the I-beam skeleton. An explosion set off on one of the higher floors here would render the same effect.

Sick with fear, Johnson forced himself to keep moving to the emergency stairs. The sound he heard next seemed terribly incongruous, the *ping* of the elevator's arrival.

Never use an elevator when there's a fire or an explosion. It's a death trap. . . .

"Holland!"

The elevator doors opened, came apart a foot and a half, then bumped closed. Johnson slammed one shoulder against them, wedging his body into the space, straining to push them apart. Fire alarms were going off now, and the elevator car was dark. Johnson never heard Preacher uncoil from the corner, didn't see the flash of his knife until the blade had dug into his collarbone.

Powerful arms sent him spinning out between the doors. A second blow slammed him onto the concrete. Now Preacher was standing over him, feeding on his pain, the blood on the soles of his shoes making the sound of flesh being peeled off bone.

"Mike-mike! Mike-mike! Holland, get out of there, now! Now! Preacher's been up there . . .

The words rang through Holland's ear seconds after she'd heard the gunshot. And still she could not move.

Holland felt sticky wetness on her cheek. It was the blood that had bubbled over Cynthia Palmer's lips and smeared Holland as she hovered over her, the woman's words like thunder dying in the distance.

Palmer was silent now, except for her breathing, fitful and hoarse. Holland understood there was no way to save her, even if the room were miraculously transformed into a surgery. She kept hearing the gunshot, and Johnson's desperate urging, but she could not bring herself to abandon the ruin. The way she had abandoned Charles Westbourne that night . . .

A gout of blood exploded from Palmer's abdomen, actually raising the sheet that covered her. Then all at once she seemed to grow smaller, the skin on her face losing its rictus, retreating across the bone and cartilage of her skull.

Holland backed away, as if watching the stricken and tortured soul pry itself from its unwanted corpse. A terrible silence filled the room, and Holland was breathing hard because it seemed something was draining all the air, even what was left in her lungs.

"God keep you. . . ."

Holland never looked back. Out of the death room, her attention riveted on the door to the walk-in closet. She hugged the wall and reached forward to clear the lock. A turn of the wrist, and the door flew back from the force of her kick.

Sandalwood and cedar. Rows of clothing, some sheathed in dry cleaner's plastic or garment covers. Shoe stands marching up one wall, built-in drawers for jewelry.

And a partly opened door at the end of the closet, the handle hanging like a broken tree bough.

Holland pushed it and saw the service corridor that separated the front units from the rear ones the entire length of the building. Diagonally on the right was the trash/recycling closet; farther down, the telephone and electronic switching center.

Which stairwell would he use? How far down would he go? Two floors, three? And then? He'd have to break into another unit, get past the owner and through it to the elevator—

But he's moving too fast. That way's too clumsy, too uncertain. He'll lose time if someone tries to stop him. It's all wrong because—

Holland scrambled out to the corridor and found what she was looking for, what *had* to be there, next to the building maintenance room: the service and freight elevator.

She fumbled for the key card, praying that the code would work. It had to: how else could residents use this elevator in an emergency? Unless they were issued *two* cards . . .

The whine of machinery startled her. Holland backed away, her gun pointed at the doors. But they opened on an empty car, the walls hung with thick padding to accommodate furniture movers.

Holland darted inside and smacked the button labeled *G-1*. She already knew how Preacher had gotten to Palmer, gotten into the building and all the way up to the penthouse, how he'd been able to tear up Palmer in the privacy of her own home. Holland was thinking about the chauffeur's cap she'd glimpsed in Palmer's bedroom, how she could have figured out Preacher's method even without it. Her mind turned to the cold, miserable fact that somewhere in the night, perhaps still undiscovered, lay another body, that of Palmer's limo driver, who—

The doors were closing when the explosion came, ripping out the walls somewhere down the corridor. The car was rocking, and now a cloud of dust billowed toward it. But the circuits were holding. The doors obeyed the computer's command.

It was the shock wave that crumpled Holland against the padding, made the car lurch, then sent it into free fall.

The sound of the alarms receded from Johnson's consciousness, pushed back by the scalding pain in his shoulder.

He was lying on his back, leaning slightly to avoid putting weight on his right side. His shirt felt sticky around the shoulder and chest, but the blood didn't matter. There wouldn't be much of it, the way Preacher had cut him. The angle of the knife's descent had been so severe that the power behind the blow had been lost. Instead of reaching deep into flesh, the blade had crunched into his collarbone, bit hard, but ultimately glanced off, slicing the skin.

The pain was like nothing Johnson had ever before experienced. The closest thing to it that he could imagine was a dentist's drill boring through healthy tooth enamel.

Johnson realized he was looking at Preacher's shoes, at the

patches of blood left behind by the soles. He forced his chin up and saw the powerful fingers holding the blade, delicately, like a conductor's baton, then the long arms, and now a face gazing down at him.

It was ten years since Johnson had seen Preacher in the flesh. After a time, Preacher's image had been scrubbed from his dreams. He had forgotten how tawny Preacher's eyes were, like a big cat's.

It all came back to him in a single rush, and the groan that stumbled over his lips was born not of pain but of the anguish of his failure. With Preacher looming over him, eclipsing the last light he would ever see, Johnson saw in the man's eyes reflections of all the victims he had ever taken. The glee and fury that danced on pinpricks of yellow mirrored the screams of women Johnson could never know, had lost his chance to help, had, in some indefinable way, to answer to. Except that he had nothing for them, nothing to offer that could possibly explain how or why he had allowed something like this to shamble out of his grasp.

Johnson cried out as Preacher grabbed his tie and jerked him up, exposing his neck.

"Hello, Arliss."

Johnson would not look away from Preacher's grinning mask. He knew exactly what Preacher wanted him to do, what any killer ultimately demanded of his victim: to stare at the murder weapon and beg, continue to beg even as the steel began to cut.

Because Johnson refused Preacher this satisfaction, he was able to see the surprise, then annoyance, that came over him.

Ping! Elevator doors opening . . . ?

Then a shot boomed out, the bullet catching the pillar next to Preacher, splattering concrete chips across him and Preacher.

Holland saw Preacher react instantly, duck and roll as she squeezed off two more rounds, which dug into the concrete in front of his twisting body.

When the elevator doors had opened, Holland had been on the floor in the corner, braced against the walls. Her arms were held out between her knees, and she had fired the instant she saw Preacher, at an angle that she knew made a hit almost impossible.

Now she was on her feet, out of the elevator, prone, the concrete tearing at her knees and elbows, as she tried to spot Preacher's legs or feet. She was hoping he'd be under a car. One round into the gas tank, and she'd send him to hell in a fireball.

Enraged, Holland rose and began pumping out the rounds. Windshields and windows exploded as she worked her way through the gun's magazine. She was going to flush him now, flush him and corner him and take him down hard. . . .

She couldn't rely on her ears, with the building alarms still going off, but her eyes picked up a blur of movement. She tracked it and began firing even before she had a bead on her target. Then in exactly the opposite direction she saw a door swing closed—the emergency exit, with stairs leading upstairs to another door, which, in an emergency, would automatically unlock itself and spill Preacher into the night. . . .

Holland wheeled around and ran back to Johnson.

"I'm okay," he gasped. "Looks worse than it is. Cobb and Maryanne are parked outside in a Cherokee."

Holland brushed away his outstretched hand and peeled back his jacket. Johnson had lied. His shirt was drenched with blood.

"We need a hospital."

"No! It's just on the collarbone. Come on, give me a hand!"

Holland helped him to his feet and draped his left arm over her shoulders. Johnson grimaced as he took his first step, but he kept moving. Holland fell in step with him, guided him to the garage doors, already open for the fire trucks, then up the ramp.

Sirens and red lights were shattering the darkness, as fire trucks and EMR vehicles scattered themselves across the street and along the drive. Men in yellow fire-retardant jumpsuits and slickers ran by, oxygen tanks bumping on their backs, their hands clutching red toolboxes, their shouts hoarse over the wail of alarms.

One of the firemen stopped and, gulping air, asked if they needed help. Johnson answered fast, telling him he had a broken ankle. It was dark enough that the fireman wouldn't see the blood on his chest.

"They're over there," Johnson said to Holland, and nodded toward the Cherokee.

"I'll take him now."

Bryant, materializing out of nowhere. Holland saw his moon face, filled with fear and concern, how gentle he was with Johnson, hoisting him so that his feet barely touched the ground.

Now Maryanne and Cobb were spilling out of the Jeep, helping Bryant, and Holland was alone, hanging back. She did not know she was staring at the top of Riverview Towers, where smoke was piling into the sky, the flames already doused by the building's sprinklers. She had no idea she was standing in the middle of the street, being jostled and cursed at by men running past her. She wasn't aware of any of this until Bryant came back for her, draped a firefighter's heavy blanket around her shoulders, and led her away.

C H A P T E R

27

"YOU'VE used up the last of your luck, Arliss. A quarter inch here or there, and . . ."

The doctor had been waiting for them in Holland's room at the Stewart Center. His name was Hooper, and he was in his early fifties, a crane of a man with wisps of gray across a glowing bald spot, and the hard, tight eyes of a battle surgeon.

Hooper ripped open a Styrette package and tapped the plastic vial with his forefinger.

"It'll handle the pain, you know."

"And put me out."

"You plan on going dancing tonight?" The doctor checked his watch and corrected himself. "This morning?"

It was half past twelve on the morning of April 5.

"Just give me something to take my mind off this."

Hooper knew what Johnson was asking for. As a cutter in Vietnam, he had discovered pills and potions that could deaden a man's wound long enough for him to go back into battle when the enemy was storming the gates.

Hooper glanced around the room, at the agents he now knew by name. Maryanne and her partner, Cobb, were in the kitchenette alcove, furiously blowing cigarette smoke through a cracked-open window. The big one, Bryant, and Claire Cranston, whom Hooper had known for years, were in the chairs opposite the bed, watching both patient and doctor. Only the other woman was standing, though Hooper detected signs of imminent collapse. This one, Holland Tylo, would not take her eyes off Johnson's bandaged shoulder and chest. She had watched Hooper's procedures with an intensity that he, who could cancel out everything around him when he worked, found disturbing. He thought Tylo could not quite believe that Johnson wasn't going to die, that she was somehow willing him what remained of her strength.

Hooper tore open a foil strip embedded with a dozen pills.

"Potent stuff. One every six hours. No more."

"You're a prince." Johnson grimaced as he reached for the medication.

Hooper packed up his kit. When he turned to leave, Claire came to him, put her hand on his arm, touched his face in the way an old lover would.

"Aaron."

Hooper looked back.

"Thanks."

"Hurry up and catch whatever you're chasing." The doctor offered a halfhearted two-finger salute. "Luck, Arliss."

As Claire saw Hooper out, Bryant motioned to Maryanne and Cobb to leave.

"Holland—"

"She stays, Tommy."

Bryant knew that tone, knew better than to argue. Johnson pushed himself up on the pillows, tore out one of the capsules and swallowed it dry.

"What do you have?"

Bryant couldn't help glancing at Holland. Baptism under fire was one thing, but what he had for Johnson would not be for her ears. He chose his next words carefully.

"The bulletins out on Preacher are back. Dry holes from L.A., San Francisco, and Seattle. But we got a hit up in Vancouver. The Mounties' new system clocks American passports, allegedly for their internal revenue people. Preacher was using a different name, but he didn't have much of a disguise in the passport photo. They faxed this down."

Bryant handed Johnson the sheet of paper, careful to hold the blank side toward Holland.

Johnson looked directly at the item Bryant had red-lined: the serial number on the passport Preacher had used.

"How did we get this?" he asked quietly.

Bryant nodded at the fax machine on the writing desk. "It's a secure line, right? I gave your office the number in case something hot came in."

Johnson checked the small print at the top of the fax: 11:17 last night. Just when the explosion started rocking the penthouse at Riverview Towers.

"The Canadians are sure about these numbers?"

Bryant nodded.

Holland watched the tension drain out of Johnson's face, the muscles going slack as though he'd taken his last breath. He looked like a man who had just suffered an irrevocable loss.

"Okay," Johnson said. "Track it down. You know the signature we're looking for. It'll be there, because there's no way the passport would have been issued without it."

Johnson handed the fax back to Bryant. "Start knocking on doors now. Call me as soon as you have confirmation. Are Maryanne and Cobb fresh enough to stay?"

"They're fine, but—"

"Make sure the three of you have secure communications. You can get to me through them."

Bryant carefully folded the sheet and stowed it away somewhere in his jacket. Then he cleared his throat and said, "I'd just as soon stay with you," in a formal tone.

Johnson knew what was eating at Bryant. He could not forgive himself for failing to be there when Preacher almost took down his boss. There were amends to be made, accounts to be settled, and Bryant was feeling that he would never get the chance.

"Tommy, you understand what that signature means to us. You're the one I can trust with this."

After Bryant had left, Johnson tested his abdominal muscles, then slowly swung his legs off the bed, rolling his neck. Gently, he touched the surgical padding and bandages Hooper had packed on his shoulder. The pill was working just fine now.

"You want to know what that was all about," he said to Holland.

She stared at him silently.

"The serial numbers belong to a batch of 'black' passports, reserved for the CIA, State, Treasury, whoever handles individuals who have to be given deep cover. On the odd occasion, we issue them to foreigners to get them out of *their* country.

"This batch is small, a few hundred, but Bryant will be at it for a while. Sometimes the paper trail is tough to follow. But when he finds it, we'll know who authorized Preacher's passport."

"Does Croft have the juice to get one? Or get someone to get it for him?"

Johnson smiled thinly. "I don't think I've thanked you for saving my life."

When he looked at her, Holland had to turn away.

Somewhere inside her, she knew what she'd done for him, but she couldn't reach down and touch that gold. She couldn't get past Cynthia Palmer, the bloody images that mocked and snubbed her.

"It'll heal," Johnson said. "It'll take time, and the hurt will be bad, but you *will* push through it.

"There was nothing more that you could have done for Palmer. Preacher outsmarted us both. Maybe if we'd had the tape from the funeral sooner, we'd have put it together right. But *I* was the one who let Palmer go out unprotected."

Johnson hesitated. "That bomb was for you, Holland. Preacher *expected* you to follow Palmer home. He knew exactly how to time his work, exactly how much pain he had to give her before he was certain she was giving him the truth.

"Then you came, a little early, but by then he was ready to fly. He knew how you'd react to seeing what he'd left for you. He was counting on your refusing to abandon Palmer.

"But his calculations were off just a bit. . . ."

"And we were lucky," Holland concluded.

"Yes."

"And we learned something."

Johnson looked at her, saw her gift for him in her eyes.

"What did Palmer tell you?" he whispered.

"Daniel Webster," Holland replied. "She told me about Daniel Webster."

Preacher had had no trouble flagging down a cab. He was white, well dressed, and had the glassy expression of a tipsy tourist.

Fortunately the driver was an Arab whose limited English precluded conversation. Preacher was just as happy not to field questions about the three-alarm fire burning at Riverview Towers.

The Arab knew the city well and had no compunction about speeding through red lights. The cab rocked back and forth on its slingshot journey up New Hampshire Avenue, where it caromed first onto Connecticut, then onto Florida, sweeping up the soft hill to the sprawling behemoth that was the Washington Hilton.

Here Preacher had parked his alternate persona, shortly after he'd checked into the Four Seasons. He was now Andrew McGee, with a full set of credentials including a California driver's license and a membership card that bespoke his good standing in the American Realtors Association.

The hotel was hosting the association's annual conference. There were fourteen hundred predatory bodies trading notes on the business, lots of self-congratulations and hearty backslapping. Preacher had gone undetected among these bottom feeders. The fact that Reagan had been shot here added a certain piquant irony.

Even at one o'clock in the morning the cavernous lobby was lively. Preacher worked his way through clots of conventioneers spilling out of bars, chatting up one another or hitting on the designer-dressed hookers circulating on the floor. He didn't see anything untoward, nor had he expected to. Johnson knew his face, who he was, and for precisely that reason had not put out a full alert, which would have included D.C. cops flatfooting it from one hotel to another, showing grimy composite sketches to bored hotel clerks. Johnson was well aware of Preacher's many talents, the surveillance he could spot in an instant, the things he was capable of if cornered.

Preacher was very careful in the corridor to his room. He snagged a valet picking up shoes left out to be shined. Preacher put a faint slur on his words as he chatted him up, but his concentration was riveted on the young Guatemalan. Preacher saw right through him. Had there been an ambush waiting, he would have read it in the man's eyes.

Inside his room, Preacher unwrapped the chocolate left on his pillow, let it melt slowly on his tongue as he opened the closet and spun the combination for the guest safe.

In terms of security, the safe was a joke—until Preacher had added a personal touch. He was very careful with the door, opening it only an inch. His fingers played over the hair-thin wires that carried electrical current from a nine-volt battery to a piece of explosive the size of a golf ball.

An ordinary burglar would have wrenched open the door and found himself with no hands or face.

Preacher set the booby trap aside and pulled out his traveling documents, a set that the honorable Senator Croft knew nothing about. Preacher was very angry about having to leave before he could pay Arliss Johnson a second visit. And Holland Tylo.

Preacher was self-critical enough to admit that some of the blame lay with him. He'd lured Johnson in and vanquished him, had been one heartbeat away from sending the knife across his throat. But he'd let it go on too long, savoring the seconds of Johnson's agony, and so had allowed Tylo to cheat him. His only consolation was that the landscape was littered with corpses. Johnson would have a lot of explaining to do, none of which would enhance his career.

There was one last call Preacher intended to make. In the end, Cynthia Palmer had been forthcoming, as Preacher knew she'd be. Now he could tidy things up and, at the same time, drill one more bit of diamond-hard pain into Johnson's conscience.

Preacher made sure he had all he needed, including his ticket for the 7:20 A.M. British Airways flight to London out of Dulles. He stopped at the front desk and was handed a small brown envelope. Preacher tore it open and out slid a freshly cut key.

Preacher smiled as he tossed the key, snatched it out of the air, then slipped it into his pocket. Crossing the lobby to the Capital Gang bar, he thought it was always a pleasure to work with professionals such as Croft, who delivered what they promised.

Preacher threaded his way through the sweaty pack and found an empty stool at the end of the bar. He signaled the bartender and ordered a straight tonic. Scanning the action in the room in the mirror behind the rows of bottles, he thought he wouldn't have to wait too long.

Wyatt Smith sat behind his desk, across from Johnson. It was two o'clock in the morning, one hour after the director had finished his appointment at Bethesda Naval Hospital.

"How did the tests go?" Johnson asked.

"There's no change, if that's what you mean. Except for time, of course. Doctors can be a pushy breed."

"Maybe they measure time differently than we do."

Smith offered a ghost of a smile. "I'd say they don't dance about on the pinhead of the inevitable. They just worry about how to treat or cut.

"But you didn't come here to talk about that. Although speaking of hospitals, Arliss, I think *you* belong in one."

Johnson had carefully gauged Smith's reaction when he'd walked through the door. Smith had all kinds of questions, but all he'd asked was, "How badly are you hurt?"

After Johnson told him, and Smith made his own assessment, he didn't press.

"You heard what happened at Riverview Towers tonight," Johnson said, ignoring Smith's comment.

"The explosion and fire. No details about the cause, but the media pegged Cynthia Palmer's apartment as the place it happened. She's the only known casualty. So?"

"I need you to understand up front that everyone who took part in this was under my orders," Johnson said. "The responsibility begins and ends with me."

Smith looked around himself, like an art auctioneer called in to appraise an estate sale.

"You do have your little secrets, don't you, Arliss? A safe house, medical help . . . You had the FBI Reaction Force tearing through the city on your say-so, then abruptly called them off without explanation. Morrison at the Bureau gave me an earful over that."

Smith's voice dropped a decibel. "What *else* do you have?"

Johnson didn't backpedal into apologies. He laid it out exactly as he'd rehearsed, taking Smith through every step, including how he had run down Holland and the deal she had cut with Croft to bring her in. When he mentioned Preacher, Smith became very still. He, too, was more than familiar with Preacher. Years ago, he and Johnson had combed through Johnson's field investigation reports for nights on end, trying to find the thread that would fashion a noose around Preacher's neck.

"Westbourne and his girlfriend, the Japanese tourists at the waterfront, Cynthia Palmer—all of them Preacher's handiwork," Johnson said.

"Why?" Smith asked. "What's brought him back after all these years?"

Now Johnson wove in the Westbourne diaries, how they had precipitated the killings, how Holland had inadvertently become enmeshed in them. He told Smith about the FBI videotape showing Cynthia Palmer, how it had come too late for him to understand that even then she had been the object of Preacher's attention.

"Tylo figured that one out, and it almost cost her her life," Johnson said. "Preacher had rigged Palmer's apartment, knowing that I or Tylo—hell, maybe both if he was lucky—would come calling. He was going to take us all out, leave nothing behind that could tie in to him or the people who hired him."

Johnson paused. "He damn near succeeded."

Smith did not speak for almost five minutes. He had that faraway look in his eyes that in combat would have been called the thousand-yard stare.

"I heard about them, you know," he said slowly. "The diaries. Every once in a while there'd be the tail end of some rumor, someone would mention how So-and-so was going down because Westbourne had dirt on him.

"I never put any stock in it. What Westbourne was alleged to have had didn't seem any more or less potent than what the rest squirreled away."

Smith looked away, speaking at the night beyond the windows.

"Who are 'the people,' Arliss? Assuming there are more than Croft."

"Only Preacher knows, which is why I want to take him alive."

Smith blinked, as if Johnson had told him something he should have picked up on earlier. He turned and glanced around the room, as though he expected to see more people.

"Tylo's not here," Smith said. "She's not anywhere in the building, either, I imagine. Nor is Bryant, and he's your best hound. I didn't see the Cherokee outside, so Jenkins and Cobb are gone too.

"You've cornered him, haven't you, Arliss? You know where Preacher went after Riverview Towers, and you're waiting on him."

Johnson said nothing.

"What about Croft?" Smith asked. "He's the strongest connection you've made to Preacher. Wouldn't Croft give you what you think Preacher can—the names of who hired him? Assuming it wasn't Croft himself."

"Not good enough," Johnson said. "Croft's a senator; he'll slip out from under all this. I'm not going to let that happen, Wyatt."

Johnson paused. "Preacher's the only one who can gift-wrap Croft for me. When I have him, I get the rest too."

"But Preacher? You can't be thinking of granting him immunity?"

Johnson looked sadly at the director. "It's better you don't have the answer to that, in case sometime the House Internal Affairs Committee calls you to testify."

Judiciary Square is a stately arrangement of two imposing I-shaped buildings separated by the Law Officers Memorial, a granite requiem that faces E Street. Because of its special significance for D.C. police, they patrol it conscientiously. Vagrants and drug dealers who might have been tempted by the low-cost housing along Third and Fourth streets have wisely moved on.

Capitol Hill Apartments and the complexes surrounding it average six stories, with a grassy quadrangle separating them from the street. The one- or two-bedroom units are generous in terms of space. The interior layouts are identical: tiny entryways, kitchen on the left, with a counter opening onto the dining area, which flows into the living room. The bedrooms and bathroom are off to the right, separated by closets.

It is the kind of place secretaries and junior office workers who keep the hive of Washington alive can afford. Because of rent control, their salaries go a little further; single women especially like to add their own personal touches. Vacancies are rare.

Holland thought the apartment cozy. The prints of 1930s ocean liners were set in smart brass frames. There was a good Indian machine-made rug on the parquet. The standard overhead fluorescents had been replaced by floor lamps with pale-pink bulbs.

Holland, in the dining area, watched Judith Trask move around in the kitchen, kettle whistling, spoons rattling in coffee mugs. She was the kind of woman who, Holland thought, would keep her dreams: moving boxes stuffed with photo albums and high school announcements and prom invitations fifteen years old; shoe boxes filled with letters from girlfriends now scattered across the country, the special letters from boys who would not recognize her today squeezed together by rubber bands and tucked away in the darkest corners.

Trask was a tall, thin woman in her mid thirties. Her chestnut hair was flat against her scalp to her shoulders, and her face and eyes were swollen from sleep. She wore a Georgetown University track outfit, the sweatpants stretched a little around her belly.

"Cream and sugar?" Judith called from the kitchen.

"Just black, thanks."

"Oreos?"

"Coffee's fine."

"I eat when I'm like this. Nervous, you know? I know I shouldn't, but . . ."

Judith set the cups down on coasters that had pictures of a Rhode Island sea town on them. She saw Holland looking at them.

"I got those last summer, on vacation."

"I want you to know that no one's going to hurt you," Holland said, looking into her eyes. "That's not going to happen."

"I feel okay," Judith said. "Really. I'm just confused."

Holland sipped her coffee. She had changed at Claire's and now wore dark-gray cord pants and a black windbreaker. The zipper on the jacket was almost all the way down, and Holland knew that Judith could see her sidearm. She wanted her to see it, to reinforce her words.

"It's just that, you know, you call me in the middle of the night, and the next thing I know you're here, telling me about . . . Mrs. Westbourne."

"I would have waited if I could," Holland said. "But there are things you might know that I *have* to know."

"I don't know very much about her," Judith said in a low voice. "I think it's terrible what happened to her."

"Have you ever seen this man?"

Holland handed her Preacher's photograph. The original had been taken ten years before; this one was computer enhanced to account for the passage of time.

"No."

"You're sure?"

"I've never seen him." Judith hesitated. "Is he the one . . . ?"

"He murdered Mrs. Westbourne. And the senator. And Charlotte Lane, the woman found with him."

Holland saw her wince at the mention of Lane.

"You loved him a great deal, didn't you? Charles was everything in the world to you."

Judith's eyes watered, and she looked away.

"It's so clichéd, isn't it? Senator and PA having an affair, banging each other on the desk, the floor—anywhere." Bitterness made her voice ragged and ugly. "But that's how it was for us, and it was very beautiful," she said, her voice softening. "He could have had any woman he wanted. God knows I'd heard about the conquests. There wasn't much I didn't hear.

"But to be with him every day, spend all those hours with him, he just didn't seem to be the man people gossiped about. Do you know how it feels when you're in a room and the whole world seems to recede? There's nothing out there—no sound, no smell, nothing to see. It's black. And you're all alone, the two of you. You've seen things about this man no one else in the world has seen. You've watched his face change a thousand times, so that by now you can tell exactly what he's thinking, what he'll say, what he needs, what he wants.

"I was closer to Charles than anyone else on earth. I'll always believe that. I think he wanted me because he knew that. I couldn't offer him beauty or any other temptation. But he still came to me, because he knew I loved him like no one else ever could."

"He came but he didn't stay," Holland said.

Judith looked at her, bit her lip. "No, he didn't. So I guess all the clichés must be true, made for losers like me."

"Did he know about your pregnancy?"

Judith shook her head. "I didn't think you could tell, not with my figure. . . . Yes. I told him. But he just shut me out." The sting of it echoed in her voice.

In that plain Midwestern face Holland saw the agony of Judith Trask, harboring a new life inside, exploding with joy yet fearful of sharing it.

"He shut me out," Judith repeated. "Didn't ask anything. Not about the baby, or how I was feeling, if I needed anything . . . I told him I wouldn't make trouble for him. I'd tell everyone the father was someone from back home. I said I'd have the baby and raise it by myself. The only thing I asked for was a little money to help me get by."

"Did he think you were going to blackmail him?"

"He knew better." She paused. "He told me he'd find me another job, a better one, somewhere else on the Hill. It'd be a civil service thing, with pension and health benefits. I'd be set. He just wouldn't give me his love."

Judith wiped her cheek with the back of her hand.

"It's not the baby, you know? I dreamed of him keeping me, maybe even marrying me one day. It wasn't wrong to dream. . . .

"When he turned away from me, I felt so ashamed. There were things he'd do to me . . . you know, sex things. Sometimes he brought in other women, and he'd watch as they used me. Sometimes I did him and them at the same time. There were pictures and videos. . . .

"I let him do that. Because sometimes, when there was just the two of us, he would hold me and caress me, and I felt so good and safe with him.

"We'll do anything if someone shows us a little kindness, won't we?"

"But you knew his secrets, didn't you?" Holland said.

"Sometimes I think I didn't know anything."

"This is about his work, Judith. The *way* he worked, where he kept things."

"He didn't keep much in his office, if that's what you mean. Nothing personal anyway."

"No vault?"

"No. He had a lockbox at First Federal. I saw the keys in his drawer. He never asked me to put anything in or take anything out."

"No place in the office where he might stash documents, computer disks?"

Judith shook her head. "His office was a mess. Stuff all over the place. I had to go through *everything* before we could close it down and turn in the keys."

"Okay," Holland said. "Maybe I'm on the wrong track here."

She tried hard to still the urgency in her voice. She'd brought Judith Trask along this far. There was only one question left:

"What about Daniel Webster? Does his name mean anything to you? Did Westbourne like to quote from Webster's works? Did he have a favorite one he referred to, a special volume he kept handy?"

Judith rose and walked the length of the Indian rug.

"No," she said, turning around. "Charles liked Madison and Jefferson. He had all their books on the shelves. It got so that I could quote a lot of what they'd written. Charles always liked to spice up his speeches like that."

Holland's hopes sank into the well of her fatigue. It had been her last chance, to take what Cynthia Palmer had given her from her dying lips and run with it to someone who might make sense of it.

Throughout the night, Holland had clutched the words like an amulet. Palmer had held on to her pain long enough to say them

before she surrendered. That made them the truth, the way a
bedside confession is the final reckoning.

But what truth?

Holland had been so sure that Judith would give her what she
needed, that she would know things about Westbourne even his
own wife would never suspect. Somewhere between these two
women who'd been savaged by the same man lay the answer she
needed. . . .

"Daniel Webster."

Holland looked hard at Judith. "Yes?"

"As I said, Charles never read Webster. But he had something
of his."

Holland was on her feet. "What was it, Judith?"

"His desk."

At one forty-five, servers in the Hilton's Capital Gang bar began
giving last call.

Seated on a stool not far from the service area, Preacher
watched the bartender slosh out the nightcaps. Eyes on the mirror, he watched the loud, boozy goings-on behind him and easily
spotted what was coming at him.

"Jesus, what a crowd! Mind if I sit here a minute, get away
from that awful noise?"

There were eight vacant stools along the bar, but the blonde
in tight-fitting black evening pants, white blouse, and magenta
bullfighter's jacket squiggled her way onto the one next to
Preacher.

"Hi! I'm Bobbie Sue."

"I'm sure you are. My name's Andrew. Andrew McGee."

"Andrew . . . That sure is a nice name. I like it better than
Andy."

The high-intensity lights in the ceiling gave away the black roots
in her blond hair. Preacher thought she'd done a good job with
her war paint, but underneath it he detected the crepe in her
skin. Thirty-five pushing fifty.

"Whereabout's you from, Bobbie Sue?"

"Oh, Maryland, just down the road."

Preacher didn't think so. The accent was closer to north Florida, from some hick inland county where the definition of a virgin
is a girl who can outrun her brother.

"You staying at the hotel, Andrew?"

"Nope. I spend all day here at the convention, enough to make
you crazy. An old fraternity brother of mine loaned me his place
while he's out of town."

Preacher smiled faintly as Bobbie Sue tried to hide her disap-
pointment. He thought she might have turned one trick tonight,
maybe two, but wanted to end the evening on a winning note. She
seemed fresh enough, maybe because servicing drunken businessmen was about as easy as her job could get.

"It's a small place," Preacher said, reaching for the check the
bartender had wedged between the glasses. "But it's nicely done
and very private."

Preacher had his wallet out, his thumb running across the edges
of the bills, giving Bobbie Sue a good look at the hundreds before
he plucked out a twenty.

Her hand felt cool on his, her nails tugging at his skin.

"I know what you mean about hotels," she said. "Your friend's
place sounds *much* nicer."

Preacher pulled three hundred-dollar bills halfway out of his
wallet.

"Believe me, it's really nice. Very romantic."

"I like men who're romantic," Bobbie Sue said breathlessly.
"They're the most generous ones, Andrew. . . ." Preacher pulled
out a fourth bill, and Bobbie Sue squealed. He picked up a cocktail
napkin and with a sleight of hand wrapped it around the money.

"Unless I'm mistaken, this is yours, Bobbie Sue."

She held his hand in both of hers and kissed his fingers, at the
same time prying loose the napkin.

"You're not mistaken about anything, honey. Now let's go find
us some old-fashioned romance."

Preacher had the cab drop them off on E Street, in front of the
Law Officers Memorial. Bobbie Sue was quite taken by the lights
playing off the stone facade, until she read the inscription.

"A friend of mine was a Los Angeles cop," Preacher explained. "He was killed in the line of duty. I like to walk by here and remember."

She shivered and huddled closer to him.

"Jeez, Andrew, you're pretty solid. You work out?"

"When I have the time."

Preacher took back the conversation, feeding her tripe about what it was like to be a real estate broker in Laguna Niguel. He tilted his head so that it rested lightly on Bobbie Sue's hair. With his coat collar up, his features were indiscernible even through a Starlite night-vision scope.

If Holland Tylo had died, as she was supposed to have, Preacher wouldn't have needed the hooker.

He thought it unlikely that Palmer had told her what she'd surrendered to him, even less likely that Tylo could have pieced together the clue *and* convinced Johnson, badly wounded, to act on her hunch.

No, he thought, there were too many variables, all of which worked in his favor.

Still, Preacher was pruning his risks. He approached the Capitol Hill Apartments from the E Street side because Judith Trask's unit faced the quadrangle in front. If there was a long-gun coverage, a sniper zeroed in on the four windows of Trask's apartment, Preacher would be able to see him now. The square was so beautifully lit that the mica in the stone blocks sparkled. There were no nooks or crannies where a rifleman could cover himself. Best of all, the roofs of the court buildings were angled slightly toward the ground. There were small catwalks between the roofs and the walls for maintenance people, but nowhere near enough room for a sniper to pull in his weapon. The barrel of the rifle would have to extend over the edge of the building.

Preacher took his time, mussed up Bobbie Sue's hair as he slowly turned his head. She laughed and scolded him, and all the while his eyes kept panning the rooftops.

Nothing.

The street, too, was quiet. The complexes along Third and Fourth streets had underground parking, so there weren't many vehicles left outside. Even with the upgraded police patrols in the neighborhood, few residents would risk smashed windows or stolen hubcaps.

Nonetheless, Preacher scanned them all, searching for anything that did not belong. If Johnson had been thinking surveillance, he would have had to settle for a van or a utility vehicle, something large enough for at least two people to operate out of.

"It's getting cold, baby," Bobbie Sue simpered. "Haven't you had enough fresh air?"

Preacher steered her onto the concrete walkway to the double front doors. He counted the second-floor windows to the left of the foyer until he came to those belonging to Judith Trask's apartment. It looked like Trask slept with a night-light.

The key that had been left for him with the Hilton's concierge stuck in the lock after Preacher had the front door open. He had to work it gently to get it out.

"That's better!" Bobbie Sue said, rubbing her hands briskly.

Preacher shepherded her across the lobby and into the small elevator. They bumped and ground their way to the second floor, and Preacher left a big suck mark on Bobbie Sue's neck, below her ear.

"I can tell you're *real* romantic!" She giggled.

He put a finger to her lips and she shut up.

To the left of the elevator, six apartments on each side of the hall; at the end of the corridor, two more. Judith Trask's was all the way down, on the right.

Preacher was still searching for the anomaly, taking the pulse of the building. The faint whistle of outside air coming through a window, then out underneath the front door into the hall; the buzz of overhead fluorescent lights. The chugging of an old heating system; faint canned laughter from some late-night sitcom rerun.

Nothing.

And just before the end of the hall, the trash closet. Preacher, gentleman to the last, had let Bobbie Sue walk ahead of him. For a time he'd watched her fine long legs. She'd served him well, given him the cover he needed. Johnson would have alerted his people to focus on a single man; an amorous couple, groping and laughing, wouldn't have registered.

"It's been sweet, *honey.*"

"Huh?"

Bobbie Sue was turning around, a smile playing on her face. She was still thinking about a nice, soft bed and this hard, well-built man with his pocketful of hundreds, when she felt something terribly hot slice through her. He caught her as she was falling. His breath puffed against her cheek, as if he were fucking her right there, except, God, it *hurt* so much.

Preacher's angle had been perfect. The blade of the modified fileting knife sliced cleanly through muscle and tissue, never nicked a rib, its tip barely touching the heart. Until he gave one final, gentle push.

Then he threw open the garbage-closet door and arranged Bobbie Sue on the plastic recycling bin. He made sure she wouldn't fall over and cause a mess before he'd said good-bye. Five steps, and he was in front of Judith Trask's apartment.

Preacher didn't have a key for this door, so he was listening hard. Faint voices . . . not the television. Someone talking, *two* people talking . . .

The vent was pouring hot air down his neck. Preacher was getting words now, snatches of conversation.

"Is that what Westbourne told you? He . . . in so many words . . ."

"It's true! . . . didn't want to know . . . the time I told him I loved him . . ."

". . . can't believe it . . . anything else you can remember . . . need to know . . ."

Preacher took a step back, drew in his breath through his mouth. Trask was not only up and awake; she had someone with her. A girlfriend? Late-night gabfest about unrequited love?

". . . anything else you can remember . . . need to know . . ."

It was Tylo in there. The certainty of it struck Preacher with such force that he had to squeeze his eyes shut. When he opened them, the gun, with its silencer, was in his hand.

There had been no surveillance outside, he was sure of that. Did that mean she had come here without *any* support?

She did that to get to Palmer. . . .

Now Tylo needed the same missing piece that Preacher had come for. She was here alone, and when she was done she would spirit Trask away. Tylo would think that Preacher was finished. The last time she'd seen him, he'd been running. She wouldn't expect him to reappear so quickly, if at all.

Preacher had calmed down now, satisfied with the explanation he'd sculpted. It was solid, with no loose ends or wishful thinking that could get him killed.

The single shot splintered the flimsy door handle; Preacher's shoulder ripped the burglar chain off the wall. The room was bathed in that rose light he'd seen from the street, and shadows fell across the carpet.

"Yes?"

"Like I said, Charles never read Webster. . . ."

Preacher lunged across the small dining area, his brain failing to make the connections he sought. Something was terribly wrong, but he couldn't understand what it was.

Why are they still talking?

His second shot was inadvertent, fired because panic had worked its way into his trigger finger. The bullet dug into the wall next to the stereo.

"Like I said, Charles never read Webster. . . ."

The voices were coming from a tape. On top of an antique chest was a cassette player, red power light staring back at him.

Preacher felt an unearthly peace, as though he were floating in warm water. Sometimes, in his idle moments, he had wondered how it would end for him. But what he'd never suspected or considered was how *suddenly* he would be taken.

Preacher was squeezing the trigger even as he was spinning around. He never heard the roar of Bryant's Mossberg shotgun. Instead, he felt its heat, then its force as it picked him up and slammed him against the bookcase. The second blast caught him just above the neck, shearing away his face and setting his hair on fire.

28

HOLLAND flinched when she heard the booms of Bryant's Mossberg. She was in the apartment across the hall from Judith Trask's, and after the deafening silence that followed she heard Judith whimper, saw that her hands were balled into fists, eyes squeezed shut.

The distance between the two women was fifteen feet, the same, Holland estimated, as between Bryant and Preacher. Nothing could take two hits from a Mossberg at that range and survive.

Holland went to Judith, careful not to step in David Cobb's line of fire. He stood facing the door, Uzi held waist high.

"Judith . . . Listen to me." Holland gently pried open her fingers. "Listen. It's all right. It's finished. There's no one out there who can hurt you."

As Judith clutched at her, Holland turned to keep her gun hand free.

"Are you sure he's dead?" Judith whispered.

Holland nodded. "I have to go back to your place now. There are things I have to do." She felt Judith's nails bite into her skin. "David is going to stay here with you. You won't be alone—not even for a second. When I come back, we'll all leave together. Okay?"

Holland pulled away from Judith's grasp, from her bewildered, wild expression.

Cobb shifted to let her pass, covered her as she opened the door and stepped out.

The hall was empty except for Maryanne Jenkins, who was covering it with a shotgun. The doors to the other apartments were closed, the units empty.

Two hours earlier, Holland, Maryanne, and Cobb had evacuated the floor, hustling sleepy tenants down the back stairs into the night, where two stretch panel trucks were waiting.

People respond better to Secret Service officers than to other law enforcement. They think that somehow the safety of the President is involved. Holland played on this, and the evacuation went quickly, the tenants on their way to accommodations laid out for them at the nearby Hyatt Regency.

Holland approached Judith's apartment. Pressed into a corner, she pointed her gun at the door, held to its frame by only the bottom bolts. At a distance of four feet, a bullet would go through both the hollow-core door and whoever was behind it.

Holland looked back at Maryanne, who had repositioned to her left, then called out, "Bryant!"

Seconds crawled by, and Holland felt her finger add two pounds' pressure on the six-pound trigger.

Preacher *couldn't* have survived, not two blasts—

"Clear! Tylo, it's clear!"

Recognizing Bryant's voice, she stepped around the torn-up door, the scent of cordite stinging her nasal membranes. The body lay in a heap at the foot of the bookcase. From the waist up, it resembled nothing human. A reflex thought, the kind that acts as a temporary shield against horror, snapped into Holland's mind: *They'll have to identify Preacher from his fingerprints. There's no face, no dental work, to use.*

Bryant was seated in the chair opposite the bookcase, Mossberg cradled in his lap. Holland thought he hadn't moved since firing.

"Tommy . . ."

The big man stirred, blinked. He looked at Holland and at the gun in his hands, and then his faraway stare melted. He took a deep breath, snorted, and tossed his head the way a horse would.

"You called it," he said to Holland. "You said he'd come after her, and he did." He paused. "I know Johnson wanted him alive, but there was no chance. The minute he was inside, he knew something was wrong. I think he saw the power light on the cassette player, put it together very fast. I know he hadn't seen me yet, but he started shooting anyway."

Bryant rose and laid a hand on Holland's shoulder. He was smiling, but his eyes were still cloudy.

"He came right to us. The way you'd rigged the place, he never had a chance."

Holland turned away, went to the stereo, and popped the tape of her conversation with Judith.

She had called Judith from the Stewart Center. Twenty minutes later, she was at Judith's apartment, sitting hard on her urgency, saying no to Judith's offer of Oreos with her coffee, praying that this woman could help her. And Judith had, by mentioning Daniel Webster . . . the *desk* that had belonged to that legendary figure . . . and had been used by Charles Westbourne in the Senate chamber.

After that, Holland had moved fast, shepherding Judith out of the apartment. Luck was holding, because the apartment across the hall belonged to Judith's friend, a nurse working the night shift at Georgetown Memorial. Judith had a key.

With Bryant and Maryanne handling the other tenants, Holland had worked hard on calming Judith. The minutes were flying by. Holland shut down her imagination so she couldn't hear Preacher's footfalls slapping in the distance, coming for her out of the darkness. She answered Judith's questions about Preacher with as much truth as she dared, painted him as a garden-variety crazy, a remote-controlled toy gone berserk.

When Judith finally understood what was needed from her, Holland got the tape recorder going. Later, she'd left Judith alone with David Cobb only long enough to slip across the hall to deliver the tape to Bryant.

The tape had been crucial. No one had had any idea how Preacher would be coming in, only that he was certain to avoid conventional surveillance. Maryanne and Cobb argued for sniper posts, but Holland said he'd be looking for those, spot them, and evaporate. So they'd put nothing on the perimeter, let him come all the way into the building.

Holland had heard the elevator door open, footsteps in the hall, but she didn't see him until he was in front of Judith's door. Through the peephole, he looked very far away.

Holland watched him standing there, listening hard to the voices inside. He must have been frustrated at first, because all he could hear were snatches of questions and replies. She was counting on his recognizing her voice and being thrown by it. Now he'd have to deal with two people in that apartment, one of whom he had to believe was armed. He couldn't ease his way in and take Judith the way he wanted to, give her his undivided attention. . . .

Holland had prayed that the sound of her voice would stoke his rage. She wanted his failure to kill Johnson to grind on him; she wanted him to see her in the red haze of his mind's eye, mocking him, her voice a siren's song, seducing him into that room where Bryant waited, his hands warming the twin barrels of the Mossberg.

"Holland."

Bryant's voice was strong, his eyes clear now, the executioner's guilt ebbing.

"We don't have to be here anymore. . . . Johnson's waiting. You have a call to make."

She felt him nudge her, then move over to her right side so that she wouldn't have to look at the corpse on her way out.

In the hall she saw Cobb with his Uzi and Judith behind him, her eyes darting around her. Maryanne was walking fast to the stairwell to bring around the transportation. Bryant motioned Cobb to follow. He held out his hand to Judith, smiling at her as he would to coax a timid animal.

Holland was headed down the hall, when suddenly she felt very cold. Bryant, already in the elevator, saw that she was hanging back.

"Go on," Holland called out. "I'll secure the scene and call Johnson."

Bryant wanted to go to her, but something in her expression stopped him.

Holland waited until she heard the whine of an electric motor before turning around and walking down the hall.

She came to the trash closet and stood very still. She didn't want to reach out and turn the knob. She was sick of wading through the blood and savagery Preacher had strewn for her.

But she couldn't erase the image of him coming down the hall. She had heard a voice . . . ? No—*voices.* The possibility that Preacher was not alone slammed into her mind. Then: *No, no way Preacher would have brought company. He worked alone.*

Yet the nagging memory of two voices would not go away, circled back on her, made her piece together *how* Preacher had approached the Capitol Hill Apartments.

He would have presumed there'd be surveillance, even though we would have had almost no time to set it up. He would have prepared for it, known we'd be looking for one man, alone. So he went out and got himself some camouflage. . . .

The metal door handle was slippery in her moist palm. She drew her weapon—with Preacher, she could not take any chances—and pulled open the door.

The woman was perched on a blue plastic recycling bin, like a sad, broken marionette. The clothes, makeup, hair, and overpowering perfume gave Holland an idea of who she might be and where Preacher would have found her.

Holland didn't bother to check for a pulse. The woman's white blouse was solid crimson. Gently she let the door close, took two steps back, and slumped against the wall, as with trembling hands she removed the phone from her pocket, hit the speed dialer.

When Johnson picked up, he did not caution Holland that Smith was listening on the extension. Her first words were, "Preacher's dead. He broke into Trask's apartment. Bryant didn't have any choice."

"Is everyone okay?"

"Fine. I'll need some uniformed Service people to preserve the scene until the D.C. police get here."

"They'll be there any minute."

As Holland gave him the details, Johnson thought she sounded better than she had any right to. But then he heard her voice falter as she struggled to distance herself from the horror. He wondered if Smith was picking up on any of this; the man's expression gave away nothing.

"Trask gave me what we needed," Holland said. "At least I'm pretty sure. We'll know in about an hour."

Johnson caught Smith's frown. "Hold on a second, Holland."

He put his hand across the receiver. "What do you want me to tell her?"

"What did Trask give her?"

"Holland, I have the director with me. We need to know what Trask told you."

The connection was silent for a moment. Johnson prayed Holland wasn't thinking of holding out on him, afraid that Smith would barge in and pull her back when she was so close.

"Trask confirmed Cynthia Palmer's reference to Daniel Webster," she said. "I've figured out what it means. All I need is—"

"Tylo, this is the director."

"Yes, sir."

"What exactly is this reference to Daniel Webster?"

Johnson noted that this time Holland didn't hesitate; she must have caught the impatience in Smith's voice. He listened to her explanation, amazed at how simple it was, his gut telling him that truly she had brought everything home.

"All right, Tylo. This *seems* to make sense. But it will also keep."

"Sir—"

"Listen to me. You've done some good work here. Don't spoil it for yourself now. Be in my office within the hour. Uniformed security will relieve you and liaison with the D.C. police.

"You have two immediate assignments. First, sit down with our Public Affairs people and tell them exactly what happened, so that they can hammer out a statement for the media. We have to be very careful here. People are going to ask whether there was anything we could have done to prevent Palmer's murder.

"Second, I need a full, written statement from you on everything that's occurred since the shooting at your home. We need a clear sequence of events and a list of all the players. What you've dredged up is going to stink. When the President calls me in, I want to know *exactly* what happened, how, and why."

"Yes, sir."

"Very well. I'll see you shortly."

Smith broke the connection and looked at Johnson.

"She's dead on her feet. Make sure she gets back here before she does something dumb."

In Croft's condo, the lights had been blazing ever since Preacher had failed to call in at the agreed time. Croft had been scanning the twenty-four-hour news services until the 3:30 A.M. report aired the story he was searching for: a shooting at the Capitol Hill Apartments, one known fatality, details sketchy because of a Secret Service quarantine of the area.

The report shook Croft. He had come to think of Preacher as infallible. The man was utterly ruthless. But Holland Tylo had escaped. Twice.

Had Preacher let the failure to kill her force him to hurry, to make him just that tiny bit sloppy?

Croft needed to know how Tylo had done it, and by four o'clock he had details, culled from his contact at D.C. Homicide. The chief of detectives, who owed his job to the senator's persuasive lobbying, told Croft that his men were seriously pissed at the Service for stonewalling their investigation. Homicide had been allowed to view the body, but the Service was waiting for its own cleanup people to move it. The coroner, smart enough not to get involved in a jurisdictional spat, had simply left.

The most important thing the chief of detectives said—without being aware of it—was that the identification found on the victim made him out to be Andrew McGee, a real estate broker from California. The chief added that it was just as well the next of kin would never see the body; the poor sonofabitch had been blown in half.

After he was finished with the detective, Croft swiftly riffled through his few options. It came down to a contingency plan he'd never really believed he would need. Now he turned it over in his mind, probed for weaknesses, found none.

The plan was audacious but perfectly viable. If properly executed, it would finally put an end to Holland Tylo's meddling, and Croft thought he had just the guiding hand he needed.

From his desk drawer he removed a magnetic diskette, slipped it into his computer, and scanned the material. There were more than enough details to set the hounds baying.

Croft checked the time, four-ten. He had a little under two hours before *Good Morning America* and the other shows came on. And there was always CNN, forever geared to run with a breaking story.

Croft made copies of the material contained on the diskette and carefully packaged each one. Then he placed three calls, to news executives who did not know his name or position but who listed him in their little black books as "Mr. Lynch," a high-level source who in the past had provided dramatic, totally accurate leads and information.

By four-thirty, Croft knew that the executives had rushed from their beds and were priming their news directors. Material from "Mr. Lynch" was on its way. Check it, get back to us, but be ready to run hard with it.

29

THE detail from Uniformed Division must have been pulling up as she'd been talking to Smith. Holland heard the clatter of combat boots in the stairwell, then doors bursting open. Four officers appeared in the hall, weapons out.

"Tylo?"

Holland glanced at the black man calling to her. "That's me."

"I'm Carswell, chief of detail. Is the area secure?"

"It's secure."

But she saw that Carswell didn't take her word for it. He fanned out his men to seal the exits. When he was close, Holland realized how young he was.

"You want to tell me what we have here?"

Holland nodded in the direction of the trash closet, then pointed down the hall.

"Two bodies. I think you'll need help."

Holland turned away as Carswell opened the closet door. She heard his sharp intake of breath, followed by a soft expletive. When he came back from Judith Trask's apartment, his eyes were wet.

Holland knew that Carswell wanted to question her, but he fell back on his training. The radio was chattering as he called in the two teams on standby, then put out an alert for someone

from Public Affairs to handle the media that would be flock-
ing. Only after he'd set up his perimeter did Carswell turn back
to her.

"My orders are to get you out ASAP."

"Let's go."

Holland followed him into the stairwell and out the fire door
into the raw predawn air. Outside, Carswell took care to shield
her from the view of D.C. police fishtailing up in their units,
scrambling across the slippery, muddy lawn.

"When they get a look at what's inside, they'll wish they never
came," Carswell muttered.

A white sedan was parked at the curb, engine running. Carswell hustled her inside, then talked briefly to the driver. The car
was already moving when he tapped on the window, gave Holland
a silent thumbs-up. She kept looking back for him long after the
sedan had jackrabbited down the street.

A uniformed officer was loitering by the security checkpoint in
the lobby at 1800 G Street NW, scanning the faces that drifted
by. There was more than the normal amount of foot traffic for
this hour, but the officer zeroed right in on her.

"Agent Tylo?"

"Yes."

"Would you follow me, please?"

"Is Deputy Director Johnson in the building?"

"I wouldn't know, ma'am. My instructions are to escort you to
the director's office."

Holland didn't press. In a roundabout way, the officer had answered her question. She began to marshal the arguments she
would use on Johnson.

The officer saw Holland as far as the double doors at the end of
the hall. Inside, an efficient-looking middle-aged woman smiled
hello and motioned for Holland to follow her. Holland, who had
never been on the top floor of 1800 G Street, took in the fine
wood paneling, the glass cases filled with trophies and medals,
the commendations in smart frames. One in particular made her
stop short.

The United States Secret Service Valor Award.

The silver disk drew Holland. Within the ranks, it was the stuff of legend, awarded to agents who had perished in the line of duty. Wyatt Smith was the only active Service agent ever to have been so honored while still alive.

"Agent Tylo?"

The secretary did not raise her voice. She understood the effect the Valor Award had on those who saw it.

Holland nodded.

They went past the director's office to the next set of doors, which opened on a formal conference room. The secretary left Holland to find her way around a table that could seat twenty, where Arliss Johnson stood pointing a remote control at a television monitor, one of six in a wall unit.

"You were right on the money, with Preacher."

At first Holland thought Johnson's subdued tone had to do with the pain and residual shock from the knife wound and the medication he was on. He had changed his shirt for a turtleneck sweater, bulky around the chest where the bandaging had been applied. Then she realized he'd been trying to corral a thought when she came in. He didn't have it yet, didn't want to give up trying, and now it was too late.

"What is it?" Holland asked.

Johnson shook his head. "You did fine," he said softly.

"It's not done yet," Holland said bluntly. "We know what Palmer meant by Daniel Webster. Judith Trask all but confirmed that."

"You *think* you know. And I'll venture you're right. But it'll have to keep."

Holland felt as though she'd been slapped. "No. Not after everything—"

"It'll keep, Holland."

Johnson hadn't raised his voice, but his tone made her stop short.

"There's a situation developing. Details are sketchy now, but when it breaks, we'll have to run hard."

"I don't—"

"Listen. You spoke to the director. You have your orders.

There's a laptop in the cabinet over there; I'll have someone bring you a pot of coffee."

He rose and slipped by Holland.

"About your report," he said. "Give the director every detail."

His brusque manner sanded away what little was left of Holland's patience. "What about the Daniel Webster reference? I need to confirm that."

"People will be reading this over your signature. Put it all in so that later no one can say that you were holding back."

The first light of day was crawling through the bulletproof windows, revealing on the conference table patches of dust the cleaning crew had overlooked. Pinpricks of high-intensity light overhead burned into Holland's red eyes, making them water. By her right hand was a tall mug of very strong coffee, which Smith's secretary had brought in for her. Caffeine, adrenaline, and raw frustration were her only company.

Holland took a sip of coffee and returned to the laptop, fingers flying. The facts weren't the problem; it was her tone she had to be careful with, keeping it dry and objective as she waded through the bloody recital.

A few times she found herself having difficulty breathing and stepped back from the work. Her anger turned on her then, working against her fatigue. Questions—about why Johnson had let Smith bulldoze him into bringing her here to write about things that were still unfolding—chased one another around her mind. The final answers were within her grasp, yet she was unable to reach for them. Looking out the thick-paned windows, Holland sensed events moving on the horizon, arranging and rearranging themselves the way a lava flow crushes and mutates the landscape. She could almost hear it, like the boom of a distant volcano.

The bells of Saint John the Divine tolled the half hour.

The door opened, and Johnson was back.

"Are you done?"

"Just have to print it."

Johnson's energy was keen, and Holland tapped into his pulse.

"What's happened?"

"In a couple of hours, this town's gonna explode." He pointed at the laptop. "You have the disk?"

Holland nodded.

"Give it to Kathy out front. She'll do the printout."

Holland shouldered her purse. "Now where are we going?"

"Kalorama. To pay Senator Zentner a visit. The van's downstairs. The networks are moving on this. You'll know all about it by the time we get there."

Kalorama Heights is a stately enclave of grand homes, located along the edge of Rock Creek Park, east of Sheridan Circle. Bryant had made good time weaving through the Georgetown morning traffic; now the van was sailing along Rock Creek Parkway. Holland gripped a handle above her head to keep from being tossed around while she watched the local ABC news.

The story had preempted everything. The national anchor, hauled in to quarterback the telecast, was talking about James Meredith Baxter, the recently convicted high-level CIA executive who'd been flushed out as a long-term Soviet spy. Baxter had told Agency and congressional investigators reams about his years as a traitor. At last count, it was estimated that he'd been responsible for the deaths of sixteen American agents in the former Soviet Union, along with countless others in Eastern Europe. The amount of technical information that had been transferred to Moscow was staggering; the effect on the Agency's morale and reputation was catastrophic.

CIA and congressional investigations had taken six months peeling James Meridith Baxter apart like a stalk of celery. In the end, they believed they had gotten everything. Listening to the anchor, Holland realized that Baxter had somehow managed to keep his trump hidden.

"The documentation appears conclusive and irrefutable," the newscaster said. "From information delivered to the media earlier this morning, it is clear that James Baxter was *not* working alone, as he himself has consistently maintained, and as investigators later on concluded.

"Throughout his reign of treason, Baxter had one powerful, invisible ally: Senator Hubert Baldwin, the senior senator from Tennessee.

Holland blanched, recalling the elderly senator she'd seen at Oak Farms. She shot Johnson a quick glance, received no reaction at all.

"Documents reveal that Baldwin had in fact been aware of Baxter's association with the intelligence services of the former Soviet Union," the newscaster continued, "and that on at least two occasions he served as a go-between for information Baxter had stolen from the Agency, to be handed over to his Soviet paymasters.

"Whether Senator Baldwin knew he was being used this way, whether he was in the pay of James Meredith Baxter or others, has yet to be determined.

"But at this time we do know that Senator Baldwin used his enormous influence on the Hill to deflect any investigations that might have been centered on Baxter. ABC's political analyst Mike Prescott tells us that Baldwin could have been covering Baxter for as long as five years.

"Mike, can you bring us up-to-date on what you've found out?"

Holland tuned out the correspondent's nasal drone while she waited impatiently for Johnson to finish his phone call.

"How much more is there?" she murmured when he swiveled around to face her.

"The networks have most of the meat," he replied. "The only reason they're offering it up in dribs and drabs is because the material is so hot. They don't trust their own confirmations."

"Has anyone spoken to Baldwin?"

"Not that I know of. Tennessee's an hour behind us. We can't be sure he knows anything's happened."

"Do you believe the material?"

"It's cherry."

Holland took a deep breath. "Have you seen any of it?"

"No. But I think you can guess where it came from."

The Westbourne diaries . . .

Holland stared at the bare trees flashing by, the hills of the park black from soil loosened by the spring runoff.

"Why are we going to Zentner's?" she asked quietly.

Johnson's tone held no pity or regret. "Because she'll end up putting Croft in prison for twenty-five years to life."

Bryant turned the corner at the Royal Thai embassy and steered up a heavily wooded drive. Holland had seen Senator Zentner's home, a sprawling red-brick Tudor, featured in the Sunday magazine lifestyle section. Stepping out of the van, she thought its most interesting feature was the front door, handcrafted honey-gold oak with a beautiful inset leaded window.

"Deputy Director Johnson, Secret Service," Johnson said to the housekeeper who answered the door. "This is Agent Tylo. We're here to see the senator."

The thin, fiftyish woman with pure white hair, who was dressed in a gray uniform, blinked like a robin. "Is the senator expecting you?"

But Johnson was already inside, Holland following fast. The housekeeper fluttered behind them.

"There's no danger, is there? To the senator?"

"None at all."

"Is she expecting—"

"It's urgent that we see her right away." Johnson pointed to sliding doors on his right. "She's in the library, right?"

"Yes, but—"

Johnson pulled the doors open, drew Holland inside, then whispered, "Close us up."

The furniture was nineteenth-century, heavy and graceless, the needlepoint seat cushions faded from sun. The curtains, like the rugs, were shiny where the fabric had frayed. All along the windows were planters, most with Asian designs, filled with exotic greenery. Curiously, there was no scent in the room save that of Barbara Zentner's overly sweet perfume.

"Who the *hell* are you?"

Wearing a powder-blue velour track suit, Zentner was curled deep in the cushions of the sofa, the TV remote control clutched tight in her hand. The set was tuned to CNN's coverage of the crisis surrounding her fellow Cardinal, Senator Hubert Baldwin.

Johnson presented his credentials, which Zentner actually took from his hand and examined.

On the inlaid-ivory table was a breakfast tray: orange juice, tea, toast with marmalade. The toast hadn't been touched, and the orange juice smelled rancid. It took Holland a second to recognize the scent—vodka, and plenty of it.

On the screen, reporters had laid siege to Baldwin's home, in the genteel section of Memphis.

"What are you doing here?" Zentner demanded.

Holland remembered those shiny, daggerlike eyes from her encounter with the woman at Oak Farms. Now those eyes found her again.

"You . . . the one who let Charlie get killed!"

Holland said nothing. Clearly, Zentner was drunk.

"I see you've been following the developments, Senator," Johnson cut in smoothly, nodding at the television.

"It's all crap!" Now Zentner was enraged. "None of it will stick. You don't know Baldwin. He's pure Teflon."

"Maybe," Johnson replied. "But he's going down on this. Take my word."

"I could have your *job* for that remark!"

"Another time, maybe, Senator. I've seen the evidence—*all* of it. Baldwin's in total meltdown. Now might be a good time to set the record straight."

"You have no jurisdiction here, *Deputy* Director. Does Wyatt Smith know you're here? I'll bet that if I pick up that phone—"

"It's Croft, isn't it?" Holland said softly.

She stepped forward, locked onto Zentner's startled eyes.

"I'm not talking to you!" Zentner said shrilly.

Holland sat down on a worn leather ottoman.

"Croft did all this for you, didn't he? He set up Westbourne, brought in the killer . . . but he did it for you and the others. The Cardinals."

"You're crazy!" Zentner whispered, a tinge of fear shadowing her words. "You don't know what you're talking about!"

"You're wrong, Senator. *I* trusted Croft too. That is, until he betrayed me."

"Betrayed you?"

"You didn't know he tried to have me killed? I'm not sure I believe that, Senator."

Holland looked intently at Zentner's ravaged face, swollen from vodka and lack of sleep, the heavy makeup starting to mottle.

"You used Croft, Senator. Westbourne had all of you under his thumb. He could make you do anything he wanted. That must have hurt, being blackmailed by one of your own.

"Then Croft offers you a way out. He's willing to take all the risks. He says he can get you Westbourne's diaries. You and the others don't think twice. Because no matter what Croft wants in return, the price is still cheap.

"Except it doesn't work out that way. *Croft never tells you he's already got the diaries.* He strung you along with promises. Until now."

Holland pointed at the television. "There's your proof. Croft is tearing Baldwin apart to prove he has the diaries—and to show what he's capable of if you don't do exactly what he says."

Holland caught her breath, suddenly aware of what she'd said. The words had been a white-hot epiphany, born in the crucible of murder and deceit. Without her realizing it, they had been floating in her subconscious, waiting for the catalyst that would pull them together.

But had she made a mistake, given away too much too soon?

"That *is* what happened, isn't it, Senator," she said, her tone flat, offering no reprieve.

Zentner dropped the remote control. Her hand shook as she clutched the glass, making the ice rattle. Orange pulp clung to her lips.

"You don't know anything," she muttered. "You don't have any proof."

Holland glanced at Johnson; he nodded back.

"That's where you're wrong, Senator," she said. "I think Croft didn't tell you how Westbourne had organized the diaries. They were on diskettes. That's what all this killing has been about—plastic."

Zentner glanced up sharply.

Good. She caught it.

"That's right, Senator. Croft led you to believe that there was only one diskette, and that if he could get it, you'd be all set for life—no questions asked, no checks on your power, no hint of your past actions. But he lied about that too. See, there're *two* parts to the diaries. He has one, and he's using it. . . . We have the other."

Holland saw that Zentner was wavering, but she didn't spare her. She leaned closer, tilted her chin slightly, and blew apart whatever hopes Zentner was clinging to.

"Your recent campaign, Senator. At the last minute, you crushed your opponent by claiming he had an illegal, tax-dodging war chest. The IRS moved in and verified it. Your opponent maintained his innocence, but no one was listening . . . and that's why he killed himself. . . .

"Only it wasn't his money in that account—the trail began at Golden West Financial in San Francisco, with money *you* put in there. The funds were then sent offshore, laundered through Caribbean and Panamanian banks, and then sent back to this country and dumped in an account that, unknown to your opponent, already had his name on it."

She paused. "Remember, Senator?"

Calling up the details she'd read on the diskette before Preacher had stolen it from her, Holland recited the names of the banks that had handled the money and the dates on which it had arrived in each jurisdiction. She gave them up one at a time, the way a poker player slowly turns over his cards, one by one, to humiliate his opponent.

Zentner had to believe that Holland could prove this and much more. Everything would be lost if the woman demanded to see the diskette. Holland was counting on the alcohol to help her now.

Zentner fumbled with a pack of cigarettes, drew one out, lit it. She smoked silently until there was a half inch of ash, and ignored it when it dropped down the front of her blue running suit.

"If I give you Croft, what do I get out of it?" she asked, staring out the windows.

Johnson cut in: "That'll be up to the attorney general, possibly even the President. I'll do what I can there."

Zentner snorted. "With your juice? Not much comfort there."

"It's as much as you're going to get, Barbara."

Holland was surprised by Johnson's familiar tone. She was learning something here—that the last few inches before capitulation were both the most delicate and the most treacherous. They had brought Zentner this far, but she had to make the crossing herself.

The senator looked around the room. Her vacant gaze reminded Holland of someone standing in an empty house that had once been a home, trying to find the memories of good times in the naked, silent walls.

"You have to choose your battles," Zentner murmured. "That's what I've always told myself." She looked up at Johnson. "You have your deal."

Johnson moved to the other side of the room to make a call. Holland drifted over, heard him talking to the attorney general, who was still at home, suggesting that for the moment she forget about the scandal erupting in Tennessee and instead pay Zentner a visit.

His second call was to Smith's office; the third to the duty officer of the Capitol Hill Police.

"The director's in his office," he told Holland. "Kathy said he's going over your report now."

"Let me go."

Johnson saw the plea behind Holland's determination.

"Let me go," she repeated. "I know where to look. I can bring it to you."

Johnson hesitated, then nodded.

"Take Bryant with you. As soon as you're inside, I want full communications to here. If it's not where it should be, get out."

Holland was puzzled by the concern in his voice, but she let it pass. After all, she thought, she was going to one of the safest places on earth.

30

THE van's heater was going strong when Holland slipped into the passenger seat. She blew on her fingers, suddenly thinking how cold it had been in Zentner's house.

"You did good in there."

Holland smiled at Bryant. He'd been miked the whole time, in case the situation inside spiraled out of control.

"You put it together very fast," Bryant said.

Holland slumped in the seat and stared through the windshield.

"It was the stuff on the TV about Baldwin. I kept asking myself why that was happening right now. The only answer I could find was that Croft was panicking. The only reason he would do that was because someone involved on his end might start to crack. He wanted to destroy Baldwin to make an example for the others."

Bryant reached for the gear lever but stopped, caught off guard by Holland's next words.

"That night at Oak Farms, when the Cardinals confronted Westbourne, they knew that even if he gave up his blackmail card, he'd still be murdered as soon as they left. Best of all, they all had perfect alibis. Every one of them left the meeting under Service escort.

She paused. "We were guarding murderers that night."

Now Bryant understood something about the emotions raging

inside Holland. In his world, those who cheated and deceived a
trust were on the bottom of the food chain.

"Johnson says you can finish this thing."

"Yes, I can finish it."

"Okay, then . . ."

Bryant slipped the van into gear. He slapped a red bubble light
on the roof, then got it and the siren going as soon as they entered
Rock Creek Parkway.

It was a little after seven. Holland began to get edgy as she
watched the morning traffic build up at the on-ramps. She
glanced at Bryant, who reached for the telephone, talking to the
watch commander at D.C. Motorized Division.

The police outriders picked them up where New Hampshire
Avenue feeds into Washington Circle. Traffic along Pennsylvania
Avenue veered to the side as the motorcycles swept by, the van
trailing in their slipstream. At the most congested intersections,
closer to the White House, police cruisers had blocked off traffic,
giving them a clear run past the Federal Triangle.

First Holland saw the Reflecting Pool; then, rising from the
morning mist, the bronze statue of Freedom atop the Capitol
dome. She watched as the motorcycle escort peeled away when
Bryant swung around to the East Entrance. Even at this hour,
tourists were huddled under the portico, sipping coffee from
paper cups, waiting for the tour of Congress in session.

"Should have used the West Entrance," Bryant muttered.
"Who would have figured rubberneckers on a day like this."

"We can call the doorkeeper—"

"Already did."

He pointed at a figure who had just opened the doors and was
shooing back the tourists. After parking the van away from the
crowd, he reached back for the small aluminum case that Holland
knew contained the Uzi submachine gun.

"We won't need that," Holland said.

Bryant shrugged, locked up the van, and set a fast pace for the
doors. Holland had her ID out. She kept her eyes straight ahead,
ignoring the stares and whispers from the knot of sightseers.

The doorkeeper passed them through without question or comment. Holland heard the doors close behind her like thunder

rolling across the prairie. Then there was only the silence of the ages, drifting down from the soaring ceiling.

"We can take it from here, thanks," Bryant told the doorkeeper as they headed down the Brumidi Corridor, passing the murals that Constantino Brumidi and his assistants had painted over the course of twenty years. "No one else is in here, right?" he called back over his shoulder.

"Not so's I know," the doorkeeper replied. "But there are other ways to get in."

Holland scarcely heard him. She was already inside the Marble Room, with its Corinthian columns and walls of variegated Tennessee marble, where the senators carried on their horse trading. A flash of memory pierced her: the first time her father had brought her here. She recalled the pungent cigar smoke and gruff conversations, how she'd blushed when the men reached down to shake her hand, pat her on the head. Holland remembered how proud she'd been of her father that day, how her imagination had danced when she thought of all the good, important things he did there.

Passing through the Marble Room, she came to the glowing cherrywood doors of the chamber and gripped both handles. Behind her, she heard the latches on Bryant's aluminum case click open. One flick of his wrist, and the case would fall away, the submachine gun would be in his hand.

Holland pulled back the doors and stood facing the threshold of the empty sanctum. She took one tentative step, glancing up at the gallery, then across the blue-and-gold carpet and the semicircle of desks that faced the Speaker's rostrum. A soft cry escaped her lips.

Standing to the right of the rostrum, partially hidden by the large flag, was James Croft.

Johnson, still at Zentner's house, was listening to Attorney General Madeline Crawford interrogate the senator.

A tall, willowy woman, Crawford favored silks and pastels and wore designer-frame glasses that added to her society matron appearance. It was extremely effective camouflage for a former federal prosecutor from Los Angeles. Her experience showed in the way she handled Zentner.

Johnson was reaching for the telephone, when he suddenly noticed that the voices had stopped. Barbara Zentner was leaving the room.

"Where's she going?" he asked quickly.

"Upstairs to the bathroom," Crawford replied.

"I suggest you send the female marshal up with her."

Crawford looked at him strangely, then understood what he was getting at. She motioned to the marshal, sending her on her way.

"You had her under a suicide watch, didn't you?" she asked Johnson. "I was wondering why she looked like a wreck."

"Who knows what she has upstairs in the bedroom. I didn't want to find out the hard way."

Crawford looked away, shaking her head. "I don't suppose you've heard."

"Heard what?"

"Baldwin, in Tennessee. He managed to get to a hunting rifle before the marshals could break down the door to *his* bedroom." Crawford paused. "I wonder what the rest of them—the ones Zentner's been talking about—are considering."

"They might decide to fly."

"They can try," she replied grimly. "My people have National, Dulles, and Baltimore-Washington covered. Names have been posted on the FAA hot sheets in case they try for a private charter. No one's going anywhere."

The attorney general crossed the room to meet an aide who was waving a fax in his hand, and Johnson made his call. He was surprised when Kathy, the director's secretary, informed him that Smith still hadn't come out of his office.

"Do me a favor, Kath? Poke your head inside and tell him it's urgent. Thanks."

While he waited, Johnson wondered if Holland had found what she was looking for. He expected to hear from her very soon. If Holland was right, Attorney General Crawford's day would go from bad to worse in a big hurry.

"I'm sorry, Arliss," Kathy said. She sounded puzzled and a little miffed. "He's not in his office."

"Say again?"

"Well, I know he *was* in there, because I saw him. Something urgent must have come up and he used the VIP exit."

Johnson knew that Smith's office had a special waiting room for people who didn't want to be seen coming to him. The arrangement was much like a psychiatrist's suite where a patient can leave without going back through the waiting room.

"Any idea what happened, Kath? Did he get any calls?"

"No. But he made one."

"Pull it up on the screen, please." All calls made on in-house phones were logged in the computer.

"Arliss, I can't do that. . . ."

"You know what hit town this morning. There's something the director needs to know, because I think he might reach out to the wrong people. I can't be sure until you give me the number."

Her hesitation was palpable, but finally Kathy rattled off the number, her voice barely a whisper. Then:

"Arliss? Are you there?"

Kathy had no idea she was speaking into a receiver that was dangling above a parquet floor, that Johnson was racing out of the house, oblivious to the shouts behind him.

Holland's eyes bored in on James Croft. Stunned, she forced her legs to keep moving down the carpeted aisle to the first row of desks.

Behind her, she heard the rattle of Bryant's aluminum case hitting the floor. Then a metallic click turning off the safety. The weapon was now on full auto.

Croft stepped around the flag, an amused smile on his fleshy lips. His arms hung away from his body, a signal to Bryant of his benign intentions. He came as far as the area between the two desks where the pages sat, directly in front of the rostrum, planted his feet well apart, and watched.

Holland was down three tiers, moving sideways now past the

mahogany desks that had been brought from the Old Senate Chamber. Holland's fingertips grazed the smooth, worn wood surfaces, some dating back to 1819. Now, just as during her first visit here as a girl, she thought they resembled oversize elementary school desks.

She was less than a dozen feet from Croft, in front of a particularly worn desk, its top nicked and scarred. Holland didn't need to read the nameplate to know to whom it belonged.

"Tommy?"

She lifted the top.

"You're covered," Bryant called back.

Holland looked into the desk and read the graffiti. Even here, in this august chamber, the honorable men of the United States legislature had indulged in schoolboy pranks. Carved in crude letters on the bottom were the names of the man who had first used it, Senator Daniel Webster, and the one who had sat at it last, Charles Westbourne.

Holland's fingers moved lightly in the nooks and crevices, her nails scraping up the ancient grime. She had to search the space three times before her touch found a slight depression, which she'd mistaken for warped wood. Holland tested the edges, and the panel came away with a squeak. Beneath the false bottom was a cavity one inch deep, six inches square. It was empty.

"Bravo, Holland!" Croft said. "I would have been disappointed if you hadn't come to the proper conclusion. Shall I show you what I found?"

With a slow, exaggerated motion, Croft dipped his hand into his breast pocket and drew out a diskette.

"This is what you're looking for, yes?"

"Put the diskette on the table beside you, Senator. Slowly."

Holland thought her voice trembled a little; she wondered if Croft had caught that. His eyes glinted at her, smooth, light opals set in pink latex.

"No, Holland, I won't do that. Technically, this is Senate property, and as such I have more right to it than you do."

"It's evidence in a murder investigation."

"A daring leap of the imagination, Holland. But then again, you have such a fine mind." Croft sighed. "It would have been so much better had you come to me at the waterfront. Actually, so much of what has happened could have been avoided if you'd just minded your own business. True, Westbourne made a stupid mistake, giving you the wrong diskette, but you compounded it by not handing it over to someone in authority—the Senate security office, for example. Or even Miss Trask."

"You would have killed her anyway," Holland said. "Or tried to."

Croft ignored that. Holland realized that so far he had said nothing that could even tarnish him, much less hang him.

"Westbourne always had such a flair for the dramatic," Croft mused. "Not that you would know that. But take my word for it. I mean, keeping the diskette here, of all places! I can't understand why it took me so long to see the obvious." He stopped for a moment, his eyes scanning the upper tiers. "About Daniel Webster's desk. It's part of Senate folklore. What do *you* know about it, Holland?"

"In the 1830s, writing boxes were added onto the desk, to give senators more space. The only one who refused to have his desk changed was Webster."

"Very good, Holland." Croft applauded softly, but it sounded very loud in the hushed chamber. "Nice to know there's still value to be had in a liberal arts education.

"And of course you realize that only senators from New Hampshire—Westbourne's state—are permitted to use this desk. . . . So when I finally asked myself what would be the safest place in the world to hide something, a place both convenient yet one which no one would dare intrude upon, I remembered Mr. Webster from New Hampshire."

Holland knew that at another time she would have accepted Croft's explanation. It was reasonable and logical, the conclusions delivered smoothly. But her senses were tuned to the breaking point, and on that fine, taut filament quivered a host of lies.

Maybe it was something on her face, a change she couldn't control or didn't even know had come over her. Croft's bemused expression hardened, and again his eyes darted up to the gallery that rings the chamber.

He didn't come alone!

The thought cost Holland a split second; her shout reached Bryant too late.

"Gun! In the gallery!"

Bryant reacted fast, twisting around so that he could cover the semicircular visitors' area with his weapon. He was raising the Uzi when the first bullet tore into him, sending him crashing into the aisle, the submachine gun spinning out of reach.

The second bullet—another soft, silenced pop—slammed into Croft's chest.

"Holland!" Johnson's voice.

She had thrown herself in Croft's direction, was crouching beside him now, hearing the awful, sucking noise of his chest wound, her gun trained on the gallery. Searching for Johnson: "He's in the gallery! Bryant and Croft are down!"

She saw Johnson then, bent over almost double, trying to use the senators' desks for cover as he came to her.

"No!" she screamed. "Don't come out from under the gallery—"

A shot splintered wood next to Johnson's cheek.

Oh, Jesus, he's moved! He's coming around to the end of the horseshoe. . . . This one's good. He couldn't have anticipated Johnson's being here, but he hasn't panicked. The alarms have gone off, but he's still hunting. . . .

Suddenly the image of Preacher slammed into Holland's mind, and with it came the thought that he had somehow cheated the grave.

He's laid out on a fucking stainless-steel-slab in the county morgue!

Her anger erupted then, her finger hard on the trigger, the big SIG-Sauer booming. Under the rotunda, bits of plaster were flying as Holland stitched a half-moon pattern.

Keep the bastard down, make him worry a little!

Because of the gunshots, she never heard the explosion that brought down Johnson, but she saw him clutch his leg and tumble into the aisle. Holland ratcheted a fresh magazine into her gun and went through the entire load as she raced to him. Her heart froze when she saw one of the gallery doors swinging wildly.

"Tommy?"

"I'm okay. Flesh wound right through the ass."

Johnson was crawling toward Croft when Holland reached him.
"He got me in the leg. It'll be okay. Croft?"

Holland removed Johnson's belt and wrapped it tightly just above his knee. Then she scrambled to where Croft lay, eyes wide open, staring at one of the mottoes over the main door.

" '*Annuit Coeptis . . . ,*' " he rasped. " '*God has favored our undertaking. . . .*' Not likely."

His hand clutched Holland's. She forced herself not to recoil at the touch of his white cold flesh.

"Wasn't supposed to be me. Why was he shooting at me?"

Then Holland did something she would not have believed herself capable of. Laying aside her gun, she worked her arm under Croft's neck and cradled his head in her lap. She bent over him, so close that some of her hair brushed across his face. She whispered consolement until his breathing slowed and she felt the hot breath of his confession in her ear.

31

REPORTS of gunfire in the Senate chamber were all over the Service dispatch as Wyatt Smith braked his car in front of the southwest gate of the White House.

He had kept an open line to the monitor at Command and Control. Extra security units had already arrived at the Capitol, with more scrambling to seal off the entire Hill. Service medical teams and equipment were inside. First reports had two agents down, wounded but not critically. As the gate officers rushed up, Smith looked from the White House to Pennsylvania Avenue, then back again. Ever since a demented pilot had plowed his light plane across the South Lawn, and then over the next months several gunmen had opened fire from Pennsylvania Avenue, security around the White House had been rethought and restructured. Smith saw more uniformed guards along the avenue; in the crowds that gathered to take pictures through the wrought-iron fence were men in college varsity jackets and long topcoats who were neither alumni nor passing businessmen. Across the street, in front of Lafayette Park, specially armored cars and utility vehicles had taken up positions, ready to give chase or to button up the avenue.

And there were things Smith knew were there but couldn't see

—the snipers on the roofs of the family quarters and the West Wing, and other things too. . . .

The duty officer at the gate delivered a terse report on the current alert level.

"Good," Smith said. "I'm going in to make sure the President stays there. Except for Service personnel, no one—I don't care what their credentials are—gets through until I say otherwise. Understood?"

The gates rolled back.

Smith left ten feet of rubber on the semicircular drive that rolled grandly past the North Lawn.

Three-quarters of a mile to the east, Holland was fighting her way through the morning traffic piled up along Independence Avenue. She had gambled on this route instead of Pennsylvania and lost; ahead, in front of the Air and Space Museum, were heavy trucks and cement mixers, yellow lights flashing, men in orange Day-Glo vests, waving caution flags.

She was in Johnson's car, siren wailing, dome light spinning. But Washington drivers are used to sirens and ignore them.

Holland spotted an opening in the left lane, stomped on the accelerator, and shot into the space, only to stand hard on the brakes. She ignored the vulgar gestures and the blaring horns that could be heard over the construction noise. Frustrated, she waited for another opening, spotted it, and pulled out into the oncoming traffic.

Her windshield was filled with hurtling slabs of metal as cars swerved to avoid her. She expected that any second now one of them would plow into her, but miraculously she got by with only fender scrapes and bruises. At Seventh Street, she took the corner hard, raced past the Sculpture Garden, and then ran a full red on Constitution. On Pennsylvania now, she kept her speed, zigzagging through traffic, tires smoking as she caromed past the taxis bunched up in front of the Willard Hotel.

Half a block to go now, dodging traffic coming off Fifteenth Street, racing toward the cordoned-off parking area, demolishing two zebra-striped sawhorses to avoid plowing into a limousine cruising into her path.

Then Holland was out of the car and running up the wide stone steps of the Treasury Department, trying to calculate the distance for her leaps, careful not to trip. Inside, under the great rotunda, she stopped abruptly, gasping. Ten seconds was all she could spare to compose herself so that the guards in the foyer wouldn't slow her down with questions.

Taking a deep breath, she fell behind the early-bird secretaries. She held her ID at face level, making it easier for the guard to compare her features with those in the photo.

"Running a little late, are we?"

Holland managed to simper.

The guard waved her through, and Holland bolted left, away from the workers herding to the elevators. Down two flights of stairs, she found herself in front of a solid steel door. The guard here, in civilian dress and armed with a submachine gun, was sharper than the one upstairs. After carefully examining her credentials, he gestured at the bottom of Holland's sweater.

"Blueberry jam with your pancakes this morning?"

Holland stared down at her waist, touched the dark, sticky mess.

"Yeah. Guess it's not my day."

"Know anything about that panic over on Capitol Hill?"

Holland shook her head. "I was just pulled in on the general scramble. I need to get inside now so I can change before I stand my post."

The agent shrugged as he pressed the buzzer underneath the desk. The steel door swung open. Holland stepped into a cement-lined silo, hurried down a spiral staircase, then stopped short when she saw the seemingly infinite corridor ahead of her. Lined with white tile and lighted by long fluorescent tubes in wire-mesh cages, this was the tunnel, the three-hundred-sixty-yard connection between Treasury and the White House.

Holland stepped onto the moving sidewalk, the kind airports use to link terminals, and began trotting, the rubber treadmill acting like a spring coil beneath her steps.

Blueberry jam . . .

Croft's face, a rictus of anguish and disbelief, flashed into her mind. She remembered how light his head had felt in her lap, the way his words had emerged on bubbles of blood.

At first she couldn't—wouldn't—believe what he was telling her. She thought it was his final joke on her, an insult wrapped around a vicious, monstrous lie. But she had kept listening, straining to hear every syllable over the hoarse grunts of wounded men, the shouts of security arriving outside the chamber. Even at the very end, as the final rattle shuddered through him, Croft did not repent but kept repeating one name over and over in a dying litany.

When he was dead, Holland turned and saw Johnson, who had crawled over to her. He was waving back the paramedics, shouting at them to attend to Bryant. When his eyes came back to her, Holland realized he'd heard much of Croft's confession, for he had the look of a man overwhelmed by a terrible truth. That was when she knew Croft had died in grace.

Johnson gripped her wrist. "Can you see it?" he demanded. "Does it make sense now?"

She shook her head violently.

"Do you see it?" he thundered.

"All right! Yes! But—"

"But it's *not over!* Memorize this—now!"

Halfway through the tunnel, over the slapping of her feet on the treadmill, Holland recalled more of Johnson's words. When he was sure she had it, he told her more: the things he suspected, the traps he'd laid, and the truths that had been snared in them. Then he pushed her away roughly, ordering her to get going.

Holland remembered backing away, remembered the look of betrayal that burned in Johnson's eyes, his shouting at her to run. The last thing she saw before the medics swarmed over him was Johnson clutching his phone, stabbing at the numbers, one arm held high to fend off those who wanted to help him.

Her breathing was becoming ragged, the warm, recirculated air in the tunnel burning her lungs. At fifty yards out, Holland staggered and almost tripped, then caught the handrail, kept her momentum, slowed when she saw the end of the autowalk. She was underneath the White House.

The corridor veered right, but that's not where Johnson had told her to go. It took Holland a minute to find the second exit, recessed in the darkness. The heat of her finger activated the security keypad, set its buttons glowing. She paused, willing her hand to stop trembling, silently playing back the numbers Johnson had had her memorize.

The keypad beeped after she'd pressed the last number in the sequence. She stepped back, her gun out and ready. Johnson had warned her not to be lulled into safety, even here, ninety feet directly below the Oval Office.

Like the door at the other end of the tunnel, this one swung open smoothly and quietly. Now Holland picked up the smell of thick lubricating grease and the dank odor of trapped air spilling out. That's how she knew no one could have opened the door recently. Still, when she entered the cement silo, her back was hard against the staircase railing, her arms stretched out and up, the sights of her gun trained on the first landing, then the next, and the next. . . .

Johnson's expression was like that of an angry cornered badger, but the paramedics ignored it as they worked on him, doing exactly what he wanted them to and no more. The bullet had gone clean through his leg, taking flesh but only grazing the bone. A dressing was applied and a pressure bandage slapped on. The medics were watching for signs of shock, but all they saw on Johnson's face was raw, red rage.

Then they moved on, leaving him where they'd found him, slumped against the cold marble of the Speaker's rostrum.

Johnson dialed the monitor at Command and Control. Within seconds he was patched through to both guard posts on the Pennsylvania Avenue side of the White House. He identified himself and gave orders to clear Holland if she came through their way.

The next call, with the same instructions, went to the Service detail stationed in the White House itself.

Johnson had to stop there. His leg was throbbing badly, and he knew that the pain, coupled with the loss of blood, would soon cloud his judgment. He had to make his decision now: gamble that Holland could beat the clock, or go for the general alert, shut down *everything,* turn the White House into a bunker.

Johnson was still considering the options when his phone went off.

It was the monitor, sounding hesitant and uncertain.

"White House posts just reported back. After talking to you, they remembered Tylo had already been cleared. Were you aware of this, sir?"

Johnson dropped the phone on the carpet, and a low, terrible groan uncoiled from deep within him.

He saw it all now: Holland racing through the tunnel, reaching the door, punching in the combination he'd had her memorize, taking that deep breath to quash her fear before she stepped into the narrow silo.

Now she was climbing, listening hard, the gun slippery in her grip.

When she reaches the top, there's another door, unlocked. Its other side looks like part of a wall in the Oval Office, the seams almost invisible. She pushes it open, expecting to see the President, ready to call out to him to come with her. She'll take him by force if necessary.

But all she sees is the President's body slumped in the chair behind his desk. Shock takes hold of her. She never hears Wyatt Smith take that one step to get close, never hears the bullet that blows her head apart or sees Smith stoop down and retrieve her gun . . . then press *his* gun—the one he used to kill the President—into her hand, slip her weapon into his shoulder holster.

Seconds later, when Smith reopens the electronic locks, his troops pile in. There's the director, eyes locked on the body of the rogue agent he just gunned down . . . but not before she got to the President.

No one would suspect that all this had been a trap, that Smith had deliberately left open the door leading from the silo into the Oval Office. Left it open because he knew that she was coming, and that this was his last chance to watch her die.

Tears blurring his vision, Johnson fumbled with his remote

communications unit, squeezing the button that would send an electronic pulse to its twin, which Holland wore clipped to her belt. It was his only way to warn her.

The unit's red eye fluttered but refused to glow, which would have indicated firm contact. Holland was already in the silo, surrounded by six feet of impenetrable reinforced steel and concrete, out of reach. . . .

Wyatt Smith swept into the central corridor that dead-ended at the Oval Office. He ignored the fierce burning sensation at the base of his spine, refused to give in to it by slowing his pace.

The secretaries and clerical staff looked up from their work. Their eyes told Smith they'd heard all about the shooting in the Senate. Now here was the Director of the Service, on his way to the President. Smith had doubled the guard here; that had not gone unnoticed.

Smith nodded to his men standing post in the hall. Their suit jackets were unbuttoned; those who carried the Uzis kept one finger on the release trigger of their attaché cases.

In front of the doors to the Oval Office sat the airman who carried the "football," the briefcase that contained the nuclear go codes. At this moment he was flanked by two agents and looked no more than a boy between them.

Smith nodded to the President's secretary, who tried to smile. Her hand dropped behind her desk, and the electronic lock on the doors snapped open. Smith paused, took one final glance at the people who had stopped to watch him, and stepped inside.

"Yes, Wyatt, what is it?" The President had been writing, his head bowed. Now he looked up. "You said it was urgent."

My President . . . My oath to protect him . . . My pain . . .

With his left hand, Smith undid his jacket button and swept the fabric aside. He wanted to speak, but all the words were ashes in his mouth.

Because Preacher, whom I spirited back from the dead, is now really dead. Because I didn't kill Croft with that first bullet, fired from the Senate gallery. Because Tylo reacted so fast, coming much closer to hitting me than she could ever suspect. And be-

cause Johnson burst into the Chamber, forcing me to take him down, stealing the time I needed to put Croft away . . . Croft dying but not yet done, and Tylo scrambling to him . . .

How much did he tell her? A few words would be enough to destroy me. So there is no choice. . . .

Come now, Holland.

Smith moved quickly, finding the switch that sealed the doors to the Oval Office. He barely registered the President's expression of surprise, had the gun in his hand before he was even aware of it. Feet apart, arms straight out, the barrel no more than eight feet from the target's forehead.

Smith heard only the hiss, felt the wind buffet him as the Plexiglas cocoon dropped from the ceiling. Even as he jumped back, his finger was working the trigger, the bullets slapping into the three-inch-thick plastic compound, creating instant spiderwebs as they squashed into fat, useless pieces of lead, the copper jackets as flat as pennies.

Smith stared at the man inside the cocoon, his arms thrown around his head. He didn't turn around, or wait to hear a sound behind him, before he spoke.

"So you made it after all, Tylo. Just like I wanted you to. You came too soon, is all. . . ."

Holland stepped from behind the door, her gun trained on Smith's back.

"Put your weapon down, sir. Now!"

"You have no right to ask me to do that." Smith nodded toward the door. "Hear them banging to get in? It'll take a while; not so long, really, but enough for us to finish here."

Holland's gun felt like an anvil in her hands. She wanted to say so much. She wanted to grab Smith by the throat and throttle the answers out of him. And she knew that even by thinking that, she was playing into what remained of his game.

"Put down the fucking gun!"

"No."

She watched Smith shake his head. And she saw one more inch of the barrel of his gun as he shifted.

"In my body I carry bullets meant for men who are so much less than you or I."

This anguished cry from a man who had come to hate his masters froze Holland. She was powerless to stop what was happening now: Smith whirling around, his body braced by his left leg, his shoulders dropping, torso clearing so that he could get off an unobstructed shot. She saw the President cower, Smith's gun rise toward her, his finger freezing on the trigger. In the last instant, Smith turned his wrist. She never heard herself scream as he jammed the gun barrel into his mouth, never heard the explosion that hurtled him against the cocoon.

32

CHIEF of White House Detail Jerry Keppler had been radioed about the shooting in the Senate chamber even before the gunfire died away. He had followed the Service imperative: When a situation erupts, seal up your own turf; don't think about what's happening elsewhere. First shots have been known to be a diversion.

Keppler had a second-stage alert in place by the time Smith arrived in the Oval Office corridor. He noticed that Smith was scanning the posts as he walked; that he made no comment to Keppler indicated that Keppler had overlooked nothing.

Keppler was six feet away from the President's secretary's desk. On the wall, above a framed photograph of her family with the Chief Executive, the red light on the status panel indicated that Razorback had someone in with him and was not to be disturbed. Later, Keppler reckoned that Smith had been in the Oval Office for fifteen or twenty seconds before the second light, amber, began to flash.

Keppler knew immediately that the electronic locks had been activated. He was turning in the direction of the Office doors, frowning, when the alarm went off, a series of sharp, persistent pings.

"Cocoon's down!" he yelled.

Keppler kept moving, his eyes missing nothing. The weapons

were out, bullets ratcheting into firing chambers. The President's
secretary, two assistants, and a Capitol Hill runner were yanked
to their feet and pushed down the hall, handled roughly by a
string of Service agents like runners passing the baton in a relay.

One agent had the airman with the "football" squeezed into an
alcove, covering him with his body; his partner was blanketing a
one-hundred-eighty-degree field of fire with his submachine gun.

"Video!" Keppler yelled.

"Video down!" someone called back.

The Oval Office is equipped with four strategically placed invisible cameras, which can be activated only at the President's discretion. But once they're on, it is possible for someone to watch
on a remote monitor located outside the Office.

Keppler knew that the President would not be taping his meeting with Smith.

"Time check!" he barked.

"Fifty-two seconds."

Keppler stepped in front of the two agents whose shotguns
were leveled at the locks and handles on the doors. He knelt, ran
his fingertips along the fine cherrywood, tried the handles, and
stepped back.

"Charges," he said quietly.

The doors to the Oval Office, solid core, reinforced with high-
stress steel plates, have locks cast from the finest alloys Diebold
produces. Even at point-blank range, shotgun blasts would only
shatter the wood veneer.

The two agents, who practiced this drill once a month, took up
positions at either side of the doors. From a foam-lined aluminum
case, they removed charges of plastic explosives the size of quarters. They fixed these to the eight hinges, then strung the wires
that fed into the detonator. Twenty-five seconds later, one of the
agents activated the twelve-volt battery. Then he glanced at Keppler, who nodded.

Making sure that everyone was covered, hands protecting ears,
eyes turned away from the flash, the agent pushed down on the
button.

The charges blew, sharp cracks sounding like splintering two-
by-fours. Both doors sagged, buckled, then smashed to the floor.

Keppler's ears rang from the blast as he hurtled into the Office. When he saw the fissures on the Plexiglas, he felt sick. But there was copper and lead embedded in the cocoon. Inside it, the President was yelling words that Keppler couldn't hear, pointing wildly at something.

Keppler saw Smith then, followed the bloody streak along the Plexiglas, made by what was left of Smith's head as he'd slid down the side of the cocoon. Now he was slouched on his side, looking as if he had passed out.

Keppler waved at the agents piling in to hold their positions. Smith's gun lay a few feet away from his body. Keppler knew what a suicide shot looked like. The only other way Smith could have been shot like that was if he'd allowed someone to jam the gun barrel down his mouth.

And there was someone in the bathroom; he heard water running in the basin. The partially open door permitted Keppler a glimpse of a weapon on the marble vanity.

Keppler motioned to an agent to cover him.

"Identify yourself!"

His voice carried over the sound of water being spit out, the faucets let out all the way. Keppler took one step, then froze as a radio unit went off. Without taking his eyes off the bathroom door, he held out his hand for the phone.

It was Johnson. Keppler heard commotion in the background, guessed that Johnson was still in the Senate chamber. Now Johnson was telling him about the body count, asking what was happening in the Office, if the President was safe and if Tylo was still alive. And where was Smith?

"Sir, the President is secure," Keppler said softly. "Please hold one minute." He turned to his men. "Stand down. Full safety. Seal up the outside. Anyone asks, we were testing a new security feature and ran into glitches."

Keppler then pushed open the bathroom door and saw the woman leaning over the sink. She looked at him in the mirror, and he saw that her face had been scrubbed pink, almost raw. Then she dropped her head low over the basin and rubbed furiously at her hairline and temples. Her fingertips came away bloody; bits of white, like grains of sand, fell into the sink. Kep-

pler recognized them as the only thing they could be: bone splinters from Smith's skull.

He turned away, took a deep breath, and spoke into the phone.
"She's all right, sir. We'll take care of her."

WHEN Holland opened her eyes, she was confused. Hospital smells were shot through with the scent from a floral bouquet on the credenza. The room was very large, done in soft pastels, with a sitting area and a minifridge under a counter. On one wall was the framed seal of the Georgetown University Medical Center.

Holland turned her head, and saw Meg in an easy chair close to the bed.

"Hi, old chum." Her words came out as a croak.

Meg rose and hugged her. She felt Holland's hands tremble and the splash of tears on the side of her neck. She handed Holland a tissue and turned away while she blew her nose, then gave her a tumbler of cool water.

"How long have I been here?"

"Six hours. The paramedics gave you a shot because you wouldn't get out of that damn bathroom."

"There was a man . . ."

"Jerry Keppler. He brought you in, handled you like fine china. He wouldn't let you out of his sight until the doctors pushed him out."

"And?"

Meg shifted from foot to foot, looked up at the ceiling. "And he asked for my number, thought maybe he and I could go for pizza."

"Pizza . . ."

"You can come too."

"Uh huh."

Holland pushed herself up on the pillows. The light fled from her eyes, and Meg knew she was remembering.

"The President?"

"Everyone's okay. The President. Johnson. In fact, Johnson's here too, raising hell because they wouldn't let him in to see you."

"Smith?"

"Johnson said he'll talk to you about that as soon as you're up to it. He asked me to tell you that if you hadn't been there, the President would be dead."

Holland closed her eyes, concentrated on the throbbing at her temples, embracing the pain because that was the only thing that would free her from the bloody images.

She had no recollection of how much time had passed before she said, "I need to wash up."

Meg rummaged in her backpack, came up with three different shampoos, expensive soap, toothbrush and toothpaste, and a new hairbrush. She watched carefully as Holland got out of bed, making sure her friend was steady on her feet. Meg was heartened by Holland's grimace when she saw herself in the bathroom mirror.

Twenty minutes later, the door opened, releasing a billow of warm, fragrant air. Bundled in a short, hospital-issue robe, Holland looked better, Meg thought, though she couldn't help wincing at the sight of the bruises on her old chum's legs and forearms.

"At least nothing's broken," Holland said as she stepped past Meg.

She opened the closet, reached for her slacks, and dug into a pocket. When Holland turned around, Meg saw two diskettes in her hand.

"That's what it was all about?" Meg asked softly.

Holland nodded, staring at them, one handed to her by a man she would have given up her life for, the second tugged from the fingers of a dying James Croft, over the strangled whispers of his confession.

"Someone else wants them now, right?" Meg said.

"I have to hand them over," Holland said. "It's my job . . . my duty."

Meg was about to protest, when she saw Holland's expression soften, a secret hiding on her lips.

"I think I need a second set of MRIs, don't you?" she said. "Just to make sure I don't have a concussion."

Meg stared at the diskettes, which suddenly appeared so delicate . . . so vulnerable if exposed to the wrong elements.

"I'll set it up," she said. "In fact, I'll have to work the equipment myself, since the technician will have been called away unexpectedly."

Holland sat in the corner of the small couch, bare feet tucked underneath the terry-cloth robe. It had been less than ten minutes since she and Meg returned to the room.

"Are you up for some company?" Meg asked her.

"Arliss?"

Meg nodded and handed her the phone.

Holland lifted her chin, letting the last of the weak afternoon sun warm her face. She needed things from Johnson. It would be a start. She listened to what he had to say and could tell by his tone that there was more he had for her, but only face-to-face.

"Maybe you should talk to Jerry Keppler about that pizza," Holland said after hanging up.

Meg shrugged. "A girl's got to eat, right? Want me to bring something back?"

"Just the dirty details."

Holland may have catnapped after Meg left. She had her eyes closed, her face still turned to the sun, when the door bumped open and Johnson, in a motorized wheelchair, maneuvered his way in. Silently he looked her up and down, scrutinizing without a hint of apology.

"*Are* you okay?"

Holland watched him navigate around the furniture. His shoulder and his upper thigh were heavily bandaged; his hair was matted, and a five o'clock shadow added another lifetime to his gaunt cheeks.

"How bad is it?"

"He winged me, is all."

"Bryant?

"Straight through the butt and out. He'll be tender for a while."

Holland flinched when he reached for her, took her cold hand in both of his.

"You saved the President's life. Never lose sight of that. Smith had it wired so well that by all rights you shouldn't have stood a chance."

"Razorback almost jumped out of his skin when he saw me coming out of the tunnel, but he recovered fast. I was in the Office for less than half a minute before he buzzed Smith in."

"Why didn't he just lock the two of you in the office? Then Smith could never have gotten in."

"There were unarmed people outside—secretaries, gofers, visitors. Smith could have had his pick if he'd been thinking hostages."

Johnson turned this over. "Gutsy move, going with the cocoon."

"You *knew* the President would," Holland said. "You once told me you were there when they installed the damn thing; you even gave him a demonstration. I guess he was impressed."

Johnson looked at her. "How much do you want me to tell you now?"

"Everything."

Johnson stretched his good leg. "For me, it began when Preacher was getting around too easily. But you thought the same thing."

Holland nodded. "He was like some damn ghost. I thought he must have had magic, someone looking out for him."

"He did. And everything pointed to Croft. I wasn't looking any further, not until the numbers on Preacher's passport came through.

"Bryant was checking, right? Any minute I expected him to call and say he'd found Croft's signature on the papers. Well, it turned out that Smith'd been the one who authorized the issue."

Holland looked into his gray eyes, swimming in pain, trying to cope with, make sense of treachery.

"So Croft had roped Smith into this. How? Why did Smith go along?"

"The director's office has been sealed. Cobb and Maryanne have been to his apartment, looking for anything he might have left behind—a diary, letters, video."

"And they found something."

Johnson looked away, rubbed his temple.

"I know that Croft needed a triggerman. He went to Smith and felt absolutely safe about bringing him in on this. There may have been others, but Smith would be his first choice. He had firsthand knowledge of men like Preacher, whom he'd worked with—"

"But you said you and Smith once hunted Preacher."

"Now I'm asking myself if, even at that time, Smith really wanted him caught. I hope I can find that out."

Johnson paused. "So now I know Smith is the conduit. He's Preacher's magic. I have to flush Smith. It's the best way to get to Preacher. I tell him about our investigation, lay it all out for him but hammer home that I'm convinced Croft's the bad boy."

"That's why you as much as told me to include the Daniel Webster reference in my report," Holland murmured. "You were giving Smith all the information Croft needed, knowing Smith would pass it on to Croft."

"Except I underestimated how quickly Smith would react. I never thought he'd be able to get to Croft so fast that Croft would have enough time to rifle Westbourne's Senate desk before you got to it."

Johnson stared at her, his voice ragged. "That's how I almost got you and Bryant killed. I had Smith in his office, going over your report. I had a line into Kathy, his secretary, who kept telling me he hadn't moved. But by then Smith was gone, out the back way, on the road to take down the last person who could connect him to Preacher and the killings."

"Croft."

"Croft."

"But Smith didn't take out Croft with the first shot."

"That was his mistake. He knew Croft was still alive after the first bullet. Reinforcements were on their way, and there you were, holding Croft. All Smith was thinking of was a deathbed confession."

"But why go to the Oval Office? Smith couldn't've thought that he would actually get away with holding the President hostage."

Johnson shook his head. "The President was the bait. I didn't realize that until it was too late. Smith set it up so that you'd follow him to the Oval Office. He made sure that security at the Treasury end of the tunnel would let you through. He was counting on your using the quickest route, one that would also bypass him completely. He knew you wouldn't be going through the front doors of the White House.

"And he was counting on *me* to think he was after the President, which is why I would send you. But all the while he had this different scenario. Listen.

"The director of the Service arrives to see the President. By now everyone's heard about the shooting in the Senate. Nerves are edgy, no one's really sure of what's going on. The boss closets himself with Razorback.

"Who knows what Smith would have told the President to waste the few minutes before you got there. Maybe some fiction about the Senate situation. But all the while, he's watching and listening for you. The second you step out of that door, one of two things happens, depending on how much the President is able to see.

"If you come out weapon in hand, Smith takes you down with one shot. He becomes the instant hero who stopped a rogue agent —one involved in the Senate shootings—from killing Razorback. At the commission of inquiry, he turns over all the information I gave him about the operation you and I were running against Preacher. My bona fides is already shot, but it gets worse: It's Smith's word against mine as to how Preacher got into the country, because you *know* that by then the physical evidence is long gone. Best scenario, I'm stripped of my rank and pension and turfed out."

"And if I came in *not* holding my weapon," Holland said, "if the President was watching what was going on, Smith would have shot him first, then me. Two seconds later, his gun is in my hand.

Maybe there's even a third shot, a self-inflicted wound, so that everyone's down when the doors are finally blown."

"At first I thought that was the way it was going to come down," Johnson said. "All I could see was him blowing away the President, taking you down with the second shot. . . ."

He was exhausted, and she felt his pain pound against her. But she had to know, and he hadn't answered her yet.

"What did Maryanne and Cobb find at Smith's apartment?" Holland asked him.

In his lap, Johnson rubbed his hands, as if he were washing them.

"Years ago, Smith was heading up a detail that was blindsided."

"In Puerto Rico?" Holland broke in. "The incident with the *narcotraficante* hit men?"

"That's the one. That's where Smith took two bullets meant for Westbourne."

Johnson paused. "Smith came out of that looking like a hero—largely because of Westbourne's testimony. But he was never the same after that. I always thought it was because he lost three men that day, and here were people giving him medals. . . ."

"Westbourne *covered* for him?"

"Smith had files in his home, notes on what had really happened, how he'd messed up. It was a career-ending situation. There were also transcripts of conversations with Westbourne, who made it clear he could have Smith's job anytime he wanted. . . ."

"And Westbourne recorded this in his diaries," Holland said dully. "So when Croft—"

She sat up. "But Croft approached Smith *before* he had the first diskette!"

"Zentner told me how that worked," Johnson said. "She and the others had heard rumors about Westbourne's having dirt on someone very high up in national security. You know how much of a ferret Croft was. He dug and dug until he had enough with which to confront Smith. Then he tempted Smith, saying that he no longer had to live under the threat of Westbourne's blackmail, that there was a way out for all of them. . . ."

"Your recommendation took Smith out of the field," Holland said softly. "He never forgave you for that. He didn't see you as the friend he could turn to. . . . You would have helped him had he come to you."

"He didn't think he needed me," Johnson whispered. "With Westbourne dead, everything was supposed to be over with. It's just that no one reckoned on you, Holland. . . ."

Later, there were different slants to the stories reported in the media. They were culled from lies and half-truths that Arliss Johnson carefully arranged and polished. But the core of each story was the same.

The gunman who'd managed to smuggle himself into the Senate chamber was positively identified as Wayne Purdue, a former Special Forces lieutenant who'd been dishonorably discharged after two incidents of violent behavior. Purdue's records at the San Diego V.A. hospital showed response to treatment by counseling and medication, but upon his release, Purdue never went back for follow-up sessions.

A search of Senator James Croft's office and residence produced several notes of a threatening nature. The handwriting was identified as that of Wayne Purdue.

According to the evidence, Purdue believed the senator was responsible for "the filthy, second-rate treatment veterans get while you fucks chow down at the trough." An FBI spokesman firmly stated that Senator Croft never brought these threats to the Bureau's attention, emphasizing that if he had, the FBI would have been able to keep Purdue under surveillance and intercept him before he went on his murderous spree.

How Purdue had been able to get into the Senate chamber became the topic of heated debate among lawmakers. In the sound and fury, the comments made by D.C. police about the murder of a prostitute in the Capitol Hill apartment complex were relegated to the back of the Metro section; they didn't even make the TV news.

No one, it seems, picked up on the fact that a body other than the one belonging to Bobbie Sue Tyler, a known prostitute, had been removed from one of the Capitol Hill apartments, much less that it never reached the D.C. coroner's office but ended up in a holding vault at Andrews Air Force Base. If any member of the D.C. police force thought that he or she recognized the description of Wayne Purdue run in the media as being even remotely similar to the mangled features of the male victim at the apartment, no mention of such a coincidence was ever publicly voiced.

Too close attention to the Croft stalking and killing was also deflected by the tragic news of the death of Secret Service Director Wyatt Smith.

During the demonstration of a new security procedure in the Oval Office, overseen by Smith, a small explosives charge was detonated prematurely. Smith, standing only a few feet away, was killed instantly.

Aides later confirmed that the President was working elsewhere at the time and was never in any danger. He was quoted as being "grief-stricken by the loss of this man who held my life in his hands."

Director Smith was to be buried at Arlington with full honors, the President in attendance.

Those who believed themselves in the know spoke assuredly that Johnson, the man who saw the threat against Croft when no one else did and almost foiled it, would become the new director.

In the peace and silence of her hospital room, Holland watched and listened. Behind the subtleties and syrupy words of regret, she detected the hand of Arliss Johnson and learned new things about him. But after a time there was nothing new being said, and the words became too sour for her to stomach. She continued working on the report Johnson had asked for and, when that was done, quietly checked herself out of the hospital.

After a sleepless night in her own bed, she went outside the next morning, to find Johnson's surveillance van in her driveway. Holland briefly raised her arm at the agent behind the wheel, threw the dead bolt to her front door. In the vehicle, she checked one last time to make sure she had everything the President would need.

.   .   .

Sunday morning at the Oval Office, and Razorback looked like any other executive who'd come to work for a few hours before going back home to his family. Over a plaid shirt, he wore a cashmere cardigan with suede elbow patches; when he rose, Holland saw the chocolate twill pants and well-worn loafers.

Holland came forward, careful not to step on the Great Seal, concentrating on the desk with its fine writing instruments, on the man himself. Still, she couldn't help but look up.

"It was you, not that damned plastic, who saved my life," the President said.

He grasped her palm and, with a practiced gesture, squeezed her elbow with his other hand. Holland caught the scent of his aftershave around the collar.

The President pointed at the bundle under her arm.

"That's your final report?"

"Deputy Director Johnson said I should bring it, sir."

The President took it from her and set it on the desk blotter. He sat back, hands folded over a slight paunch.

"The people at the hospital tell me you're going to be okay. True?"

"Yes, sir."

Holland felt his eyes drift over her, more curious than probing.

"You've been hearing a lot of garbage in the media, haven't you? I think the lies bother you as much as they do me. But this time, we had no choice. If anyone were ever to find out how close Smith got to me, our security would be a laughingstock. The Service would be demoralized; it would take years to fix the damage." The President paused. "Still, it rankles, doesn't it?"

"Yes, sir, it does."

"I know something about you, Agent Tylo, what you've had to live with. I wouldn't have wished this on anyone, least of all you."

The President drew a thumb over the pages he'd taken from Holland.

"You put in everything you know, from the beginning, in sequence?"

"Everything, sir."

"Then let me tell you what you haven't heard yet." He tapped a crystal letter opener over a short pile of envelopes. "Letters of resignation. One from each of the remaining senators who gloried in being called the Cardinals. Nothing holy or powerful about them anymore. I can't prosecute them, because that would tear the country apart. You think people hate politicians and Washington now; it'd be nothing compared to the avalanche that would bury us all if word of what happened got out.

"The one thing I can do is turf out this pair of bastards." He looked at her shrewdly. "Except that doesn't really cut any ice with you, does it?"

"The people in question were part of a murder conspiracy, Mr. President," Holland said. "That's pretty thick ice."

"Only if you have evidence, Agent Tylo. And even then, that's subject to interpretation."

"I understand, sir."

"No doubt you do. But that by itself doesn't do much for you, does it?"

Holland didn't reply.

"I take it you're staying on in the Service?"

"I've requested and been approved for an indefinite leave of absence."

"You think it'll be impossible for you to work in the Service again because of the rumors about how you held a gun on your boss until he sent himself to his Maker?"

"It's crossed my mind, sir."

"Let it go," the President said softly. "I understand the limitations of this office better than most people. But let me tell you one thing that's gospel: only you and I know what really happened in here. The agents who came in later have all been interviewed by me personally. I made it very clear that it would be highly detrimental to their careers if there was even a suggestion, from whatever quarter, that you might have acted inappropriately."

The President shifted in his chair.

"I have this place for at least another year. Then four more, if that's the way things are meant to go. For that long at least, you have nothing to concern yourself about."

"And later, sir?"

"By then, Agent Tylo, people won't remember and they won't care. Except the man sitting in front of you. In five years' time, when I'm spending Christmas morning with my grandchildren or fishing for Idaho trout, I'm going to see your face and say a little prayer for you."

The President rose. "Heal, Agent Tylo. Heal, then come back to us."

"You've been very kind, Mr. President. Thank you."

His voice caught her as she reached the door. "I recall asking Johnson for two specific items. Did you include them?"

"Of course, sir."

The President found the diskettes underneath a report whose heading caused him to frown, but he was in too much of a hurry to pay attention to that.

Slipping the diskettes into his computer, he remembered what he had said to Tylo. Staying in the White House was *not* necessarily "the way things are meant to go." You *made* that happen. The Westbourne diaries *would* make that happen. Because he was safe now. The information Westbourne could have used to black-mail him was at his fingertips. And with the diskettes, he'd have the complete and undivided attention of every major player on Capitol Hill who was mentioned in Westbourne's catalog of sins.

The drive was running, but the screen remained blank. The President tapped keys, swore softly, then again when the second diskette came up white. Now his hand was reaching for the phone, to get Tylo back before she left the building.

Holland had reached the guard post at the corner where the West Wing corridor intersects the hall leading from the Oval Office. If they were going to stop her, this was where it would happen.

She slowed her pace, focused on the Service agent who sat behind a small desk. His gray eyes played over her face, stayed there even as he picked up the phone on the first ring. Holland didn't hear his murmured reply. It really didn't matter, because she'd seen the truth in the shiny curiosity and suspicion in his eyes.

"It's for you," he said.

"Agent Tylo. It seems you've provided me with the wrong items," the President said, straining to keep his tone light.

"No, Mr. President. I delivered exactly what I was instructed to, my report and the Westbourne diskettes."

The President eased into his chair. The woman's voice was perfectly calm, not even a ripple of a lie.

"But the diskettes are blank, Agent Tylo."

"I wouldn't know anything about that, sir." There was a brief pause. "The only thing I can think of, Mr. President, is that something may have happened to the diskettes while I was in for an MRI. I believe you have my medical report there?"

The President wet his thumb on his tongue and flipped through the pages until he saw the hospital papers.

"Yes, I do."

"It was a very hectic situation, sir. I can't even recall exactly how I was taken out of your office, much less what happened when they got me to the hospital. But it is possible that in all the confusion, the radiologist didn't follow every rule in the book. For example, all my clothing may not have been removed, or it may have been left close enough to the machine for the magnetic field to have an adverse effect on the diskettes."

The President pinched the bridge of his nose.

"An adverse effect," he murmured. "Tell me, Agent Tylo, is that what you believe really happened?"

"Yes, sir. Because I have no other explanation."

"I see. So it would follow that the information on those diskettes is irretrievably gone. No one could possibly resurrect it."

"Yes, sir. If, as you say, the diskettes are blank, it's gone. Take my word on it."

The President hesitated. A former litigator, he knew there was a time to retaliate and a time to cede.

"I *will* take your word, Agent Tylo. And because of that, I'm sure I'll sleep well at night. Don't you agree?"

"Yes, sir. Very well."

"Have a long and successful convalescence, Ms. Tylo."

"I appreciate your thoughts, Mr. President."

. . .

"Everything okay?"

Holland handed the receiver back to the agent. "Yes. Thanks."

The agent rose and held out his hand.

"Just remember. Guys like him"—he nodded in the direction of the Oval Office—"they only rent space."

Holland returned his grip, smiled, then moved on. In the end, Razorback understood very little about those who protected him, the things they held sacred, the loyalty to each other that was the crucible of their creed.

But she was grateful that the President was an astute, well-informed man, who understood modern technology like the magnetic disks, how electromagnetic fields could burn out their core, wiping out all the data . . .

Wiping out all those sins we might be so tempted to embrace . . .

ABOUT THE AUTHOR

PHILIP SHELBY lives in Los Angeles, where he is currently working on his next novel.